LIBERATOR'S LIGHT

The Hero's Code

Book 4

A.R. KNIGHT

ONE

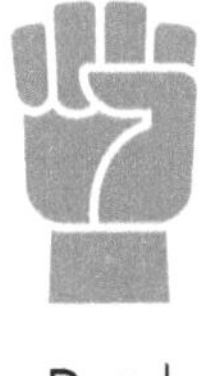

Raid

Sacrifice the whole to save the part.

Aegis glared at the words, left by his daughter Celice on his Tama, coded in so the wristlet's screen showed them every time Aegis looked its way. He swiped the phrase off so he could see the plans and project them to the waiting twenty with him in the cargo plane's hangar.

A ship sprang first from his Tama, and then from the linked projector Celice had hooked up into the plane's boring backside. She'd also found enough parts and people to get the propeller-driven craft in the air for the first time since before Aegis had been born.

Two pilots sat in the cockpit, shuttling the combined Paragon and normal strike force over the deep, dark Pacific ocean. Their target sat minutes away, enough time for one last look at how they were going to hurt Ziran, the company stealing the world.

No, not stealing, capturing. Taking by force.

"At last count," Aegis started, doing what he could to keep too many sleepless nights from his voice, "Ziran has

1

five drones on the ship. Another squishy squad beyond them."

"Standard orders?" asked Particle, a Paragon who'd proven their worth with an assault rifle more times than Aegis cared to count.

"Standard orders." Aegis gave an eye-sweep across the fighters. They all wore drab black now, protective, tactical gear taken wherever they could get it. No Paragon blues anymore. "Normals, signal if you spot a drone. Don't engage. Your job here is to get to those controls and turn the boat our way."

Because the Paragons needed those supplies. Weapons, food, anything that could be used. Aegis watched the boat's projection spin in the hangar's center. The leak hinted there might be something more interesting in that vessel's hold. Celice wanted it investigated bad enough to ask her father on this one personally.

He'd get it for her.

The two squads, half Paragon and half normal, split apart and pulled on their parachutes. Up front, the pilots flipped on the warning light. Aegis made himself ready, tried to quiet his stormy thoughts.

Just like the old days. Another mission, difficult odds, but ones he, Aegis, the people's protector and a living legend, would be able to overcome. He'd come back from near death stronger than ever, and he would prove it again tonight.

Except Aegis had been proving it, day after day and hour after hour since Mila and the healing tank in the Factory's basement put Aegis back together. He'd battered drones by the hundreds, led assault after assault in the two months since Mynx disappeared and her machines switched sides.

For all that effort, Aegis had damn little to show.

"Almost to launch," Aegis spoke into his Tama as he took his position at the hangar's end, where the ramp would lower any second. "Things okay back home?"

"Focus, dad," Celice said.

"Just seeing if you were paying attention."

"Ziran doesn't have all the eyes yet. I've got a grainy feed, but don't get reckless. You're too far out for back-up."

With a squeal that belied the plane's age, the door dipped open. Air pulled at Aegis, whistling through his cropped hair and scruff. Behind him, clicks sounded as his team checked their gear, settled into position.

"So long as we have evac," Aegis said.

"She's nearby," Celice replied. "Let's hope you don't need her."

"Let's hope."

The light above Aegis flared green. Champions didn't hesitate so Aegis led the way, stomping down the ramp and leaping into a silver night sky. Below, the ship laid out long, its running lights a beacon against the black water.

A familiar rush found Aegis as he fell, seconds ticking off in his head as the fall buffeted his arms, legs, stomach. The team followed behind him, leaping and pulling their chutes as ordered.

Aegis didn't reach for his.

Contacts in his eyes linked to Aegis's Tama, flooding data into his retinas as he fell. The ship, highlighted in a neon green, grew large as an altitude ticker sprinted down in his vision's upper-right corner. Containers stacked on one another dominated the ship's surface, steel towers with narrow gaps between rows. The Tama found, highlighted drones and patrolling guards in those gaps with a bloody red. A dire Christmas.

When the ticker hit two thousand, Aegis pulled the chute. Flaring up, the chute pulled Aegis back, though the holes scattered through the fabric kept up the Champion's momentum. He'd cut them himself in a meditative moment earlier that day, knowing the precise number from a time long before the Paragons existed.

Back then, the U.S. military controlled Aegis's drops. Back then, they told Aegis how to be efficient, how to maximize surprise. Not too many years later, Aegis turned that training back on his owners. Fought and won his freedom.

Aegis bunched up his knees, guiding the chute towards a landing on a container tower. The ribbed metal shone silver under the moon and stars, just clear enough for Aegis to roll as he hit. The impact jolted his knees, clacked Aegis's teeth against each other as he slammed across the container. His right hand moved on instinct, releasing the chute as Aegis left the somersault and sending the canvas billowing off into the night.

His arrival didn't go unnoticed.

Alarms sprang up fast, new and blinking lights firing up across the ship as someone barked orders from loudspeakers. Those accessories played in the background as Aegis focused on a more immediate threat: two drones, flanking him on the container's either side.

These machines, revamped gladiator drones, looked like frying pans with a few too many handles. Directional jets sprayed out from their bases, while weapons lethal and not dotted those metal arms. The drones had a white coating now, blazed over with an orange Ziran logo to make sure Aegis knew just who would be shooting him.

"I liked you better before," Aegis said to the closer one, near the ship's middle.

The black metal and Paragon blue paint *had* looked cooler.

He took two long steps to cover the container's width

and leapt off its lip. Hot energy met him, another Ziran tweak. Azure flashes accompanied pain as Aegis's tactical gear proved unable to handle the heat. Burns, though, didn't meet the same measure as hard metal shot inside Aegis's heart.

And lasers didn't stop the Paragon's momentum.

Aegis hit the drone hard, sending the machine flying backward as its jets tried to compensate for the extra kilos. The machine's job grew harder as its fellow, continuing to fry Aegis, proved fine with friendly fire. White plates turned black as energy struck home, following Aegis as he climbed into the three-meter-long drone's middle.

A clock ticked in his head, and when it hit zero, Aegis punched down with both fists, abandoning his trek. His hands broke through the drone's softer build in its center, jagged fragments slicing up Aegis's skin.

The Champion growled away the pain.

The drone followed its programming, flipping itself over. The move put the drone's jets facing up, sending the machine rocketing down towards the ship's deck. Aegis tried to free his hands, get away. His suit, his skin snagged on metal and wires. Kicking his knees up, Aegis pushed with his feet, breaking free as the drone struck home.

The ship's deck crunched as the drone and its human pancake struck, plates crumpling in as the machine's momentum overwhelmed a deck not exactly built for a Champion slamming into it. Aegis felt the steel snap under his back, bend against his shoulders, tear beneath his head as the drone pushed him through. The machine itself stuck, its peripherals lacking the weight.

Aegis landed on rust-red grating, staring up at the drone's sparking, battered corpse. His body tweaked, twitched as its cells fixed themselves. With a groan, Aegis sat up, stretched his neck left and right. His suit hung in little more than shreds, and the crash had spun off his belt and the extra gear to somewhere Aegis couldn't see.

The Champion's eyes found plenty else, though. The thin lower-deck hallway should've been where the guards spent their nights, or served as additional cargo space for Ziran's toys. Instead, Aegis saw bright blue lines bisecting the hall from floor to ceiling on his left, the way leading towards the ship's bridge.

On the walls around him hung hasty signs, plastic ones thrown up against the green-gray metal. In bold white on red, letters warned against continuing further. Against agitation and complaining.

Against anomaly abilities.

"You alive, Aegis?" Particle's voice came in over the Tama as thumps, gunfire, and at least one crackling explosion filtered through the deck's newest door.

"Alive and moving," Aegis replied, standing up. His own ability kept the drone from killing him, but Aegis felt the aches as he stood. He'd need days after this to get back in fighting shape. "Something weird down here."

"Great. There's things normal and dangerous up top if you're available?"

Aegis snapped his view up to the sparking drone. Right. Take the ship and he could figure out what lay below later. Ignoring the hallway and its beckoning, Aegis turned to the closer wall and punched a dent near his waist.

Did it again a meter higher.

"On my way," Aegis said, nodding at his handiwork.

Backing up, Aegis took a single step and leapt. His right foot caught the bent metal foothold, giving Aegis enough leverage to punch a handhold for himself and secure his left foot's grip. Looking up at the drone, Aegis squatted, gave himself as much push as he could, and jumped.

Reaching up, his hands caught some broken deck plating, the razor edges adding to the cuts Aegis already collected on the mission. None would scar, all would be gone by day's end. The pain filtered out, experience and focus doing their work to keep the Champion climbing, pushing, punching, and tearing until he once again saw the night sky.

Fire interrupted the stellar beauty now.

Around Aegis, Paragons and commandos landed, their chutes snapping off as the combined force found drones and Ziran guards rushing to meet them. One gung-ho soldier, on Aegis's left, rounded a shipping container stack silhouetted by blue-white spotlights. The man aimed his rifle—a kind long outlawed, but Ziran must have found a stash—at another Paragon, a graying woman just rising from her suit.

"Cover!" Aegis shouted, breaking towards the guard.

The gun's noise said Aegis wouldn't get there in time. The Paragon's ability said it didn't matter.

The guard, trigger pulled, found himself standing five meters ahead, the fired bullet striking him in the back. He hadn't stepped, hadn't ran forward, but just appeared there. Aegis blinked as the man crumpled, glanced towards the Paragon and caught a wink.

Aegis wanted to sigh, but more targets closed in on the landing zone. If this had been a real Paragon operation, one run with more planning, more established teams, he'd have known what the Paragon could do. He'd know where to be to use her abilities.

Instead he'd wasted seconds playing defense when none was needed.

The old days had been so much better.

Three more guards followed the first, calling out their downed companion's name. This time, when Aegis nodded at the Paragon woman, they understood each other. The guards sighted on Aegis, brought up their weapons.

And a god stood among them.

Aegis struck fast and with finality, dropping a guard with each fist and the third with his forehead in a crunching smack. He knelt down, picked up a rifle off the unconscious guard.

"Give me a shot, Particle," Aegis said.

The anomaly, taking their birds-eye station on a container tower's top, yanked Aegis's vision towards a drone making mayhem near the ship's aft. The normals, coming in later, were landing at the boat's back, around the bridge. The drone took advantage, its weapons working to spray incoming chutes and their charges with glittering fire.

"Can't hit that from here," Aegis replied, breaking into a run.

"Then get closer."

Aegis held up a hand as he ran, hoping his new partner would understand. Smaller container towers littered the space between Aegis's landing spot and the ship's bridge, some glowing as drone fire or Paragon abilities missed their marks. Between and around the blocks, Ziran guards, drones, and Paragons did a dangerous dance.

Not one Aegis had time to join.

He jumped, and Aegis felt the Paragon partner jolt him forward, once, twice, and a third time. He kept moving between the jolts, falling back to the ground. The last boost slammed Aegis into another guard, knocking the soldier flying into a beet-red container. Aegis didn't do much better, losing his footing and stumbling into a somersault.

Those, at least, Aegis understood.

The Champion left the roll with a kick up to his feet, keeping the momentum going. Every second spent, his allies lost more lives. The rush closed in Aegis's vision, pushed away his aching bones.

The guard, shaking her own head, lurched off the shipping container, its red the bottom share of a steel two-stack.

"Bad idea," Aegis said, jumping again.

The guard looked up in time to see Aegis land on her shoulders, kicking off and sending her back to the ground. The boost brought him up, enough for his partner—did her ability have a range?—to shunt Aegis higher. He flew up and over the containers, landing on the far side in the last flat expanse before the bridge.

A helipad, occupied.

The white-and-orange vehicle's blades already whirled, pilots in the cockpit and doors sliding shut. Aegis caught a foot disappearing on the 'copter's opposite side. Aegis wanted to lunge after it, wanted to until Particle whipped his vision back to the drone and its continuing devastation.

"Priorities," Particle said. "We can take the helicopter later."

"Not if it gets away," Aegis growled, but he broke past it anyway, skirting the pad and hustling towards the bridge.

As he went by, the helicopter did what helicopter's do: its blades spinning up, the vehicle lifted off the ship's surface in a rapid rise.

"Bring it down?" Particle asked as Aegis jumped a rail, the drone only meters away.

And risk killing people fighting on the ship's surface? Who knew what was on the 'copter anyway?

"Find a way to track it," Aegis replied. "Secondary objective."

Ahead, the drone spun around, its disc shape showcasing a pockmarked beating where desperate normals had tried to fight it. Above and behind the drone, like strange clouds, more normals descended, chutes fluttering.

Saving lives. It's what Champions did.

Aegis brought up his stolen rifle, held the trigger as he ran at the drone. Bullets sprang out, meeting their objective with colorful sparks and nothing more. The drone returned fire, its own flashes burning Aegis's bare skin. More pain to shrug off.

The drone must've decided that its attacks weren't doing much, because it accelerated towards Aegis. Jumping, Aegis met the drone in the air, going for the machine's center, that vulnerable circuit nest begging for a bullet absolution. After carving up his skin on the last drone, punching through metal wasn't high on Aegis's to-do list anymore.

Not that the drone cared. It swerved as Aegis jumped, shifting its lip to catch Aegis in the gut. His legs beneath the drone, his arms, right hand still clutching the rifle on top, the Champion tried to find breath and failed. His lungs couldn't expand, the drone shoving them both in a wild acceleration along the ship.

Desperation took over. Aegis held down the rifle's trigger as the drone's speed kept him pinned to its front. This close, the rifle's bullets still bounced off, but a few found softer homes, chewing into the drone's middle. The machine altered its plan as it felt Aegis's fire, acting way too damn smart and braking hard.

Aegis's momentum carried him off the drone, flying out over the sea. As he fell, he aimed the rifle up, played out the clip into the drone's bottom-facing jets. Aegis hit the water hard, its ice seeping in fast as the Champion tried to take a breath. Overhead, once again, those bright stars vanished.

The cause this time?

A big ol' fireball where the drone had been.

"We've secured the ship, conducting clean-up now," Particle said as Aegis bobbed in the waves. "That you out there, Champion?"

"Nice work," Aegis replied. "I'm going to need a pick-up, Particle. And a towel."

As drone pieces splashed around him, Aegis looked over at the ship. Another raid, another win. But it wouldn't stop Ziran.

Not yet.

The Routine

KAT WAITED for five pizzas shoved in a special pack that'd keep them warm for the trip. She sat at a greasy, dough-colored table over tile last cleaned, she imagined, a decade ago. Muddy melted snow piles paired with the TV screen hung in the corner, dangling entertainment for waiting customers. Some talking head barked through another raid, earlier that morning, on a Ziran freighter.

The Paragons at it again, resorting to terrorism in their final flailing moments.

Two months after the drones swapped sides and the Paragon years already held a place in horrified history. Kat's existence as a tracker relegated alongside humanity's past nightmare regimes, as if she'd knocked on doors with designs to destroy the families within. That the Paragons kept anomalies safe, kept normals safer, went unsaid.

To do anything else would be to risk angering the machines floating outside.

Kat pulled the grey hood up over her head, uncut bangs drifting around her eyes and slicing up the behind-the-counter view as she looked away from the TV.

Unarmed machines supervised by normal humans spun up pizza dough, minced tomatoes grown in condensed gardens in the restaurant's back. This place kept its quality where it mattered: the food. Outside the crust, they didn't give a damn.

Which made it perfect for a former tracker trying to get her forbidden friends some lunch.

Minutes later, pizza pack strapped to her back, Kat rejoined a particular puppy digging at the wet grass outside. Brown and freshly exposed, Chicago's lawns hadn't yet found their spring vigor and, if Seeker had his say, they never would. The husky seemed to regard any opportunity to create a hole as one not to be missed, no matter how many times Kat tried telling him no.

Admittedly, she wasn't good at it.

"Here," Kat said, handing over several pepperonis the joint's owner sent her way. A tiny gesture that ensured she stayed a repeat customer, though the man didn't know Kat's choices for lunchtime options were slim.

Seeker snapped up the delivered delectable, then another, and a third before Kat showed an empty palm. The husky flicked his eyes back towards the pizzeria and huffed.

"Moderation, my friend," Kat said, heading off down the sidewalk and pulling Seeker along.

A pod whisked by, ferrying people in its tinted orb to destinations unknown. The wheeled sphere made nothing more than an ear-tingling hum as it went, the tires crunching a louder sound than the batteries boosting it along. Kat would've called one, would've saved herself blocks hiking through the cool air, except pods weren't private.

Ziran would be listening.

Ziran always listened now.

Kat's arms swung as she walked, her left one outpacing her right, its lightness still a new sensation. The Tama that'd been there gone, along with the wristband to hold it. A small plate sat on her skin, covered by a long sleeve, waiting to get plugged in. It would have to wait a lot longer. No way Kat would be strapping a Ziran-made device to her any time soon.

Weed, the Paragon acting now as the Chicago lead—as if such a thing really existed anymore—still had his Tama and claimed Ziran hadn't infiltrated all the Paragon systems. Aegis, the Champion returned from the dead, apparently had one and hadn't been tracked down yet. All the same, Kat had a hunch Ziran kept its cards close.

If your enemy was content to give their position away, why not let them?

The sun faded fast, a sudden shade not belonging to a passing cloud. Kat caught the reflection in a nearby window as she walked, a gladiator drone bringing its truck-sized body along the avenue. A normal patrol that, a few months back, would've made Kat feel secure, safe and protected. Now she turned her face away, bent down as if to tie the laces on her boots.

Ziran knew her face. Wexley knew her face. He might have higher priorities now, but Kat figured he'd come after her eventually.

Or was that vanity talking? Wexley had the world to fight for now. He probably didn't remember Kat existed. He wouldn't take the time to order drones out to find her.

Kat kept her hood up anyway.

Five blocks later, in a ragged residential neighborhood where single-story ranches spoke to century-old construction long left to founder as money made moves elsewhere, Kat picked up some Seeker droppings and swept a look around.

For all the upheaval, humanity powered on. People took trains and pods to their jobs, or set themselves up in home offices. Kat could see heads glued to monitors in front room windows. Some few joined the sidewalk with her, often muttering into their Tamas as they took their meetings on foot. Nobody did what Kat wanted to: scream out a question asking whether everyone had lost their minds.

She'd seen what anomalies could do. Lost her family to one when her sister's cells bent the wrong way and sent Kat's parents, their house, and the sister herself into the next life. Kat held no particular love for those humans afflicted with abilities, but she'd made a home in the house the Paragons built. It'd functioned, it'd been clean and clear.

Now Chicago marched to a fearful drum, overseen by and obedient to a machine swarm demanding that its citizens carry on. Send their emails, file their reports, and make the economy move without thinking about who really benefited.

"I liked it more when I just had to catch another moron," Kat said, turning up a driveway with cracks destined for weed incursions.

"Who you calling a moron?" Smoke, a Paragon who'd embraced the no-uniform look to shag out with lounge wear, called from the house's cement porch.

"Nobody," Kat replied, slinging the pack off her back and dropping it near the door. "Lunch is served."

"Keep it hot this time?" Smoke eyed the pizza box with something between desire and disgust. "If I'm eating this again, I—"

"You're welcome to get it yourself."

Kat didn't wait for Smoke to find a comeback and went inside, Seeker pawing after her. They both knew Smoke wouldn't go many steps from the house, where a drone might get a good look at her. The machines seemed to know Paragon faces at a glance—how Weed squared this with his refusal to believe Ziran had Paragon system access, Kat couldn't fathom—and responded to a potential catch with verve.

When help arrived, the anomalies weren't even finding bodies anymore.

Inside, makeshift moxie abounded. Oddball pairings huddled over screens set up on haphazard tables, power cables making a footfall maze liable to trip any inattentive newcomer. Anomalies and normals, the few who cared enough about the Paragons to want them back, swarmed through the space. A dishwasher hummed behind it all, and, deeper in the house, the laundry machines continued their constant vibrations.

"Where's Weed?" Kat asked a man standing just inside the door, his eyes on the big front window.

The hour's appointed watchman, Smoke's secondary for the shift.

"Briefing room," the man said without sashaying a look Kat's way. "They're not letting up."

"With all the wins lately, why would we?"

The man frowned, but didn't offer anything else to go with Kat's sarcasm. Humor died fast after the drones turned, despite Kat's attempts at resuscitation. Not that she'd stop: a little laughter was the only thing keeping her sane.

That, and hoping for a sign.

The briefing room would've been a joke anywhere else. A cracked cobblestone patio out back now hid beneath a scavenged lime green party tent, a screaming decorative failure embraced through necessity. Kat kept her criticisms quiet: her own apartment, now left fallow once she'd discovered tracker drones keeping tabs on it, would've failed any design reviews.

She did, though, miss Todd. The surfer AI managing her life back there had been a constant pleasure. Did Todd still exist, chatting with an empty apartment? Wondering where the woman requesting daily, late, brunch orders had gone?

Seeker pulled Kat's focus to the gathering, a solid six-person event, unfolding before them as Kat walked through the rear sliding doors. Weed held court, a projector linked to the man's Tama spewing a blueprint up against an old black chalkboard. Kat didn't recognize the layout, but the words up top reading *Power Station* answered the question clear enough.

"Why? Hit this and we'll knock out the north suburbs for three days," Weed said, the scraggly man nonetheless standing straight before his charges. Calvin had mentioned he'd liked the man.

Calvin.

Kat pressed her eyes shut for a second. Opened them back in equilibrium.

"And why does that matter?" Weed continued. "Every day they don't have power, every day business is disrupted, we swing them back our way. This is a long war, and we'll win it with small victories."

Looking at backs, Kat couldn't tell if Weed's audience took the man seriously, but when Weed dismissed them all to get suited up, the five members forming Rookery squad —Weed and Beth, the Elemental leader sharing power in the place, went with Chicago landmarks as squad names for variety—popped up to gather gear.

"Annoy the citizenry enough and they'll want you back?" Kat said, letting Seeker loose to dash around the yard.

Weed, swiping away the projection, scratched at his nose and shrugged. "It's something to try. More, it keeps us going."

"And getting killed out there."

"Better that than wallowing in here. At least we're trying, and we're not alone. Aegis—"

"Took another boat. Guess how many Ziran's got out there?"

"You know?"

Kat collapsed into a folding chair, its stiff cushion providing precisely zero comfort, "Of course I don't know, but it's gotta be more than one." She shook her head, glanced up. "Anything?"

Weed grimaced, matched her head shake, "We haven't heard anything more. Gordon hasn't sent a word in a week."

The tracker had vanished with a few anomalies on a mission to see exactly why missing Paragons and Elementals were just that: missing. The drones, given Wexley and Ziran's repeated proclamations that anomalies were to be destroyed, should've been leaving bullet-riddled bodies in the streets. Instead, anomalies seemed to just disappear.

Kat read enough novels, saw enough movies to have ideas aplenty about where they might be, what might be happening, but so far nobody caught a trace.

Calvin had been one. Weed described the day, back when Kat had been in the hospital under a dizzying drug dive to get her through dire emergency surgery. Calvin and some other Paragons, Weed included, tried staving off the world's end with a hit on a drone repair center on Chicago's south side. The mission came off as a success, with Calvin being the only casualty.

Fire and drones everywhere, Weed said. They couldn't

see what happened to Calvin, couldn't risk going back to rescue him.

Kat had given Lob, the Paragon doing the in-and-out jumps on the mission, a good punch anyway. Now he left rooms whenever she entered, and Kat didn't feel one tiny regret about it.

"So, the pizza's here?" Weed said after a long breath.

The man at least had the grace to look embarrassed about asking.

"You want a piece, better get in there," Kat replied. Weed gave her a nod and took the advice.

Overhead, the sunshine died again, this time in the slower, more natural fashion. Raindrops followed, striking the canvas with hollow, splattering thuds. Kat stared at the chalkboard, tried to find something meaningful in its blank, black surface.

At least Seeker, chomping at the droplets, had fun.

The rain became a downpour, thick enough that even Seeker sought refuge beneath the canvas. The clattering storm made so much noise, misted up the yard so thick Kat didn't notice the bag fly over the fence until a body followed. Seeker woofed as Kat stood up, her hand vanishing beneath her jacket to the snub-nosed pistol she kept with her now. Guns felt wrong in a Paragon world, but strangely right in the new dystopia, ready to end an enemy's life as easily as Kat's own, should the circumstances go too far south.

Seeker's barks pulled Kat's hand away, their tone suggesting less a break-in and more a return. Pulling up her hood again, Kat broke cover and dashed across the yard to the body, her boots already squelching in the soaked, muddy grass.

Gordon Holyoak looked like he'd found some enemies. Bruises littered his face, and Kat saw the man's scalp where some hair had gone aggressively missing. His outfit bore tears and holes, some going all the way through to bloody lines in the tracker's skin.

"You alive, man?" Kat asked, kneeling over him, taking Gordon's face in her hands.

His eyes didn't keep the suspense long, fluttering open at her touch. Scruff competed with mud for space on Gordon's face, though the rain turned the latter into brown rivers as Kat pulled Gordon up. Seeker bounded about them, woofing and helping not in the slightest.

"Hey," Gordon said, words a whisper over the rain. "Grab my bag?"

Leaving Gordon draped over her shoulders, Kat leaned down, picked up the duffel making a new home in the mud pit yard. Sweeping her left arm around Gordon's waist, Kat turned back to the house.

Standing behind it, some with guns raised and others with arms out, ready to deploy whatever magic their cells had given them, were Weed and Beth's makeshift army, or at least the fifteen or so ready to play. Weed and Beth stood at their head, both with arms folded, eyes peering out from the canvas.

"Some help, maybe?" Kat called. "It's Gordon, and he's hurt?"

"How'd he get over the fence, Kat?" Beth asked.

The woman, an Elemental leader and one whom Kat wouldn't mind going a few rounds with in a no-holds-barred ring, took the new world like it was a new outfit. She pulled the disaster around her like a coat and used it to cover flaws, striding around her diminished forces like some savant who could, with enough grit and grime, get the Elementals and their disenfranchised Paragon friends, back on top.

When Kat mentioned Beth had been behind innumerable attacks on Paragon property, had nearly killed Kat herself with a dirty anomaly trick, Weed hadn't done much more than turn away. They needed every anomaly now, no matter their past.

So Kat caught her would-be killer's orders and carried them out with one forced smile after another.

Why?

Because staying here offered her only chance at something more than the streets. She'd given her life to the Paragons, and they'd repaid her with a career to call her own. Resurrected a broken teenager and taught her how to fight, to trace a rogue anomaly, to stare down a wall of assholes like this one and punch right on through it.

"He pulled himself over," Kat said. "I saw him."

"Looking like that?" Weed asked.

Gordon straightened, hissing as he did so. "All me. Wouldn't mind getting out of this rain, though?"

Weed and Beth pulled a paired frown that would've been cute if Kat wasn't considering pulling her gun and gut-shotting them both right then and there. The Paragon leader, possibly reaching real deep, found his heart and waved Kat and Gordon forward. As Kat and her friend went, several anomalies followed Beth's signal and broke out from the line. They swept passed Gordon, heading for the fence. Another popped into the air with a flute-like noise, fluttering upwards like a leaf into the downpour.

A risky move to use such an obvious ability in the open, but better than risk the whole house to some waiting ambush.

Weed and Beth wanted an immediate debrief, but Gordon demurred, claiming a chance to clean-up and get some first aid took precedence. Kat helped the tracker downstairs, to a wide basement expanded with judicious anomaly abilities to extend beneath the whole backyard.

The Elementals, who had some experience building makeshift bases, divided up the new, calcified-white chamber into various rooms, including a three-bed micro hospital.

Gordon went from shower to bed, with Kat helping apply bandages. Seeker, their apparent protector, curled up his soaked self at their feet, blue eyes watchful.

"You're staying quiet," Kat said as the silence ate away. Gordon hadn't said so much as a word, save recurrent thank-yous as the recovery commenced. "I'll let you get away with that for a minute more, then I'm gonna lose it."

Gordon chuckled once, then turned his beat-up face Kat's way, "I'm not talking because I'm trying to figure out what I have to say."

"There's your problem. You can't overthink it. Just talk, Gordon. Who did all this to you, and why? Did you run out on another girl?"

Another chuckle, this one sadder.

"It's not who, Kat. It's what. I didn't get it all, but I found enough. I've got a location."

"A location for what?"

"For the anomalies," Gordon said, a smile threatening his lips. "They're alive, Kat. Calvin's alive."

Family Life

RHIMES STALKED the objective beneath palm fronds. Hiding small arms beneath a billowing shirt and shorts proved trickier in LA weather than Chicago's, but the operative and his team made do. Across the street and approaching from the opposite side, three mercenaries completed Rhimes's four-member squad.

They backed up the main weapons: a metal duo skittering through the neighboring yards. The tracker drones, roach-like robots with sharp edges aplenty, would be taking the lead.

Rhimes could care less about turfing off the opening responsibilities. Any attack carried the most danger in its first moments, when plans went awry and intelligence failures became evident. Better to risk robots that could be churned out by the hundreds every day than a single normal life.

At least, that's what Rhimes told Wexley, who didn't argue.

"Last check," Rhimes said. "Go?"

His three operatives clicked an affirmative, and the two

drones, sitting somewhere to Rhimes's left behind a white fence, followed with their own okays. Their target, a two-story bungalow with a modern design, all creams and dark wood, sat ahead and looked, like most places on this residential street, to be deserted.

If only.

"Let's get it done," Rhimes said, triggering the op.

Reaching into the loosely buttoned shirt, Rhimes pulled out a combo gun from its shoulder holster. Double-barreled and designed by yours truly, Rhimes had the Factory turning these babies out fast enough to equip Ziran's entire force. A little switch swapped the weapon between lethal and not, a discretion becoming more important by the day as Adriana's influence pushed aside Wexley's bloodier instincts.

Rhimes didn't know what Adriana did with her prizes, but at least she kept the body count low. Any revolution came with casualties, but Wexley wanted those drones turned to anomaly execution real quick till Adriana convinced him otherwise. Not quite the equal-opportunity society Zhan-Yo had preached.

Regardless, Rhimes set the pistol to stun and closed with the house at a light jog. To his right, he saw his operatives head into another house, one co-opted from its bribed owners for today's event. In a few seconds, Rhimes would have rooftop cover. In fewer, the drones would be inside.

The tracker drones had their own lethal bent, but they'd be prioritizing a nerve agent, one that would send a victim's body into static shock for enough hours to get them where Adriana needed them to go.

Where that was, Rhimes didn't know. He hadn't asked. Enough anomalies could read minds that Rhimes kept his own life as need to know as possible.

A helicopter buzzed along overhead, its noise masking

the tracker drones as they carved through the house's back windows. Rhimes watched the entry on his Tama as he took cover behind a parked pod on the street near the house. Now came the delicate dance between observing the drone's progress and keeping his own eyes ready in case the anomalies decided to take flight.

Then again, there'd be noise aplenty. Anomalies didn't run quiet.

On the Tama's screen, Rhimes caught clear video as the tracker drones scampered inside. His chosen view veered sideways as the machine scaled the wall to the ceiling, ready to pounce on any incoming body. The second drone crossed the kitchen fast, getting itself on a wall opposite the glass doors where anyone coming to investigate would—

There. A man, holding a coffee as he rushed into the room, eyes wide. He turned, shouted something back into the house, and noticed the drone, more than a meter long, hugging the wall.

The dart, fired from a joint in the drone's front right leg, one of six knife-like limbs, stuck in the anomaly's neck. The man staggered back a step, dropped the coffee, then fell into its expanding brown pool. Rhimes winced as the man's head cracked on the tile. A nasty concussion coming with that one, most likely.

Then again, he'd take that over the anomaly getting his ability off.

The drones held their position, waiting for the new bait to work. How many could they add to their collection? Intelligence gathered by these same tracker drones and aerial surveillance suggested at least five anomalies— Elemental members, all—lived here.

"Movement on the second floor," came a buzz from Rhimes's second on the mission, the one providing rooftop cover. Brielle had a switch Rhimes envied, going from smooth-talking philosopher to strait-laced sharpshooter in a second, and now she had her competence game on. "Taking shots?"

"Only on exit," Rhimes replied. "Let the drones do their work. The quieter, the better."

In the couple months since the takeover—Wexley kept promising he'd find an official name for when Ziran toppled the Paragons worldwide, but he hadn't yet—civilized society swapped between outright panic and sustained disbelief that anything about their lives had changed at all. Markets, manufacturing, and good old fashioned day-to-day took their time getting settled, but as the sun kept rising every morning, more and more cities, countries, and governments found themselves remembering the before and reverting to it.

All out warfare in the streets threatened to disrupt that careful balance, so Wexley and his shadowy backers said. Rhimes had to be quiet, focused, and sharp. Take out the anomalies, let people get their lattes. A balance.

Two more shapes showed up in the drone cameras. Together, neither with drinks in their hands, the man and woman, both past middle age, looked at the fallen target and waited. Rhimes slid his fingers along the Tama, zooming in on the pair. The drone catching the shot had itself squeezed onto the ceiling, nestled behind a fan, but it'd be seen if the two dared look up for more than a second.

With a closer look, Rhimes saw what he suspected: the woman's fingers moved, as if playing a piano in the air. The man's eyes had a faraway bent to them, in shock. Tapping on the Tama, Rhimes sent a different command to the drones.

No more waiting. Time to go on offense, before the anomalies finished whatever nonsense they were planning.

His Tama vibrated. An outside call. Not taking that now.

Instead, raising the firearm, Rhimes swept around the car and made for the house's front door. Sunlight glinted off gutters. Two twirling sparrows flitted by, oblivious. Some children splashed and shouted in a pool across the street. Rhimes held his focus, looked down the barrel at the rose-red door.

It opened. A face looking back inside the house as the door swung wide. The older man. Rhimes fired. The upper chamber hissed, popped, a quiet launch muffled further by the gun's design. The man jerked as Rhimes's shot hit him between the shoulders.

Wexley's main man picked up speed, breaking into a run as something large crumpled inside, metal grinding on wood. The Tama vibrated again. Behind Rhimes, he heard more feet running. His two agent back-up.

"Second floor," Brielle said. "Teenagers in the windows."

"Anomalies?" Rhimes asked as the man he'd shot stumbled onto the cement porch.

Rhimes reached the man as he turned, stuck a left foot against the victim's heel and slammed the man down. Just before the anomaly's head had a rude encounter with the concrete, Rhimes slipped his left hand beneath it. Earned a scrape against his knuckles for the effort, but the anomaly didn't leave a bloody splatter, instead blinking fuzzed eyes up at Rhimes as the numbing drugs did their work.

"Unclear," Brielle said. "They're together. Three."

"That's more than reported," Rhimes said, aiming back toward the open door. A quick Tama check showed two missed calls and static on the drone feeds. "Family?"

"You're asking questions I can't answer."

Rhimes signaled his back-up to wait, watch the opening while he moved inside. Using the door for cover on his left, Rhimes looked right as he entered. A dining room, fresh flowers in glass atop dark wood. Chairs positioned properly. Framed photos on the wall, the kids smiling. Nobody waiting for him.

"Can you hit them?" Rhimes said, fishing in his belt for help. Vague art sat against the teal inside wall on his left now, the door covering his back, the two outside covering the door and Brielle doing what she did on the opposite rooftop.

The house blueprint flickered in his mind. The stairs would be behind him, to the right. If the kids grew frisky, they'd make noise.

"I can," Brielle said. "They've shut the door. One's opening the window. Go?"

The stunning rounds were dosed for adults, not kids. Hit someone too tiny and the drugs might knock them out permanently. The younger ones might not even be anomalies—powers weren't always inherited. Balance that against one being an adolescent bomb.

Protect his people. Ziran could always claim the whole family had abilities later.

"Go." Rhimes said. "And signal medical."

Its own risk, bringing innocent help into the play before he'd secured the site, but Rhimes liked to think he hadn't lost himself yet.

"On it."

Rhimes snapped around the dining room entry, covering the opening leading into the kitchen. Soft cream carpet met bronzed tile where the kitchen began, the ceramic getting itself swamped with the golden and blue fluids found in the drones. It leaked out to the left, beyond the drywall arch where Rhimes couldn't see.

Glass shattered again as Brielle took her shots.

"Watch the exits," Rhimes said, clicking twice to clarify the order went to his two on-the-ground agents. They'd split, one back and one front while he cleaned out the inside. "Nobody gets off the property."

"Medical's incoming," Brielle said, voice chill, almost happy. "Two down. Third one's hiding behind the bed."

Rhimes approached the kitchen entry. Listened and heard twinkling twitches. A drone's last gasps, functions fighting for their lives. He debated calling out, giving surrender a chance. Doing that would out his own position, but might spare the woman, or his agents, or himself.

Instead, Rhimes looked into the kitchen, watching right, where the microwave, a shiny new model, served him well: its glass finish gave a distorted mirror view into the living room, where two long, shiny bodies showed drones that'd had better days. Nobody else stood with them.

Rhimes took a breath, embraced the cautious fear always haunting him at times like these, and went through the arch.

The drones showcased their demise: a long winding cut scythed through their bellies, less like a sword and more like a painter with a razor brush stroke. Their innards spilled circuits and coolant all around, dooming the home to a makeover once this adventure ended. The second drone, hugging the ceiling, had crushed a coffee table in its fall, adding wooden bits to the mess. A TV mounted over a fireplace, walls covered in more family photos.

Children's drawings had their place on the fridge behind him. Good ones, too: strong crayon strokes.

Rhimes went forward, rolling his feet with the gun up.

"Third one tagged," Brielle said. "He went for his siblings. Medical three minutes out."

Rhimes clicked in reply. The wall on his left wrapped around the home's central stairs. He followed it to the end, washing around the edge to the last square. A half bath on the right, door open and nobody inside. The living room empty all the way through.

Just the stairwell going up. He wanted to ask if anyone had seen the woman, but there'd be no point. His crew would've spoken, they were good. A glance behind Rhimes confirmed his agent had a place in the backyard near the pool, weapon aiming up. Every window covered, every door spied.

Time to talk.

"Give it up," Rhimes shouted. "Your family's down. Whether they live is up to you!"

No reply. Rhimes gave it three heartbeats, then took another step towards the stairs. A rosy chime jerked his attention to his right, towards that TV. Someone turning it on. The screen went to a splash selection, icons aplenty. Rhimes recognized one glowing towards the top, signaling a link with someone's Tama.

They whirled through the icons, hit one then another, and Rhimes felt his fear melt into resignation. A chosen video started to play. Kids, probably the ones upstairs, laughing and running around the pool. Parents, both in Paragon white-and-blue uniforms, sharing a drink with their casual-clothed grandparents. Dots connected themselves, as they always did.

"Then save your grandkids," Rhimes called up the stairs. "Don't be selfish."

He couldn't tell the woman she'd save herself, that she could see them again. He wouldn't make false promises, not now.

"Door's opening," Brielle said. "Kid's room. It's her, but I don't have a shot. She's staying behind that door."

"Going up," Rhimes replied.

A maple stair, light wood with a carpet running up the middle. Cheery teal, matching the walls, the pool water on a bright day. A dead light hung above him. Vacation photos on either side, so crowded as if the family couldn't bare a naked patch. Rhimes kept moving, fast now, and cleared the hall in time to see the woman walk through the door ahead on the right.

"Take the shot!" Rhimes said.

The drywall on his right split open, a flickering green line slicing through towards Rhimes. He fell back, slipped and rolled down the stairs, landing on his back with his gun facing up.

A crack rang through the air. Loud, sharp.

"She's down," Brielle said. "So's Jesse."

Rhimes swung up to his feet, pounded the stairs and swerved into the room, pistol up and ready. Three teenagers lay about the room, collapsed and unconscious. Posters conquered the walls, an unmade bed the room's centerpiece. The target, a fatal red blossoming beneath her, laid on it. Beyond her, sharp gashes broke through the house walls, tearing down into the yard where Jesse, Rhimes's third agent on this mission, had lost his bottom half.

Rhimes let the pistol fall to his side, watched as medical pods rolled up, as more drones poured in from above.

So much for quiet.

BRIELLE CAUGHT him on his way out. The Ziran office in central LA now served far more than the telecommunications crowd, its stories up and down taken by the forces keeping normals in charge. Rhimes had slipped into a glass-coated elevator, ready to make the thirty floor descent to the showers, a locker, and then a quick walk to the nearest bar.

He'd need three rounds to sleep tonight.

"I didn't have any left," Brielle said as she stood next to him, wearing a white-orange Ziran jacket. Always the loyalist.

"We carry two per target," Rhimes said. "If you—"

"The kids, Rhimes. They moved, I used up my stuns. I wouldn't have fired, but she went for Jesse and I thought she'd get you next."

Rhimes watched the offices roll by. Still full as the afternoon crawled towards evening. People hard at work on the revolution. Some probably spinning up a story about what Rhimes had just done. An anomaly family, plotting terrorist acts, taken care of by noble Ziran agents.

Heroes all.

"You made the right call," Rhimes said. "I'll take the heat."

Wexley wouldn't be happy they'd lost the woman. Or, check that, Adriana wouldn't be happy. She wanted them alive, and Wexley gave her that so long as the anomalies left the streets.

He'd crossed the finish line with Wexley, but the game kept on going. Now he punched a clock, pulled a trigger, and waited for the end.

"We'll do better next time," Brielle said.

"Jesse won't."

Brielle's lips pressed tight as the elevator found its ground home. Rhimes went out, angled towards the locker room. Brielle followed him to the door, pressed her hand against it when Rhimes went for an opening.

"I'm worried about you," Brielle said. "You haven't

been yourself lately."

Rhimes stepped back, gave the locker room door some space in exchange for a potted fern. His hands stayed in black old-school leather jacket pockets. The pistol, reloaded, hung against his chest.

"Who has? You?"

"Respectfully, Rhimes, this isn't about me." Brielle waited, as if she'd presented a platter for Rhimes to load up with feelings.

"It's been a bad day. Bad week. We just lost an agent, and I need a drink."

Brielle turned her face ever-so-slightly, narrowed her eyes, "I get it. Deflecting. Done it myself. But if you want to open up, you can always call."

"Appreciate it," Rhimes replied. "Now, can a man take a shower?"

"You do need it," Brielle said, then she gave Rhimes a single press on the shoulder and headed off.

Inside the locker room, Rhimes lost his clothes and found the shower. Turned the temp up high and waited for steam to fill every corner, the water roaring away from several faucets. Nobody else shared the space, whether because Rhimes hit the right time or because he looked like bad company.

He checked anyway, confirming the room empty, before burying himself in the steam. On his left wrist, fighting through the water with its smart, Ziran design, Rhimes eyed his Tama. A swipe sent the screen, bright enough to see in the clouds if Rhimes brought it up close, to the messages.

The man had tried to call twice, then went for a text. A location, a time, and a request.

The dead had come back to life, and they wanted burritos.

On The Wind

CASSIDY TOSSED THE VOID, the tiny reality tear cutting several strands and their hanging, pink-white dragon fruit to the ground. Dessert, again. Behind her, three teenagers watched.

"Control," Cassidy said, letting the void dissipate. "It's the first thing you have to learn, no matter what you can do."

The teens stared back at her, and Cassidy wondered how much they understood. English wasn't their language, and she'd only picked up Thai's basics in the couple months burned out here in the wilderness. Nonetheless, the kids seemed to get her intent, and their nods provided some hope all these demonstrations weren't useless.

Because if they were, Cassidy might go throw herself in the sea.

Three more small voids finished the lanky cactus's fruit supply and the quartet filled their makeshift packs. The hike back passed in conversation, the teens talking with each other and Cassidy swatting the mosquitos plaguing every step. Back at the camp, at least, netting and smoke would keep the bugs to a manageable level.

Eventually, Apinya insisted, Cassidy would stop noticing the things altogether.

Overhead, the moon and its attendant stars gave light to the walk. Whenever she could trust the path ahead, Cassidy let her eyes wander up, looking for moving dots among those stellar objects. Every plane passing by brought with it some hope, some despair.

A dream that she might get back to Pacifica, see her kids.

Not really children by now—older than the anomaly teenagers following her, definitely—Cassidy didn't know how her family reacted to the new alignment. The new society.

Ziran kept changing the takeover's name, testing the branding and deciding what would play best with a populace confused, frightened, and, if they were anything like the anomalies in the camp, wanting stability more than anything else. Going by the drones hunting overhead daily, Ziran planned to get that stability through genocide.

Apinya wanted to find a plane. They'd set the plan after fleeing Bangkok months ago, filled with vengeance and go-get'em spirit only to find the airports clogged with murderous machines. Apinya's face, as with all the Paragons, had a target attached. Cassidy and Thane tried once by themselves, betting on their exile status to slip through Ziran's net.

That'd cost several lives and put Bangkok's smaller airport on lockdown for three weeks. Apinya said he could see the fires from the camp, kilometers away to the north.

So they'd decided to place their bets on the other Champions. On anomalies closer to the Factory who could make the rescue happen, save the world while Cassidy taught some orphans how to keep from killing themselves with their genetic miracles.

"Here," Cassidy said, pulling a dragon fruit free and lobbing it to a thin, old, man covered in bug bites. He sat on a log near a small fire, staring into the flames like the answers to all his problems could be found flickering therein. "It's delicious."

Thane caught the fruit with one hand, slid an eye towards it as Cassidy plunked herself on a stump nearby, "It's the same thing we've had every night this week."

"I asked the cacti. They won't grow anything else."

"Shame."

Thane's fire sat near the center, with a spiraling outgrowth stretching many meters in all directions. The camp grew over the months as Apinya's messengers found anomaly communities all over southeast Asia and prompted them to come here for refuge. Cassidy wondered how the drones hadn't found them yet, hadn't staged a massive assault, but Apinya never seemed to worry.

Perhaps he had another anomaly in his pocket, one keeping the growing group hidden. Regardless, they numbered several thousand now, and Cassidy figured someone would make a mistake soon.

"When they find us," Cassidy said between bites into the black-specked, soft fruit inside, "are we going to run again?"

"Fight," Thane said, not looking up from his fruit, the fire. "Apinya's already decided. He believes we can destroy enough drones to make a stand. Serve as a symbol to the world."

"And then?"

"Die. That's how the path ends. Every drone Ziran makes is a lethal weapon. Most anomalies have useless abilities. Of all the ones we have gathered here, less than a hundred would be helpful in a fight."

"What happened to all that optimism on the island?" Cassidy asked.

"I am optimistic when it's earned. All of my old plans are worthless, devised for a world that no longer exists. I'm struggling to find a way to a new one."

Cassidy might've tossed off the gloomy words had Apinya, or another anomaly, said them. Coming from Thane, especially in his present, withered state, she could only look at the dirt and shuffle it with her feet. The thin sandals, woven together by some anomalies with practical skills, did nothing to keep the dirt from her toes, did nothing to counter Thane's pessimism.

The man saw so far when he couldn't run a single step. He would be deep in thought now, rushing from one scenario to the next hunting for a chance. Variables mixing and splitting in a probability blender. Thane had described it once as an intellectual adrenaline rush, un-ending until something pulled him from its sweet grasp.

For now, Cassidy left Thane to his half-eaten fruit and the fire. She finished hers and eyed their tent, a shallow thing that nonetheless served to keep them shaded during the hotter and hotter days. The locals said only a few months and they'd have the monsoons, more rain than Cassidy could imagine drowning the camp and everything around it.

At least they'd be cooler then.

Apinya held court at the camp's center, achieving zen with such ease and at all times that Cassidy avoided the Champion whenever she could. He took the disaster with an infuriating grace, adopting a sage-like posture as he taught incoming anomalies Paragon maxims and meditation techniques. Cassidy remembered when the world had considered Apinya a psychic, a manipulator able to change dreams and desires for anyone. Apinya pacified villains, instilled courage in the hesitant, and inspired whole scientific fields at conferences.

Cassidy would know—she'd watched simulcast streams of Apinya giving teachers around the world motivation to deliver the best for every student. She'd felt his touch on her mind back then, a slight fleeting thing that nonetheless washed away the frustration with funding for supplies, with the class clowns and her own rep salary. The feeling died within a day, but Cassidy went back to it often, remembering the sensation and embracing it whenever the grading, the lessons, seemed too much.

Now, Apinya delivered his targeted gospel to three.

Cassidy tilted her head as she approached, trying to identify the group. They appeared to be in uniform, all standing as Apinya spoke, the Champion's own fire dwindling to coals behind him. Neglected, an oddity. Apinya tended to keep his fire large as a motivator, a signal that a Champion still lived at the camp's heart.

Apinya caught Cassidy's approach before she announced herself. The Champion matched Thane in age, but where Thane's body bore a thousand battle's scraps, decades worn out with little nutrition and care, Apinya had a lively sheen. The man no longer held any hair on his smoothed head, but wrinkles made few advances on his face, and wiry muscles roped the healthy limbs sticking from Apinya's grass-woven robe.

"Just when we need her, she appears," Apinya said as Cassidy shuffled into the light. "Cassidy, meet our three newest friends."

Cassidy gave the trio, all turning around, a wave. She kept her hands—always whispering, always waiting to throw a void—by her sides. Getting a better look at the new arrivals, Cassidy saw trials. Their uniforms sported tears, stains, and their faces had battered bruises and gashes. The young man on the left had an eye wholly swollen.

"They come to us from the city," Apinya said.

More? Cassidy thought any anomaly this close would've fled Bangkok by now. She kept her question quiet, letting a raised eyebrow ask it for her.

"Newly arrived there as well," Apinya continued after a planned beat. "By way of a Paragon jet. It seems our friends across the sea would like our help."

"If they flew in on a jet, then where is it?" Cassidy asked, refusing to let hope sneak in. "You didn't land in the swamp?"

"We were forced down by drones," said the one-eyed man, revealing his Canadian origins as he spoke. "We expected it, though. The jet's in one piece, and safe."

"This one," Apinya said, nodding towards the speaking man, "has a rather wonderful ability."

"Can we trust her?" the woman said, glancing back at Apinya. "We were told to get you and only the ones you think would be useful. There's not much room."

"Not much room?" Cassidy asked. "On the jet?"

"It seems the Paragons aren't quite as content to let our world die as I thought," Apinya said. "Aegis has returned to us, and he needs help." Apinya frowned, waved at the camp. "However, should this jet become broader knowledge, I'm afraid we may start a panic."

"Because people might want to leave this paradise?"

"Because a jet like this can take you far away," the woman said. "We're only going to Pacifica."

"Then what are we waiting for?" Cassidy asked, the first hopeful jolts finding their way through her repression. "Apinya, you know who's worth bringing. Let's go."

"Therein lies the problem," Apinya said. "We can't. The jet is no longer in our control."

THANE MOVED FASTER than Cassidy expected. Upon meeting the pilots, the anomaly insisted the mission be started immediately. A squad to go free the jet and take off with it back to Pacifica. The drones would no doubt be waiting, but with a fast enough strike, they could be defeated and the jet used before reinforcements arrived.

Apinya attempted to delay the action with a bureaucrat's litany, an odyssey into possibilities political and otherwise that would descend upon the camp should he disappear along with the upstart society's more powerful anomalies.

Thane growled at that. Cassidy had a better response.

"You're a Champion for the world, Apinya," Cassidy said. "At least, that's what you told us back when you and your friends ripped apart what we knew and replaced it with what you wanted. You have a responsibility to act."

Whether Cassidy's words or the combined stares from the ten other anomalies making up the camp's strongest set —Daw and Kamnan among them—convinced the Champion, Apinya relented. With the time ticking into early morning, fresh coffee swam through the group as they packed, pitched ideas for breaking the drone's hold on the jet, and gave last regards to friends and family they'd be leaving behind.

Cassidy had her own goodbyes to say, waking up and delivering a thank-you, an encouraging word, and a final line to the orphans she and Thane had saved from the village house so many weeks ago.

"You're not coming back?" said the young woman leading the pack, who'd stuck together in their own tent enclave. Their bleary eyes couldn't hide some sadness, a rogue tear dripping down here and there.

Cassidy had been their surrogate parent, a role she'd fallen more and more into as swampy days and nights passed in the jungle. Boredom blended with a former parent's desire to see the wayward children find their way in a hard world that would only be getting harder. Now, she'd be passing them off to the camp at large, and Cassidy willed them to find their places in what would be confusion after Apinya left.

"The Paragons still here won't know what to do with you all," Cassidy said. "Don't let them make your choices. Listen, then decide for yourselves. Trust your own judgment. Stick together."

"You sound like those posters in back at the base," one of 'em quipped.

"Those posters had the right idea," Cassidy fired back. "When we win, come find me. I'll make sure you get what you need."

"What if you don't make it?" A boy asked, his voice sounding like Cassidy's doom was more or less certain.

"Then you'll have to rely on yourselves, like you've already been doing," Cassidy said. "But I'll be fine."

Whether or not Cassidy believed that herself didn't matter.

The trip to Bangkok's northern, and smaller airport, Don Mueang would've eaten the night except for the second pilot in the trio. The young woman had the fourteen members gather in the dark on the camp's southern edge. They assembled, wary and tired selves sporting makeshift packs and bright souls. Cassidy felt the nerves as she joined with Thane, the anomaly rustling up some anger to put himself at a healthy equilibrium.

Nerves, but not fear. These Paragons, these anomalies,

were ready for a fight after weeks spent hiding in the muck and the mire.

Apinya, too, transformed. Now in a more mission-appropriate shirt and pants, the Champion held his ever-present walking stick along with his tongue, keeping silent except to give the pilot permission once the last anomaly had arrived.

The pilot, holding a lighter and using its candle to navigate, put herself at the group's center.

"Stay still," the pilot said. "This might take a minute, and when it starts, it'll feel strange. Try not to freak out."

"Is that an explanation?" Thane muttered.

"She talks like you," Cassidy said.

Thane huffed a laugh.

A breeze, an every-so-often pleasure this deep in the jungle, rippled through the woods. Trees moved, leaves shook, and Cassidy felt the cooler air kiss her sweat-matted hair. Kiss, and then flow right on through it. Her body filled with the wind, at once feeling light and diffuse, her arms and legs less like limbs and more like shadows, sensations, dreams.

Beneath her, around her, Cassidy could sense Thane and all the others, even as the ground where they'd stood slipped away. Trees blew by, Cassidy rushing around them, over ferns and under the canopy until, with an upward surge, she rose over the leaves. Only she wasn't really there, at least so far as she could tell.

She couldn't see anyone else either. The setting moon, the stars, and a vast dark stretch ending with Bangkok's approaching lights. The breeze carried her—carried itself? Cassidy didn't seem to have a body anymore—south at a sprint's pace. Far faster than trudging through the thick foliage.

Adrift, Cassidy found herself embracing the journey.

Conscious thoughts failed to form, sensations instead dominating as her wind-self flowed towards the city and, once she'd passed its outskirts, towards the airport's flashing runways.

There, isolated on a concrete stretch apart from other planes, sat a thin Paragon private jet. It showed the Paragon's white and blue colors, sparkling beneath spotlights. Four drones surrounded it, two gladiators on the ground and a couple patrol machines hovering overhead. A capable, if not strong defense.

Cassidy didn't get a warning. The breeze swept them towards the plane and she found her feet touching the ground in a stumbling run as physical laws once again took hold. Cassidy would've fallen if a reach hadn't found the jet's rear wheels to grab.

She'd been slow.

The shouts came fast, crisp as the Paragons around her reformed and did their duty. Cassidy saw Daw flickering as one Paragon blitzed out pure yellow daggers at the nearest gladiator. The bolts struck the softened drone, bursting into angry crackles that ate away the machine's metal. It started to turn, bring a functioning weapon to bear, only for Thane, now several meters high and roaring, to mash the gladiator's metal skull to putty.

Overhead, an aerial drone tried to counter, its guns ratcheting up only for the spotlights nearby to swing themselves like giant clubs and bash it from the air. The Paragon doing that damage sat in a squat at the jet's base, eyes closed and hands pressed to his temple.

The second gladiator found its fire, sending bullets and worse streaming towards the jet. Ignoring the Paragons to destroy their escape. Cassidy saw the shells impact their plane, assuming the whole plan to be lost in that second, only to see nothing. Precisely nothing. Every attack hitting the aircraft seemed to vanish, as if it'd been sucked into one of Cassidy's voids.

Oh. Right.

Feeling the rush to her fingers, Cassidy threw her right and left, each void leaving a cold snap as it left her body. Heat replaced that snap fast, flushing her face as the voids hit the second gladiator, turning a single drone into a three-piece scrap pile. Behind her, Cassidy heard the other aerial drone crash to the concrete, a lethal green fire consuming its insides.

"Shall we go?" the one-eyed man announced, standing next to the jet's entry.

"Please," Apinya replied.

The pilot touched the jet, shivered, and smiled as the aircraft's boarding door swung down. "She's ready now."

Cassidy, forming up next to a shrinking Thane, could only blink.

Anomalies. Always a surprise.

Pocket Planning

THE HAT SUFFOCATED HIS HEAD, bright red and bearing a logo for an LA team Aegis neither knew nor cared about. He wore it alongside a generic pastel jacket, a shirt and jeans combo built for beachside happy hours. The waves weren't far away, morning sun making its golden impression on the white-caps, their constant crashing a background interrupted by names shrieked into the air. The coffee stand's drink delivery system added zero charm and much efficiency to the boardwalk's breakfast crew, a population growing as Aegis drew those Paragons worth a damn to his fight.

Beneath his sneakered feet sat sanded boards, and Aegis found his eyes drifting down, picking out gaps showing white grains below. Crabs and the seagulls waiting to eat crumbs parlayed around the waking crowd standing in a shuffled line.

Back in Manhattan, in his big tower, Aegis would've had his beverage choice waiting for him after leaving the shower. Warm and perfectly prepared. Now he waited behind stiffs getting set for retail shifts and the few diehards ready to hit sales as soon as the boardwalk shops opened their doors. Up and down the beach signs waved from storefronts, declaring deals in big, round numbers.

The Paragons might be reeling, Ziran and its corporate backers might be installing a new worldwide order, but swimsuits and souvenirs still needed selling. The economy must continue.

"Don't forget my mocha," Celice said, her voice catching in Aegis's ear. "With the extra shot."

Aegis glanced up, winced at the people still before him. Celice took their situation better than he did. She snagged incoming challenges and turned them into to-dos, dishing out tasks and getting them completed while Aegis . . . well, while Aegis waited in line for coffee.

It'd been easier, decades ago, to use his righteous spirit to declare the world a corrupt and messy place. He'd stood before the cameras, his visage beaming out to all the suffering people, saying a fix would be coming. The wars, the poverty, the hunger would all end, thanks to the Paragons and their superhuman saviors.

Behind him, on the beach, some kid broke from his parents with a kite. The red and green bird and its attendant string took the air, riding the breeze with aplomb. They seemed happy enough. Secure enough. Just like so many did when the Paragons kept their promise.

Then why did so few rise up in protest? Where were the normals ready to leap to Aegis's side and fight for the better world he'd made?

"You going to punch in an order, mate?" said a dull-eyed dude standing behind him.

Apparently lines moved faster than Aegis remembered. Then again, it'd been a long time since he'd stood in one.

Maybe he was too privileged.

The screen accepted Aegis's taps, directed him to pay his reps in a cheery tone. Aegis held his Tama against the terminal, and the same voice congratulated 'Reed' on his successful payment. Mathieu and Celice put that one together, creating accounts and personas to go along with the Paragon's sudden need to keep themselves secret.

When they'd asked Aegis what he wanted his new name to be, the Champion had suggested his original. He hadn't used his birth name in public since adopting Aegis. The government, to keep his family and friends protected, scrubbed out any references to Aegis's former life. It seemed safe enough, but his daughter insisted otherwise. Something random, something with zero connection anyone could draw between its syllables and the person they protected.

So 'Reed', random enigma, stood off to the side and waited for his order. His Tama called to him, buzzing with another hail, another message. He couldn't take those here, not with so many people around that might hear, but he could read. The little missives stacked on the wrist-sized screen, some detailing the day's operations, others yesterday's results from around the world.

Attacks on Ziran facilities, defensive moves to protect Paragon and other anomaly groups. Jabs and blocks, stabs and deflections.

He recognized the game, because not all that long ago Aegis had been on the other side.

The Paragons cut off the world quick, toppling the big players and forcing resistance underground. Just like today, people looked around and decided that, if they could feed their families, keep their homes, then it wasn't worth taking up arms in resistance. Particularly when the enemy wasn't some insane other, but neighbors with genetic accidents.

Guerrillas fought back regardless. Small actions, assassination attempts. Aegis himself took a sniper's round to the cheek that knocked him out for an afternoon. Eventually, one step at a time, the Paragons and their Champion leaders smashed the cells and cemented their control.

Would Ziran do the same thing to them?

Up above, a gladiator drone, all white and orange in Ziran colors, floated overhead. Omnipresent now, those things.

"Reed?" a woman asked, holding a drink carrier to go along with her own order. "It's been calling you for a few minutes now."

GETTING to the Paragons didn't take some secret codes, some fantastical effort. Aegis wandered through a beachwear store, heading straight for the back. The shop wasn't officially open, but the unlocked doors let Aegis in as easily as they'd let him out minutes ago. In the back, nestled between sandal racks and children's floaties, a thin door marked Employee's Only waited.

Aegis glanced at the knob. Let his lip curl up in a small smile as he looked back, confirmed the swimwear blocked any sight lines. The Champion stepped forward into the door and came through the other side, the shop long gone.

Above, where a ceiling might be, a constant deep blue glow stretched to seeming infinity. Around Aegis, people bustled, watching their Tamas or each other. Clicks and snaps sounded as squads armed themselves from racks lining dark walls. Neon green signs marked entries and exits like the one Aegis had just used.

Some led to hotels with Paragon-friendly ownership, where anomalies could get their rest. Others led to restaurants, to gyms, to anywhere else in roughly a hundred kilometer area a Paragon might want to go. Tied cables ran out one dimensional door to draw power, Internet, and spread it all around to tech inside.

Pocket, the anomaly who'd made the space, lay in its center. Aegis went near her with the drinks, making his way across the crowded expanse to his daughter's claimed area for Paragon intelligence. Seeing Pocket stole away Aegis's smile: she'd been plied with stabilizing drugs, plugged into IVs and catheters, stuck in a forever hold to keep this place alive.

How many times had Pocket made places like this, smaller but just as focused, to give the Paragons a platform to stage an assault? Even to prep for a particular show? Pocket would pick her people, pick her sites, and stretch the world's physical boundaries to make space. Afterwards, she'd walk out an exit, exhale a deep breath, and the miniature realm she made would fade to nothing.

Over Pocket's head, tied to a big screen they'd dragged in, a counter in teal numbers ticked down. Aegis watched it, running the math in his head.

"One day left and we move again," Celice said, snagging her drink off the tray and giving it a look. "You went to a machine, Dad? Again?"

"It's right there," Aegis replied. "Easy."

"Which you equate with good for some reason."

Aegis pointed at the counter. "I equate it with time. Do we have the next site picked out?"

"There's a housing development back towards the city," Celice replied. "There's enough vacancies that we shouldn't have much competition."

Finding a place that wouldn't wonder about several hundred new occupants appearing overnight took work, particularly when they had to repeat the process every week or so. Any longer on the cot and Pocket might not survive. After she'd rested for a couple days, up sprang the dimension and their raids could start again. A necessary pause.

If she collapsed her dimension with everyone inside it?

Not even Aegis's healing would save him then.

"And the next one?" Aegis asked.

"Next three," Celice said. "We're getting better at this."

His daughter kept a chirpy vibe, a hard reversal from what, Aegis had been told, her demeanor had been while Aegis sat in the vat. His surprise recovery dominated their father-daughter relationship, with Celice trying to stuff Aegis into every backroom, non-combat role she could find. As if Aegis had returned made from glass.

Aegis followed Celice back to her workstation, a computer plethora with every monitor racing through readouts Aegis couldn't parse. He knew his way around a Tama, but Celice operated in a different sphere. One that seemed to always find distractions.

"Here's today's targets," Celice said, as she'd said every morning since the war really started, since they'd returned North America. She swiped on a monitor, the screen flipping to five columns split into rows, each one detailing a different objective. "A good set today, minimal risk. Ziran's trying to adjust but it's slow. Like we're not a priority."

"Because we aren't," Aegis said.

"If you're about to say that they're thinking about the world and we're thinking small, I'm gonna get annoyed."

Aegis shook his head, "Last night, on the boat. A helicopter took off with people inside it. There were cells too."

"Empty ones."

"You know what they were labeled."

Celice turned her chair around, cocked her head at her

father, "We know Ziran's taking anomalies when they can. That's not a surprise."

"But transporting them overseas?" Aegis leaned past Celice, pointed at another big, wide screen showing action reports by media, by people catching things on their Tamas. "See all these? The teams Ziran sends around? Why risk anything when a drone could eliminate a target from afar?"

"Your supervillains are coming back to haunt you, dad," Celice said. "Let's say Ziran is taking anomalies. Where, and for what?"

"I want to find out. Add it to the list."

"Higher than number one?"

"No. That stays."

Mynx and Maya had top billing. The Champions, last reported at the Factory, hadn't been seen since Ziran's takeover. Mynx would never freely give up the Factory and its drones, her pride and, if not joy, obsession. Celice and Matthias had people scanning every channel, watching every feed. Aegis had anomalies that could read minds lingering as close to the Factory as the Champion dared, hoping to steal useful thoughts from a wayward employee.

Nothing yet.

"I want to attack again," Aegis said.

Celice rolled her eyes, tapped on her Tama. A call screen popped up, answered within a second by a man who'd stabbed Aegis in the back.

"You here?" Celice asked. "Can you come over and talk my father off the ledge?"

"THREE TIMES," Zhan-Yo said, meeting them at a narrow conference table. Pocket's micro dimension didn't have much for privacy, so the table and its attendant chairs sat apart, but without walls, doors. The ground beneath them had a violet halo, calling them out from the dimension's otherwise dark environs. "We've tried three times and it's always failed. It's always cost lives."

"We've made it farther every attempt," Aegis said, leveling a look at Zhan-Yo, Celice, and Mathieu. A far different crew than the Champions he used to work with when the world was in crisis, but, aside from himself, the other Champions were fighting Ziran in their own regions. "The next one, we might break through."

"Farther?" Mathieu said. "Aegis, we haven't made it in the front door. Ziran's turned the place impenetrable, in no small part because you've made it clear the Factory's our only real objective."

"Hey," Celice said, and Aegis saw the way her hand migrated to Mathieu's wrist.

"Because it *is* our only real objective," Aegis countered. "The Factory makes most of the world's drones. They're all controlled from within those walls. We take it, Ziran's effort is over."

Zhan-Yo held up a finger, then took his Tama and swiped from the screen onto the table. Names listed out, split across from locations. Zhan-Yo slid a finger along his Tama and several names highlighted, including one that had Aegis growling before he caught himself.

"I'm not going to argue with that," Zhan-Yo said, "but I've been in your position, Aegis. I wanted a swift end to the fight, but I wasn't prepared to achieve it. Instead, I went halfway, and ruined everything."

"If you're talking about the bomb, then you're right," Aegis replied.

"Dad." Celice continued playing mediator.

"We can't take the Factory as we are now," Zhan-Yo

said, throwing Celice a respectful nod. "We need more help, and I'm working to get it. Reinforcements are coming that can swing the balance in our favor."

Aegis pointed at one name, "Thane? That's your idea of a winning card? He'll try and kill us as soon as he gets in here."

"Apinya disagrees."

"Apinya? You've been talking to Apinya?" Aegis stared hard at Zhan-Yo, hands pressing on the table. That this man, this murderer, would be going behind Aegis's back and—

"Dad," Celice said, louder this time. "Can we talk, outside?"

THE SEA BREEZE cooled Aegis's temper. Back on the boardwalk, coffees in hand, father and daughter walked along a pier out over the waves. Blue sky, sunshine, salt spray smell. Families laughing, a few fishermen casting their lures into the surf.

"He's taking over," Aegis continued, insisting on the thrust despite Celice's constant counters. "Now Zhan-Yo's going behind my back, getting the other Champions on his side."

"He's doing what he's good at," Celice said. "We all are. Zhan-Yo knows strategy. You know how to hit people really hard."

"Thanks for that."

Celice smirked, "It wasn't just you last time either, you know."

Sure, but back when Aegis and the other Champions pulled together, they'd been on the rise. The insurgent force, sure of their cause and their inevitable victory. Aegis could be, had been, the standard-barer while Mynx, Apinya, and the others dealt with the fine print.

And Celice's mother had been there too, fighting alongside him, making sure Aegis didn't do the stupid things he too often settled on. Just like Celice did now.

"We made mistakes back then too," Aegis said, finding an empty spot and settling his elbows on the wood rail. "Compromises that took off some shine in exchange for cleaner wins. Fewer bodies. I don't want to repeat those."

"That's where Thane comes in?"

"We used him first as a hammer. He and I would crash on in together, the blunt instrument delivering Paragon justice to anyone defying our control." Aegis rubbed his chin. He hadn't had to shave since Maya did her thing. Stronger than ever, maybe, but his body had changed. "Your mom would cool him down after missions, bring him back to a stable state."

Celice kept quiet.

"It worked fine until it didn't," Aegis said. "We thought we had'em all, until one moron with a gun decides it's time to go out shooting. Your mother had Thane in her arms, calming him down, when the bullets hit. I don't know how many, it didn't matter. He had her neck snapped before the man stopped firing."

Even Maya couldn't bring someone back from the dead. She'd tried anyway. Wasn't long after that the Champions split up. Too much trauma and not enough time to heal.

"Not his fault."

"I know," Aegis said. "I know, I know, I know. Dammit. But he's unpredictable, Celice. He could do the same to anyone. To you. To me."

"If we don't get inside that Factory," Celice said, "a drone's going to do what Thane might. Ziran's going to erase the Paragons from the planet, and anomalies along with them. Zhan-Yo's right to try this."

Aegis put a hand on his daughter's shoulder, "Then, when the time comes, you stay away from that one. From them all. I buried your mother and I won't bury you."

SIX

Dinner Dialogue

CHICAGO DWINDLED IN THE REAR-VIEW. Its great buildings, a skyline Kat hadn't been without for so many years now, vanishing with the rain. The interstate, crowded with pods racing in synchronized efficiency, shot on towards the horizon and beyond. They'd be riding it that far and farther.

Gordon, patched up and resting, sat sleeping next to Kat. His breathing came with the telltale rustling suggesting a coming cold, one Kat had no desire to catch, had no options to avoid. Taking separate pods on a cross-country trek seemed stupid, cold or no, and a plane would've been dumber still.

The drones would've shot Gordon if he appeared at an airport. Then they might shoot Kat too, just because.

Gordon didn't have a locale, but he had a rough idea. A region pulled from a tracker's ping. Gordon sold the story back at the small house, with Paragons and Elementals crowded around him, looking to learn where their friends had gone.

He'd been walking around Ziran's headquarters,

trying to find a way inside that wouldn't end with his insides out. An anomaly—Gordon figured the culprit to be a disgruntled Paragon—flashed their powers at a drone, damaging it with some acidic spray and drawing attention. As the drones descended, Gordon found his ping, ran by while feigning a panic, and slapped the ping onto the anomaly.

Drone fire clipped Gordon as the man fled, but the machines had their metal hands full with the Paragon. Slipping and sliding from one pod to the next, from one side street to another, Gordon made his bloody way back.

"And the ping is?" Beth asked, the Elemental looming over Gordon's legs at the cot's end.

A corner lamp couldn't compete with computer monitors and their splashing blue light. The glow squeezed between the shoulder-to-shoulder circle, hitting Gordon with a striped shadow silhouette.

"Still working," Gordon said. "Heading west fast."

"Wait," Weed, next to Gordon's right, spoke up. "You said the anomalies are alive. A ping doesn't tell you that."

"But their direction does," Kat said, sparing Gordon a few breaths. "If they were just killing the anomalies, why fly them far from town? Ziran must want them for something."

"You're making a big guess," Beth said.

"Hi, I'm your reality. I'm desperate and need a big swing to turn things around, so how about we just ride with this idea?"

"Because we can't afford to chase dreams," Weed said. "Aegis gave us our orders. Harass and hinder as much as we can until he and the other Champions set things right."

"I'm telling the truth," Gordon protested, looking so pathetic in that bed.

"No one's doubting you." Weed shrugged. "I just can't

risk lives chasing after a drone that's already across the Mississippi."

"Then you don't have to," Kat said. "Just do me a favor: keep an eye on my dog."

KAT WATCHED HER TAMA, a video playing on its small screen. Tap, her apartment's AI, sent it to her weeks ago, the recording from months before. The AI had a programmed reflex to record happy moments, things Kat might want to relive. On her Tama, Calvin played with Seeker. Kat wasn't there—at an Elemental meeting, most likely—but the anomaly and Kat's dog danced around the apartment, playing with a toy rope. Calvin laughed, trash-talked the husky, who didn't mind in the least.

A sappy video, a cheesy one. Not the thing Kat would've gone for on her own, would've gone for a few months ago.

"Then again, what hasn't changed?" Kat muttered.

Around her, Kat felt her suit, its gadget array nestled into her wrists, against her waist, legs, and resting on her head. Its every object purchased and integrated to capture those anomalies just like Ziran's drones were doing now. Back then, she'd done it for the money. As a means to survive.

Now?

She could use them for something a little more impor-tant than reps.

"Are we there yet?" Gordon asked, sitting up.

"The suburbs?" Kat replied. "You missed them."

"Oh no." Gordon shook his head, looked out at the highway. At the pod's screen showing the ludicrous hours it would take to get to LA. "Don't suppose you brought a deck of cards?"

The ping put Gordon's anomaly well north of the city, but even Kat's reckless nature didn't suggest sending two humans in against whatever Ziran was doing there. Kat figured the drones guarding all those anomalies had to number in the hundreds, thousands.

Could Mynx's Factory make a million of the things?

"Never owned one," Kat said.

"What, cards?" Gordon replied. "Never? Not even as, like, a souvenir?"

"Who would I play with? Seeker?"

"I wasn't always gone."

Kat left a lip corner upturned as she looked back at her Tama, the video with Calvin and Seeker looping back through another play.

"And you never seemed that sad," Gordon continued.

"I wasn't sad, and I'm not now," Kat replied. "Just because I didn't choose to be like you, doesn't mean my life wasn't a good one."

Gordon put his hands up, "Peace, Kat. This isn't a short trip, and I don't want to spend it fighting."

"Then how about planning?" Kat said.

"For something we don't know or understand?" Gordon said. "My *plan* was to get a good look at the place and go from there."

"Suppose you're right," Kat swiped away the video on the Tama, sat back against the seat. "I don't know, Gordon. How would you like to spend the trip?"

"Movies?" Gordon nodded at the pod's console. "There's a few thousand on there, I think. Don't know the last time I watched one."

"I saw enough in the hospital."

Those had been bleak days. Gordon stopping by here and there, but with the Paragons collapsing, everything and everyone had been on edge. Kat, largely immobilized, had to decide whether to embrace the chaos and sink into the dire news or escape it all. She'd done the latter, especially when Calvin never replied, when Gordon said he couldn't find the anomaly.

Easier to escape, one fantasy hour at a time.

"Yeah," Gordon said. "But I bet you haven't seen my favorites."

Kat closed her eyes, let her lips smile again, "Okay Gordon, pick one. Wow me."

In Gordon's defense, the comedy-drama blends making up his pod playlist turned the day's travel into quick work. With the pod zipping along the kilometers, Kat and Gordon embroiled themselves in ridiculous affairs, their laughter, absurd stakes, and heart-warming conclusions softening the trip's edges until the pod slid into the first night's destination.

Lincoln, nestled in barren Nebraska fields, looked largely untouched by the revolution. The University dominated, though Gordon directed the pod to stick to the city's outskirts. Kat would've suggested sleeping in the damn thing if not for Gordon's own wounds. Dressings needed changing, showers needed taking.

And, if she was being honest, sleeping in an actual bed rather than a shared couch seemed like a good deal.

The chain hotel the pod picked—Gordon put in their rep budget and it chose accordingly—eschewed personal anything, letting the pair check in through a screen at the entry. The keys dropped down in a slot, along with a stale recommendation to try the hotel's in-house restaurant, also fully robotic.

"Just delightful," Kat said as they made their way down a featureless hall to their designated room. "Why don't I travel more often when it's so much fun?"

"Hey now," Gordon said. "The movies weren't that bad, were they?"

"They were fine," Kat said, dropping the cynicism. "Thank you."

"Oh, don't thank me yet." Gordon swiped the key, unlocking the door into another spiritless chamber. Two beds awaited them, along with the standard TV and flower prints on the walls. "We've got two more days of this."

Two longer days, but at least the scenery would be more interesting. Kat held to that idea as they took their turns in the shower, reviewing their sparse suitcases for new clothes, and finally heading back outside to find somewhere to eat. Their pod sat in its charging station, sucking up power. Gordon angled for it until Kat put a hand on his arm.

"I'm not getting back in that thing till tomorrow," she said. "How about right there?"

Their hotel stood over a classic off-the-highway neighborhood, with few houses and chains aplenty. Drive-by industry thrived even more with pods around, as travel became cheap and nobody had to blow reps on gas or car insurance. Kat's father, back when she'd been tiny, had pointed to these weird oases as a future-past blend.

Time doesn't take everything. At least not right away.

Then he'd grin, ask Kat to pick a place, that's where they'd go, all four of them. Smiling, laughing, and—

"You know what you want to order?" Gordon said, the laminated menu book on the speckled white table between them. "The burgers look good. Is it too cliche to get a malt and fries?"

"Never," Kat replied.

She'd been eying the dessert drinks herself. The restaurant wasn't a diner, but more one that plugged its menu with trends from across America. Too many pages, too many options, and too much atmosphere.

From the outside, the restaurant—*Americana*—looked like a fun place, with neon and memorabilia running along its wooden siding. License plates, old and new, coated the walls. Signed photos from various celebrities, most Kat didn't know, decorated the entry. Gordon figured they weren't real, but who knew and who cared.

At least this place had real humans serving, though those seemed to be the only ones in the place. Kat checked her Tama again. Only nine. Not exactly late, but then she ran on Chicago time. Maybe Nebraska took things differently.

Or maybe . . . Kat caught motion, looked up as a person who definitely was not the young man who'd sat them came their way. This guy looked double Kat's years, sported earrings and silver swished-back hair matching his chef's apron. A long burn went up the man's right arm, easily visible when he set both palms on their table.

"Don't know who you are, but I know what you are," the man said. "And I don't want you here."

Gordon looked stunned, as if the tracker could never expect such rudeness thrown his way. Kat had played around Chicago's darker places, though, where being polite rarely matched reality. Spending too much time in the pod had wound her up too, so when the man's demand offered to flip Kat's switch, all the pent-up energy gave her the go.

"Who do you think we are?" Kat said, planting her elbow on the table and her chin on her hand, staring at the man.

"Trackers have a way of walking," the man replied. "A way of looking around that I don't happen to like."

"Because you're an anomaly operating under the radar?"

The man sighed, straightened and nodded towards the restaurant's door, "I asked you to leave."

"C'mon Kat," Gordon started before Kat waved him off.

Not moving, she cocked her head towards the chef, "What's your problem, guy? You know trackers aren't operating anymore. We're nothing now. Just normal people. Like you."

The man had his head shaking before Kat finished. "Don't care what you are now. People like you pushed my friends into the Paragons. You don't think, you just pull your triggers. Claim it's all for the good." He stopped himself, pointed now towards the exit. "Please, just go."

Gordon tried again, and this time Kat let him. Together, they scooted from the booth. The chef gave them room. Gordon took advantage, but, standing, Kat faced up to the man. She read his eyes this close, the lines in his face. This wasn't anger talking, but experience, exhausted experience.

"I'm sorry about your friends," Kat said, then waved an arm at the quiet restaurant. "Sure you want to kick us out? Doesn't look like you've got business."

"That's not your problem." The man flushed, more in his leathery throat than anywhere else.

"Let's walk away, Kat," Gordon whispered.

"Nah, not yet," Kat said, folding her arms. "Know what you learn to do quick as a tracker? Read people, understand when they're lying, when they're hiding something."

The man folded his own arms, matching Kat. "Leave."

"What's your ability?" Kat said. "Making a perfect medium-rare every time?"

Gordon grabbed Kat, pulled her around, "What are you doing?"

Kat freed herself, put a step's space between her and Gordon and the man, a human triangle between booths.

"They're all anomalies, Gordon," Kat said, pointing to the man, the hostess, the boy who'd sat them at their table. "How about everyone in back, too?"

Now the man's flush vanished, those burly arms falling free. His head shook again, but without any heart.

"Why does it matter?" Gordon asked. "Who cares if they're—"

"Because they're hiding, Gordon," Kat said. "They're hiding here instead of fighting. The Paragons are dying every day, and they could use the help. Instead this guy's in here making milkshakes with, what, five? Ten anomalies?"

"Thirty-four," the man said, straightening. "All refugees from your Paragons, or the drones that came after. We don't want any part in your war."

"My war?" Kat laughed, feeling a little crazy slice into it. "Haven't you read any history? Don't you know what happens to people that don't stand up when their number gets called?"

Gordon looked between the two, lost. So long as he kept quiet, Kat didn't care. Calvin, as much as refugee as these people, threw himself into the fight. That this guy would dare keep so many anomalies on the sidelines . . . it didn't seem fair. Even if their abilities had no place on the battlefield, they could still cook, clean, fix things for the Paragons who could fight.

"I know the local Paragons all died the day Ziran took over," the man said. "I know some didn't wake up when the drones blew up their building. I know that's what they'd do to us. It's not the brave thing, but we've got kids here. Mothers, fathers, families. They don't belong in this fight."

"They might not have a choice," Kat shot back and, again, the man shrugged.

The chef didn't seem like he would be budging. He made no calls to action, had no epiphany about embarking with his crew to wherever the closest resistance cell resided. Kat couldn't call herself a diplomat, and she had nothing left to say.

Instead, giving in to Gordon's urging, Kat turned and the two left the restaurant. They stopped by another, robot-driven place and snagged some spicy takeout, wandering back in the dark to their hotel room.

"You had to fight with that guy?" Gordon asked as they settled in. "You really had to?"

"I don't know why," Kat said, staring at her fried rice like it might hold some answers. "I've never felt a part of anything before. Not till now, and seeing us all cramped in that house, fighting to survive, while these people just sit on the sidelines?"

"It's their choice, Kat. Their lives, their choice."

"They're choosing wrong."

"The Paragons tried to make choices for them, and look at what's happened? Maybe that's why we're here at all."

"The Paragons?"

Gordon nodded, and for once, Kat figured he might be right. Aegis and his Champions, their rigid code. She'd slipped around it through her normal genes, but for those anomalies, nothing had really changed. Before, they'd been hunted by trackers. Now, drones.

"Then what are we doing, Gordon? Are we helping the wrong people?"

"The way I see it," Gordon said, snapping cheap chopsticks apart, "is we're getting our friend back."

That, at least, was a cause Kat could get behind.

Promotions

WALKING through another person's house put Rhimes on edge. Then again, he didn't notice his nerves much as he went through the thick doors separating the Factory from Mynx's personal home. The big barriers were so alien from normal office spaces, homes, anywhere that they tended to wipe away your thoughts.

Rhimes, washed up and wrung out from yesterday's assault, having burned the day in debriefs and office work, eschewed tactical gear for a loose gray suit. No holsters, no weapons, so he passed the scan from Wexley's personal gladiator. The drone stood tall just past the doors, eyeing Rhimes in its implacable fashion.

"See? All good," Rhimes said to the machine.

The drone didn't answer except to, with all four arms, gesture Rhimes ahead. Even so, as Rhimes took those first soft-shoed steps, a buzzing companion slipped from the gladiator's back to follow along. Ready and willing with a stunning dart or, should the situation escalate, a lethal one, the hovering drone took its meter-back position behind Rhimes's head.

Security took a paramount position these days, what with anomalies all having Wexley's face topmost on their target boards. At first, even before they'd assaulted the Factory, Rhimes wanted to know what Wexley planned for this part.

How do you defend against people that could be anyone, be anywhere, could level a city with a nasty look?

The answer, according to Wexley, was make sure they were too damned afraid to act. Then, while the anomalies hesitated, use the drones to capture or kill'em first. Thus far the strategy worked, albeit with some Paragon cells refusing to die.

Rhimes attributed the stubbornness to Aegis's reappearance. The Champion's revival gave a spine to the scrambling Paragons, pushed them back from a disorganized brink and into an annoying force. When Wexley sent Rhimes the meeting request, Rhimes figured the continuing campaign would be the main subject.

Hopefully the meeting would be short. Rhimes had somewhere to be.

Mynx's main house had a clean, mild luxury to it. Ocean design mingled with a disinterested efficiency to create a white, glass-filled, and bright inside. Soft woods and elaborate rugs. Framed black-and-white photos from the Champion glory days. Mynx even had a few magazine covers, those print artifacts, up in lights. Not so much to be cliche, but enough to let a visitor know their host had a reputation.

That host, right now, sat in a tube deep beneath the Factory. Rhimes estimated fewer than five people knew Mynx's ultimate location, or whether she lived at all. He'd gone down to look at her himself, partly to gauge the Champion's prison and ensure it wouldn't pop her free anytime soon. Partly, too, to look at a legend without needing to shoot her.

Because for all the talk, for all the hopes and dreams pushed by Zhan-Yo and now taken up by Wexley, they were still fighting against the people that'd defined Rhimes's world for decades. Aegis and his crew might've turned into dictators, but at the start they were true heroes. Flying around the world and sometimes beyond it to turn away danger wherever it rose.

"Getting distracted?" Wexley asked, waving Rhimes his way from the sliding glass door leading out to the vast porch. "I'd tell you to indulge in whatever you're thinking about, but we're pressed today."

"Pressed?" Rhimes asked, following Wexley's direction outside, where the sea breeze mingled with the warm sun.

The porch held sway over a nook between the steep cliffs and their ocean cousin. A carved path led from the white wood platform down to the sand and the waves beyond, while behind, stones and sparse trees provided a barrier between the house and the Factory's churning cogs.

Wexley took on a fitting look, loose button-up flapping, his sunglasses thick and hair styled up to an aggressive slice. Rosy red burns marred the image, though, carving up and down the man's arms and chest, visible through the shirt's thin fabric. Victory's price, Wexley called it.

An anomaly could've cleared away those scars at any major hospital, but so far Wexley had let them be.

"Aegis and his annoying crew hit another ship last night," Wexley said. "Five more came through unmolested, but even so. He's a blight."

"We're trying to track them." Rhimes fell back on the words he'd practice on the pod ride over. "They move often, and not in ways we understand."

"Because they have an anomaly helping. That's always

the answer, Rhimes. When someone cheats now it's not because they're clever, but because they found someone who can break the rules without trying."

"Right," Rhimes said, taking the offered sparkling water Wexley held out to him. A half-eaten salmon salad graced the porch's long glass table, embedded screens displaying news scattered around the plate. "We'll find them eventually."

"That's why I called you here," Wexley said. Ziran's leader and thus, by extension, the world's, waved his own glass towards the ocean. Grim gray shapes moved on the horizon, Ziran freighters bringing parts to the Factory. "I don't need *you* finding Aegis. I need you supervising that effort. I need you managing my security. I need you looking across this planet we find ourselves controlling and making sure it stays that way."

Rhimes fought to keep a neutral expression as Wexley spoke. Waited until the man paused, read the knowing, slight smile on Wexley's face and knew Wexley expected Rhimes to say exactly what he was about to speak.

But the truth was the truth.

"I'm not a manager," Rhimes said.

"You lead a squad very well," Wexley said. "Back in Chicago, you ran our entire off-board enterprise. You can't call yourself anything but a manager."

Rhimes opened his mouth, and Wexley put his free hand on Rhimes's shoulder.

"This is the part where you say yes," Wexley said. "There's nobody I trust who can handle this. I won't have you out in the field, where any anomaly might get lucky. You're going to be here, at the Factory, working with me to define a better future." Wexley set his glass down, took the hand off Rhimes's shoulder and offered the other one for a shake. "Stake your claim on history, Rhimes. Be my general."

With the drone and its deadly weapons buzzing behind him, Rhimes did the only thing he could: he shook.

WEXLEY DIDN'T WAIT LONG to put his general to work. As soon as the handshake ended, Rhimes's Tama blew up with incoming messages. All pre-programmed, and all placing Rhimes into initiatives spanning the globe. There were assaults aimed at clearing out Elementals in London, a coordinated cyber tracking effort in China meant to lock out methods Paragon communications, and, of course, drone deployments on every continent to review.

Most important? Find the Champions still living and ensure they were dead or captured as soon as possible.

Leaving the Factory, Rhimes called a pod and set a particular course, swiping away the squawking demands on his wrist and leaning back into the thin seat cushions while LA's cityscape scrolled into play.

He'd started with Ziran as a security guard, a low-level way to make good on his military experience in a world that no longer needed militaries. Competence climbed ladders, and before all that long Rhimes found himself standing outside the top office. Met a woman named Sylvie as she left a one-on-one with Zhan-Yo. She sized him up, took out a small notebook, wrote a place and a time on a page, tore it off, and handed it over.

Now Sylvie occupied a grave somewhere in that city and Rhimes employed a trick she'd taught him: never take a pod right where you want to go.

Rhimes left this one blocks away, yet well within rough-and-tumble construction, demolition. The stadium destroyed months ago still absorbed LA's industry into its removal and renewal, drones and humans alike swarming around the site, their evidence left in warning signs, caution tape, and closed businesses.

Not that the flags warded off Rhimes's target. The man occupied a bench, burrito in hand and bag with Rhimes's own choice holding a spot on the tanned wood seat. Across a street closed to traffic, the stadium's shredded hulk hid behind scaffolding, tarps, and moving bodies, both mechanical and not. Bullhorns mingled with anonymous beeps mingled with the blaring daytime music accompanying labor everywhere. The day shift transferring into night, the clean-up an all hours affair.

Rhimes took the seat, adjusted his jacket, kept his eyes straight ahead. Zhan-Yo, next to him, leaned forward in his straw hat, thin flower-printed shirt and white shorts showcasing knobby knees, legs a little withered from their time in hiding. Sunglasses hid the man's eyes, salsa made a dripping line down his chin and landed on a well-placed lap napkin.

"Long time," Zhan-Yo said.

"Not that long," Rhimes replied. "Tell me you have a reason for asking me here beyond burritos."

"You want one that bad?"

Zhan-Yo's voice crackled, verve hiding behind the bites. If Wexley offered up cold efficiency, Zhan-Yo sounded like the true revolutionary, always a breath away from some epic speech.

"A burrito?"

"A reason to leave him," Zhan-Yo replied.

"It's not what I expected," Rhimes said. No reason to hide things from Z. The boss had always been perceptive about his employees, if not always his own goals. "You think you've won and then you find out there's so much more, and it's so much worse."

"Worse?"

Rhimes reached over, looked in the bag. A burrito, some chips. He took the latter out, crunched into the salt. Wished he'd brought some water.

"I'm not going to say anymore till I figure out what you're doing," Rhimes said. "Nobody's heard a word from you since London."

"Learned about that, did you?"

"The world saw you get put on a platform, your head about to go for a ride."

"When it didn't, I changed sides."

The boss continued while Rhimes swapped from his chips to the burrito, digging into the adobo chicken while Zhan-Yo detailed a cloak-and-dagger journey over the Atlantic and the broad American middle to get here. Necessity cemented alliances between him and Aegis, between what Paragons they could find and the normals who'd once fought to undermine them.

"Most people want equality, freedom," Zhan-Yo said. "They don't want wholesale destruction or genocide."

"Wexley would call it control." Rhimes wiped his hands, his mouth. It'd been a damn good burrito. "Hard to let living bombs walk free."

"A human doesn't have to be an anomaly to cause damage." Zhan-Yo nodded at the obvious before them. "Aegis and I are a start. If Wexley could be convinced, if we stopped the raids and the drone attacks, we could form a common world together."

"If Wexley could be convinced to do what? Give it all up?"

Zhan-Yo sat back on the bench, looked up towards the sun and a drone coasting by overhead, "Everyone has their motivations. What are yours?"

"I joined Ziran for a job. I helped you for a cause. I

never signed up for an extermination, but that's what this is. I'm not gonna claim to be some idealist, but I thought this was about more than a body count."

"If you remind Wexley of that, he might see things as you do. On his current course, there's no getting away. He'll either lose or win, but he'll be a monster either way."

"Okay, so I do what? Walk in there and say hey, buddy, how about you chill for a minute and call this whole thing off?"

"Not you." Zhan-Yo reached inside his shirt's front pocket, one decorated with a peach-colored orchid. He pulled out another small notebook, just like the one Sylvie used. He tore out a page without writing on it first, handing it to Rhimes. "Her."

A boring name, an interesting address. A care center in Chicago's northern suburbs.

"Who's this?" Rhimes said.

"She'll tell you," Zhan-Yo replied, standing up and stretching both arms tall over his head. "She has the key to stopping Wexley long enough, maybe, for him to reconsider."

"She must be something."

"She most certainly is that. Stay in touch, my friend. It just may be we can stop this from getting too much worse."

BACK AT THE FACTORY, Rhimes looked around a blank office. The space opened into a view over the busy, churning drone floor and, given the various hooks in the ceiling, had been designed for some prototype work before its current assignment. No art hung on the walls, only a prefab desk and a rolling black chair occupied its center.

A Tama hook-up and a monitor waited for him.

As the afternoon dwindled, Rhimes burned through

the messages, the assignment reports. He delegated with uneasy speed, relying on Wexey's given command—to order, not to do—as a guide. At first, Rhimes heard the questions in people's replies, the confusion at his tonal change. Silences peppered conversations as Rhimes's partners, agents, and techs expected Rhimes's usual burden bearing that didn't come, not this time.

"Can't," Rhimes said when Brielle asked why Rhimes wouldn't be owning a raid personally. "Wexley changed my job description. Promoting me, and now I'm promoting you."

"You think I'm ready to run a team on my own?" Brielle asked.

"If I didn't think so, I wouldn't be asking."

"So where are you going to be? Behind a desk?"

Rhimes sighed, reached in his pocket and pulled out Zhan-Yo's paper. Reread the address. He'd spent the last few hours signing death-and-capture warrants on anomalies across the globe. Each one brought with it precisely zero satisfaction. He'd wanted to fight for something, or get paid to protect someone.

Now he felt like the world's most high-tech rat catcher, chasing out the vermin before they ruined the party.

"I'm going to take a short trip," Rhimes said, and when Brielle started to ask about a vacation, he cut her off. "Just need to clean up some leftovers at the main office."

"Chicago? Pack some warm clothes."

"Been there once or twice." Rhimes tapped his Tama, called a pod for pick-up. He'd check flights on the way, there'd be a red-eye available. "Do me a favor, Brielle, and don't get yourself killed."

"You too, boss. You too."

EIGHT

Hard Landing

WHEN THE JET took a sharp turn north, Cassidy swore the wingtips touched the waves. Sunset brought the flight into focus, the speed run towards California and the Factory close to completion and now interrupted, according to the Paragon pilots, by heavy drone presence. Their planned landing zone coated by flying machines double-checking flight numbers, passenger lists on incoming aircraft.

Something the Paragons, no matter their anomaly abilities, couldn't fake.

"Stay calm," Apinya announced across the jet's inside, words that did little on their own but, when backed up by the Champion's subtle mental nudge, quieted Cassidy's urge to fire off a void.

With Thane next to her, another bombs-out plunge to the water didn't seem all that impossible.

"You swam this far last time," Cassidy muttered to Thane, who had his eyes fixed on a portable Tama. Another article on Ziran's global reach, its proposals for a post-Paragon world. "You could do it again, right?"

"Yes."

Thane offered nothing more and Cassidy didn't ask.

All told, the hours burned in the air had gone quiet. Cassidy herself had slept for quite a few, and then she'd fielded questions from other Paragons who'd never been across the ocean. What was California like, what they should be ready for.

Cassidy gave them a decade's outdated information, but they seemed happy, and Cassidy couldn't kid herself: it felt nice being a teacher again, feeling needed and useful. If her students this time happened to be adults, older and younger than herself and with mixed English understanding, so be it.

As the aircraft neared Pacifica's coast the pilots broke up the party. Turbulence, likely unnatural and forced by Ziran drone patrols, would be likely. So Cassidy and Thane sat, strapped into their seats, Thane in his Tama screen and Cassidy looking out the narrow window.

The northward turn completed, the jet surged into a rise, screaming up and leaving the waves behind. Cassidy didn't understand why until an anomaly across from her, Daw, pulled back from his window with wide eyes and a hard grip on his seatmate, his mentor and seemingly omnipresent guard, Kemnan.

"They've found us," Daw said, voice carrying through the jet, its interior quiet, the plane's electric turbines running soft.

"Trust the pilots," Kemnan replied, the stoic man keeping his eyes forward. "They have done this before."

As if putting Kemnan's words to the test, the jet juddered, swinging left and right as its ascent continued. Outside, the waves came together into a blue mass, single cloud wisps getting in the way. New shapes swung into view, white-orange blots resolving themselves into various drones as they streamed up after the jet. The drone engines left hazy streaks behind the machines themselves, blurry slashes against the far away ground.

Cassidy glanced at Thane, frowned. From this high, no way they'd survive a fall.

"We've been sighted," the primary pilot, the same woman who'd joined them all with the wind and carried them to the plane, said. "Anyone who can take out a drone from within the plane, have at it. Everyone else, stay seated and strapped in. There will be sudden drops."

Sudden drops?

Through the window, the drones made their intentions clear. Cassidy saw their weapons give notice, bright flashes searing up and past the plane. Misses, despite the jet not being exactly nimble.

"Warning shots," Kemnan said to Daw, who'd continued pestering the man about what they should do. "They will force us down if they can."

"Why?" Daw asked.

"Because crashing planes is not stable behavior," Thane said, setting the Tama in the armrest slot next to him. "Ziran doesn't want to explain a crashed jet. They do not want panic. They want normalcy."

More flashes. The jet turned east. Two anomalies that'd traveled from Bangkok unstrapped themselves and headed aft. Cassidy didn't know their powers, but given the determination on their faces, the pair looked ready to deliver drone destruction.

She could've done the same if an open door or window existed to throw her voids. From inside the plane, though, Cassidy would just break the craft apart. So she watched, offered a nod when one glanced her way.

"So they won't hurt us?" Daw continued.

"An algorithm," Thane said. "A clock ticking both by

time and distance. As we approach the coast, the drones will change their tactics."

"And then what?"

"We see how good these pilots are."

Kemnan threw a glare Thane's way, "There's no need to scare him."

"Daw is not a child," Thane looked past Kemnan, at Daw. "Does he need to protect you?"

Daw shook his head, bailed on the conversation by turning back to the window. Kemnan settled into a frown. Thane went Cassidy's way next. The jet shook again, its nose tilting down.

"Did I handle that well?" Thane asked quietly.

"What?"

"You and Apinya have made clear over these last months that loyalty is more than power itself," Thane said. "If I am to find a place here—"

The jet froze, fell. Cassidy's stomach leapt up her throat, nerves spiking. She rose, the seatbelt digging into her waist. She might've screamed, except she couldn't find her breath. Next to her, Thane grew, leveraging that fear to make himself as invincible as he could.

Smoothly, the jet thawed and swept forward, arresting its fall and streaking towards the California coastline. Cassidy saw the drones now above them, turning to pursue an aircraft that must've looked like it was in a terminal decline.

"Now," Thane rasped, his throat shrinking, his mind returning. "They will attack in full."

The drones did as Thane suggested, laying out more white-hot energy, but supplementing these shots with physical rounds. The jet stopped and started, froze and thawed in a racing descent. Every time the plane seemed to lock in place, Cassidy heard the clanking sounds as bullets blinked off the jet's unbreakable hull.

The other pilot, the one that'd kept the jet invincible back in Bangkok, doing his part.

The dance between vulnerable acceleration and plunging safety turned quick against the Paragons. The drones closed, picked up their fire, and Cassidy found her stomach going longer and longer between pauses. The plane, too, rumbled and cracked as incoming shots slipped through the shielded seconds.

At least the altitude drop put them closer to the waves, to the sandy cliffs marking landfall. Again Cassidy could pick out the whitecaps, could see a winding road with a few pods zipping along it. Back in Thane's drop safe distance?

Thane, though, wouldn't be able to save more than Cassidy.

The thought pushed her eyes up and down the plane. Most Paragons on board sat in near-panic, hands clutching friends or partners or armrests. Daw had himself flickering, while Kemnan stayed stoic, staring straight ahead and ready to take whatever life gave him. Thane kept a stronger state, occasionally glancing over Cassidy to see out her window and muttering to himself. Apinya's eyes were closed, no doubt engaged in some mental maneuvering.

Back on Mynx's island, Cassidy had dealt with the other anomalies like resources. Some became friends, yes, but everyone understood their lives were fragile things. Easy to lose amid an anomaly power struggle.

Here?

Everyone was on the same side, taking up the Paragon mantel to try and stop a drone-driven anomaly genocide.

Cassidy unsnapped her restraint, wobbled to her feet. Thane asked what she was doing, where Cassidy was going, and she ignored him. Went straight towards the cockpit and the forward exits. The two anomalies that'd responded to the initial call for help with the drones were next to the closed cockpit door in states that said they weren't really there.

The woman had herself sitting on the floor, her eyes shut and head sat back against the plane's wall. A thin bloody line ran from her ears, but Cassidy saw her chest rise and fall. Across from her, the man stood stock still, hands clasped over his chest. Despite the jet's twisting and turning, the man never lost his footing, didn't seem to move at all. His eyes, open, saw through Cassidy.

Whatever the pair did, Cassidy couldn't see it from inside. She kept going, pressing on the cockpit door's handle and swinging it open. The golden coast laid bare through the cockpit's front window. Sandy rocks, tall trees came closer with speed. Bullets and energy bolts lanced around the view's edges, splashing down into the sea or breaking into the rocks.

On the right, the man making the plane invincible did it again, locking his arms against the instrument panel. The jet shuddered, its nose pointed down, and Cassidy stuck her hands out to either side, pressing to keep from falling forward.

"Shut that door and get out!" called the woman on the left. "You should be strapped in, not up here!"

The man freed his arms, freed the jet, which lurched back into level flight. Several alarms blared.

"You have to land," Cassidy said. "We can't help you fight while we're in the air."

"We land, we get swarmed," said the woman, banking the plane south as it put the ocean behind. Now any hard landing would be on rock, not water. "There's no escape if—"

"There's no chance if you don't drop us on the road," Cassidy said. "Do it!"

"What do you—"

"She's right," the man said. "I can keep us safe when we hit. We're losing too much air to keep going."

A louder bang, a wild alarm forced Cassidy's point. The woman cursed, noted the jet's tail had been blown through. The jet began a slow spin, plunging down and around. Nowhere near that road. The twist threw Cassidy from her hold, sprawling her to the jet's floor. Glass shattered as the drones, continuing their attack, struck home. Bullets ran through the fuselage, the openings busting the cabin's pressure and popping Cassidy's ears.

Somewhere in there she bit her tongue, the iron blood taste flooding her mouth. Scrambled instincts, bruised muscles. Fire's searing smell tickled her nose and brought Cassidy back into focus.

"I can't dodge the tree," the woman was saying. "No power left."

The voids called, and this time, Cassidy answered.

She flung the first in a wild throw, the reality tear slicing through the plane's nose and hitting a thick tree right in their descending path. The void severed the trunk, turning a solid barrier into a loose one as the jet skipped off the half-standing tree. Metal blew everywhere, and the clip accelerated the jet's spin.

"Nice shot," the man said, glancing her way. "Can you move that cliff?"

The jet's next obstacle covered the horizon, a beige wall destined to splatter the plane and its occupants into pancakes. Cassidy figured the man's invulnerability trick wouldn't do anything to stop their momentum, turning the broken plane into a casket.

Unless Cassidy could break the path.

She threw a second void down and ahead, cutting through the plane beneath the two pilots. Their seats suddenly resting on nothing, the two pilots fell through the hole, plunging out and towards the ground. A rough landing, maybe, but a chance at life. Whirling back around, Cassidy sent another void slicing through the plane's undercarriage.

Metal ripped and vanished, exposing earth meters below. Smoke and fire shrouded the view, the crashing plane's dying gasp. Daw and Kemnan fell through the hole. Others followed as Cassidy threw one void then another, cutting holes in the plane until it broke apart, her own section spinning off on its own momentum.

At least she had a nice breeze.

Cassidy's cockpit door frame tumbled and she fell free, joining the debris, the bodies, as the Paragons plunged towards the road. She'd hoped they were close enough to survive, close enough to land with broken bones but alive.

She'd been wrong: the tree she'd severed lived on an outcropping, and Cassidy's makeshift escape funneled people into free-fall a hundred meters over the ground or more.

Abilities flashed as the Paragons tried to save themselves. Cassidy's own hair blew into her eyes, the wind rushed against her, and she figured this last stomach-churning fall would be the end.

At least she'd died doing the right thing, trying to save her friends.

STEEL ARMS STAVED OFF DISASTER. Cassidy, rushing through a last mental I-love-you to her kids, found the impact hard but not life-destroying. A solid shock rang through her bones, the air blew from her lungs, but she lived, and opened her eyes.

A drone held her in a single claw. The gladiator, a four-armed monster, held the invincible co-pilot in the limb opposite Cassidy. The drone dug its claws into their cargo, with Cassidy feeling the cuts along her skin, into her back. She cut off a shout, instead straining her neck around to try and figure out what the hell had happened.

Evidence wasn't hard to find: the drones that'd been attacking the shuttle dove in to save its occupants. Falling anomalies found themselves scooped up by metal saviors, the drones now rising back into the sky with their prizes.

Why hadn't the machines let them fall?

Cassidy didn't have an answer to that question, but she did have voids. Even as Cassidy sought to call them up, their drone rose quick into the air, putting a void attack into question. She'd just been saved from a fatal flaw, did Cassidy really want to take another?

"What's going on?" Cassidy shouted.

"I don't know!" the man replied, himself snug in the drone's grip. "I can't get free."

"Wasn't talking to you," Cassidy said, but as the drone wasn't giving her a reply, the man would have to do. "Why did it save us?"

Beneath them, the California cliffside fell away. Sweeping coastal pines came into play, a beautiful view if not for the situation. Cassidy squinted, caught some of those trees swaying, falling in a path trailing them.

"I think we're being taken somewhere," the man said, stating the obvious with resigned calm. "Ziran's been capturing anomalies, but we're not sure why."

Oh, good. Cassidy could've died nice and quick, but now she'd get the lab treatment instead. Thane's stories about years stuck in a Paragon facility, drugged up and left alone, rose around her. Not good, not a life she could stand.

"Are you okay if I destroy this thing?" Cassidy said.

"Go for it. I'm going to be fine!"

Of course he would be.

Cassidy twisted, trying to get an arm into position. If she threw the void just right, she might not destroy the whole drone right away, might get a chance at . . .

She flung the narrow, cutting void. It sliced through the drone's mid-section and the thing's neck. Sparks rained out, wires spread like spiders, and the machine went into a steep dive. Exactly what Cassidy didn't want.

"Another great shot," the man said. "Guess you're dead now!"

The drone's claws loosened as its programming failed to account for its new severed state. Cassidy tried to get the claw beneath her, tried to get the drone's metal bulk in the way.

Later, Cassidy insisted she'd have managed it. That she would've rode the drone's carapace to the surface in style.

Thane ensured that didn't happen. A barreling monster, Thane launched from the woods in a leap too messy, too brutal to be majestic. All taut skin and flying spit, Thane crashed into the drone's flailing upper body and wrapped it in his grip as they crashed down. Pinned between the drone's claw and Thane's hulking self, Cassidy asked, far from the first time, how in the hell her life had turned into this.

They landed in a crumpling bang, pine needles flying everywhere. Scrapes added their pain pings to Cassidy's new repertoire, the drone's body bouncing away, fire and debris going with it. Thane breathed behind her, angry huffs that found their way calmer each and every breath.

"Well then," the invincible man said, stepping around a

broken tree. His clothes were shreds, but the man's body didn't have a single scratch. "That sucked, didn't it?" He winced. "Think that was our last jet, too."

"Aegis," Thane growled as Cassidy pulled herself away, rubbed her arms, and looked up at the sky. "Where is he?"

Cassidy didn't catch the answer. For the moment, she felt only the forest beneath her feet, the fresh air coming into bruised lungs. The trip had been a disaster, but here she stood for the first time in so many years. Her children weren't an impossible distance away anymore. If she wanted, if she could get the chance, she could go . . .

Home.

NINE

Wreckage

ZIRAN ATTACKED THE JET.

The distress signal came in hot. Aegis heard the report, pulled himself away from another ship raid planning session. A rescue roster would be slim: Pocket's purple-black hideaway held fewer anomalies than usual, most out on evening missions securing supplies, ambushing drones, or catching some much needed rest.

Celice and Mathieu, though, held their positions, basking in the azure screen glow. Aegis came up behind his daughter and she didn't even have to ask why.

"They've got two anomalies scrambling the drones from inside the jet," Celice said, clicking between the screens. "They're not very effective."

"What does that mean, 'not very effective'?" Aegis asked, trying to parse what he saw on Celice's screen. One monitor held a black expanse with a sapphire cross in the middle, surrounded by swirling red squares. On the screen's right side, a big grass-green blob approached. "Are they going to make it or not?"

"I don't think so," Celice said, bringing a finger to her

lips. "We should've directed them further north, away from here."

"Transporting them over land has its own risks. Ziran's getting closer every day, and we need to move fast. Can we get them any help?"

"Nothing that's going to make a difference in the fight."

"But after?"

Mathieu, walking over from his station, leaned in and looked at the monitor, put a hand on Celice's shoulder. "When those drones finish, there's not going to be much left to find."

Celice frowned, matching her father's look at Mathieu, though she didn't have Aegis's narrowed eyes. "When did you get so callous? There's always hope."

"There's a difference between hope and delusion," Mathieu replied. "Not everything works out."

"For you, maybe," Aegis said, ignoring Mathieu's rolling eyes. "Celice, get me anyone free and a pod. If there's a chance Apinya makes it out alive, I'm going to take it."

"Mathieu, you heard my father." Celice pushed back her seat and stood. "Get us a pod."

"Us?" Aegis asked.

"You see anyone else here willing to follow you into that mess? No? Then I guess this is father daughter day."

Aegis might've smiled, might've laughed, but on the screen behind Celice, those red squares converged. The blue cross slowed. Another mayday warning played quiet over Celice's speakers.

His team was in trouble, and Aegis wasn't there.

· · ·

THEY FOUND debris well before the crash site. Churning up a highway in a pod disconnected from Ziran's grid, one reprogrammed by some Elemental refugees to allow manual control, Aegis and Celice slowed as they passed by a broken wing sticking from the sand like some crude grave. The sun chased the afternoon, sending glare across the ocean and into their rounded glass vehicle. The roadway itself had zero occupants, all normal pods rerouted away from the scene.

The stated cause flashing over local Tamas? Landslide.

Ziran, always good at covering its tracks.

"Can't say that's a good omen," Celice muttered as the pod went past. She had her hands on the manual control stick, an awkward metal arm popped up from the pod's floor. "If we start seeing bodies—"

"We won't," Aegis replied.

"You think they all made it out alive?"

The jet's mayday signals had stopped by the time Celice and her father boarded the pod. The jet's wind-blown pilot, covered in scratches and broken glass, appeared as they climbed in, declaring the plane lost. Seconds later came Ziran's stay-away message. While Aegis couldn't know the jet's ultimate fate, its escape seemed the least likely option. The powers some on the flight had might ensure survival, if not perfection, and injured anomalies on foot didn't stand much chance against pursuing drones.

But Ziran wasn't interested in death. At least not right away. And even a body might prove useful for whatever Ziran was doing.

"Taken," Aegis said. "All of them."

"Then why, exactly, are we here?"

More sheet metal flakes dotted the road, with Celice

navigating around them. Cliffs rose on their right side, basking orange.

"Because some might still be fighting," Aegis said.

"And we're going to turn the tide?"

Aegis sighed. Celice had her weapons, including new guns armed with the EMP rounds Ziran itself had put together to fight Mynx's drones. The Paragons reverse-engineered the bullets after finding enough around Wexley's gambits back in Chicago and now everyone had some on their belts. Aegis, too, had his near-invincible fists.

Neither one would hold up long against a drone attack.

"Relieve and rescue," Aegis said. "They might have hidden themselves too. There's a chance."

"There's always a chance," his daughter repeated.

That chance came not too many minutes later, in the jet's still smoldering shadow. The bulk sent its black smoke skyward, while broken rocks and split trees framed the wreck. Bullet casings and burned slag across the road, bushes, and dirt told the assault's story. Not just a plane crash, but an annihilation.

And not a single body.

"Almost eerie," Celice said, stopping the pod and popping its dome open. "There's nobody here."

"We'd have sent a rescue crew," Aegis said, joining her out on the asphalt. "Even if everyone on this plane had been an enemy, we would've done the minimum."

Celice eyed him, "You would've made sure they were dead."

"If that was necessary, yes. I won't flinch away from what we had to do to keep the world safe."

"I bought into all that, you know. But claims like that one might be why Wexley wanted you gone."

"It has nothing to do with the Paragons," Aegis said.

"That man wants power, plain and simple, and he didn't like us having it instead."

A sharp breeze ripped through, turning the smoke their way. Aegis went forward towards the wreck, not exactly knowing what he might find but figuring their journey deserved at least a look. Celice followed, her eyes up towards the stars, watching for drone lights.

"Zhan-Yo says different," Celice said. "He thinks Wexley, like him, wants a more equal society. You, ever think about doing that, back when you were in charge?"

"We made society equal," Aegis replied, getting near the jet's nose and, with his legs helping, pushing the fractured mess aside. No bodies crushed beneath. "Rich and poor were closer than ever before. Basic rights didn't see skin color, gender, citizenship."

"They damn sure saw anomalies and normals."

"Because you can't look past powers. I'm sorry, you just can't. Anyone that could level a block or heal any disease with a blink needs to be treated differently than . . . " He tried to find a suitable example that wouldn't sound insulting to the woman standing right there, a normal. "You get it."

"Maybe that's why it's the normal who's running the world now," Celice said. "You never saw us as a threat."

Aegis didn't have an answer to that and shrugged. Took another long look around the wreck. No evidence, no trails to follow. He called out Apinya's name several times, loud yells that carried up and down the cliffs.

"They grabbed every single one," Aegis said when nothing came back. "Every single damn one."

Celice had the pod turned around, the route back to Pocket and the old strip mall hiding their current headquarters, when the road before them split apart and vanished. A new hole, right in the center, eating up the yellow line. Celice stopped the pod and Aegis jumped out fast, drawing his drone-zapping sidearm and looking for a target.

"Sorry!" A woman shouted, back behind and up the cliffside. A Tama—not hers—glowed nearby, casting her face in gray-green light. "Didn't know how else to get your attention."

Waving next to her, Aegis recognized Samir. The anomaly had a neat ability, great for safeguarding valuable people or pieces. He'd been the co-pilot on this particular extraction, and his presence here meant . . .

Aegis's mind blanked at the next body around the tree. Thin, withered, but as bright-eyed as ever, Thane met Aegis's look with a mocking glare. No matter how hard Aegis tried, Thane's stare seemed to say, Thane would always survive, always come back.

"Dad?" Celice said, joining him outside the pod. "You going to put your gun away?"

"That's Thane," Aegis replied. "Right there, that's the man that killed your mother."

"The old guy? I thought Thane was a big monster?"

"Only when he's angry." Aegis moved, put himself in front of Celice. "Stay behind me. I don't know what Samir's doing, or that woman, but Thane isn't a friend."

The woman on the cliff, the one who'd shouted, seemed to share Celice's confusion. She looked back and forth between Aegis and Thane before throwing up her arms and waving Samir forward. The Paragon led her down the bushy, sandy rocks while Thane stayed right where he was, matching Aegis second for second in a staring contest that meant so much more.

Last time they'd met, Thane had delivered Aegis a near-death beating. Sure, hours after, Aegis and his Paragon reinforcements, Mynx included, had brought

Thane low through sheer firepower, but the one-on-one embarrassment still lingered. Worse, Aegis didn't have that back-up now. If Thane decided he wanted to send Aegis and his daughter on a fast trip to the great beyond, Aegis might not be able to stop him.

"Celice," Aegis said. "Don't wait. Get in the pod and go."

"What?"

"Thane won't be able to catch you if you leave now. Go, then call Ziran if you don't hear from me. Tell them to send the drones. Let their army smash themselves on him."

Maybe Wexley and the drones could win. Deliver one good death for the planet.

"Dad," Celice said, making no move towards the pod. "Why do you think he's here?"

"How should I know?"

"He's standing there with Samir, near the crashed jet. Maybe Apinya was bringing him over the ocean?"

"Never."

As Aegis spoke, Samir and the woman reached the bottom. She threw a head-shaking look back up towards Thane, then the pair strode right up to Aegis. Samir, his clothing shredded, nonetheless looked perfect. His newfound partner, though, bled from scratches all across her body, with little cover left from the torn rags operating as clothes. The woman stuck out her hand, and when Aegis hesitated, Celice reached out to shake it.

"Cassidy," the woman said.

"Celice. I would say it's a pleasure, but I'd rather ask you both if you know what happened?"

"Not yet," Cassidy said, cutting off Samir before the man could jump into his recount. "I think there's some air that needs clearing first."

"You think?" Celice replied, nodding at Aegis.

"I do think. As much as I'd like a shower and some real clothes, what I want first is an apology and a promise. From him, and from you."

Thane made his approach while Cassidy spoke, after it became clear to everyone that the beef between Aegis and his longtime rival wasn't the only stick in their current mud. The old anomaly kept himself svelte, so Aegis holstered his weapon and held one eye Thane's way while his attention otherwise settled on Cassidy's story.

A lifetime disrupted by a decade on Mynx's prison island. The words felt unreal as Cassidy spoke them, and Aegis once again found his world shaking. He'd thought, as the lead Champion and Paragon banner-carrier for so long, that he understood the world Aegis and his friends had created. Instead he kept running into niches that escaped Aegis's understanding, his knowledge.

He knew Mynx had the island, of course. Knew that Mynx used it as a dumping ground for anomalies that were impossible or inconvenient to kill. A life sentence for a nuclear bomb. Aegis assumed the anomalies dropped there inevitably murdered each other, or at best eked out some forgotten existence until disease or time took care of the problem.

Yet here stood someone bearing that choice's scars. Aegis couldn't recall Cassidy's crimes, but Paragon justice held an absolute edge. Little sympathy and little recourse for the accused, because anything else would mean risking anomalies going wild. How many juries could get swung by a single anomaly with mind-bending powers? Impossible. If an anomaly didn't want to join the Paragons, then they were a threat, and they—

"Dad? Are you going to apologize like she's asking?"

Cassidy had an eyebrow-raised look his way, just like a

teacher who knew he knew the right answer to the question, but had her doubts whether he would say it.

"You want me to say we created a flawed world," Aegis said.

"Very much," Cassidy replied.

"Why does it matter? You're off the island now, if the place even exists any more."

"Because I came back here at your Champion's request. He wants us to help put the Paragons back in control, and I'm not sure that's a good idea, seeing as you're a bunch of spiteful asses."

"Quite the thing to say if you're traveling with that one." Aegis threw his glance towards Thane.

"Oh, the guy you kept trapped, drugged in a basement for most of his life?" Cassidy reached out, put a finger against Aegis's chest. Celice's eyes went wide at the move, her hand drifting towards her waist, but Aegis shook his head her way. "You've caused so much pain for so many people, and yet here we are, nearly dying, just so you can do it again. So yes, I would like you to say you're sorry." Cassidy took a breath, a slight flush kissing her cheeks as she hit her crescendo. "And if that sounds like I'm talking to a kid, it's because I think I am. A kid who doesn't know any better, and who needs to grow up if he's going to get my help."

Aegis blinked as Cassidy withdrew her hand, as she folded her arms. The vanished asphalt patch lingered to his right, a reminder that no matter how much Aegis might want to indulge his aggressive instincts and show Cassidy why threatening him wasn't a great idea . . . perhaps threatening her wasn't the best plan either.

Besides, scrambling around these weeks with Pocket had proved a continual point: society didn't seem to regard the Paragon's destruction with despair. If Ziran wasn't better than the Paragons with their drones, they weren't much worse. Seeing your life's work pass from the Earth with a shrug had a way of making one re-evaluate.

"You want an apology," Aegis said, "then earn it. I'm not perfect, never claimed to be, but Mynx put you on that island for a reason. This is your opportunity to fix it, and I'm willing to give you that chance."

"That's the best you're going to get," Celice added. "Best I've seen anyone get, really."

Cassidy considered, then let her arms fall free, "I don't exactly have many options. But what about this guy?"

Thane came up alongside Cassidy, still glaring at Aegis.

"You said Apinya brought you?" Aegis asked, and Cassidy nodded. "Thane, Apinya brought *you*?"

"We had a plan," Thane said slow, his voice raspy and weak. "A plan that still has a chance if you can be smart for once in your life."

"Guess we'll find out," Aegis said, feeling Celice's worry his way. She thought he'd be throwing a punch right about now. And he wanted to, oh how he always wanted to send Thane right to the dirt. The jet, though, kept smoking around them. All those Paragons and Apinya vanished. Now wasn't the time for rivalries, reckonings. "I'm not forgiving you, but we're in a bad spot. We could use your help. Really."

"With one promise," Thane said. "We win, then we go free. Records cleared."

"That doesn't sound like you. Where's the world takeover? The grand plans?"

"One step at a time, Aegis." Thane's withered, thin lips curled into a smile. "One step at a time."

TEN

Late Night Dining

THE VENDING machine didn't impress. With the hour pushing eleven and dinner's influence fading, Kat had gone snack searching. Chips and candy abounded, along with some granola bars that looked like they were a decade past their expiration date. She wanted something with more substance, more peanut butter. She hovered a finger over a selection, biting her lip and wondering if this was the right call. If Kat bought it, she'd have to eat it, and then she'd be too full to choose a different one, so . . .

The damned restaurant bugged her. It'd killed the night's mood right away, then festered through a bad movie and Gordon's descent into an early bedtime. His excuse? That if they were going to be arguing about this all day tomorrow, he'd better get his rest.

Not a bad plan.

Kat glanced down at her t-shirt, pajamas. An outfit not worn outside her apartment in years, now gracing the dusty, sepia hotel hallway. The ice machine gurgled, perhaps in judgment.

"You don't look so good yourself," Kat said to the brown, square box.

Not that it stopped her from getting ice. The tap water needed everything Kat could throw into it tonight.

Walking back, candy bar and ice bucket in hand, Kat caught glare through the hallway's far window. A white light mismatching with the hotel's own glow and gone in a smooth moment. A random person might not know what they'd just seen, might not care, but Kat had too much conditioning not to catalog the sight, match up its probable cause: a drone.

Kat dropped the ice outside her room, kept the bar and took a bite as she went to the hallway's end. The smeared window, spotted with winter's muddy remnants, offered a damaged view: across the parking lot and to the left sat the restaurant and its anomaly cadre. The drones—Kat counted four—circled the building. The machine's bulk suggested gladiators, Ziran's bread and butter machines for anomaly collection.

Two broke from their aerial surveillance, landing in the lot and approaching the restaurant's entrance. The drones sparked up lights on their shoulders and chests, bathing the neon sign in a harsh white intended to make any lurking ambush blind. The hovering pair shifted towards the restaurant's back before landing themselves, approaching with heavy steps Kat could hear.

Any anomaly in Ziran's new world had reason to fear, had to expect a drone might arrive at any moment intending to kill or steal them away. Still, Kat found it hard to square tonight's attack with her and Gordon's arrival. Coincidence seemed too simple an explanation.

She wouldn't find any answers in the hallway.

Gordon didn't take long to rouse once Kat mentioned the drones. Flipping on their room's bright lamps and chucking Gordon's bag onto his bed helped too. Experience had them throwing on their gear fast, ready to go by the time Kat finished her bar. Gordon's long, dark jacket hid weapons in a dozen pockets, gray tactical pants and vest providing hideaways for tools many and murderous. Kat's own white tracker's suit, loaded with wrist launchers, a hooded helmet complete with a vital-monitoring visor, tuned Kat's temp to her fighting ideal as the pair left the hotel.

"And you think we're responsible?" Gordon muttered as they strode into a quiet parking lot, a few pods parked and dark in lined spaces left over from another era.

"Don't know," Kat replied, "but I'd like to find out. I have enough things to be guilty about without throwing some scared anomalies in the mix."

She'd have to move quick to make a difference: the drones hadn't waited for the trackers. The restaurant's entrance—Kat couldn't see the back from ground level—had its doors broken in, its sign split apart and sparking across a battered front walk. Flashes poured through shattered windows, sizzling static snapping the air as anomaly abilities parried drone weapons and their hard claps.

"Still fighting," Gordon said, glanced at Kat. "Last chance?"

"We've taken lives for a long time," Kat said. "Let's save a few, shall we?"

She didn't wait for Gordon, breaking into a run. With a quick snap, Kat armed a grappling hook in her left wrist. Another jerk sent her right loading two silver orbs, tweaked by the Elementals to have some fun with her more mechanical opponents.

The two trackers crossed the hotel's lot, then the street before the restaurant under cloudy skies. Kat's suit pegged the temp in the low sixties and breezy, a perfect setting for a rumble. One marred by a sudden, blue-flamed pillar bursting from the restaurant's center and climbing into the air. Gordon swore, Kat pulled up from her run, and both watched as embers flew from that pillar. Not tiny sparks, but large shapes gliding down to the roof, the parking lot.

One landed two meters from the tracker pair, its glowing form cooling, resolving into a teenage girl. Behind her, the fiery line dwindled and vanished, leaving smoke in its wake. Kat ran forward, stuck out a hand to help the girl up. The fire child looked at Kat's face, screwed up her own in a breathless fear, the girl's hands pulling back and starting to glow.

"Wait!" Kat said, reaching up and retracting her visor. "Human, see? I'm on your side?"

"Our side?" the girl asked, shaking her head, then she looked back towards the restaurant. The other embers resolved into more anomalies and younger children. All scrambled towards the restaurant's edge, trying to get off the roof. "The drones are—"

"We get that," Gordon said. "You're not going to beat them. You have to run."

"Run where?" the girl stood, turning her glowing hands back towards the restaurant. "This is our home."

"Not anymore," Kat replied. "Are there more inside?"

The girl nodded. As she did, something groaned in the restaurant, and three gladiator drones burst up through the ceiling, landing on the weak roof. Anomaly powers, varied in light, sound, color, sprayed from panicked hands, minds, bodies towards the machines in a fluorescent wave. The drones didn't care, their own attacks piercing through. Darts and worse struck the fleeing anomalies, driving some off the roof into long falls to the concrete. Others vanished behind the roof's lip, picked off and dropped.

It didn't matter whether there were more inside. Kat and Gordon would be pressed to save the ones out here.

"Find pods," Kat told the girl. "We'll keep them busy as long as we can."

"You go up," Gordon said, going around the girl, who still seemed confused. She'd have to figure things out, the trackers couldn't waste more time. "I'll take under."

"Sure." Kat flicked her visor down as she went for the restaurant, its programming already finding ideal grapple spots. "Send me after three drones."

"You've got the fancy suit," Gordon called, breaking right as they neared the restaurant and aiming at a gaping hole in the front wall.

A suit designed for anomalies, not for gladiators, but Kat held her tongue and fired her grapple anyway. The steel cable launched from her wrist, found purchase on the big, now broken, sign lingering over the roof. Kat bent her knees and jumped as she ran, twitching her wrist enough to start the grapple's pull.

The cable yanked Kat forward and she swung her legs up, letting them catch the restaurant's front wall. Pumping, Kat ran up the wall's side as energy bolts blue and white glitzed above her. Calls to dodge, to attack, to run rang out between repeated drone commands to stand down. Bullets struck with a softer touch, clueing Kat into their rubberized make, a disabling rather than deadly approach.

Ziran must really want all these anomalies alive.

Hopefully that meant Calvin still survived.

Kat crested the roof, detaching her grapple from the sign as she scrambled beneath its wire frame. Ahead, the drones pitched a winning war against an anomaly rabble. Beside Kat and going the opposite way, jumping off the roof and getting caught in more burning, teleporting geysers, were children. Older siblings led the younger ones, yelling encouragement as they leapt.

Behind them, their parents delayed, distracted the drones.

Kat's visor highlighted the fighters, splaying out the fifteen adult anomalies still struggling in mint-green halos. The three drones in ruby red, each one with its four arms targeting and delivering. The gladiators marched forward, heavy feet cracking the broken rooftop with every step and activating embedded jets whenever tiles crumpled away.

Against a trained Paragon force, Kat figured fifteen anomalies might win, might even win handily if their abilities hit the right marks. At a glance, these didn't measure up. She saw one throwing orange-glowing silverware, the forks and spoons striking the drones and melting into hot liquid, leaving zero marks and doing no damage. An older man jabbed his fists at nothing, his punches striking home on a drone, annoying it enough for the machine to shoot him with several darts at once.

Another waved her arms, creating cracks in the air that caught darts leaving drone cannons and stuck them in place, at least providing some value. Some others flung their abilities, drenching the drones in sticky liquids, icy rains, or violet rays.

None did much beyond attract devastating attention.

Kat could do better than that.

Breaking into a run right at the drones, which spread the restaurant's roof even between them, Kat flipped open her left wrist, tapped a couple buttons on her Tama. A program spun into motion, ticking a tock to buy an opportunity. Kat snapped her wrist and sent her grapple flying again, this time at the leftmost drone.

The piercing steel hook zipped right at the machine, only for the drone to see it, to jerk its upper right arm at a speed too fast for humans to match, and catch Kat's grapple.

Good.

The Tama program triggered, and Kat's visor crackled as every radio frequency found itself coated in targeted gibberish. Every single command in Mynx's library, all designed to get the drones to stand down, to fly home, to retreat, blasted out in every language the drones supported. Weed bet Ziran wouldn't rewrite the entire codebook, not all of it and not right away. Kat hadn't been so sure, but a chance beat out nothing at all.

"Run, you morons!" Kat shouted as she snapped her grapple, flying towards a hesitating drone.

Stares followed her as the anomalies caught the suited tracker in their midst, or rather, saw Kat's form skip through the burning air. The tracker heard a few calls to run, to pick up fallen friends, and then she found herself with her feet planted on a four meter tall gladiator. The drone's metal face seemed stunned, its eyes blank as it dealt with the command onslaught.

Maybe Weed had it right.

With the grapple tying her to the drone's arm, Kat went to her belt with her right hand. Pulled a new tool punched together back in Chicago, a thin battery with twin prongs just waiting for a completed circuit. Holding it in her right hand, Kat waited, breathed, took a look back to the parking lot.

The girl proved to be better than scared after all: pods zipped into the space, with the anomalies climbing in them. Parents dropping off the roof found their families, pushed their children into the vehicles. Ziran could track the pods, of course, so they'd need to ditch them before long, but—

The drone's face buzzed as it moved, those implacable

eyes finding Kat. No pupils, no whites, but Kat felt the stare anyway. And she sure as hell saw its other arm reaching for her.

"Almost a minute," Kat said as she slacked the grapple, dropping to the roof and away from the reaching arm and leaving the steel line in the drone's grip. "Not bad, Weed."

She stabbed the battery into the drone's right foot, the clawed, white-metal thing proving an ample target. Kat aimed for the gap between armored slats, a thin band hard to hit if you weren't standing right on it. The spikes bit in, the battery did its thing, and the drone froze as hard current melted its wires, overwhelmed its transistors.

Kat's left shoulder swung hard as something struck her. The culprit bounced off unsteady roof tiles, a stun dart rolling away on the slates. The tracker whirled from the dead drone to see its two pals focused on her.

"Gordon?" Kat yelled, the suit sending the transmission to the other tracker on their localized connection. "Help?"

Eight arms, each loaded up with very unpleasant things, fired.

Kat dove forward, hoping the drones would assume otherwise. The gambit failed when the drones covered every option, and Kat felt two heavy thuds strike her head, her back as she rolled on the roof. Her vision blurred, a ringing blared away Gordon's response, and Kat's lower body went numb for a terrifying moment.

But her momentum kept Kat moving. Her instincts, honed by too many anomalies in too many terrible situations, told Kat to twitch her left wrist. The grapple responded, nearly breaking Kat's arm but shooting her up and away from the firing field. Kat hit the fried drone's arm hard, adding more stars to her shocked skull.

Kat figured she'd pay for these concussions sometime, but that would be later. She could die now.

She clung to the dead machine's arm, scrambling to put the metal between her and the drones, as it stood on the restaurant roof, the tiles beneath its feet already feeble with their falling brethren. The rubber bullets, the darts from the other two drones pushed the creaking roof over its fractured edge, and the dead drone tipped backwards. Not the ride Kat expected, but as the other two drones marched closer, trying to get a clear target, the tracker would take anything to get her away.

She wanted to help the anomalies, not die for them.

The fall didn't last long. A split second's collapse ended with a shrieking, crackling noise as Kat and her dead drone struck something beneath them. Something that didn't support the drone's weight for more than a moment. Kat, her head swimming, her legs flopping, her visor telling her one bad thing after another, rode the second fall to the ground, where the landing jarred her loose.

Lying on her back on the drone's chest, Kat stared up at a night sky washed out by lights. Not the restaurant's, not the nearby street's, but those two damn drones. They loomed overhead as Kat snapped her wrist and recalled her grapple.

"Kat!" Gordon shouted, his voice, his real voice, coming from nearby. "Thanks for the assist! Drone crushing drone!"

Eight arms rose again, aimed again. Kat wanted to move, found her legs jelly.

"Gordon?" Kat yelled. "Help?"

She started a roll, going left, towards the restaurant's side and a roof still standing. She brought her right arm across when a dart struck near Kat's shoulder. A miss followed by a rubber bullet's hit, this one right into Kat's chest. Her suit took the brunt, the bullet took her breath. Coughing, wheezing, Kat turned her head to see Gordon limping towards her.

The tracker had panic and pain all over his face, his duster torn and a stunning dart sticking from his leg like some terrible extra appendage. Behind him, out the windows, Kat could see the pods streaking away, the anomalies on the run.

The metal claw cut her view as Kat felt heat from the drone's jets. Its steel fingers closed around Kat's body, cinching tight and pulling her up. Gordon, drawing a gun, fired off a round. It bounced off the gladiator, the bullet disappearing into the chaos. Gordon fired again and again, each shot going around Kat, striking his big target and doing nothing as Kat's captor rose into the sky.

Facing up, Kat saw the burning reflection in the drone's chest as the machine rose, its armor marred but still gleaming white. Its partner, functioning and well, took up the chase, descending into the collapsing restaurant after Gordon. Hopefully, the man would realize they'd done what they needed to do and run.

Hopefully, Gordon would get away. Hopefully, Kat wouldn't lose her two best friends to this damn war.

"Tell me where we're going," Kat whispered to her visor as the drone kept rising higher and higher into the sky.

The visor, pulling their speed, the drone's battery capacity, and likely destinations, laid out a list in mild yellow across Kat's aching eyes. They were moving fast, and moving west.

ELEVEN

Loyalties

ANOTHER CHAMPION CAPTURED ALIVE. Wexley delivered the news as Rhimes rose into the air over LA on a public flight to Chicago. His boss wanted a video call, a long chat about what Apinya's apprehension might mean for their strategy, but Rhimes begged off. Claimed the late hour and daily debrief deluge prohibited any conversation. Besides, Rhimes argued in fast-flying messages from his first-class seat, the drones took Apinya and the other incoming anomalies to a safe, secure place. They had time to plan, to decide how Ziran could broadcast the big win.

Adriana saved Rhimes then, taking Wexley away to celebrate. Rhimes ordered his own whisky to toast the woman and her timing, and the robot carts wheeling up and down the aisles delivered the drink in seconds. Its standardized smoky flavor cut in as Rhimes reflected on the woman, who'd come in hot to Wexley, Ziran, and their revolution.

Reps, vocal support in meetings, and a drive to push Wexley further and further all endeared Wexley to Adriana, and Rhimes couldn't blame either. The two belonged as a power couple, falling into each other's gears as though by design. As soon as Wexley had the Factory secure, Adriana passed off her other businesses—Paragon uniforms weren't in high demand anymore—to various executives and moved right in.

The anomaly testing had been her idea, and Rhimes hadn't fought it. Adriana pushed for it right away and Wexley gave her the clearance, gave her everything she asked. She threw herself into the idea from the start, securing space, the drones to make it work, and directing Rhimes and his teams to focus on capture over kill.

Not that Rhimes minded that much. While he figured the anomalies weren't going to a luxury hotel after his team took them away, at least they weren't bloodstains on the wall.

Adriana fed Rhimes and Wexley talking points too: test the anomalies, find their secrets, and learn how to shut them off. A teen taken for that noble effort would be looked at differently than one shot in the street. An anomaly father stolen in the night could be pitched as a risk to his family, his neighborhood, with the bright hope he might someday be cured and returned.

Just when Rhimes started believing Adriana might be sincere about the whole thing, she flung into the final number: with enough time, they could learn not only how to turn anomalies off, but which abilities to turn on. Pick and choose among the loyal ones, those that could do the most good without turning traitor to Ziran's cause.

Now Adriana worked an hour north doing just what she said.

Rhimes landed, taking in a wet, misty Chicago spring kiss. The drone tapped Rhimes on the shoulder and the soldier started, looked back at an empty plane. The little serving bot announced something about regulations and the next flight, so Rhimes hot-stepped it off, already back on his Tama while his feet carried him on a much-memorized trek from tarmac to taxi.

He took a second glance at Zhan-Yo's scribbled address and dumped the numbers, the name into the pod's glowing screen. The machine spat a rep fare at him that Rhimes waved off with his private account. Ziran would've comped any pod ride Rhimes took, but some things were better off the books.

Speaking of those, Rhimes's Tama held great reading material. Overnight drone and mercenary raid reports pooled in with the passing minutes, most laying out successes and failures across several clear-cut columns. Lives reduced to variables, x's and o's against a black background. They'd hit seventy-percent success last night, a new high and a top mark on the upward curving graph building since Ziran's drone takeover.

Rhimes didn't have to wonder why the machines and their minders had improved: simple attrition. The drones could go out night after night, with repairs for damages churned away at the Factory and other tireless centers. Any anomaly on the run, meanwhile, needed food, first aid, sleep. They'd make it past one raid—like this group in Nebraska that thought they could outrun Ziran's grasp—but by the second they'd be weaker.

By the third, they'd be captured or dead.

The Nebraska encounter kept Rhimes's attention as the pod slotted away from O'Hare on a road-bending climb around the city's center. The lead in Omaha tagged the raid with an exceptional event badge, something Rhimes put in as a way to signal Paragon or Champion activity. Tapping away, Rhimes skipped over the typed description and went right to the recorded drone camera feed.

He watched the damn film five times, every replay hoping it would end different. Kat should've been splattered across that rooftop, or buried in that burning restaurant's glowing corpse. Rhimes didn't know the other one helping her, caught only in a glimpse towards the end. The man probably went with those anomalies. He'd be rounded up when the drones kept up the attack tonight.

But Kat?

The drone had her going to a holding center in Kansas. They'd test her there, find out whether Kat had any anomaly powers, and when they discovered she was just a normal . . . Rhimes rubbed his face, looked out at the shopping centers, billboards laying out the summer's concerts. As a normal, she'd be charged with interfering. Locked away.

Too good for someone who'd about put a bullet through his brain. Who killed some of Rhimes's best soldiers near that frozen lake.

One call, two messages, and Kat's journey changed its course. No prison cell for her. Adriana could always use more healthy bodies for the experiments. Kat ought to be a good one, fit and perfect for an early, fatal failure.

Making the moves didn't prompt some satisfying blossom, some wild laugh. Rhimes did nod towards the pod's ceiling, towards the ones he'd lost. They would understand, would know Rhimes wouldn't ever forget about them.

And now they'd be avenged.

ZHAN-YO'S ADDRESS proved a pretty one. Isolated deep in the woods and on another lakeshore, the pod dropped Rhimes in a place so very at odds with the life he'd led since . . . childhood? Late spring flowers abounded, and while the hour still clocked in early, cooks and their coffee buzzed around. Early morning kept up its gray-scale presentation, the drizzle dotting Rhimes as he left the pod.

Rhimes went up to the front doors, expecting the sliders to open at his approach. Instead, they stayed shut. Someone's daughter came up behind him, waving her Tama towards a camera peaking out from a potted fern on the door's left side, and the entry opened. Rhimes took a step after the woman, playing the trailer.

"Stop, please," came a sharp, short voice from nowhere. "I assume you don't have a card, or you would know how to use it?"

Rhimes backed up, held his hands free. He'd gone without the tactical gear today, choosing a light button-up and jeans as a standard civilian backdrop. His weapons and gnarly outfits waited in his suitcase, which sat in the pod down the drive racking up rep fees this very second.

"I'm trying to see Regina?" Rhimes asked.

"Regina who?"

"Regina Porter."

The voice went quiet long enough for Rhimes to wish he'd stopped for coffee. Instinct told him Regina Porter's name had a long list of requirements attached, hoops to be jumped through before anyone could go in to see her.

"What did you say your name was?" The voice asked.

"I didn't," Rhimes replied.

"Mind sharing it? We can't let anyone in without a name. Policy, you understand."

And here came the turning point. Rhimes could give his name, and it'd be flagged. Wexley might get a note on his Tama right away, and within ten minutes Rhimes would have himself on the defensive from the world's ruling company and its leading man. Did he want to face all that, just because Zhan-Yo gave him a note on a bench?

Just because a revolution for a better world seemed to be heading for dystopia?

"Sorry," Rhimes said. "I'll come back later."

The voice didn't respond and Rhimes ditched back to the pod, squeezed inside, and told it to go get him that coffee. The hands went over the face again and Rhimes breathed. Not his nerves, never his nerves getting to him. The idea, though, that he'd turn against Wexley. Ridiculous. Stupid. He shouldn't have flown out here at all.

But.

After Zhan-Yo killed Aegis, Rhimes had been the man's personal bodyguard. He'd escorted Zhan-Yo from one hideaway to another, picked up food, laundry, and anything else Zhan-Yo needed. They'd spent nights in sleeping bags and days watching the world from quiet construction sites or dark bars. While Rhimes could sit and spend hours without saying a word, Zhan-Yo proved the opposite.

Like the man needed Rhimes to believe, Zhan-Yo streamed out his vision over and over again. The telling, the goal was never identical, with variations introduced every time Zhan-Yo completed his revolution. This time there would be a committee pulled from everyone at random, that time anomalies and normals would elect their leaders, and the last killed the variance altogether: regionalized representation, normal or anomaly status be damned.

Rhimes respected that one the most: stop dividing people by something they couldn't control. Skin color, language, family history, all that crap didn't matter compared with what a person did with their time. Put everyone on the same slate and maybe Rhimes would have fewer reasons to carry a gun, fewer reasons to pull the trigger.

The pod's chosen coffee shop had a bright feel to it, a local place with character and real people behind its counters. The pod dropped Rhimes off at the door and went to find a corner to nestle into. Rhimes read off the menu, chose a scone and a mocha, then took a seat at a wobbly wooden table. Driftwood painted over with cheeseball sayings mobbed the walls, interspersed with family photos that must've belonged to the owners.

"Here you are," said the barista, dropping off the delicious double dose.

"Question for you," Rhimes said before the young man could rush back to the counter. Not like the coffee shop had a hundred customers now anyway.

"Sure?"

Oh, that awkward nervousness. Rhimes figured he had to have been that way some time too long ago. How quick it died when lives started hanging on your actions.

"Let's say you've got two friends, and they don't like each other anymore," Rhimes said, and while the barista kept looking back towards the counter, he seemed to be listening. "One asks for your help with something important, but it would make the other mad. Worth the risk?"

Rhimes winced inside at his own explanation.

"I don't know, sir," the barista said. "Guess it would depend on how important, and which friend you liked more."

The barista didn't wait for Rhimes to follow-up. The boy didn't exactly drop a wise pearl there, but what did Rhimes expect? Clarity from a kid less than half his age?

Nah, if he really wanted answers, he'd have to go to the source.

Rhimes pulled up his Tama, dialed in the number and let it ring. Two sets and Zhan-Yo picked up.

"I'm here," Rhimes said.

"And?"

"Haven't gone in yet. They'll know, he'll know when I do."

"He's going to find out eventually," Zhan-Yo replied. Static swarmed in the background, as if the man had a window open as his pod streaked down the highway. "You have to make the right choice."

"I get it, he's got some secret woman stashed away here," Rhimes said. "What I'm not seeing is how that's going to be worth turning my life to dirt."

"It's because she'll know the words."

"What words?"

"Every drone has a failsafe. Aegis told us. Mynx put it in there, but we've tried hers, and it doesn't work," Zhan-Yo said. "Wexley must have replaced it."

"Or deleted it."

Zhan-Yo's laugh came through, "He's afraid of anomalies, anything stronger than humans. There's no way he's going to take away the only weapon he has against the drones. We need that passcode."

Rhimes leaned back in his chair, looked at the cafe's walls. All those happy people, unbothered by raging machines, raging anomalies.

"I get it, you use it on one drone and it gets changed again," Rhimes said. "It's a bad plan."

"No. You get it, you get into Ziran's headquarters there, and you send it out to all the drones. Every single one at once. That buys us enough time to do what needs to be done." Zhan-Yo took a long breath. "You see?"

Rhimes could've said Wexley would make more at the Factory, but he didn't have to ask. Didn't have to press why Zhan-Yo wasn't out here with some anomaly hit squad doing this job. The rest of'em, all those sneaky Paragons, would be hitting the Factory with all they had. Probably get some worldwide coordination on this, hit every drone manufacturing place on the planet at once.

A bold move, maybe the only play they had. Now Rhimes had it. The whole book. He could call Wexley and he'd scramble the code, make it random, unknowable. Then it'd be a slow slide to an inevitable end.

"Why're you telling me all this?" Rhimes said. "You didn't before?"

"Because you went to Chicago," Zhan-Yo replied. "You trusted me this far. I'm trusting you in return. Billions of lives are waiting for you to save them, Rhimes. Please."

"I'll think about it."

"Don't think too long. Things are in motion that we can't stop. Tell me when you have the code."

Rhimes clicked off. Stared at his mocha, took the scone and tried a bite. Sweet, with little orange flakes. The barista eyed him from behind the counter. Maybe the kid had heard the conversation, not that it mattered.

He finished the scone, half the mocha, then stood. Made his way back to the counter and waited behind two high schoolers and a harried delivery guy. The barista asked what he'd like.

"Know someone who'd like to make a rep or two?" Rhimes asked.

This time, the barista didn't look so confused.

TWELVE

Showers and Surprises

Basic needs competed with lingering trauma as Cassidy watched the pod drive away with Aegis, Thane, and Samir, leaving her alone with Celice amid the jet's wreckage. She wanted water, a shower, something to clean the cuts she'd sustained while falling into a forest, and you know what, Cassidy could've really, would've really liked a salve for the scars in her mind.

Time and again she'd overcome the nerve-searing shock when a companion, a friend left life behind. Cassidy had the usual trials growing up: relatives passing here and there, funerals and eulogies and the reckoning with time's inevitable march. Once Mynx ditched Cassidy on the prison island, though, that march became a visceral sprint.

At first, anomalies tore each other up. Desperate for any advantage, or just because their deeds back in civilization had rendered them unfit for anything resembling society, the fiends air-dropped onto the island sometimes required severe put-downs. That's where Cassidy had learned to split someone with her void, learned how to look death in the eye without blinking.

"It never gets easier," Celice said, Aegis's daughter looked at the still-smoldering ruin. The flashy metals shone against the starlight, the cliffs obelisks in the night. Celice inspecting like some detective, her Tama's light sliding around the nooks, as if some Paragon might be hidden beneath the rocks. "These missions, even before all this, we'd lose people every day."

"Are you a mind reader?" Cassidy asked, staying on her far side of the street.

The ocean lay out this way, a black expanse broken by the occasional moving glows provided by ships heading south to LA's docks. The crashing waves had the same comforting sound they'd always held, an echo from a youth growing up on Oregon's coast. Exhaustion came in with the surf, and she had an urge to lie down, right here in the dirt, and sink into sleep.

"Not really," Celice said, "but you'd have to be a bit of a monster not to think about death after all this."

"They might not be dead," Cassidy replied. They were shouting, Cassidy realized, into and over the breeze, the waves. Easy to do out here, when you weren't thinking about the walls, about who might be listening. "The drones seemed like they didn't want to kill us."

"The anomalies never leave that camp," Celice replied, crunching her way over to meet Cassidy, her inspection apparently over. "None that we've found. Ziran's snatched some good Paragons, strong ones that could've made it free from almost anywhere, but we've heard nothing." She glanced at her Tama. "The pod's almost here."

"Then what?"

"We go back. Get cleaned up. Look at what we've learned and plan the next mission."

"To save Apinya."

"And the others," Celice countered. "We sent the jet to

Thailand for Apinya, yes, but not him alone. We need fighters. You and Thane and all the other Paragons on that plane."

"What if I'm tired?"

Celice laughed, "Then you'll fit right in."

CASSIDY HAD the pod stop halfway back at an all-night convenience store. On LA's outskirts, its shelves had brand names Cassidy recognized. She'd had a taste in Hawaii, but that escapade had been too quick, too frantic for any reverie. And as much as Cassidy wanted a shower, as soon as that pod made it wherever Celice had it going Cassidy would be chained down again.

Running her fingers along the drinks in the store's big fridge, Cassidy spotted the ones her kids loved. The logo styles had changed, of course, but the names remained the same. The flavors too. She could fill a cart with their favorites now, could remember the stock grocery list like it was . . .

"Know why I asked to stay back with you?" Celice asked, stepping into the aisle and making Cassidy flinch. She covered it by pulling a bottle—lemon lime energy something—and dropping it in Celice's basket.

"Because sharing a pod with Thane and Aegis would be a nightmare?"

A slight smile, sad and sarcastic at the same time, "He killed my mother, you know." Cassidy raised an eyebrow. "Thane, I mean. An accident."

"He was angry," Cassidy guessed.

"He had every right to be."

"That's one helluva perspective," Cassidy said, taking Celice to a different aisle, one with skin care, soaps, shampoos. Who knew what the Paragons actually stocked back at their scruffy hideout. "I've gotta be twenty years older than you and I don't think I could let that go."

"Had enough revenge already. It's not as fun as it seems, or as satisfying."

Cassidy figured she let the jury stay out on that verdict for a bit. While the drones stole her away, torching the machines didn't exactly make her feel like an avenging angel. No, that would wait until she made it up north, until she found her former husband and had a nice, long chat.

That would come later. For now, she'd dumped enough into Celice's basket to clean herself up, to give her another outfit when her first finished disintegrating to rags, and the pair went through the checkout. Celice swiped her Tama and they went back into the parking lot, empty save for their pod and another pulling in.

Cassidy pulled out her drink, nodded to the curb at the store's front and Celice took the hint, taking out her own bottled iced tea.

"You ever do this before?" Cassidy asked as they picked their spot, sat down with their feet on the concrete. Behind them, yellow-white lights seared away.

"Sit outside a store?" Celice shook her head. "Not really."

"We used to get ice cream, my family and I,. It was nicer where we lived. Not so many highways, not so many buildings. But we'd take our cones and sit out on the curb just like this." She took a breath and Celice didn't butt in, leaving Cassidy to continue sliding down the memories. "At the time, the Paragons felt new. It'd been years already, but you don't change everything overnight."

"Can only hope so."

"We'd keep the focus on the smaller things. School. Sports. The weather or the next new videogame they wanted." Cassidy took a sip. Tasted the same, sweet and tangy, as it always had. "While at night my husband and I would argue about what would come next. How could you tell your kids about their futures when it all might go up in smoke when they turned thirteen?"

"Thirteen?"

"The tests. The anomaly exams the Paragons put every kid through." Cassidy shook her head. "I understood why, we all did, or at least that's what we told ourselves." A sigh, Cassidy bit her lip. "I wasn't there when it happened. Couldn't hug them, tell them it'd be okay, because I was on that damn island."

Celice didn't say anything. She drank, she stared at their pod. Cassidy waited, and perhaps hurt because she figured the two were forming some connection, spoke with a sharper edge, "Nothing to say?"

A shrug, "The island might not be Mynx's best idea, but the alternative? We would've been like Ziran is now. Take everyone that commits a crime and stuff them in a cell. Or kill them." Celice put her drink down, swiped on her Tama and called the pod. "When this is all over, you make it through, at least you can go see your family."

"That a promise?"

"Not one I can make," Celice said as the pod pulled up, "but one you can earn."

Pocket's inter-dimensional hideaway didn't have running water. For that, Cassidy had to take a separate pod to a nearby hotel. She rented a room using a name and account Celice gave her, pulled herself together and took a much-needed nap in a real bed while the others set about planning. In some ways it was a blessing to be a bit player: she could curl up in the cool sheets while everyone else stayed up trying to save the planet.

• • •

THE CALL CAME LONG before Cassidy wanted to wake up. The sun was well along its morning jaunt, but yesterday's adventures didn't lend themselves to sleeping in. Nonetheless, Celice spoke through the room's phone, told Cassidy to get herself together and meet in the lobby. After her second shower—not quite as good as the first, but still amazing after so long in the Thai swamps—Cassidy changed into the t-shirt and raggedy jeans from the convenience store and headed down.

Celice, unchanged from the night before except the growing bags beneath her eyes and the black baseball cap on her head, had a coffee waiting when Cassidy stepped from the elevator. Little preamble brought Cassidy through the bland lobby and outside, where she expected a pod to be waiting.

Instead, nothing. A lot with a few idled pods and sunshine. Palm trees lining the hotel's border.

"What, is there an invisible pod now?" Cassidy said. "Another anomaly that can make us float away on the wind?"

"Not quite." Celice kept a straight face beneath that ball cap. "How's the coffee?"

Cassidy drank. A little murky, and she'd prefer it with some milk, but again, after the island and the swamps she wouldn't complain.

"Best I've had in a long while," Cassidy said and Celice nodded.

"Good, keep drinking and follow me."

Cassidy pulled the cup from her lips, "What?"

Celice went right, towards the road and a sun-blasted sidewalk. Across the street businesses were opening up, retailers pulling closed signs down and putting open signs out. Birds lingering in bushes made themselves known. Cassidy realized the shoes she'd bought at the store last night didn't fit all that well, rubbing her feet with every step.

Not that the irritation mattered next to whatever the hell Celice was up to.

"The plan," Celice said, "requires you to keep drinking that coffee till it's gone."

"What happens then? I turn into something?" You could never be too sure with anomalies. "And what's the rest of this plan?"

"Can't tell you yet. Always a chance someone could read your mind. Or break you."

Cassidy stopped beside the hotel's end, dangled the cup over the thin ferns making a home in the brown mulch there.

"You tell me, or I dump this right now."

"It's for your safety and mine." Celice, down on the sidewalk already, turned back towards Cassidy "I don't even know the rest. Just to get you to drink that and walk this way."

Of all the injustices. How much had Cassidy done for Thane, how much had she gone through just so he could pursue all his crap, and now, again, she was getting hung out into some scheme. Thane had to be behind this too: Aegis didn't know Cassidy at all, and if Celice didn't know the plan, then she wouldn't be the one offering Cassidy up for it.

"If it helps," Celice said, "Thane's weak. Really weak. He's using all he has for this. He said you were the only one he'd trust with this part."

"He said that?"

Celice didn't blink, didn't shrug, look away. Straight on with those cold eyes. Cassidy wanted to wince that someone else could be as damaged as herself. She pulled the coffee back from the brink, slugged it back.

She'd never make it north to her family, not without help.

"You know," Cassidy said when she finished the whole cup, "we never trusted the Paragons. Not ever. This isn't helping."

"Don't need you to trust me. We just need you to do what we say."

"Again, not helping."

But she followed Celice down the road anyway. Five blocks as the day heated up. A cloudless sky gave the sun free reign, and the star used it. Celice didn't talk and Cassidy didn't ask her to. The shopping strip malls, the labs for meat and vegetables, shifted between one another until they leveled out into a park. Green space, all manicured and ready to be enjoyed.

Cassidy counted five kids on the playground already, parents chasing them around. Celice turned into the park, but kept away from the families. Instead, she steered Cassidy towards an empty field.

"Can't say I understand what's going on here?" Cassidy said.

"Wait," Celice replied. "Stand here. Stay calm. You'll be okay."

Celice put her hand on Cassidy's shoulder as they reached the field's center, gave the anomaly a nod. Then ran. A flat-out sprint that had no obvious spark until, until . . .

Damn it.

They flew in fast, from all sides. Three gladiators from above, two tracker drones from below bursting through the bushes. Their alarms wailed, warned pedestrians to stand back. Cassidy felt the voids leap to her fingertips as she whirled, trying to decide which one to destroy first.

"Stand down," said a gladiator as the drones

approached, white-orange color schemes wildly out of place in the natural park.

Cassidy would've, should've split the drone in half with a void. She twitched an arm that way, but stopped. Felt the coffee on her tongue, heard Celice speaking in her mind.

Wait, stay calm. Thane's plan.

Beyond the drones, Cassidy caught the kids watching, their parents scooping up the toddlers and carrying them away. If she fought the drones now, there was a chance she could die. Could inflict those children with a sight they'd never forget.

"Fine," Cassidy said. "You want me? You got me."

They came in slow then, steel claws tearing at the grass. The tracker drones and all their legs gleamed, the big roaches coming in close. One gladiator decided to play the lead and when it came within a meter, Cassidy turned its way, flipping both hands up into a lovely double-bird.

She felt a prick, a thud hit her back. The numbness came fast, her knees giving way in a breath. At least the grass gave her a soft landing. At least she didn't feel the drone pick her up.

She did see, as her vision dimmed into a tunnel, those panicked parents and their charges looking back her way. On those faces, Cassidy didn't see hate.

But she saw fear, and not aimed at her.

Revolutionaries

THE COLD BASTARD watched the drones take away his friend—girlfriend? Love?—without a word. Aegis, arms folded, shared the stare from the restaurant across the park. Inside, behind big sun-catching windows, the trio explored coffee, waited on eggs, and left a seat open for Celice to join them. Street clothes abounded, not a Paragon whisper among Thane, Zhan-Yo, and Aegis. The big villain himself stayed thin, desiccated.

Thane's wheelchair sat near the entrance, tucked away between a tall fern and a bored hostess.

"I've put her through a lot," Thane said finally, turning his sharp, sunken eyes back to them. "She's handled every-thing well."

"So close to remorse, and yet so far," Aegis replied. "As if you know what the word means."

The pod ride back to Pocket's hideaway the night before had been a studied exercise in silence. Samir sloshed the jet's story all over the trip, giving Aegis openings to ask the pilot questions and avoid noticing Thane. Not a look, not a word, not a pat on the back for the anomaly that might save Aegis's dream.

Because, sitting here and in that pod, Aegis wondered whether a dream requiring this was worth saving.

"You would do the same and you know it," Thane said. His voice came out quavering, so dry and weak. Hard to understand how the man beat Aegis last time they met. "You can't change the world without sacrifice."

"Big words before breakfast." Aegis cast his eyes along the restaurant, hunting for the drone that'd deliver the first round. The machine hadn't emerged from the kitchen yet, but the several other occupied round, linen-topped spots showcased delectables. "But here we are."

"Here we are indeed," Zhan-Yo said, standing and giving Celice a short bow as the woman took the fourth chair at the table. "We are on the move?"

"Didn't you see what happened?" Celice asked, taking off her baseball cap and shaking out her short hair. "Cassidy's on the board now."

"As is my associate," Zhan-Yo said. "It's time we put ourselves into play."

Aegis pointed a finger at Thane, "He stays home. No matter what."

The old man didn't push back. Didn't say anything. Vanished off into his own head again, exploring scenarios Aegis couldn't imagine, or something like that. During all those years they'd kept Thane locked, drugged away, Aegis learned to save his offence for the spoken word, not the silent second.

"He'll perform his part," Zhan-Yo smiled. "Now is not the time for grudges, no matter how deserved."

Aegis grunted, Celice rolled her eyes. The eggs came, and the foursome kept it quiet as they devoured breakfast. They knew the plan, understood what came next.

And you never knew who, or what, might be listening.

AEGIS RAN his hands over the selection laid out on the spotted, laminated blue counter. A coffee machine burbled nearby, its neighboring bagel box a counterpoint to the death machines cool beneath the Champion's fingers. Sun came in from the right, muted by drawn blinds but enough to cast his daughter in a good light as she went about filling her own belt with lethal means.

"First time in the field together," Celice said, clicking a magazine into its compartment. No normal rounds here—bullets were hard to come by—instead, all the magazines had their contents tweaked for mechanical murder. "Hard to believe."

"My mistake," Aegis replied. He found a baton, its top rounded and silver. Ready to conduct some electricity. He picked it up, flicked the thumb switch and felt the buzz in the black weapon. "You've been ready for a long time."

"What makes you say so?" Celice grinned as she looped three grenades onto her gear. "Was it that I tracked Zhan-Yo all the way to London, that I beat him straight on? Or—"

"Before all that," Aegis said, and Celice picked up the tone, watched as Aegis set the baton in his keep pile. "When you had Mynx come to Manhattan. When you worked with her to convince me I'd better start thinking about the future."

"How's that make me ready for field duty?"

"Because you're thinking about what comes after the next punch," Aegis replied. "As long as humans exist, we'll be beating each other up over something. There'll be winners and losers, but if you can look a little farther ahead, you'll be on the winner's side more often."

"Fighting for all time?" Celice sighed. "Dad, you know how to take a nice moment and turn it sour."

"Maybe that's what I am now. Sour."

"I'd call it bitter. That's right. You're a bitter old man."

Aegis quirked a smile, looked over at Celice and waved a second baton her way, "Watch out, or this bitter old man's going to give you a lesson."

Celice stretched her arms over her head, "A lesson in what? Grumpiness?"

The baton flew fast when Aegis flipped it, wheeling hard at Celice's stomach. She caught it, rolled off the chair with the move and came up standing, baton pointed back towards her father.

"See? I never let my guard down either," Celice said. "All your sayings, your lessons. I listened."

"Can see that." Aegis nodded. "You're ready."

"Are you?" Celice frowned, came over to the counter and handed the baton back. "I know Mila patched you up, that you've been punching out these machines, but you've tried the Factory before."

Three times. At first, when they finally made it to LA from London, via cross-country treks, Aegis barged up that way. He'd punched through a gladiator before realizing two dozen more stood in his path, before realizing even he'd get knocked out trying that one solo.

The second attempt came coordinated. A varied assault with LA's Paragons and Elementals teaming up in a big raid. They'd had the firepower, but the wrong strategy. A big force rolling up and demanding satisfaction, with the media alerted to showcase Ziran's downfall, only to be set upon by machines and Ziran's human commandos from all sides. A drastic retreat, too many anomalies captured or killed.

After that, things had gone dark for a month. Aegis and

the others licked wounds, reached out around the world to find support. Zhan-Yo rebuilt his underground network, finding sympathetic normals who didn't want all out slaughter to replace Paragon rule. That reality pushed Aegis towards the third try.

Because if Zhan-Yo rallied everyone to his cause, if the man who bombed out a stadium managed to orchestrate a world-freeing, war-ending mission, then Aegis wouldn't have a chance to bring things back. The Paragons would be over. Done forever.

So he'd found his loyal crew, a small ten anomaly task force. Darted from Pocket's dimension deep in the night, burrowed their way with an ability all the way up to Mynx's old house on the coast. Dodged the front door, came right at those stairs ready to go.

And found too much metal waiting for them.

That'd been the worst one. The tracking drones bursting from the sand at their feet, the gladiators rising up over the cliffs. Knowing they were done before the fighting even started. Aegis called for the evacuation and seven made it.

Since then he'd kept quiet, killing the panicked voices every time they spoke up to say he'd failed.

"She'd do a little more every day," Aegis said. He'd sat in that vat, suspended in chemicals. Itching everywhere as the enzymes, proteins, whatever did their work. "Come down, hit me with what she could spare. Reeves would send a drone down with her to carry Mila back when she finished."

"Didn't know someone could be hurt that bad and still live."

"Wasn't my body that took the longest. My mind, Celice. Mila didn't just put my bones back together, but she found my brain, oxygen starved and battered, and put that back too. Synapses by the millions."

Aegis planted his palms on the counter. Mila was missing too. Vanished with Mynx. Everyone assumed the two Champions were hidden in the Factory.

"You sure you have that many?" Celice said, tilting her head, raising an eyebrow.

"Hey."

"You take a lot of punches, dad. The evidence is grim."

Shaking his head, Aegis shoved himself back, headed towards the apartment's living room. "Quit shooting easy targets and get yourself ready. This one's it."

Zhan-Yo agreed when Aegis told him the same thing. Despite his breakfast comments, the fighter, bomber, murderer, and leader had his two tachi laid out on the bed. Aegis locked onto the blades, feeling the cutting, spine-tearing edge as one stabbed into his back. That'd been in Chicago's dark underground, in a grime-covered substation or something. An ambush with traitors and—

"Are you focused?" Zhan-Yo asked, tightening a wrap around his right wrist.

"Focused?" Aegis asked. "What the hell else would I be thinking about?"

"Thane, for one."

"Maybe it's you. Maybe I'm distracted because the guy that stabbed my back is giving me orders."

Zhan-Yo nodded, "I did what I thought was right. Just as you did when you formed the Paragons and destroyed my family's freedom."

An old bubbling rose in Aegis's throat. The heat rushed up to his cheeks and he felt, knew the argument coming. The lines about how safety and prosperity necessitated some sacrifices. The Paragons had evidence proving how much better the world ran with the Champions at the helm, and why couldn't everyone see that, and . . .

"The difference with you and me is that we had the tools and the will to keep trying until we got our way," Aegis said.

"And to hell with anyone who tried to stop us."

Aegis joined Zhan-Yo at the window. The apartment nestled into a huge complex, one of several secured with reps and a little nudging.

"Way back, before all this," Aegis said, "Most of the Champions served their countries. They were drafted, markers to say this or that nation had the newest super weapon."

"I know. I lived it. I woke up every day expecting one of you or a country with a distaste for the world to decide it wasn't worth keeping around."

"As paranoid as me then."

"You showed us a way forward," Zhan-Yo said, drawing a curious look. "We flailed without ideas as anomalies appeared, and then here you are with the solution, albeit an imperfect one."

"Imperfect?"

"Exclusions create classes, which eventually turn on each other. Keep your trackers, your Paragons, your incentives for anomalies to choose a stable path over a disastrous one. But give us a place, some power and some purpose."

"Normals like Wexley, you mean."

"You already have anomalies like Thane." Zhan-Yo gestured outside, the drones floating by. "Wexley is smart, strong, and twisted by the world you and I helped create. We—"

"Please don't say we can save him. That doesn't work. Not once it goes this far. I've seen his type. He'll die before he surrenders."

"Maybe, but let that be his choice, not ours."

THE POD DROPPED them up in the valley hours later. A foursome. Aegis, Celice, Zhan-Yo, and Particle. Three agents and their hammer. Everyone had slim backpacks, had belts loaded with everything possible.

Evening encroached, turning blond sand and rock into violet-orange waves. Brush crackled in brittle wind like the stones beneath their boots. A coyote barked, only heard and never seen. Aegis checked for snakes, found none.

Celice had particular fears, see.

Particle took the lead, stepping off without any fanfare after an Aegis nod nudged the mission into its active state. Zhan-Yo's last message confirmed things were a go. His ace, the one in Chicago, hadn't checked in for a while, but Zhan-Yo had faith. The target knew what to do, would execute the mission.

Aegis found he didn't much care about the specifics. Getting another crack at the Factory, at Wexley would be enough.

"Laces, dad," Celice said, and Aegis glanced at his boots. The left one hung loose, the strands lingering on the thin asphalt. "Don't think we need you tripping when the fighting starts."

Distracted. No excuse.

"Perhaps we will be lucky." Zhan-Yo watched Aegis tie up the boot. "Maybe all the drones will be receiving an update when we arrive."

"Hope and reality are two different things," Aegis said, joining the other two and starting after Particle. The anomaly's footprints stood out clear in the dirt, stepping over and around sprigs and crackled bushes. Not a single one disturbed. "Wexley won't let us rescue Mynx without some fun."

"We could run." Zhan-Yo played the scene, jogging past Aegis before turning back, wearing a limber grin. "Sprint right past the drones until we get to the Champions. You know how to run, don't you, Aegis?"

"Learned it from you," Aegis replied. "How many times did they find you in Chicago?"

"Hi," Celice interrupted as they walked. "It's the young one here asking you two to grow up?"

"That's the secret," Zhan-Yo laughed. "The older you get, the younger you get to be. Nobody's going to tell you different."

Even Aegis chuckled at that one, though he didn't agree. While Mila's work had made the bullets, the bruises, the beaten bones holding him together fix themselves, Aegis didn't know yet how long her work would last. Which firefight, thrown punch, or stabbing knife would get through his refurbished self and put a more permanent end to him.

"Okay, Z," Aegis said with an exaggerated huff. "You win this one. The drones come after us, we run." He held up one finger, skin almost glowing in the descending light. "You'd better stick tight to me if that happens, because I'm not coming back for you."

"Spoken like a true Champion of the people."

Aegis stopped, found his fists ready to go. Zhan-Yo seemed to sense the move and turned, looking back. The older man's wrinkles, laughing eyes, and the cigarette hanging from Z's mouth took the edge off, just a little. He'd still stabbed Aegis in the back.

Still blew up a stadium with innocents gathered inside.

"You know," Aegis said. "I'm starting to think you're not necessary anymore."

Celice, between the two, flicked her eyes back and forth. She might've said something, but Aegis ignored it. This wasn't her fight.

"And I'm wishing you'd stayed dead," Zhan-Yo replied.

Aegis took a step forward, boot crunching into the hard-packed dirt, "If I hadn't crashed Gatete's party in London, your head would be on a pike."

"Then at least I wouldn't have to listen to you." Zhan-Yo reached back, put a hand on a tachi hilt. "What a wonder you are, Aegis. So powerful, and so short-sighted."

"Guess which is about to matter to you."

Another step. Celice planted herself in Aegis's way, shouting at them both to stop. Aegis pushed past her—he wouldn't hurt Celice, not ever, but she wasn't stopping this. Zhan-Yo dropped his hand from the blade, gave Aegis a little wave, and ran.

Leaving the Champion to give chase.

After all, Zhan-Yo fled in the Factory's direction. Aegis could deliver well-earned justice, and still complete the main mission.

It was a beautiful day for a run.

FOURTEEN

Test Subject

THE DRONE STOPPED several times over the night and through the next morning, always letting Kat off its big arms into a fenced pen. Skylights washed out the stars while other drones looked on as Kat found water, bathrooms, and other captives like her. Tracker instincts went wild as Kat caught faces, vacant stares as the others stood or laid down in the dirt. Even without their abilities—though some wore unnatural scars as evidence—the anomalies made themselves known by their condition: Sedated, all of 'em.

The machines left Kat alone save when her chosen gladiator, the same one that'd flown her all the way from Nebraska, hovered back onto the scene. Its batteries charged, the drone loomed over Kat before flashing its lights and extending its arm. Another leg through the chill air.

Calvin's name kept whispering in her ears as Kat checked her Tama, her suit's functions at every stop. Those told her the drone's course kept going west towards the Factory. Everyone knew that captive anomalies went to some big camp out that way. A camp that seemed right on Kat's projected path.

So why try to break free? Kat would get riddled by drone fire for her troubles, and even if she lucked into an escape would be nowhere with nothing. Maybe if she had people to get back to, if she had a cause to rejoin, her motivations would be different.

Weed and his crew were watching Seeker. Gordon was probably following her west now, pod crawling along the highways. Neither needed Kat scrambling, hurt, pursued.

So when the drone offered her its arm, Kat climbed in. Did her best to find a comfortable way to curl up in the steel fold. A few hours sleep crept into the trip's crevasses, interrupted at last by the glowing sun and the ocean's sparkle on the horizon.

California.

Beneath her, barricaded behind thin walls thrown up with haste's handiwork, Ziran's anomaly camp made its gridded, efficient appearance. Crammed into a valley, the camp nestled between two beige hills, a soft-flowing exit heading towards the ocean and another, at its front, providing a crowded roadway access. As Kat's drone flew in, she counted pods aplenty on those streets, picking up and dropping off people in Ziran's easy-to-pick-out orange and white uniforms.

Other drones marked Kat's approach, smaller machines swarming the skies. Three pulled up alongside Kat's carrier, each one turning an olive-green light her way. Kat fired up a glare, stuck out her tongue at the last one. They beeped as they caught her image, then the trio formed up in a line, angling towards the camp's right side. Kat's gladiator followed.

Scaffolding abounded the white-orange camp, permanent structures erasing the tarp-and-pole approach that'd brought Ziran's idea forward from conception. The camp's left side, tucked against that hill, had the largest buildings. One already completed towered, at four stories, over everything else.

The big Z carved onto its roof, blaze orange on white tile, would've been a great target for some spit had Kat's drone flown her close.

Padded dirt paths paved the way between smaller structures, including big tarp tents where Kat imagined her anomaly partners burned their nights away. Those same anomalies clogged the paths now, shepherded along by Ziran guards with sparking stun batons. Gladiator drones stood at various points, scanning the crowd for any anomaly thinking they might use their powers.

None did.

More sedatives, or resignation against impossible odds?

The gladiator settled on a circular patch after following the small drones. The patch sat between two large tents, one labeled A, the other B in those big orange letters. Stylized, too, in Ziran's swooping modern font.

Never willing to be basic, these guys.

Kat stepped off the drone's arm, letting her mask stay over her face. The display confirmed the mild temperatures, her own rumbling stomach, and that the suit itself retained its capabilities after the Nebraska fight. Kat had burned some stopover hours fiddling with the joints, wiping away ash stains from the restaurant fire. The watching drones didn't care then and, by the way no machine advanced on her now, that apathy stayed the same.

"You!" A real, human somebody called Kat's way, and she saw the armed and armored woman approaching. "Stay right where you are." The guard glanced up at the gladiator drone, the big machine standing still. "Sedation status?"

"Negative," the gladiator replied. "Target is not an anomaly."

The guard stared at the drone. Machines weren't the only things that froze when their programming broke. Kat jumped through her own mental hoops: she'd arrived at Ziran's anomaly camp, but she wasn't an anomaly. A normal human stumbling into a place where they didn't belong, particularly one like this, tended to wind up dead.

Not good.

"It's wrong," Kat said. "I was hiding with other anomalies. I just, I mean . . . " Kat looked down at herself, sent the mask receding so the guard, curious now, could see her face. "My power's not much. I don't use it."

The guard, holding that sparking baton towards Kat like she might pass it for a relay, strode up to the tracker. The woman's own face, visible in the orange-tinted visor, put the guard old enough to be Kat's mother. Wrinkled eyes drenched in suspicion, mouth in a thin frown.

"Show me," the guard said. "Prove that machine wrong."

SHOW *me what you can do.*

Kat heard the words in a field. Grass left to grow reached beyond her shins. The air four meters away in every direction shimmered, an effect brought by the Paragon standing five meters in front. The Paragon had her eyes closed, blue-white uniform resplendent. A small table stood to her left, dotted with sodas and snacks.

On the table's other side sat another Paragon, bored but with his Tama raised. The man's hair frizzed out, a detail Kat couldn't understand why she remembered except that she needed to focus on something, needed to hold on to something while her dreams were put to the test.

"I can't," Kat said. "I don't know how."

Her parents told her an ability would come naturally. She'd feel it, like a new arm, a new hand. She'd woken up on her thirteenth birthday breathless, waiting. Now, a week later, she still felt nothing.

"That's fine," the sitting Paragon said. "Remember, ninety-nine percent are normals. We'll just need to confirm it's not latent." The man took a breath, glanced towards the other Paragon. "Run the tests."

The shimmering air intensified, blurring out everything except the grass at Kat's feet. The Paragons, the blue sky smudged. She'd heard about this, saw it presented in the school's auditorium at the year's start. This would be the make or break moment.

Kat closed her eyes, clenched her fists, took a deep breath and *hoped*.

An electric shock came first. Then a piercing scream. Something stabbed her leg, while her left hand went numb, as if coated in ice. A million tiny legs crawled across her scalp. And while Kat had her eyes shut tight, she could suddenly see her family being held at gunpoint by some shadowy figure. Her father called to Kat to save them, to do what she knew she could.

Nothing came. Nothing went. When the session ended, Kat took the offered water, candy, and a sticker with the Paragon's blue P and the words *I've been tested* in cheery red. She waited in a chair for twenty minutes with other kids like her, watched by the school's nurse and a medical drone for any side effects.

Kat's future washed into the great normal river. No powers, no Paragon life working alongside her parents.

When the nurse told her she could go, Kat went to math class, like everyone else in her grade.

KAT KICKED THE GUARD. Hit the woman's right shin with enough force to send the guard slipping to her knees. The tracker caught the guard's lurching baton in both hands, bent the weapon and the guard's wrist so the baton's flickering end found a home in the woman's helmet. Sparks shivered, arced over that white armor, and the guard collapsed.

The darts dug into Kat's shoulders even as the guard fell. One, two, and a third into her lower back as the watching drones bounced into action. The sedatives hit hard, fast, and Kat didn't even manage a step before she joined her guard in the dirt.

Only to get herself dragged forward, other guards coming and pulling off Kat's mask. She felt a different pinprick to her neck, a surge fighting back against the numbing sleep.

"Don't go out on us now," rumbled a harder voice. "Not after a show like that."

"The feisty ones get express treatment," skittered another woman, younger and high-pitched. "Third this week, right, Terry?"

"Our shifts always get the good ones," the man— Terry?—agreed as he hoisted Kat back up to her feet, not that she could stand. The woman slid herself beneath Kat's left shoulder while Terry took his place beneath her right. "People always talk about peace and quiet, but where's the fun in that?"

Kat blinked, a slow, tedious affair spiced up by two rolling medical drones, a meter tall apiece, zooming by their trio towards the downed guard. On-site benefits for the team.

The guards carried Kat away from the large tents, angling towards the bigger, completed building on the camp's other side. At their shouts, the guards cleared space in the shuffling anomaly lines, drawing the occasional glance and little else from the powered people. Kat tried to keep an eye out for Calvin, but in the uniformed mass, with the sun glaring down, everyone seemed to look the same.

Strange to be carried while numb. Kat could tell, by virtue of air on her face, that she moved, but otherwise it seemed like she drifted across the camp. A ghost out in broad daylight, haunting nobody, scaring nothing. And, like a ghost, she went in by her own way.

The building with its big orange Z on the front rose high, its entry split into rows dominated by marching anomalies. Guards and drones towered over their subjects with a placid disinterest, either lazy or confident in their sedatives. Kat didn't get much chance to decide which before her captors had her at the left line's end, cutting right to a glassy overhang.

A spectacled man leaned back in a bargain-bin black office chair resting on cheap gray tile. Behind him, the building's bright corridors awaited, swarming with anomalies getting shuffled into various rooms. Kat found herself pushed up against a white desk with orange trim. Images and words in a blue-and-white color scheme leapt from the desk and hovered before her eyes.

"Have a new one for you," said Terry. "She's feisty."

"What am I supposed to do with her?" Spectacles asked, raising some very bushy eyebrows over his eyeglasses. "Do you see an opening? Is there not a line behind you, one that you have, without any need, cut?"

"She hit Sarah," said the woman holding Kat's right shoulder. "She's dangerous."

"Think that might be because she's wearing all that gear?" Spectacles looked Kat over. The stare, at first a casual review like someone observing a misfit garden, sharpened. "Wait. I believe I recognize this one." The man leaned forward in his chair, waved away the screens with his hands. "What's your name?"

When Kat didn't answer right away, the man shot a frown at the two guards, "Tell me she's not so sedated as to be useless?"

"Them's the rules," Terry said, keeping Kat balanced under his shoulder. "Anomalies act up, they get knocked out."

"Except she's not an anomaly," Spectacles replied. "Rhimes flagged her, and Adriana's approved. She gets the suppressor."

The hell was the suppressor? Kat tried not to seem like she was listening, that she cared. Not that hard to fake when all her body wanted was to lie down right there and sleep.

"You just said she's not an anomaly? Why's she getting that?" Terry asked, and Kat silently thanked the guard for solving her problem.

"Terry, is your job to ask questions?" Spectacles said, adopting the smug grin that seemed to come free with authority positions everywhere. "Or is it to follow orders?"

Terry slipped out from under Kat's arm, letting her lurch to the side. The woman reached around Kat's waist, stabilized the tracker. Kat caught Terry make a particular gesture with one hand before he turned and walked away, muttering something while the spectacled man laughed.

"Room three's ready," Spectacles said, turning to Kat's sole helper. "Drop her, lock her in."

. . .

THE SIDE EFFECTS should be minimal. The shot would sting when administered. Did she have any questions?

The machine, a slender medical drone, sat on its wheels in Kat's shock-white cell. Kat, arms and legs tied together with thin plastic, looked up from the floor at the two meter tall computer. On the outside, the drone looked like someone had run a knife in strange patterns along its matte orange coating—Ziran branded, because of course. The lines carved out little sections that could emerge and retract based on the drone's needs.

And right now, it very much needed to stab Kat with a greenish-yellow liquid. The syringe and its long needle emerged from one of those lined sections, aiming towards Kat and waiting for her approval before descending.

"I can override it if you don't say yes," Spectacles said. He'd a personal interest in Kat's well-being ever since she showed up at his desk.

"Not gonna," Kat said, the words coming out mushy.

Her throat hadn't recovered much, and everything lower still seemed disconnected. Kat had her head, her eyes and her ears and nothing more. Like a dream, and Kat wouldn't have minded waking up.

"Please confirm," the drone repeated. "I cannot proceed without your stated agreement."

The Paragons and their laws. Apparently Ziran hadn't seen fit to reprogram all the medical robots yet. No doubt they would. Wexley might make the bots offer all patients a new Tama plan with Ziran as part of every procedure.

"Kat," Spectacles said. "Time's wasting."

Kat told the man to do something delightful with himself.

"Fine." Spectacles shrugged, gave the drone the override. "Be that way."

The jab came without ceremony. A quick stick, the needle in, the liquid following, then back out with a blood drop easing down Kat's arm. Another slat on the drone opened, bearing a tiny white pad. The drone wiped up the red droplet, slid the pad up to cover the injection site. The machine's metal arm, a chromed stick, pressed the pad into Kat's skin to stick it.

All through the process Kat found hope: she could feel it. The poke, the pad's press. The numbing hits she'd taken were wearing off. The ties around her feet and her hands rested lightly, a loose capture made by guards too used to sedation pay attention to technique. They'd be tough to shake, but not impossible.

Ideas.

The medical drone retreated, vanishing through the room's door. Spectacles stayed where he was, watching Kat through the window.

"How fast does this work?" Kat asked.

"Any minute now," Spectacles said.

"Any minute?" Kat kept her voice thick, sleepy.

She sent some test twitches down her legs, to her fingers. Found nerves waiting, twitching. Fingertips touched each other, toes curled. Biceps contracted. The moves came with delays, slower and weaker than Kat would like.

But she could work with this.

Kat let her mouth open, some drool escaping as she let her head fall forward to rest against the hard ground. Her arms and legs left to go limp. Her tied hair flopped over her head.

"Kat?" Spectacles asked. "Are you all right?"

Kat mumbled something back. Random sounds. Soft nonsense.

"What are you feeling?"

A grunt this time. One fading off at the end. Kat threw a spasm into her right side, arm and leg jerking once, violently against the floor. The zip ties scraped. She felt the chill tiles. Tasted the sanitizer in the air.

"Kat?"

The cell's door opened. Footfalls. Kat stayed quiet. Eyes open. Spectacles leaned over her, held his hand over her mouth to feel for her breathing. Kat held the air in, waited for him to check the next vital sign.

Spectacles moved to Kat's neck, a slow reach. The man smelled like coffee. His clothes over-worn and under-washed. A pencil pusher not ready for field work.

In other words, a perfect target.

Break Out

BRADEN the barista's break finally rolled around. The kid knocked on the pod, jolting Rhimes from the Ziran action reports, messages, and administrative crap that'd consumed his morning. Folding his arms and putting on a half-lidded, lazy frown, the barista shrugged when Rhimes asked if he was ready to go.

"Sure, I guess," the kid, added, as if that cleared things up.

"Going to need a stronger affirmative," Rhimes replied, but he slid to the pod's right side anyway, clearing a spot in the vehicle. "We're not going shopping."

"Good, cause I gotta be back in thirty minutes." The barista poked his head in, looked around. "You're not some kinda predator, are you?"

"Would a predator ask you to help him get into a care home? You want the reps or not?"

The money greased palms, calmed suspicions, and the kid closed the pod door behind him. Rhimes told the craft to get moving and the pod complied, pulling into warm-lit suburban streets. A cloudless sky echoed spring's sunshine, a happier mood than Rhimes could claim. Big trees offered buds as the pod returned to the forested path leading up to the home.

This time Rhimes had the pod drop them off halfway up the driveway where a trail intersected with the asphalt. Voices off to the right gave away a walking group too far off to get any specific words, but enough to give a relaxing vibe.

"That's your opportunity," Rhimes said to Braden, whose eyes had grown large, whose arms had returned to their fold. "Nothing illegal, nothing dangerous. Just get their attention."

"And I'll get the reps?"

Rhimes held out his Tama, Braden tapped his. The transfer went through with a happy chime. A strange milestone, paying off a kid to do the dirty work. Then again, how often throughout history had fate's lever moved through an unlikely actor?

Braden jogged down the path towards the voices, the teen's attitude reinforced by payment delivered. Ziran's security chief sent the pod for a ride, telling it to come back to the home's entrance after twenty minutes spent circling the blocks.

If Rhimes hadn't escaped with Wexley's sister by then, he wouldn't be needing the pod.

Hiking up towards the home's entrance, Rhimes stayed off to the right near the trees. The walking prompted a realization, one that hadn't hit home through the flight, the pod rides, and the deal making with Braden, barista extraordinaire: if Rhimes made it out with Wexley's sister, how would he convince her to give up the drone codes?

"Dammit, Zhan-Yo," Rhimes muttered.

The revolutionary would get Rhimes killed yet.

But Zhan-Yo didn't want genocide. Compared to Wexley, that was enough.

BRADEN MADE his move as the home's entrance came into view. Rhimes heard the kid shouting, falling back on the idea they'd discussed: some strange man chasing after him, needing help and all that. Braden's teenage voice obliged, cracking into high falsettos that shattered the artificial calm around the place. Birds leapt from their perches, and the orderlies that had been ready to tackle Rhimes earlier found themselves checking their Tamas.

Two, clad in their cream-colored uniforms, hustled out through the main entrance. One gave Rhimes a lingering look as they rushed by, but Rhimes disarmed the stare with a polite nod. No aggression here, just someone who wanted to try again.

Those glass double doors, closed and locked, waited. The speaker sat to the right, its black circle daring Rhimes to hit the call button and ask for Regina Porter again.

He'd played it nice once. Not a second time.

Rhimes went right towards the door. Didn't until he'd closed within a meter. Planted a foot, and struck out with his military-grade, steel-toed boot. The kick struck the door's vulnerable middle, splintering, breaking the glass in a satisfying spider-web then shatter progression. The shards hit the floor in a thick rain.

And Rhimes ran. Barreled forward like a truck with broken brakes.

Beyond the double doors, the care home's lobby opened up into a meeting space built for calm. Cushioned, olive-colored chairs that must've been decades old arrayed around basic round wood tables. A skylight let in some natural color while the walls gave themselves away to photographs showing residents enjoying themselves around Chicago's various sites.

The lobby gave Rhimes options.

An elevator to a second level sat on his right while two corridors, straight ahead and left, offered chances. The odds would've been even except for one tiny detail: Wexley wanted the best, and he wanted it efficiently. Straight ahead to the back, the home's biggest and best room.

The lobby's guest smattering—some families having lunch with their loved ones—looked up as Rhimes trucked through. Not a one rose to get in his way, not a one moved to trip him. No heroes.

Good.

If the home had any employees ready to step up, they stayed hidden as Rhimes went through the lobby into the corridor and found himself wedged in a hallway between a zen garden and closed doors to residents he didn't care about. The carpet collected his steps, kept things as quiet as Rhimes could want.

The hallway t-boned at its end, the left choice offering a roundabout return to the lobby while the right hinted at rewards through a glinting black-and-gold sign suggesting room zero-one lay that way. With a quick glance left to confirm no charging security—none showed—Rhimes made the pivot as clean as his boots allowed.

Room one and its star occupant appeared up faster than Rhimes expected, its rose-red door and black name-plate breaking up the beige wall on the left without preamble. There wasn't a handle, just a Tama scanner.

Hmm.

Shouts carried down the corridor, not the panicked kind but the calm, controlled calls from a well-trained crew responding to an emergency. Of course Wexley would put his sister in a place versed in breakouts, break-ins, anomaly events. Of course they'd react to Rhimes's smash-n-grab with a complete, measured response.

So much for chaos carrying Rhimes and his quarry out of here. Braden the barista's valiant efforts on the nature path would've wrapped by now, so the orderlies would be coming on back. Worse, far worse, would be any drones called in to assist.

Rhimes stared at the door. Took a deep breath. It looked sturdy enough, but he had to hope the home cut its budget somewhere and left these things flimsy. He led with another kick, angled right above the Tama scanner. The blow struck the wood, left a mark and little else. He tried again fast.

A chip fell out. As big as Rhimes's thumb.

Not a good sign.

To his left, back down the corridor, Rhimes caught shadows advancing against the building's quaint sconce lighting. Time to throw it all in, hope those kicks did enough work to weaken the door.

The inflection point. Every mission had it. The lever that would either doom everything or propel him towards success. Sometimes, that lever came at the end of a gun's barrel. Others, Rhimes put his fate in his allies and his enemies, trusting them to make the right and wrong choices.

Most often? The lever came down to him.

Rhimes put his muscled bulk behind the rush, leaning in and leveling his charge right above the black circle marking the door's lock. Right where his earlier kicks had gone about their business.

The door opened. Swung aside as Rhimes reached it, revealing a curious woman clad for an afternoon inside. Rhimes snapped up the details in the frantic millisecond before he slammed into Wexley's sister: her curled hair, fresh face, bemused air. The look of someone so used to routine that they never believed it could be broken.

She flew a meter without touching the ground when Rhimes hit her. Regina's feet touched first, their grip on the carpet flinging her backwards hard enough that she bounced before sliding to a stop. Her hair splayed out on the ground behind her, and Rhimes heard the halting, gasping sounds as Regina tried to find a breath.

Rhimes cursed, slid the door shut behind him. The motion let him confirm no inside latch, no way for Regina to guarantee her privacy. Wexley might've paid for the nicest cell, but this was still a prison.

Regina's box held a queen bed cloaked in forest sheets, a single black walnut nightstand adorned with a framed family photo Rhimes recognized—the same one had a home on Wexley's desk in Ziran's headquarters. On the right, a recliner and coffee table played host to dime novels stacked in teetering rows, leaning against each other at odd angles.

No TV, no Tamas.

"Sorry," Rhimes said as he approached Regina, leaned down to help her up. "I'm trying to get you outta here, not kill you."

She coughed. Wheezed. Wind definitely knocked from her lungs.

The door jittered. The lock clicked as someone's Tama gained clearance.

Rhimes scooped up Regina in his arms, like a princess, albeit one in a robe and slippers. She coughed again, but her open eyes studied Rhimes as he angled for the big windows at the room's rear.

No chance getting through all those guards, but he might break through all that glass. Roll outside with only a few cuts.

The door opened. Someone shouted at Rhimes to stop. The air near his ear *whooshed* and a stunning dart stuck into the wall next to the big windows. An intentional miss or not, the point was made: Rhimes wouldn't make it out without a hit to his back.

Hostages didn't make for a sound strategy. Chain a body to you and now you're carrying it everywhere, and a live one like Regina was a sure bet to turn against him.

Better to play for surprise, find an opening.

Rhimes stood Regina up straight, raised his hands to the orderlies and their shouts to move real slow. He faced his pursuit, the foursome looking bulky and not so much angry as thrilled that their day-to-day had been so gloriously interrupted. These guys had ages that ran high enough to lose cherished careers to the Paragons and their anomaly law-and-order mandate.

All four locked eyes on Rhimes and his straight arms. Four stun guns aimed at his chest. Rhimes waited for the trigger, the pull. None came.

"Who sent you?" asked the orderly on the right, the oldest in the crew. More interesting than the question came his tone: honest curiosity.

"Tell us," said the next one, younger and eager. "Was it him?"

Oh.

"Regina?" Rhimes said to those steady stun guns and the rigid faces holding them. The foursome didn't seem to breathe, but they all tilted their heads in unison, a downright creepy move. Rhimes tried not to flinch. "What're you doing?"

"Answer the question," said the third, a woman who'd spent more time in the weight room than either of the first two.

"Now," growled the fourth, long and lanky, squeezed in against the wall.

Lie to an anomaly? One holding four darts to his zero?

"Zhan-Yo," Rhimes said. "He thought you could help your brother."

After a long several heartbeats the foursome began to shake, twitches that looked like simultaneous seizures. As though they were fighting to control their own bodies.

"Come on," Regina said from her own self, taking Rhimes's arm and walking forward. "Push through before they remember who they are."

"Remember who they are?"

Regina, in those slippers, in that robe, followed Rhimes as he elbowed his way through the orderlies. They fell over around him, gasping for breath, tugging at their beige shirt collars.

"I sent them scurrying deep inside themselves," Regina answered as they tromped down the hallway. "A vacuum in their minds that I filled for a short time."

Behind them, a loud curse erupted, and Rhimes broke into a run.

"Could've held them longer."

"They were nice to me. Push too deep and there's no coming back."

One more anomaly to stay away from.

OUTSIDE, flashing lights said the cops were on the scene. Drones would've been alerted. Wexley would find out soon, might already know.

Rhimes's Tama hadn't vibrated once since he'd crashed through the care home's door. Had Wexley learned Rhimes was a traitor at that moment?

Worries for another time.

"Together," Regina said, her long, thin fingers gripping Rhimes. "it's been a long time since I've done this to so many."

Rhimes counted five human officers, two drones. The drones hovered on the sides, letting the officers use their armored pods as barricades. Like the orderlies, the police wielded stun guns, poking out from behind their curved glass cover as if Rhimes was going to unleash hell.

He wasn't, but Regina might.

The police shouted when Rhimes led Regina outside, their words rolling over one another while the drones turned their lights up high. Another impossible situation, but maybe if Rhimes went hard right, pulled Regina with him, they could . . .

"Surrender," Regina said. "Trust me."

What choice did he have?

"Don't shoot!" Rhimes said. "I'm done. I give up."

The officers came forward, cautious. One took the lead, holstering his stun gun under more cover than Rhimes ever had on his Ziran missions. The man held out cuffs, and Rhimes let the officer slip them on.

"You're coming too," the officer said, nodding Regina's way. "We've got questions."

Rhimes didn't need to see too well to sense the surprise from the other officers. The way their heads tilted, their moving, muttering lips suggested their arresting colleague broke protocol.

"Into the pod, both of you," the officer said, slapping the machine with his Tama. The armored door obliged, its thick glass rimmed with a warning orange glow. "Straight downtown."

Rhimes obliged and Regina followed, the officer helping her into the pod. The door shut behind her, prompting the other officers to ask questions, words that barely came out before the pod jolted forward, its doors hard locked against any forced exits.

The drones, their prey apparently captured, spun off into the early afternoon. Rhimes, Regina, and the gentle pod wheel grind rolled towards the road.

Regina turned towards Rhimes, the two, particularly Rhimes, doing a good job filling out the pod's only seat. Wexley's sister shook her wrists, then her head. Sighed.

"He's going to need at least a week to recover," Regina said, her eyes slipping out the pod's front window, a guilty conscience hiding itself.

"The officer?"

"He fought at the end. When he realized what we were doing."

Rhimes didn't have much to stay to that. He'd have fought too, in the officer's place. Not that it did any good. Regina discarded her guilty conscience quick, reaching into her robe's pocket and pulling the little, ridged card serving as the cuff's key. An officer's Tama could unlock the things too, but in a digital world, having an analog back-up wasn't a bad thing.

"Did he start fighting when he gave you that?" Rhimes asked as Regina plugged the card into the narrow block between his cuffs.

"He started searching," Regina replied. The cuffs popped off, and Rhimes rubbed his wrists. "Sometimes they don't notice what's happening if I keep them close to what they want. When they notice, they look for a reason. Are they dreaming, are they ill?"

"How long does that take?"

"Until they remember what I am."

Rhimes leaned forward, tried swiping a destination on the pod's console. The police had its route locked down, with a black box pop-up demanding Rhimes's ID to change course. Lacking any such number, Rhimes swiped away the request and instead looked at the map, the destination.

"Where are we going?" Regina asked.

"A nearby station. Your ability work on machines?"

"It does not." Regina looked askance at him. "Tell me, did you kidnap me without any plan at all?"

"Today, I'm improvising." Outside, the pod rolled along city streets, meshing with traffic as it passed by strip malls, schools, and forested parks. Rhimes tapped the pod window's glass with a finger, testing the feel. "Too thick to break."

"I suppose I should start getting my story straight," Regina said, leaning back into the pod's couch. "Help, he threatened me. It was so scary, I didn't know what to do."

"Fits you." Rhimes went to his Tama, swiped up his Ziran console. His access would let him flag a nearby drone, command the machine to stop the pod and give them a chance to escape.

When the Tama connected to Ziran's servers, when the white-and-orange logo blinked up in a spirited start, Rhimes felt his blood go cold.

A kind little rectangle with rounded corners appeared in his Tama's center. In it, cream text on a light gray background told Rhimes what he'd been waiting, dreading to hear.

Blocked. Exiled.

Hunted.

SIXTEEN

Arrival

UNION STATION HAD CHANGED. Cassidy shouldn't have been surprised—she hadn't been to LA since childhood, a family vacation gone well. Now creaky trains gave way to floating ones, bottoms held up by magnets as they glided to and from their destinations. The people boarding them had changed too: heads down, feet shuffling, no looks towards the drones standing around the station or the ones funneling in new arrivals.

Ziran logos hung across the glass window wall, giant banners dripping with slogans about prosperity, equality, protection. Cassidy saw the results around her, watched the group grow over the hours since she'd been picked up that morning.

Her captor drone had set Cassidy down outside the station, barked some instructions while holding a weapon to her head. A thin fence guided Cassidy to the entrance's left side and into the station itself, ending with a makeshift pen. Golden poles with red velvet ropes walled in her temporary home, decorations yanked from their holiday purpose and thrown into a more sinister one.

The barrier wasn't meant to stop anyone, only ward away curious pedestrians. The gladiators, naturally, did that better than any fencing. As for the anomalies in the pen with Cassidy? They slumped about, some sitting near the wall, others on spare benches dragged into the space. A portable toilet lingered in the back corner, the lone concession to needs. Against the back wall, nice and centered, two windowless wood doors held a sign across their handles reading *Closed*.

On the way in, the station's announcer broadcast arrival times in strait-laced tones. Furrowed glances went her way as she alone walked within the ropes, and Cassidy caught the feeling passengers scanned her face to be sure she wasn't someone they knew. Once confirmed, some gave her a slight nod, others turned away, they all never looked a second time.

She followed the velvet ropes to the pen, three anomalies already waiting. One had his head lolling back over a bench. The other two lay sprawled out on the tile. The cause became clear as the lone Ziran security guard, a chipper young man in the same uniform Cassidy used to know from Ziran's stores, approached her with a pill.

"It'll keep you calm while you wait," the man said.

Off to the right, some poor soul began a contract to play piano across the station's central area.

"Calm like them?"

The man didn't faze. His smile held. The hand holding the pill stayed level. The other scratched at his nose.

"Exactly," the man said.

"Do I have a choice?"

"You do not."

Being a piece on a chessboard came with certain drawbacks. Cassidy had to go along with the plan. Improvising an out now, throwing voids around and causing chaos might hurt whatever steps Thane had underway. At least, that's what Cassidy preferred to think, preferred to believe.

That preference let her to return the young man's smile, find the words to say, "Well, then what are we waiting for?"

She took the pill from the man's hand, kept her eyes on his so that he felt compelled to do the same. With Cassidy's left hand, she let a void, a very tiny one, leap to her fingertips. As Cassidy slid the pill towards her mouth, she flicked the void up from her waist. The ripping hole caught between Cassidy's tongue and the pill, zapping the capsule into nothing. The void tugged at Cassidy's lips, and a painful prick announced a hair had been sucked away, but when Cassidy dispelled the hole, the young man still kept his straight smile.

"Yum," Cassidy said.

"Glad you liked it," the man replied, and his shoulders settled, that hand made another stubble scratch. "Thanks for not making a scene. I hate having to call the bots over."

"Does that happen a lot?"

Nods. "More than you'd think."

"Not so sure about that," Cassidy waved behind the man, towards the benches. "How long are we waiting here?"

"Until we hit a car's quota," the man shrugged. "Could be an hour, could be all day. It's been slower lately."

"Less supply?"

The man started to answer, then seemed to remember he was, in fact, talking to that same supply. A flush played around his collar and he stepped aside, "They don't tell me that. I'd, uh, take a bench early. They go fast."

"I bet," Cassidy said, taking the invitation to walk around him.

She felt the man's eyes on her, following her walk until

Cassidy picked a bench for her own. Slate gray with a slight give, the bench had drone claws beat on the comfort scale, but not much else. Sitting set Cassidy's mind to the more important question, one that'd lingered in the fringes during the drone ride, the arrival to this noxious place.

Thane wanted her here for his plan. Why?

Or, if not here, then wherever Ziran would be taking them.

Thane knew her power, knew Cassidy's inclinations. She'd spent a long time on Mynx's prison island. Putting Cassidy in another cell wasn't going to generate good feelings. Might, in fact, push her to do something rash. Provoke a response.

Draw Ziran's attention.

Okay, so maybe her part in Thane's plan wasn't all that complicated.

Cassidy swept another look at her fellow anomalies lying around the pen. Several hours leaked by, with Cassidy burning the time watching arrivals and departures blow through on the station's giant screens. The air inside made a gradual shift from coffee-pastry breakfast to greasy fryer fare for the lunch crowd. More anomalies trickled in, all taking the man's offered pills and most looking dazed even before they took the bite.

More than twenty filled the space when Ziran's man whistled, the clock heading towards the afternoon's middle. Like closing off an opera, he moved a velvet rope across the pen's entrance, then turned to face the crowd.

"Afternoon, recruits!" The young man beamed as he waved, apparently needing both words and motion to get the attention of his strung out subjects. "We're ready for your next steps."

"Oh joy," Cassidy muttered, trying otherwise to keep herself as vague as everyone else.

Imitating a zombie was harder than expected. Especially when the dark wood doors swung open and two more Ziran members—these two in heavier gear, with rifles openly displayed on chest-crossing straps—waved the ensemble through. The other anomalies jerked and stumbled, some crawling. The original Ziran greeter came in behind, waking up sleeping prisoners with hard slaps to the face.

Cassidy feigned her stumbles, dragged her right foot and tried to look at nothing as she walked. The anomalies around her looked like they came from anywhere, everywhere. Some had designer clothes, jewelry dangling from ears and rings on hands. Others looked and smelled like sewers or the dusty city outskirts. Still more stank of saltwater and spices beyond Pacifica, as if they'd come right here from some Ziran prison barge.

The doors did little to prep Cassidy for the other side: a classic feel opened into a futuristic platform, one so new and spotless that she had to wonder if Ziran had built this up in the last two months. Would have, until she noticed the faded logos imprinted on the tiles.

Paragon 'P' signs, scrubbed away until only the grooves remained.

"You new in town?" a beefy, dread-locked man grumbled, shambling next to her. His details suggested a dim present, but Cassidy saw brightness in his eyes. "Staring at those things like you don't know what they mean."

"I know what they are," Cassidy said as they kept moving onto the wide platform. A pristine mag-lev track, all blues and glowing, sat in the recess before them, a red warning line blanketing the edge. "I just didn't expect something so modern here."

"Put in a bunch of things for the summit," the man sighed, a rumbling bass. "Shame how that turned out."

Right. Apinya had mentioned that back in Thailand. A tragedy that, somehow, failed to move Cassidy all that much. The Paragons groomed enemies aplenty, about time one struck back hard.

"Shame how *this* is turning out," Cassidy said, flicking her eyes back and forth around the group.

"Knew it'd happen eventually," the man replied. "Name's Vick. You?"

"Cassidy."

"How'd they get you?"

"Took a walk in a park. Bad decision."

A laugh, no bitterness anywhere. Other anomalies noticed, a few made the effort to get closer. Eavesdropping maybe, or just looking for companionship before the end.

"Know where they found me?" Vick asked and didn't wait for Cassidy to answer the impossible question. "Right in my own damn house. Work all night slinging bottles at the pharmacy, go home to catch a breather, and I get metal in my face."

Cassidy winced, "Sorry."

The Ziran trio, who'd spread out to cover the anomaly assembly, announced their train would be here shortly. Cassidy noticed the young man had traded his pills for a stun gun, his young hands gripping the weapon tight as if it might spring away from him.

How many Ziran employees found themselves shifted to this, how many were told to ditch their retail counters, their tech support cubicles to stand guard over their fellow humans?

How many said no?

"What's your deal, Cassidy?" Vick asked. "You have any tricks?"

"A few." The voids, ever ready, tingled her fingers. "How about you?"

"A few she says." Vick shook his head, pointed at the tunnel to where a light brightened. "I might as well say the same thing. Hope they're good ones, where we're going."

"Where are we going?"

Vick eyed her, "You really are from outta town. There's only one place this train goes. One way trip too."

"You don't seem sad about it?"

Now Vick's spark dimmed, just a fraction. "What's to be sad about? Last couple months, they've taken my friends, my family. Might get to see some, if I'm lucky."

The mag-lev train rolled in, settling to a stop before Cassidy. Doors opened, leading into clean seats. Vick went straight across, settled onto on. Cassidy took the one next to him. The Ziran guards didn't follow the anomalies onto the train, a bold move until Cassidy noticed the ceiling overhead: tracker drones, their centipede bodies, clung every few meters to the train's roof. That they'd dive down and cleave apart any brave anomaly seemed certain.

At least the seats were cushioned: a marked improvement over that bench.

"Your whole family and friends were anomalies?" Cassidy asked Vick.

"I was traced a long time ago. The tracker was a good dude. Hell, might still be a good dude if these guys haven't killed him yet."

"So you worked for the Paragons."

"More like I worked for whoever they told me to. That wasn't a problem. You get used to it, and having reps isn't bad."

The train launched, a smooth acceleration from Union station and up onto the raised track. Cassidy caught the mountains, the ocean beyond the buildings to her left on a glittering horizon beneath the sun. Heading north, then.

"Your family, though?" Cassidy asked. The idea that

Vick's brothers, sisters could've all been anomalies . . . what about her kids?

"Not my blood family, you understand?" Vick raised a sleeve, pointed at a little tattoo. Numbers and letters in green-black ink. "That's our trace number. Our tracker, good dude like I said, got all his traces together and we got these to commemorate. Happy hours, baseball games." Another head shake, but a wistful one. "You go in thinking you're gonna get used, but instead you wind up finding people like you who understand, who get what you're going through."

"That's who Ziran took? The other ones this tracker traced?"

"Now you know why I'm here," Vick said, before shifting his back her way to look out the window. "Figure I'll get one more good look at home."

"You might come back."

Another laugh, "Nah, Cassidy. I've seen a lotta people leave on this train. Never seen one come back."

AN HOUR later the train shot from a rocky valley into a tan plain. As the vehicle slowed, Cassidy caught fencing and huge tents out the windows, including one multi-story building that looked as solid as anything back in the city. Ziran wasn't playing around out here.

There'd been rumors in Thailand about anomaly capture, that Ziran wanted anomalies for wild experiments rather than just slaughter. Nobody verified what was happening and, in those swamps, nobody could do anything about it, so Cassidy relegated the buzz to the background. Here, seeing all those whispers whirl into something real sent the wrong rush through her nerves.

Vick whistled.

"I didn't want the Paragons to win," Cassidy said as the train pulled into its stop. "I thought they were awful, what they made anomalies do."

The doors dinged open. Someone outside ordered everyone out. The drones on the ceiling shivered, tracking the movement as anomalies rose from their seats. Vick pulled himself to his feet, then offered Cassidy a hand.

"Bad to worse, my friend," Vick muttered. "Guess we won't have to worry about that much longer."

They joined the shuffling anomalies leaving the train, exiting onto an open-air platform under guard by gladiators around the sides and aerial drones hovering above. Several more Ziran soldiers—Cassidy switched up the term because these guys wore heavy armor, not the tour guide getup from the man back at the station—waved the line on, splitting them into three. Each one went towards a box-like station manned by another Ziran worker, each one monitored by a gladiator.

Beyond the stations sat the camp's inside, including that big building.

"I wouldn't give up yet," Cassidy said. "Things could change."

Vick nodded, put a hand on her shoulder, looked like he was about to say something when an anomaly just in front stopped. A skinny dude, the guy froze, then shook his head, hands flying up to his scalp. The line bunched up around Cassidy, Vick, and their impediment, and Vick took the lead.

"Hey buddy," Vick said. "You all right?"

Over the footsteps, the overhead announcements, Cassidy had a hard time hearing what the man kept muttering to himself. She stepped closer, would've leaned in except Vick shot her a warning look, reached out with his right hand to push Cassidy back.

"Steady now," Vick continued, slow and even. "Don't try what you're thinking about. It's not worth it."

The man shrugged off Vick's arm, glared at Cassidy's newfound friend. The anomaly's body seemed to shift with that motion, blurring and snapping, as if struggling to retain its shape.

"They're taking everyone," the anomaly said, voice reverberating as he spoke, face waving like water in the wind. "I can't, I won't let them take me too."

Vick put his hands palms up towards the man and Cassidy swore she saw a thin, teal line, the same color as those pills, stretch between Vick and the shifting anomaly. Saw a connection, the anomaly taking in a deep breath, eyes closing, and saw that connection sever with a shot's ringing bang. A second followed, Vick and the anomaly both hitting the ground as a gladiator's hovering form moved overhead. The heat from the drone's jets blasted Cassidy even as she crouched, tried to get to Vick.

A hand grabbed her arm, orange, white and armored, "Leave'em alone, or you're next."

The guard pulled her left, away from the bodies. Cassidy struggled at first, found those voids calling, and she would've launched one, would've blown up Thane's plan right there if the gladiator drone hadn't picked up both bodies and carried them away towards that big building.

Two bloody pools stayed behind, the shuffling anomalies stepping around them without another word.

Opening Move

AEGIS CAUGHT the terrorist in a shaded limestone canyon, a gash between two larger hills his Tama put near the Factory. Zhan-Yo posted up on the right in smooth alcove cut by a long-dried stream. The man had his own Tama out, frowning at the screen. Farther up, watching with a finger on the gun on their belt, Particle leaned against their own rock. Behind Aegis, Celice would be coming up, more complaints on her tongue.

She'd lashed him over the last hours as they'd run through the brush, the dirt, the rocks. A litany that started as a plea and ended as an accusation. Aegis tuned in and out, not bothering to offer a reply even as Celice's arrows found their marks time and time again.

No, the Paragons weren't perfect. No, the Champions weren't always ideal.

Further than that, Aegis would not go. In those depths he would only find a nihilistic madness.

"He has her," Zhan-Yo said as Aegis approached. "Rhimes is moving forward. They're in the city now."

The success threw Aegis and he covered his surprise

with a studied stare at the ground, at the several pebbles and a single tired spider trying to find cover beneath them. Zhan-Yo's gambit had passed its first big test: Rhimes stealing Wexley's sister from her enclave.

"They have the codes?" Aegis replied.

"Code. Singular. And if she doesn't have it, then nobody does." Zhan-Yo looked Aegis over. "I have some extra water if you would like?"

"I'm trying to kill you."

"Can't it wait till after we stop the world from ending? If you're lucky, I might even die in the raid. Then you won't have to worry about getting your hands dirty."

"My hands are plenty dirty."

"Dad," said his daughter, scuffling her way down into the canyon. "Please."

Aegis had his hands open, resting on his thighs. A deep breath. The run had been long, more exhausting than Aegis expected. It'd also done that damn thing exercising tended to: cleared his thoughts, especially once Celice stopped her haranguing. Zhan-Yo had the right argument, the better view.

Defeating Wexley and his robot army had to take priority, and Zhan-Yo would either be around for a proper slaying after, or the drones would solve the terrorist's equation.

"Fine," Aegis said. "You can live for now."

"Hurrah." Zhan-Yo looked to his right. "Particle, please tell me we're nearly there. If I have to walk one more kilometer, I might give up."

Particle shoved themselves off their rock, closed with the group while everyone took a requisite water break. Aegis, Zhan-Yo, and Celice had dust over every centimeter, but Particle had kept themselves clean. Their walk came along without any noise, and nothing about their bearing suggested the slightest concern for the group's infighting.

"We leave the canyon that way," Particle said, and Aegis felt his eyes jerk to the canyon's far exit. "That'll put us over the Factory's docking entrance. It's guarded, but our approach should let us get close without an alarm. We neutralize the drones at the entry, call in the reinforcements, and then it's your show."

Particle finished with a flicking look between both Zhan-Yo and Aegis, as if to imply they weren't sure who's show, precisely, but definitely not their's.

"If you're ready," Particle added.

"They're ready," Celice said, and Aegis noted she'd once again put herself between the Champion and Zhan-Yo.

Smart, that one.

Aegis took over pole position, with Zhan-Yo and Celice bringing up the back. Particle stayed on the Champion's right as they stalked down the canyon towards the lip. Aegis would draw any initial attention, Particle would divert as long as possible until Zhan-Yo and Celice could clean up. A simple strategy that should work so long as the drones didn't outnumber them by a high margin.

"They will swarm," Zhan-Yo had said, back in Pocket's dimensional hideout. Thane, Zhan-Yo, Celice, Mathieu and several others huddled over the table beneath the purple-black glow. "We need them to."

"Because?" Thane asked.

"When my man triggers the shutdown, we'll need to destroy as many drones as we can. Not because it will slow down Ziran, but because it will buy us more time to get to Wexley."

Take the leader, win the war. Their guiding principle for this assault, for everything that would come after Aegis crested this cliff. Ziran would fall along with Wexley, confusion creating chaos that the Champions, the Paragons and any normal allies could wipe up.

Of course, Ziran hadn't fallen when Zhan-Yo vanished. Another, worse body simply stepped into his place.

Aegis glanced back, saw his daughter. Like Particle to Aegis, Celice stayed a few meters away from Zhan-Yo. Space to act should it be required. Should the opportunity arise. Everyone here had their professed objectives. Aegis had no doubt second, secret ones lay unsaid. He hadn't pummeled Zhan-Yo to pulp out here in the rocks, but a bullet or a knife to the back when things were secure would do the same.

The canyon made its exit through a narrowing dip. Sunlight caked overhead, rocky shadows playing about Aegis's body as he approached the end and the blue sky beyond. The cover from the high walls drained away to scraggly brush when Aegis, crouching low, moved out. All conversation between the team ceased as the mission truly commenced, a silence covered by buzzing insects and an occasional howling breeze.

Sloping down in what might've been a waterfall in some distant past, the canyon's last meters gave Aegis time to crawl beneath spindly brush. The brittle branches tugged at his uniform, snapping off as Aegis kept moving. His knees and elbows ground against sand-coated stone, warm and rough.

The lip had no lead, appearing without preamble as Aegis found the edge with his arm. Below and beyond sat the Factory's loading dock and the gladiators guarding it. The two drones watched as cargo pods and the crewmen working them, assisted by more mundane machines, moved raw materials in and completed creations out:

boxed up drones making their exit, waiting to be shipped to some far off region.

Another wrinkle: the plan hadn't counted on civilians being present.

But no plan was ever perfect.

Aegis's Tama vibrated and the Champion glanced at his left wrist, readied the go signal. Everyone else in position. Time to save the world, or die trying.

A familiar feeling.

Pressing his feet against the rock, Aegis popped up into a running leap. He launched off the lip, soaring into the air for a stomach-flipping several seconds before hitting the street below in a roll. His bones burned at the effort, Aegis's ability knitting them whole by the time the Champion stood up straight.

The loaders, their helping drones, and the two gladiators stared at him. The larger weaponized machines had the most intense glare, their red eyes standing out as the sun cast them into silhouettes. Aegis waited for the recognition before remembering he wasn't clad in Paragon blues this time. Practicality mattered more than publicity today.

"Run," Aegis announced to the humans. "You don't want to be here anymore."

To punctuate his order, Aegis broke into a sprint, bursting past the workers towards the two gladiators. The guarding drones realized his purpose before the others did, raising their four arms and activating systems too varied for Aegis to recall. The various hums and clacks finally triggered a response in those loaders, sending them scrambling to their pods. The helping drones gave no such cares, feeding Aegis an idea.

Reaching out with his right hand as he ran, Aegis gripped a boxy loading machine's side. Planting his left leg on the next step, Aegis pulled the hapless machine in between his body and the big gladiators. Mynx's monsters took the adjustment in stride, holding their fire and instead stomping forward on grinding metal feet.

Two ways to deal with gladiators: either hit them straight on and hope Aegis could puncture the power generators in the thing's chests, or duck and cover long enough for disabling fire to have an effect.

Aegis had a decided preference.

He pushed against the loader drone, the machine barking its own alarm about personal injury risk, a call for saner times. The gladiators heeded the alarm as much as Aegis did: not at all. Though they towered over the loading drone, Aegis's squatting shove made the big machines opt for clearing the cover. Aegis felt the jolts as metal claws sliced into the loading drone, felt the pull as one gladiator ripped the poor robot away.

Aegis charged.

The time between sighting a target and acting to remove it, Mynx had said far too many nights ago, ticked in at the milliseconds. Raising a weapon, getting a bead on Aegis would take slightly longer.

The gladiators, though, had a problem: behind Aegis, clustered in their firing field, were all those workers getting into their pods. Missed shots might cause innocent, collateral damage. Acceptable within certain parameters, if certain risks—like if Aegis might cause more death himself —were met.

Aegis by himself? Attacking two drones in front of a sealed stronghold?

The gladiators held their fire, instead swiping at the Champion. Aegis didn't have any bullet-dodging abilities, but slipping around heavy punches? That he could do.

The drone moving the loader aside had its lower arms angled right, where they'd shifted the loader. Its upper two pounded down towards Aegis, attempting to squash him flat, while the other gladiator knelt for an ankle-level swipe. Aegis didn't so much see the moves as *feel* them, an instinct honed by so many duels against one nefarious foe or another. Bouncing off his left foot, Aegis stretched into a dive, jumping over the swipe. The twin hammer blows came faster than Aegis moved, catching his legs and knocking Aegis's knees into the concrete.

To stay still meant death, so Aegis ignored the nerve-jangling impact and ducked his shoulder, tucking his legs into a momentum-saving roll forward. On his back between the right gladiator's legs, Aegis stared up into orange-white metal death.

And kicked.

He'd burst through walls, broken bones and backs with a hard kick from legs packed with the power that came with having no injury risk, no fear of the consequences. Aegis struck the gladiator's knee joint, a neon orange disc that should've popped out of place, should've sent the drone to a one-kneed surrender.

The leg didn't budge. Aegis cursed.

Mynx kept making those damn upgrades, building every version stronger. Now Aegis couldn't even hurt the things?

The gladiator juiced its leg jets, hopping up and back from Aegis, exposing the Champion to the other gladiator's weaponized aim. No civilian danger now. Four arms, each one with their own dart or bullet-blasting barrel, locked in.

"Too late," Aegis said, hoping he'd timed it right.

Rounds slammed into the gladiator's side, sparking blue lightning across its torso, its head, and those weapons. Particle and Celice laid into the drone from the lip above and Aegis found himself smiling as the gladiator failed to fire, as the machine jerked, its wires and circuits burning out.

His view snapped. One moment, Aegis had victory in sight and in the next his neck wrenched around to see the other gladiator, the one that'd tossed the loader aside, taking up its fallen friend's mantle. Arms coming up, weapons ready to work.

Aegis rolled towards the dangerous gladiator, shoulder-chest on the concrete before popping up with his arms to a straight stand, sliding in his feet to make a narrow profile. Bullets flared, lighting up the spot on the concrete where Aegis's head had been. Chips flew, hot casings seared Aegis's uniform from back and front as the drone pincered him with live rounds.

No room left.

Kicking off his right foot, Aegis reached for the gladiator's lower left arm. He felt hard impacts as several shots struck home, the bullets slicing into his clothes, ramming the armored vest beneath. Aegis's right arm went numb, and something in his abdomen squeezed acid agony through his stomach as a point-blank blast hit home, but the move brought Aegis inside the drone's reach.

Even numb—an experience Aegis had felt more than he cared to admit at various villain's hands—the Champion worked his right arm, then his left to scale the gladiator. The big drone tried to pick Aegis off, but he ducked, swung, scrambled to the machine's back. For all its polished gleam, the gladiator's attachments meant hand-holds were not hard to come by. Some metal ends, running way hot by now, burned Aegis's hands when they landed, but he threw the pain away.

There'd be time to feel it all later.

Getting to the gladiator's head, Aegis pulled back his left fist, swinging and denting the drone's skull plate. Off to his right, Aegis saw the first gladiator, still taking rounds from Celice and Particle, get its faculties back. After Ziran captured a gladiator using EMP rounds, nobody in the group expected to get the same results here. They just had to slow it down long enough for . . .

Zhan-Yo ran in from the back right, having taken a longer way down from the lip to the battlefield. Coming around a sloping, scalloped retaining wall, the revolutionary leader paid physical dues to his cause with his dual swords. Zhan-Yo didn't try to slice the staggered drone, a move that might've broken his blades on the armored plating, but worked like a surgeon, stabbing in between joints and severing connections. First one leg then the other flared out, sparking and collapsing as the drone's ability to control its stance fell away.

From above, Aegis had a beautiful view as Zhan-Yo took his blades to the fallen drone's head, completing the coup de grace with a casual finesse. Aegis would've clapped if he hadn't been whaling away at his own target, battering aside the lighter armor up top. Now, wires and metal revealed themselves, ready to be grabbed, torn, and tossed.

The gladiator shot up, a rumbling rise forcing Aegis to grab the drone's fractured head to hang on. Just like the drone on the Ziran boat, the gladiator assumed Aegis wouldn't survive a fall from a huge height, and this time he didn't have water to drop into.

Great.

Aegis, hoping his numbed right hand could keep its grip, punched with his left. He felt his fingers get around wires and pulled, ignoring the cuts as metal fragments sliced on the exit. The gladiator shuddered, but the rockets kept their burn. Beneath him, Zhan-Yo and his kill fell away. Celice and Particle watched him from the lip, holding their own shots.. The workers finally had their pods running, the three vehicles rumbling away from the Factory at speed.

The breeze picked up again, the setting sun, freed from any shade, felt warm on Aegis's back as the gladiator ascended. Aegis punched again, this time breaking the head's joints clean off. The drone's metal skull fell away, leaving Aegis on the shoulders of a machine heading for the stars.

What a way to go that'd be, the original Champion rising up and up until he burned out in the atmosphere? Or would he suffocate first, fall unconscious and dive into an unceremonious splatter?

That was a chance Aegis couldn't take. He had a legacy to preserve, a legend to protect.

So he let his right arm loose, bunched his legs, and kicked off the drone into the air.

EIGHTEEN

Seek and Find

SHE HAD to find Calvin before Ziran found her.

Kat sat up from the display, taking another look behind her at the body on the floor, then to the fabricated door, as shiny a silver as everything else in the thrown up building. She'd locked it upon entry, throwing a sliding bolt. Analog security everywhere proved a bonus, because Kat hadn't been able to get anything useful off the spectacles man.

She'd tripped him first, pressed an elbow to his throat while pinning him with her weight. If the man had been a body-builder, Kat might've been in trouble, but pushing pencils meant he couldn't get the leverage he needed. When he went limp, Kat made a tough calculation.

Leave the man unconscious, take a risk that he'd pop back up and sound the alarm. Kill him and maybe Kat could buy herself some time, but she'd be adding another body to her count, another life to her conscience. In the moment's fury, like when she'd gunned down Wexley's mercenaries on that frozen lake, Kat could make the fatal move without regret.

But there? In that cell with a syringe-toting drone staring at her in silence?

She took the shot from the machine and injected it in the man instead. He'd called it a sedative, maybe it would keep him out longer. After pushing the syringe, Kat searched the man's pockets, took the ID badge off his shirt. His Tama had already gone dark, doing its level best to keep its owners secrets.

Then Kat fled, spent the next two hours moving around the base trying to figure out what the hell was going on way out here. The fluorescent, artless hallways folded into one another, pasted on signs giving vague clues to places like 'engineering' and 'specimen analysis'. Every time she encountered a door sealed with a Tama scanning lock, Kat went the other way.

When the tracker ran into someone walking by, they kept their head down and so did she. Water cooler conversation didn't have a part to play in this place, not that Kat minded. She stumbled on the cafeteria eventually, six sparse card tables served by several vending machines. Along the room's back wall?

Drop in offices for the busy worker bee.

And one was occupied, the door slightly ajar. Nearby, a lonely soul grabbing something from a vending machine on the right. Kat went to the machine on the opposite end, read depressing options for every energy bar flavor she could want. Waited until the other eater grabbed his prize and left.

Rolling her feet, keeping quiet, Kat went quick to the open office door. Listened, heard a voice humming to herself. Kat peeked in, saw someone scrolling through what looked like a frightening message box. So many unread, high-priority items littering the screen. Ziran keeping its bees busy.

With her right hand, Kat put the slightest pressure on the door, its thin frame moving like air. A sliding step in, her prey still humming, Kat's approach unnoticed. At least until Kat shut the door, spun the bolt.

The woman turned, her expression all innocent curiosity. As if nothing bad could happen here in this warped sanctum.

"Hi," Kat said, "and sorry."

Kat hit the woman, palm up, right in the nose. The woman's head flew back and Kat, yanking the woman's chair away from the desk, gripped the exposed throat and held tight. Too many struggling seconds later, with Kat spending them all telling the woman to stop and she'd live, and the lady finally passed out.

Propping the lady's body at the office's end, where anyone slamming the door open would find they'd mashed it into a colleague, Kat settled into the chair and started tapping.

"Accounting," Kat grimaced as she swiped away the messages, the spreadsheets filled with numbers and formulas. "No thanks."

Kat's opinion on accounting notwithstanding, the woman left her electronic life impeccably organized. Once Kat cleared away the open programs, she stared at clean, labeled options directing her towards the camp's staff, its rosters, experimentation schedule, and other juicy choices Kat would've explored if she had any time.

She went for the roster first, a dynamic database that turned every anomaly here into variables. Height, weight, genetic background paired with names and zero other description to create an impersonal listing. Maybe the clean sheet made it easier for the lab's staff to run its tests, but for Kat, it looked all too familiar.

As a tracker, Kat had looked at a database not much

different than this one for a long time. Names paired not with physical stats but financial ones. Reps and contracts listed out one after another so Kat could focus on her most productive anomalies. Prioritize catching similar powered fugitives to increase her revenue.

Nowhere did the Paragon's tracker database add any color, nowhere did it describe an anomaly's mental state, their home life, whether or not they enjoyed the contracts forced upon them by an all-powerful entity.

Kat shut her eyes, rubbed her forehead, tried to ignore the slimy sick feeling oozing around her abdomen. There were obvious leaps but she wouldn't make them. Wouldn't try to bridge the gap between the Paragons and Ziran.

A bridge didn't seem as far as it had a minute ago.

Swallowing, wishing she'd bought a drink from the vending machines outside, Kat tapped into the search bar and entered Calvin's name. Tapped the little magnifying glass, an icon that'd been around before Kat existed and that hadn't ever changed, and stared at the message appearing front and center:

No results.

What?

Kat tried again, read her typing to check for any errors.

No results.

She sat back in the chair, tried to think. Maybe the search wasn't targeting the anomalies, maybe it was broken. Maybe the list was old.

"It's not broken," said a low voice behind her and Kat jerked around in the chair, falling out into a crouch. With a push, Kat could send the chair rocketing back into the woman, who leaned, butt on the floor, against the office's back wall. "The headache is much worse."

The accountant felt around her nose with one hand

while the other massaged her throat. Her eyes found Kat, and Kat found that same curiosity she'd seen when the tracker first broke into the room.

"I take it you're not supposed to be here?" The accountant said.

"Your nose isn't broken because I didn't need it to be," Kat replied, buying time to try and find an explanation or a way to stop the accountant from calling for help. They were too far apart for a scrambling knockout and Kat didn't have any guns. "I'm not trying to kill anyone here."

"That's a relief," the woman replied, letting her hands fall to her sides. "Most of the anomalies that break out rack up casualties before they're put down." At Kat's blink, the woman shrugged. "Not that I'm inviting you to try and beat their score."

Kat judged the distance from the woman's hands to the door. She'd have to sit up, reach, undo the bolt, then pull the door open and get around it to flee. Too much time, too much distance. The accountant would need help, but . . .

"You're not screaming. Why?" Kat asked.

"Because we're not supposed to," the accountant replied. "It's in the training Adriana provided to us all. Studies show anomaly encounters are more often fatal if the anomaly is agitated." The accountant leaned forward, put a finger on her own cheek. "You're not agitated, are you?"

Two cards to play here. Kat could go with the anomaly-on-the-lam approach the accountant already believed, or she could hot-swap to something else. Spin up some jam about being a spy, maybe, or a Paragon soldier out for vengeance. Or the truth?

No, never that.

"Agitated enough." Kat moved her left hand off the

chair, held it aloft like she might be trying to cast a spell. "Choose: help me or I put you under, and it won't be so nice the second time."

"What do you want?"

No hesitation. Kat could appreciate that.

"I'm trying to find a friend. He came here with me, but I don't see him on the roster."

The accountant looked over at the screen, "May I?"

"Slowly."

Kat stood, shifted towards the door with her back to the wall while the accountant went past her, took the chair. Looked back at Kat and waited, helpful and earnest. The tracker had to reset again. She'd never met a hostage this cooperative.

Either Ziran dearly loved their employees and would give up secrets to save even one life, or Adriana and Wexley never thought someone would dare attack their people.

Then again, hadn't this whole situation come about because Wexley took Mynx hostage and, as a reward, found himself the drone king?

Kat dished the accountant Calvin's name and, at first, the accountant did the same thing Kat did.

"Tried that already," Kat said when the same pop-up appeared.

Rather than be frustrated, though, the accountant just nodded and swiped over to a different database, this one much smaller with different values displaying next to every anomaly name. The columns listed progressions, treatments, and next injections. Without giving Kat time to parse the new panorama, the accountant ran Calvin's name through another search.

Bingo.

"Him?" the accountant asked as the database centered

on Calvin, showing he'd be starting his third cycle today. "You said you came in at the same time?"

"Where is he?" Kat countered.

The accountant was the hostage, she'd be answering the questions.

"Top floor," the accountant replied, turning towards Kat and folding her hands in her lap. "He's at the last stage. It's always a show. Are you going to kill me now?"

Kat curled up her nose, "No. Count to a hundred, then you can leave."

"And go where?" The accountant smiled again, a soft one that spoke of zero complaints, only a soft acceptance. "This is my job and, for now, my home."

"Then you should find a new one," Kat replied. She slipped the bolt with her right hand, nudged the door open. "And soon."

The accountant said nothing as Kat left, shutting the door behind her. The cafeteria had more people now as the afternoon veered hard into evening. Kat caught the lines for the energy bars, the energy drinks, the salty snacks and realized she had no idea where these people came from, where they lived. Their uniforms held a sci-tech mix, with drab green maintenance scrubs on a few contrasting with Ziran office standard on the rest. One armored guard sipped some soda through a straw near the exit, idly watching her Tama.

Not a one had gone towards Kat's stolen office. All might come to the accountant's defense if the woman made a noise.

In other words, time to go.

Kat quick-stepped it from the cafeteria, her tracker gear catching looks. The guard, too, squinted Kat's way as she went past, but break-time must've held sway and Kat made it out un-accosted.

The building, fabricated as it was, had only a single elevator and a rickety one at that. The shaft ran through the building's center—so far as Kat could tell—and it paired its path with a double-wide stairway. Kat gauged the elevator as she came close, saw the glowing down button as another maintenance man waited, eyes on his Tama.

Too much risk in the machine. Elevators could be stopped remotely, could be turned into death cages. Better to be free.

The stairs proved loud but clean, flimsy metal steps matching the silver aesthetic and bouncing with every footstep. Kat's own noise mingled with plenty others going up and down in a constant ping-pong barrage. Co-worker's conversations muddled along beneath the banging, once again prompting Kat to wonder how the hell people could be so normal in a place like this.

Could someone really adapt that fast? Decide a paycheck could be worth taking in anomalies and subjecting them to who the hell knew what?

Empathy threatened to make in-roads, to humanize the people in this building with Kat, but she hit the top floor before anything truly dangerous de-railed her plan: free Calvin, then get away, preferably burning this place to the ground in the process.

The top floor didn't give a penthouse impression. Kat left the stairwell slow, cracking the door and sneaking a look before going all the way into a hallway that could've matched the one she'd left below meter-by-meter. The only difference? Fewer doors.

Restrooms lay to Kat's left and right, and beyond those the hallway continued without another feature until an abrupt end near the building's edge. Tama-locked doors covered with red warning signs closed those sides, and Kat let them be, turning her focus to the main doors before her.

Across the hallway sat an opaque double set. Unlike the thin, chromed crap elsewhere in the building, these doors had heft, had a white paint with the orange Ziran logo in the center. They also had a Tama lock. Authorized personnel only signs labeled each door too, confirming the lock's purpose.

Kat went up to the door, stuck her ear up close. Heard nothing, though she couldn't tell whether the doors blocked the sound or if the accountant had been lying about Calvin's locale.

Another tough choice. Break down the doors and blow her stealth, or try to hide and wait in, say, one of those bathrooms for another hostage-taking opportunity?

The slow-go had its appeal, but Kat's nerves burned already. The accountant wouldn't wait forever, even if she actually counted to one hundred at the slowest pace known to man. And if Calvin was in there, if they were doing something to him, then every second Kat waited outside could be his last.

Taking a deep breath along with a long step back from the Tama lock, Kat gauged her feet, her legs, and those doors. She could use a gadget to break through, but maybe . . .

Kat took one long lung and snap-kicked, sending a booted heel smashing right into the Tama lock. The little screen and scanner didn't stand a chance, shattering into black plastic and glass. An alarm sounded before Kat's foot returned to the floor, a tinny thing that re-affirmed the building's hasty construction. The lights didn't even change: no dire red, no rapid locks.

The tracker didn't stand waiting, but slipped to the

right, putting her back to the wall and the double-doors on her left. Another deep breath, another bet.

Something clicked in the doors, and Kat felt a thud as a bolt moved. A second thunk followed and the doors swung open. Kat caught nothing as she looked left, biting back a little curse. She'd hoped the people running the experiments would be dumb, would come charging out into the hallway ripe for a surprise knockout.

Instead, these guys had tactics.

"Whomever's out there, give it up," some man barked, his voice coming out modulated. A helmet, then. "We have reinforcements coming. You're outnumbered."

What a negotiator, this guy.

"Okay," Kat said without moving. "Okay. Don't hurt me. I surrender."

"Then come around with your hands up, your face clear."

"I don't think I can walk. I hurt my leg kicking the scanner."

The negotiator or his fellow guard didn't wait, but wrapped around the door's side as Kat finished talking. The man had a stun gun raised and ready, would've pulled the trigger except Kat launched herself at his ankles before he cleared the doorway.

Kat's dive hit the man's calves and drove him back, a stumble that might've left him standing except Kat used her left hand to yank the man's right leg forward. As the man fell, as voices started shouting—Kat cringed inside as she heard several drones spit out their mechanical demands—Kat kept her legs moving, pushing herself into the fallen man.

Cover was cover, even if it lived.

The penthouse finally lived up to that Ziran promise: the wide room lacked any tile floor, instead housing a white-and-orange mat from end to end. Windows arrayed floor to ceiling around the space, granting a spectacular sunset. A motley drone, scientist, and soldier arrangement enjoyed that view, and Kat figured even the five anomalies standing center would've appreciated the look as a last sight before their long dark.

With her right hand, Kat fought the struggling guard for his stun gun. The guard's pal, his voice giving the negotiator away, ran over with his own stun gun aiming for a point black shot. One that would've struck home if the tracker hadn't rolled. Kat's left arm bore the brunt as she shifted her tackled guard over her chest, hoping to feel the stun gun's thud strike the man.

The negotiator held his fire. Waited till the tackled guard, on top of Kat, completed the roll over. Lying on her back, exposed, Kat stared at the stun gun's barrel and the utterly set face of the man who held it.

Behind him, looking her way with his jaw just about dropped to the floor, stood Calvin. A drone rumbled next to him, syringe extending towards Calvin's left arm. An arm that led to a hand, one spread out on the floor.

And Calvin's right hand?

As the tracker drones, those metal centipedes standing watch broke their cover, as the other anomalies gave in to their desperation and started to move, Calvin reached for her.

NINETEEN

Back Home

THE HOUSE, windswept and weatherworn, bore Chicago's spring in the old leaves, the dirt and twigs clotting its gutters. Winter's leftovers clung to the nooks, bearing the afternoon breeze and the half-cast skies as best they could. A two story piece belonging more on an east coast cape than a suburban avenue, Rhimes appreciated the oddity. He took the front steps slow, hand on the white rain-slick railing, feeling the wood steps creak beneath his boots.

He'd stayed here for years while working for Ziran, swapping between Zhan-Yo and Wexley in roles sliding towards the dark and dim. Now he'd been cast out by Wexley and sent Zhan-Yo an update, one Z had answered with a single word:

Go

Z would have to wait a minute. Behind Rhimes, Regina came up the walk with a tourist's wandering eyes. Back further the borrowed pod trundled back into the street, off to collect another passenger. Rhimes had bashed and smashed his way from the Ziran one kilometers off to the north, a desperate move that forced the pod's emergency programming into play, ditching the pair off the highway's exit.

They'd slipped and shuffled through damp neighborhoods before picking up two more pods in sequence, Rhimes digging up old aliases and their dusty rep accounts to cover his tracks. He'd last used these to hire up mercenaries, buy weapons, and manage Wexley's little Elemental killing spree in a way the Paragons couldn't trace back to its owner.

Funny how some things come back around.

"This is your house?" Regina asked as Rhimes tried the door.

A manual lock, and still bolted. He had to assume the key was . . . Rhimes walked three meters to the right, bent down and lifted up the thin siding. There, nestled in some insulation, sat the tarnished object. Right where Rhimes had left it months ago before heading out to capture a gladiator drone with Wexley.

"I asked you a question," Regina said as Rhimes straightened.

She had her arms folded as if Rhimes, who guessed he had a few years on her, was her kid.

"Heard you," Rhimes said, plunging the key into the lock and turning. "It's not."

"Then whose is it?"

Rhimes pushed the door open. Smelled the dust, the heavy air left to founder. Dark wood floors, crown molding, and a stair heading up. No pictures on the light blue walls. Chilly inside too, the furnace either dead or cut off by Ziran's exacting accountants: why pay for a place no longer in use?

"It's Ziran's," Rhimes said as Regina followed him in. He let her go past him into the hallway before shutting the door, locking it behind her. "I'm hoping they've forgotten it."

"With my brother, that's a bad plan."

"Sometimes all the plans are bad."

Rhimes went past Regina, glanced at the basement door along the hallway. The arsenal had been emptied, spread around to the hired guns that'd brought down that drone. All except a choice few left behind, ones useless against machines but just fine for flesh and blood.

"So that's why we came here," Regina said in the kitchen, when Rhimes opened the cabinet over the fridge, pulling free a briefcase packed with ceramic knives. Fragile but almost undetectable. "You think some knives will get us into Wexley's office?"

"Last resort," Rhimes said, taking three and tucking them into his jacket, one into his sock. He held the last one out to Regina, flipping it in his palm so the black leather hilt stuck her way. "Here."

"I don't know how to fight with a knife," Regina said, curling her lip and staring at the blade.

"When you're desperate, you'll figure it out." Rhimes nudged the hilt Regina's way again, and when she made no move, he sighed, reversed the blade to put the hilt in his palm. Slid it up his sleeve and nocked it there. "Or not."

"Tools are for those who need them." Regina's eyes traveled to the pantry. "Tell me, does Ziran stock its hide-aways with food?"

"So long as fresh isn't a requirement, eat up. Then we're moving on."

Regina found some rock-hard cereal, cement-solid peanut butter, and a few edible energy bars. That last seemed appealing until Rhimes tried the faucet and found the water cut off too.

"Your brother's cheap," Rhimes said, twisting the faucet back.

"He's spending it all on me," Regina quipped, nibbling on the chocolate granola slate all the same.

Rhimes's Tama chimed: the pod he'd summoned waited outside, ready to bring them downtown. The two headed for the front door, Rhimes leading, hand reaching for the lock.

The door blew in. The shockwave sent Rhimes flying back into Regina, bowling them both onto the hallway's floor as splinters rained around them. His ears ringing, eyes stinging, Rhimes sat up and looked into a suppression drone's small, floating sphere. Non-lethal but plenty dangerous, the ball hovered over the porch as its chosen weapon retracted.

"Move," Rhimes said, voice sounding small and tinny through his numbed hearing. "Backyard."

Regina seemed to understand, getting to her feet and heading towards the kitchen. Rhimes followed, getting two long steps in before the kitchen's all-glass sliding patio door copied its front brother, shattering with a concussive bang. Rhimes grabbed Regina as the shards flew at them and charged to the right, through the door and down the basement stairs in a stumbling run.

As they hit the bottom, Rhimes reached for a light switch and found that, too, useless. With only a blue sliver making it through the open doorway, Rhimes more felt than saw Regina push away from him, backing into the room's center.

"How did they find us?" Regina asked.

"You know what your brother does, right?" Rhimes asked, ignoring an aching ankle as he brushed glass off his shoulders.

"I thought you'd figured out a way to disappear?"

Rhimes waved his glowing Tama at Regina while looking up towards the doorway. Those drones were non-lethals, but that didn't mean they couldn't make Rhimes hurt a whole helluva lot. Not to mention, if he and Regina didn't get going soon, Zhan-Yo's plan wouldn't have a chance.

And if Zhan-Yo failed, then Rhimes would get a traitor's treatment.

"I hoped he wouldn't find us this fast," Rhimes said. "Guessed wrong."

Regina backed away, put her back against a wall illuminated by Rhimes's Tama. Around her hooks told the vanished arsenal's story.

"Stay away from me," Regina said as Rhimes watched. "The worst I'll get is a ride back home."

Well that hurt, but Rhimes couldn't blame the woman. Self-preservation and all that. Instead, he ducked back towards the stairway. Beneath the wood steps sat old crates and boxes used to ship the weapons, and while the crates themselves were empty, the crowbar used to open them hung right in its spot. Rhimes hefted the black, dusty bar, tried to feel like a badass.

Tracker drones robbed that feeling, their sharp steel legs skittering as they took over for their floating suppression brothers. Rhimes heard the clicks up above as they shifted from bright tile to thick wood. The man reached for his Tama to cut the light, then stopped.

The drones could see in the dark.

"What are those things?" Regina said, her eyes tracking over Rhimes's head.

Rhimes heard the question and listened, instead, to the tracker drone's claws reach the stairs end. Lifting the crowbar, Rhimes started moving that way, planning to deliver an overhead bang before the drone could react. He brought the crowbar up, leveled his left shoulder, and felt something snag his weapon.

"There's two of them!" Regina yelled, clarifying the panic as Rhimes pulled away from the stairs to the room's center, tugging on the crowbar.

The drone couldn't keep its clawed grip on the weapon and Rhimes tugged it free, stumbling back, readying himself as the two tracker drones, their silver centipede carapaces slithered towards him from either side. Both reared up like cobras, the small slits hiding their dart-firing guns opening.

No way Rhimes would go down that easy.

He picked right, taking a step and swinging the bar like a baseball bat. The hit crunched into the drone's midsection, bouncing off the drone's armor with the slightest dent, a loud ring. The darts fired. One stabbed into his back, a second into his left shoulder.

They burned, and Rhimes lost his left hand as he swung the crowbar a second time. He went overhead, angling for the tracker drone's eye, and never made it. The machine swerved its spine, jerking back outside Rhimes's reach. Again like a cobra, the drone lunged forward after the swing, pushing Rhimes to the ground. A leg swatted the crowbar, sending it rolling across the floor.

Its metal mandibles looming over his head, Rhimes winced at the steel maw while his body went numb. At least, with two darts, he might lose consciousness. He definitely wouldn't feel the pain if these things decided to tear him apart.

Behind him, Rhimes picked up Regina's voice, muttering *please no* over and over again. Suppose he must've done something right if she didn't want him dead.

Rhimes couldn't feel his Tama vibrate, but he saw the screen light up. An incoming call from the person he really, really didn't want to talk to right then. Thankfully, he couldn't answer the Tama even if he wanted to.

The tracker drone sank down, rested two sharp legs on Rhimes's chest. With one other, the machine extended a steel claw and tapped the Tama, accepting the call. Wexley's face, sun-bathed and sun-glassed, filled the screen.

"Rhimes, you don't know how much it hurts me to see you like this," Wexley said. To his credit, Wexley did sound hurt, did sound tired. "Stabbing me in the back right when I need you the most?"

"You wouldn't listen."

Rhimes didn't have the lungs to speak in more than a whisper. Tried to find some strength anyway, do something not to look, sound so weak. The drone pressed its claw deeper, tearing through Rhimes's shirt, marking his chest.

"Listen to what?" Wexley asked. "What's the problem, Rhimes? What is so bad that you have to take my sister from me?" Wexley brought up his hand, took off his glasses and rubbed his eyes. "I don't even get what you're trying to do, taking her to that old storehouse."

"That's not—"

"Hey, drone," Wexley said, "is my sister there?"

The drone tilted, snaked a claw into Rhimes's arm, cutting deep. Rhimes couldn't feel a thing, but he could see the red drop in the Tama's light as the drone yanked Rhimes's arm up over his head, giving the Tama a good view.

"I'm here, Wexley." Regina found her spine somewhere: Rhimes heard no trace of the whimpering. "Leave the poor man alone. He didn't know what he was doing."

"That I don't believe for a minute. He didn't hurt you?"

"No. I think he wanted me for something."

Not saying what. Regina wasn't giving up right away. Rhimes couldn't exactly see a way outta this disaster, but knowing he wasn't all alone felt a bit better. Not that he'd be feeling anything for much longer.

"What he wants doesn't matter. Stay away from him," Wexley said. "I have a pod coming for you to take you back." Something crackled through the Tama, an alarm's steady fuzz. Wexley swore. "Have to go, Regina. Love you."

The Tama call blinked off, something Rhimes only knew because the drone extracted its claw from his arm. Freed, Rhimes's numb limb dropped back to the ground, the Tama's screen blank before his eyes.

Now came the execution.

The drone standing over him straightened, keeping Rhimes pinned but not exactly going in for the mauling. Its partner, with no preamble, sped away, metal legs scurrying up the stairwell's side for the door above. Rhimes knew enough about drone tactics to find the move strange: tracker drones used their numbers to confirm kills. The partner shouldn't have left until Rhimes was a cold corpse.

Not that the remaining drone couldn't handle the job. Rhimes saw a leg, sharp point visible in the Tama's dull glow, angle for his throat. Rhimes couldn't feel his legs, his arms, his anything, so he tried to keep a straight face. Determined, unafraid. Regina, at least, would be able to tell Wexley that much.

The crowbar smashed the drone's glassy left eye. Shards scattered as the machine fell to Rhimes's left, freeing the fighter from its clawed press—not that Rhimes could do much with that freedom. Regina advanced, swinging the crowbar again and striking a steel leg. The blow didn't do much, but neither did the drone attack the woman.

Wexley's own commands. Rhimes tried to laugh, coughed instead as his lungs struggled to get enough air. Ziran's drones wouldn't dare hurt the man's sister or the man himself, lines Rhimes had made sure Ziran's personnel added in an early update after taking the Factory.

"Get away," Regina said, as if the drone would listen to her. "Leave him alone!"

Caught between directives, the drone faltered. Regina smacked it again, Rhimes catching the hits from the corner of his left eye. The machine wanted to snake around Regina, get to Rhimes and finish the mission, but every time it made a move, Regina bashed it again.

Overhead, the house shook. Shouts and bangs bounced in echoes through the hallways. More glass shattered. Rhimes thought he caught tactical commands, but who the hell else would be here? Everyone he worked with was caught up in Ziran's missions now, and none would choose loyalty to him over security with Ziran's—

"Would you hurry and get up?" Regina barked, laying another golf-like blow against the drone's encroaching head. "This isn't my style!"

"I'm trying," Rhimes replied, his mouth mushy. "Two darts is a lotta drugs."

Rhimes needed time, and the drone wasn't stupid enough to give it to him. It moved right, pulling Regina with it, and when it feinted towards Rhimes again, she scooped the crowbar in another all-out smash. The drone scuttled beneath the blow, lying almost flat on those shiny legs, and ran up along Rhimes's chest.

"Don't, you ugly bastard!" Regina yelled, charging after the machine.

"Well, damn," Rhimes said as the drone rose up and slashed down with its claws.

Even with the darts, Rhimes felt those cuts.

TWENTY

Rise Up

CASSIDY ESTIMATED THIRTY bodies clustered in the windowless cell, hemmed in by cheap fencing and gladiator drones all too willing to keep their guns pointed at the prisoners.

Thirty bodies, and every last one jumped when the anomaly, a girl crouching in the corner, screamed.

Not in terror but with bright, energized anger.

Beneath a broad tent split into six of those large pens, a space near the base's middle where, Cassidy gathered, anomaly shipments would be clustered and sorted, the shout galvanized the captives. Cassidy couldn't explain it: one second, she'd been staring off towards the beige hills, wondering how Vick had died so fast, and the next? Charging towards the fence with the other anomalies.

No, she could explain it: another ability breaking the world.

The voids leapt to her fingertips, ready to fire as Cassidy crushed in with bodies bending one physical law after another. Some anomalies leapt into the air, darting up through the tent or diving towards a guard without heed for tactics. Others burst into flame, threw fantastic light globes, or melted into the ground only to appear next to a gladiator drone and beat on it with useless fists.

The drones did what they were designed to do: all four arms erupted in targeted fire, bullets streaming into the crowd. Some back pocket in Cassidy's mind realized she was going to die, they all were, but that same anomaly shouted again and that doubt vanished. Instead, Cassidy bounded on a wounded, falling body before her and used that height to throw a void at the nearest gladiator.

The invisible knife sliced through the air, found its target, and swallowed the drone's metal skull. Wires tore up and away from the thing's body, its arm cannons halting, collapsing. Another anomaly followed Cassidy's attack, running up to the drone and, with a touching hand, shrank the gladiator to a human's size while growing his own.

The big anomaly roared, the crowd roared with it, and, as Cassidy's voice came down from the call, a pinpoint laser turned the newly giant anomaly into a casualty. The riot cried, turned their attention to the anomaly's killer.

Cassidy turned too, voids ready to shred Ziran's monsters and their base until nothing remained save cinders and ash. Stepping off her human platform, Cassidy started to merge into the crush until another hulking anomaly, barreling by with some warrior song spilling from his mouth, smashed Cassidy's head with his shoulder.

She spun, fell, and would've been trampled if her little escapade, her void tossing, hadn't put her at the pack's back. Some bare feet crunched her legs, one pressed her hair into the dirt, but she breathed. Lived.

Found her sanity.

From the ground, packed dirt cool against her cheek, Cassidy saw beneath the fences, out the tent and towards the building's base. What had been a makeshift metal sheen now clouded with dirt, fire, and a drone-human morass. Hard rounds cracked their way through the air, splitting shouts demanding calm and a deeper sonic mixture defying description: anomalies and their abilities breaking, snapping, booming, and reverberating.

Cassidy felt like she'd warped back to her teenage years, stuffed in a crowded basement listening to motley bands wail away on random instruments.

In the chaos, though, lived opportunity. The island had taught Cassidy that much.

She pushed herself up, pulled together the fighting she saw, the blazing powers and the burning guns, and tried to form a strategy. Celice said Cassidy coming here was part of some plan. Had Thane or Aegis orchestrated the blow-up, the uprising? And if so, what was the goal?

On Cassidy's left came the younger woman, the yelling one who'd kick-started the rampaging rush. The woman shouted again, cupping her hands around her mouth to give extra oomph to the order, the call to crush Ziran's machines and their murderous caretakers. Cassidy felt the urge, but it slid off her logic, her self-control. Like the Duchess back on the island, knowing an anomaly was the source removed the threat.

"What are you doing?" Cassidy said to the woman, upping her voice to be heard.

"Taking a chance," the woman replied, looking Cassidy over. A frown said she wasn't impressed. "Why aren't you helping?"

The answer to that question came through their feet, came with a different, warmer breeze blowing by. One that didn't smell like the sea or the scattered brush but like ionized gasses, electric energy churned out an engine. Cassidy took the woman's arm, pulled her back from the struggling mob. Throwing a void, Cassidy sliced apart the fencing, letting the two walk out the tent's back and under the open sky.

"That's why," Cassidy said, pointing towards the southern horizon.

A dark, shifting cloud sped towards the camp. Drones of all kinds rocketing towards the anomaly prison break.

"They won't try to sedate us," Cassidy continued. "They'll sit above us, massacre us, and Ziran can start again when we're dead in the dirt."

The woman shook off Cassidy's hand, glared as the cloud came closer, "So you want to give up? Run? Those won't work."

"Neither will fighting like a mob."

Cassidy saw motion, a flash in the sun as a tracker drone, all bright metal, dropped off the tent's top and scuttled towards the pair. The Void pushed the woman aside—she fell into the dirt with a curse—and launched two small black holes at the machine. They tore the drone apart, sending sparking halves to either side.

Nodding at the busted drone, Cassidy extended a hand to the woman, one she took then released with a hiss.

"I think you burned me," the woman said.

"Sorry," Cassidy replied. "But that's what I'm talking about. We need a plan, and we need to get all these people on board fast."

The woman looked from Cassidy to the destroyed drone, picked herself up from the dirt, "Okay, but don't get me killed."

A born leader, this one.

"No promises," Cassidy said.

· · ·

LISSY, the screamer, had some good tricks. With Cassidy feeding strategies gleaned from months hiding in Thailand and years leading anomalies on the island, Lissy manipulated the camp's emotions with every cry. With Cassidy spawning voids to cover her advance towards the center, Lissy launched into a shrieking cadence.

The blasted out ring, forming naturally as the anomalies and the drones fought an ever-widening perimeter, let Lissy turn as she called out, catching the battle's parts with her cries. Lissy's first shout fell into the raging, blasting, punching rabble like water on a wildfire: she dampened the anger, inspired caution. Even that first step made an immediate difference as anomalies looked around themselves, following Lissy's instructions to work together, find ways to defend and attack in equal measure.

Cassidy listened as Lissy repeated the cry in the other directions, her voice ringing out over heads metal and human. Gladiator drones towered at the edges, some falling while others still fired ceaseless rounds into defenseless or, if they had the right powers, defended anomalies. Up above, anomalies that could fly tangled with suppression drones, fists and random objects striking welded spheres that didn't hesitate to shoot back.

Bodies fell, shrapnel joined them.

And that dark cloud came ever closer. Before it, orange now as the sun set to the West, the Ziran building boiled at its top. Windows broke as anomalies, guards, and drones tangled in a fight Cassidy couldn't make out, didn't understand. Lissy might've seen it as an opportunity, but the small group up there wouldn't help the war down here.

"Phase two!" Cassidy said as Lissy wrapped up the first call.

"I need to catch my breath," Lissy replied, trying to do just that.

Cassidy whipped a void past the screamer, a spiraling black hole that swallowed incoming fire from a rogue gladiator. The machine tried to switch targets only for a neon-blue blade, appearing from the ground like some lost spike, to sever the drone in two. Cassidy couldn't tell who'd spawned the thing, which fizzled out into azure embers after its attack.

"C'mon Lissy, now's not the time," Cassidy said, trying to look everywhere at once.

"Okay, okay." Lissy straightened, took in more air than Cassidy thought possible, like a bird puffing up before a song, and belted out the command.

If the first call inspired caution, solidarity, then Lissy's next carried focus on her words: fall back and form up. The battle lines around the camp frayed as anomalies with better abilities crashed ahead while weaker ones died or fell behind. Just by watching the gladiator drones and seeing which ones blew apart, which ones came closer, Cassidy could read the conflict. The camp itself provided its own page to read too as those tents fell, collapsing as anomalies and drones threw wild attacks.

As Lissy's shout, repeated again and again, reached their ears, the super-powered prisoners back-pedaled. Some anomalies threw up solid-colored or glimmering shields while others projected shadows or bent light, causing drones to fire into the air or at empty ground patches. Gradually the chaos came together, anomalies finding themselves surrounded not by deadly metal but by allies. Explosions died away, though the drones continued pouring gunfire into the anomaly defenses, fire that failed to find homes.

This was what Thane wanted, why he'd sent Cassidy here. He knew she could command a rogue anomaly force, knew she would understand how to keep them alive because she'd done it for years on that island. He knew, he saw Cassidy cared about those children in Thailand, cared about her family over here.

He knew she'd try anything to get these anomalies out safe.

And, damn it, Thane was right.

Now, Cassidy still had no idea how Thane could've guessed a battle would break out, but that would be a question for another time. Preferably, one that didn't have a twilight sky filling with metal monsters.

"Now what?" Lissy said between long inhales. "I dunno if you noticed, but those drones are still coming."

Cassidy, though, wasn't watching the drones anymore. She held her focus on the building's top, where the fight kept going in earnest. Bodies occasionally fell through broken windows to land on the ground below, and a flame's glow spoke of bad times inside. The incoming drones, too, seemed more focused on that conflict than the anomaly force gathering outside.

The anomalies needed two things to live: an escape, and a distraction to keep the drones away. Cassidy had an idea for the former, maybe that building could serve as the latter.

"Lady?" Lissy repeated.

"Train station," Cassidy said. "That's our only ticket out. Get everyone on it."

"And you?"

"I'm going to get us some cover."

"Works for me."

Lissy's lackluster heroism cut a smile onto Cassidy's face as she made her way straight ahead. The anomalies, as Lissy hit them with another command, one that had Cassidy feeling like she needed to head to the train station if she wanted to live, went left. They popped, flew, ran, or straight up teleported past Cassidy. The ones keeping up the shields held them up throughout the move, the multi-colored display walking with the crowd.

The drones on the ground, the Ziran guards followed, their guns quiet.

They'd been trained, programmed well. Cassidy burned up if she threw too many voids, most anomalies had similar costs for their powers. All these people would get tired, would find their abilities unresponsive eventually.

Then it'd just be clean-up.

Unless Cassidy could change the equation.

As they walked, the anomalies grumbled and growled, spoke suggestions to each other. Battle strategies mixed in with quips about making it out alive. Soldiers drafted into an immediate army, and the scene matched it: Cassidy smelled the sweat, the fear tamped by Lissy's manipulation. Shredded clothes, ash drifted by on the breeze. Thuds vibrated the ground as the multi-ton drones shifted their bulk. Beyond it all, the building's alarm continued to sound, a warning far to meager for the situation.

As she neared the last of the line, Cassidy felt the voids come to her fingertips. She would have a second, maybe, before the drones realized she wasn't protected. That would have to be enough time.

Her forehead grew warm, her arms hot as Cassidy's heart pumped faster and faster. The last two anomalies squeezed by her with concerned glances, walking backwards as their weird barriers—one a milky white oval, the other a cascading static square like an old TV—kept covering the move. Cassidy ducked between them, looked at the building and what stood between.

Eight gladiators here, with twice that many Ziran guards. Machine and human alike stopped their creaky pursuit as Cassidy cleared the barriers. Rifles raised, the gladiators tilted their gun-cannon arms. The sun's last efforts turned their white paint purple, the orange a murky black.

The swarm approached, flew over, around the tower. An oncoming, unstoppable storm.

"I surrender," Cassidy announced, and swept her arms up.

The energy bled from her hands, shot straight down her fingertips and raced into the air, all those voids whispering to Cassidy that now was the time, that they could race out and destroy the enemy.

It'd been a bright day, an early morning. She'd had a coffee in her hands, watching from the driveway as her son threw a basketball at the driveway hoop, the kid's backpack waiting in the lawn. The ball went up, hit the rim, and bounced towards the street. Behind her, the door opened as her husband ushered out Cassidy's daughter, ready for her own school-ward walk.

The car, a big SUV like so many on the street barreled towards the ball, towards her son chasing it. Cassidy didn't think, didn't do anything except follow the voids and their instincts. She threw out her hand, sent a spinning black hole towards the oncoming car. The void ate the front wheels, tore off the bumper, and sent the SUV into a sparking, shrieking halt as its front end smashed into the asphalt.

Her son, her daughter stared at the car. Cassidy's husband only looked at her.

Together, the voids linked, flew, a spinning disc wide enough to sever a tower. The drones, the guards, Cassidy watched it fly over their heads. As her hands went up, the heat came with it, burning Cassidy up like a fever to end all fevers. Her vision blurred, her knees bent, and before the first bullet fired her way, Cassidy hit the ground, already gone.

TWENTY-ONE

Ring The Bell

KICKING off suspended Aegis in the sky as his upward momentum fought, and lost, against gravity's pull. Around him, the sunset blinded his eyes with purple and orange. The drone's rockets, shooting up forever, splashed Aegis with heat. Not all that far below, Los Angeles spread like an urban blanket, and off to the right, Aegis caught the ocean, sparkling.

His ears recognized the fall before his stomach, the wind roaring as Aegis began his plummet. Began and stopped as his sideways kick launched him into the hillside. A tall pine caught the Champion, branches making a clawed cushion as Aegis tumbled, broke, split and shattered his way down too many stories to the dirty, dusty, needle-covered blanket at the bottom. Tears and pops abounded between his joints, his brain banged inside his skull like a rattle sent ringing, but the man didn't die when he finally found the ground.

Up through the canopy, Aegis could pick out the first, the few stars brave enough to pierce LA's city lights. He took his breaths shallow, wiggled his toes, blinked a few times. A tiny fireball, far above, gave evidence to the drone's end.

Aegis laughed. Another one to add to his score.

He curled up, stood up, brushed up and down on his shredded uniform. His ears found their way back from stunned silence to shouting, calls from his daughter and Particle saying his name. Twisting his neck back and forth to kick out the kinks, Aegis put his feet back into motion.

It'd been one helluva an opening round, but the team had made it to the second.

The breeze blustered as Aegis left the forest, as he skittered and slid down the hillside back down the Factory's big entrance. Zhan-Yo stood astride the downed gladiator like some conquering king, his tachi angling towards the concrete. Celice and Particle, seeing Aegis hadn't become one more casualty, took up cover behind the drone, weapons at the ready.

"Am I too late?" Aegis called, jogging onto the scene.

"For once, you're early," Zhan-Yo replied.

Celice rolled her eyes, but Aegis caught the barest hint of a smile that meant the world.

"What's he waiting for?" Aegis asked, glancing towards the big, shut door. "Is he scared?"

"Wexley's cautious. He's looking at us, trying to figure us out. Asking what I'm doing here."

"Then I'll tell him."

The wind whipped as Aegis went up to the loading dock, catching in the concrete walls and blowing back and forth, anxious to escape and not knowing how. The big door bore the Paragon logo, a golden version inlaid, upon close inspection, with a circuit board's etched lines. There wasn't a knocker, wasn't a way to get the thing open from out here.

"Wexley!" Aegis called. He couldn't see the camera,

but Mynx had shown him years ago that it lay right in the P's offset circle. The Champion put on his best hero mug, glared at the invisible eye. "You have a friend of mine in there. Let her out, or I'm coming in. You choose."

Nobody replied.

"Good job, Dad," Celice called. "Really scary stuff."

Aegis held up a single, particular finger. Zhan-Yo sighed loud. Particle, wisely, kept their thoughts their own.

"Aegis!" Wexley's voice, loud and clear from the camera, overrode the snapping wind. "Thank you for saving me the time to hunt you down. The world's ready to move on from your mistakes, and so am I. Please wait another moment and you'll have what you're looking for."

Not quite the monologue Aegis expected. Most villains in their triumph would go on for far too long about this or that grand ambition, a mystery until Apinya, in one eye-opening chat in the Paragon early days, revealed that villains wanted recognition. Wanted their greatest foes to understand their goals, the who, what, where, and why that was their destiny.

After that, Aegis did everything he could to punch'em out before the idiots began talking. Saved time, and none deserved anything better.

Wexley held true to his word. After giving Aegis another breath for his body to repair, the loading dock grumbled its way open. A gradual rise, centimeter by centimeter, giving glimpse to the drones holding serve on the other side. Gladiators, trackers, suppressors, and who knew what else lay in that metal morass.

Aegis whistled. Cracked his knuckles.

His eyes swerved, zeroed in on a point behind the drones. A lift's control panel, barely visible between all those weapons, the glistening silver and steel. Leave it to Particle to keep their focus on the objective.

Three gladiators formed the front line as the door completed its rise. Twelve arms loaded for death spun up. Beneath them, the tracker drones lurched forward, their spikes biting into the concrete.

Aegis grinned, felt that wind at his back, flowing around him and into the now-open doorway. Lowering his shoulder, Aegis took a long step forward, alone.

And, in the next instant, so very not.

Fading in ahead to Aegis's left came a huge, fist-swinging figure. Thane's muscle-bound, spit-flinging anger beast nearly matched a gladiator drone in size. His haymaker came in from the wind, striking with a crunch, sending his four meter tall target collapsing back into the drone force.

On Aegis's right, a young Paragon crouched, hands pushing outward. The Champion didn't feel anything, but the drones on the formation's right side crumpled in towards each other, their metal parts slamming and sticking tight. Rolling in from the wind after the man came one of Apinya's recruits, Kamnan, and the older man blitzed the collected drones with a hot light, melting the clump into a bright, burning ball.

Still, Aegis had his own gladiator front and center. He faced it, stared at those weapons, and broke into a charge. He kicked off as two hands gripped his shoulders from behind. Aegis felt his clothes, his body, everything freeze. A sitting target.

Until a second anomaly popped Aegis and his rider forward. The gladiator raised its guns only to find Aegis no longer several meters away but right in its face, the Champion's momentum carrying his invincible body into the gladiator like a cannonball. Aegis crunched into the machine's chest, his protection brooking no damage, his speed cracking the drone's armor and driving the machine back.

Aegis snapped into motion as the two hands dropped away, Samir lunging for the damaged drone. At a touch, the Paragon locked the dented gladiator into invincible stasis, saving Aegis a shooting but keeping Samir within kneeling reach at the gladiator's feet.

Perfect for those tracker drones and their slicing claws.

"Celice!" Aegis shouted as he went for one on the right.

The silver drone cut around the gladiator, going for Samir with its front mandibles. Aegis punched down, delivering enough force to reroute the drone into the concrete. Sparks flew, Aegis felt the blow crack a knuckle.

By the time his second hit struck home, breaking the tracker drone's centipede spine, that knuckle had itself back whole.

Behind Aegis, shots rang out in a staccato pop. A second tracker drone took the hits and changed tactics, leaping onto Aegis's back and scrambling towards the Champion's head. The machine's claws sliced his uniform, cut deep in the Champion's skin, and while Aegis threw his arms back, instinct told him he'd never get a grip in time to save his own life.

Pain seared hot in a flash and Aegis shouted, expecting to find a lethal cut following. Instead the pressure on his body vanished. Aegis whirled and saw, as more drones and anomalies crashed into each other, Thane holding the tracker drone high. The thing's claws scrapped against Thane's skin, drawing red lines on the man's taut, mottled flesh.

Thane yanked the tracker drone apart. Holding onto the metal and its slicing claws, Thane went to work on the machine horde, laying about and shredding drones wherever he struck.

It'd been a long time since Aegis fought with Thane, a long time since that anomaly had claimed the Champion's love. Aegis would never forgive the monster that moment, but right now, with everything at stake, he could appreciate having the creature on his side.

"Letting go!" Samir called.

The big drone snapped back to life, found its aim, only for EMP rounds to cascade into its bulk. Zhan-Yo's hired guns, Mathieu's commandos, rolled up in several pods, forming up with Celice and Particle to deliver covering fire as the anomalies set up for an advance.

And they struck now.

With the Paragon force emerging from the wind, the combined anomaly abilities overwhelmed Wexley's greeting party. Bolts, blasts, and blitzes struck smaller drones from the air and littered larger ones with fires, acid balls, and electrical shorts. Machines blew apart, fell dead to the ground, or turned to fight their fellow drones in a maniacal break with their programming.

Aegis leapt into the middle, following Thane and falling into a rhythm with the bigger anomaly. As Thane went high, Aegis went low, ducking the monster's wide swings to pick up a tracker drone and throw it into Thane's claw-shredding backhand. A suppression drone riddled Thane's right side with stunning darts, ones that bounced off the man's hide, and Aegis took the drone's focus and turned it into an advantage: the Champion gripped the ball-like machine and threw it into another gladiator's hip, smashing it apart and cracking a hole in the gladiator's armor.

That gladiator turned to see its attacker, only for EMPs to strike right in the small hole.

"Thanks for the opening," Particle said, their voice

crackling in through Aegis's earpiece. "Progress is on schedule."

"What schedule?" Aegis said, rolling away as Thane engaged another gladiator, the dance getting too hot for him.

"Mine," Zhan-Yo replied. "I have our wind rider getting reinforcements, but they won't arrive immediately. We need to get inside the Factory where we can defend ourselves. "

"Doing just fine out here," Aegis replied, rushing towards another tracker drone to bash apart.

Their advance carried the anomaly-normal strike force past the loading dock lips, bringing them just inside the building itself. Without the tight concrete confines, Aegis caught the Factory's vast levels, all lit up in bright white on black-blue metal floors kept clean by even more drones. Here, even with the fight's constant noise, Aegis could feel the Factory's lines churning out more machines, ones that might leap off the final leg and go right into the fight.

With open space above and below, with every drone able to fly or climb, Aegis's group could get hit from any, every angle. While they numbered several dozen now, those numbers would fall fast without surprise on their side.

"Keep going!" Aegis called, his voice getting through the earpiece and echoing over the fighting. "Once we're in, split to your objectives! Don't wait!"

The drones seemed to sense the turning momentum. Either that or some Ziran supervisor decided to save her machines for a better battlefield. The few remaining gladiators backed up, triggering their jets as they made it within the Factory and launching upward and out of sight. Tracker drones and their airborne suppression brethren fled too, most getting blasted apart for their trouble.

Aegis's group ran forward, the normal commandos defaulting to covering fire. Thane, already leading the way, ignored any and all planning, instead breaking off to the left and charging along the Factory's broad main level. Aegis formed up with Zhan-Yo, Celice, and Mathieu just inside the entrance, the Champion eyeing the main lift.

"What about the maniac?" Celice asked, pointing after Thane.

"He'll draw attention," Zhan-Yo said.

"And if he dies, so much the better," Aegis added. "I'm on Mynx. You three get to the command center."

"You're not going alone," Celice said.

Aegis would've accepted help, would've taken an ally or seven with him, except new noises drew their attention. Particle, watching the loading dock doors, snapped eyes. Outside, new drones landed, gladiators smashing into the pods the commandos had driven up. Behind them, too, new alarms rang out in the Factory as security systems came online.

Celice snapped up her rifle, squeezed the trigger to send a bullet flying over Aegis's shoulder. It struck an opening panel, perforating a turreted cannon on the other side. Sparks rained down. Commandos and anomalies alike called out other guns coming into view, the Factory rising against the intruders.

"You can't spare a soul," Aegis said, breaking for the lift as the everyone around him flew into life-saving action. "I'll get Mynx, you stay alive."

"Just be fast!" Celice replied, already aiming, firing away at another target.

Bullets flew, lasers flashed, anomaly powers flared from every surface as their reflections caught on the Factory's polished skin. Beautiful chaos, a mission risking everything. Aegis found his adrenaline pumping as fast as his legs as he reached the lift, slammed the button sending it lower. Terrible, deadly, and missing from his life for too long.

The Champions once made their names with strikes like these, teamwork triumphing over impossible odds. Now he was at it again, one last time saving the world.

Did it get any better than this?

TWENTY-TWO

Office Rumble

DEATH STOOD before her dressed up like a Ziran guard in orange and white armor. His rifle, ready to fire, angled at Kat, her feet kicking, slipping on tile. No cover, nowhere to go. She reached up with one hand, shielding her face as the guard went for his trigger.

Kat had faced death before. Been real close, and at no time had her life flashed before her eyes. At no time had the moment slowed down to make room for some last introspection. This time was no different, though it sure seemed strange: one blink, the man had his gun on her. The next, a reflective circle flew between them.

The guard pulled the trigger, the gun fired its guts into the thrown circle, one made from the same floor Kat sat on. In another fractional second, the circle flew on by, clattering in the hallway. The man still had his gun, still had his hand on the trigger.

But Kat had a moment.

She twitched her left wrist and two silver orbs flew out, banging against the guard's visor. He stumbled back as Kat rolled over, covering her eyes. The bright flash went off, visible beneath Kat's eyelids as a purple-green flare. The tracker pushed up with both arms as shouts, screams, and orders rolled through the room.

Something sliced at her ankle, tore her boot, but Kat kept her footing as she went further into the room. Anything to put distance between her and the guard's rifle. Something hot whisked by her right ear, and Kat opened her eyes to see what looked like a cluster of orange-burning bees buzzing near her. The swarm shot back behind her as Kat whirled, the anomaly insects catching a charging tracker drone.

The bees darted in and out and *through*, each molten mark eating the drone. The machine faltered as its wires cut, its processors fell apart. Several seconds and the drone hit the floor, a perforated husk. The bees zipped away in search of more prey.

Kat would be happy never tracing that anomaly.

Not that tracing was the moment's biggest issue: the tower's top floor erupted into chaos around Kat, with drones and Ziran guards tangling with anomalies sniffing a chance at freedom. Across the long, wide space with windows all 'round save the left side where the hallway traveled, conflict rose, quick and brutal. Guards and drones lanced out stunning darts at anomalies, some hitting and others getting blocked as Calvin, ripping away the floor, threw up thin, stiff barriers.

The bees swarmed down the line. Their leader, a woman with tangled hair going head to toe and more ink on her skin than anyone Kat had ever seen, directing them with waving hands.

On the room's far side, several guards clustered around someone Kat couldn't make out, even though she could hear the woman's loud voice calling out commands.

Defend, take them alive, kill the intruder, all the good stuff.

There was a plan: get to the lady behind the guards, and Kat might be able to buy a truce, get the madness to end. Get out alive, and not alone.

Kat found Calvin, caught his eyes for a long second until they widened and the anomaly disappeared through the ceiling as it collapsed. Kat would've gone forward except that guard who'd been a tile away from shooting her wanted a second round.

Recovered from Kat's stunning orbs, the guard had his gun up again pointing her way. Kat, on her feet this time, flicked her left wrist to get the grappling hook back. She fired up, jumping at the same time as the guard shot. The stunning dart snapped by her legs, a thinner target than her body. The grapple found a hold in the ceiling, one Kat kept until the dart slipped by.

Releasing the grapple, Kat hit the floor in a run, closing with the guard as he brought the rifle across in a swing towards Kat's head. A predictable haymaker. Kat bent at her waist, letting her head fall to the side and the rifle swish through the space. With her left hand, Kat went right a gloved uppercut, bashing the guard's chin. His head snapped back, the man's arms falling out to his sides as the guard backpedaled.

Right into perfect kick distance.

Falling into the practice so many bar fights at *Carver's* had honed, Kat lashed a flat-footed strike to the guard's stomach. The man's armor made it feel like Kat kicked a wall, but the guard himself wasn't so sturdy. The man fell on his butt, sitting up for a nice follow-through.

Kat flipped feet, steadying on her left and bringing her right for what should've been the clincher, except for a loud crack, a whistle that went right by Kat's ear. The bullet struck and sheared through the window behind Kat, cementing the round's status as live and deadly. Kat gave up on the kick and went left, putting the room's entry and its narrow cover between her and the triple-guard phalanx on the room's opposite end.

Either Ziran knew Kat wasn't an anomaly, or they'd decided to stop playing around.

The slip into cover gave Kat a second to re-evaluate the fight, and she caught a vast silence, both in sound and in action. The burning bee assault died when a tracker drone, dropping from the ceiling, bore the woman to the ground, stabbing her with some knockout drug. The other anomalies that'd been waging war a breath ago seemed to be quiet, though the room hummed as a whipping wind creased through broken windows. Drone parts scattered through what Kat could see, with various bodies among them.

The leading lady called out different commands now, ordering the drones to clean-up, her guards to advance, and, in an interesting twist, someone to get reinforcements sent up from the Factory fast.

Reinforcements for what?

The guard Kat had been fighting started to get up, so Kat reached out, put a hand on the guard's shoulder. The man froze. Careful to keep herself hidden behind the doorway, Kat spoke soft, slow.

"Try anything, I break your neck," Kat said.

"They'll break yours in a minute," the guard replied. "I'll wait."

Kat couldn't argue with that. She heard the drones, the guards advancing down the room towards her position. They could've swarmed her, but their hesitation made sense when the elevator behind Kat dinged a new arrival.

Why risk anything, anyone when they had their target trapped?

She needed to change the situation.

"Stand up," Kat said. "Now."

The guard, thankfully, didn't question her. With Kat helping him, the man rose to his feet fast. As soon as his soles were flat on the tile, Kat pushed him around the corner. Behind her, several more guards clattered their boots from the elevator, one calling for Kat to surrender.

"Don't shoot me!" Kat's prisoner called as the tracker pushed him, with herself close behind, around the corner.

When the guard's pals didn't fire, Kat pushed her hostage forward, angling ever-so-slightly towards the room's middle.

"Get him out of the way," the woman ordered.

Kat heard the tracker drones, heard the guards behind her snapping their guns up. She shoved her hostage, sent him stumbling towards the woman's protection. On Kat's right, a tracker drone dropped from the ceiling, claws swinging towards her. A sharp sting bloomed along Kat's right arm, leg.

The tracker dove.

Calvin's hole didn't have much wiggle room, but Kat didn't match the man's size. She flew through face first, squeezing between two hanging lights to fall onto a dented desk. The hit compressed her lungs, boggled her brain. Glass, already shattered on the desk's surface, nicked her forehead.

Before Kat could grasp where she'd gone, hands grabbed her and threw her off the desk. Bullets slammed into the space she'd been, blowing holes in the furniture. Kat swore, a hacked whisper of a curse, and tried to back up further. Tried, anyway, until she saw wood-and-metal lines streaming up past her, weaving a taut web across the ceiling's hole.

"They've got a dozen ways to get down here, so let's move," Calvin said. "If you're all right?"

The top level's glassy glitz traded its style for a processing center's power, albeit with the windows still surrounding the edges. Desks and workstations coated Kat's landing room from end to end, monitors glowing with demands for user names and passwords. Beyond screens, most desks had cases with vials, many a familiar dark red. The kind Kat had running down her own arm right now.

"I'm so far from all right," Kat said.

Calvin looked unscathed from the fight, his Ziran t-shirt and flimsy pants making the man appear more like some thrift store monk than an anomaly prisoner. He'd gone from Paragon buff to a gaunt look, his eyes puffy and a new black-haired beard putting scruff around his chin. Still, Kat saw the man she'd been chasing right there and couldn't resist a tight hug.

A tight hug that Calvin stopped, pulled apart, looked at her.

"Woulda said the same thing till you saved my life," Calvin said.

This time they met with their lips, a quick press cut short by ripping, shredding sounds. An awful way to ruin what should've been a damn blissful moment. Kat's own pain, her frustration and exhaustion flipped to a white heat.

"We're gonna talk more about what just happened later," Kat said as they turned to the tracker drone's progress. "Who's the woman upstairs? She seems like the key to this whole thing."

"Adriana," Calvin said. "This is—"

"One sec," Kat said as the tracker drone dropped through its hole.

The slice-and-dice machine hit the same desk Kat and Calvin had used as a landing pad, straightening itself up just in time for Kat's grapple to spear the drone through its front mandibles. The steel hook dove deep into the machine, and Kat didn't flick her wrist when she yanked it back with both hands. Barbed, the grapple ripped wires, cut circuits as Kat pulled, finally popping out the hole it came in with a sparking disaster in tow.

The tracker drone lurched towards them, unsteady, still trying to fulfill its mission. Trying, anyway, until Calvin stabbed it with several metal slivers pulled from another desk.

Any triumph died with a lock chirping open on the room's doors. Kat and Calvin both dove down behind another desk, huddled shoulder to shoulder as the guards made a banging entrance.

"Tell me you've got a plan," Calvin said.

"Sure, we get Adriana in our hands, then we get her to let us out," Kat said. "Easy."

"So easy."

Despite her confidence, Kat didn't really know what the hell they were going to do. Calvin might be able to suck another hole through the ceiling, but they'd get caught eventually. Breaking through the windows meant a dive to a hard splat. Three stories down to dirt meant they might not die, but a broken leg would be just as bad. A firefight without any weapons—Kat's grapple aside—wouldn't go their way either.

She might want to turn Adriana into a hostage, but Kat couldn't make that a reality.

The lighting above Kat changed, dimmed as a deep blue lattice grew up and around the two. Calvin moved in close, his shoulder brushing into Kat's, the anomaly's right hand held high, left planted on a receding ground. Ziran's guards shouted, one squeezed off a harmless, ricochetting round.

"Buying us time," Calvin said, "till you figure out this easy plan of yours."

With her back against the lattice, Kat noticed an interesting detail outside the windows: drones sweeping towards the building. The sky turned white and orange in the sunset's lingering glow, glints flashing off polished carapaces.

Were all those robots here for her? For Calvin?

Kat's hand found Calvin's planted palm. All those gladiators would destroy them, no matter how much tile Calvin wove into a shield. The anomaly noticed the drones too, swore, but kept his barrier growing. Now the sapphire sphere brushed up around Kat's back, weaving its seal around the desk. Its farthest strands extended over her head, dripping down into her view like snowflakes expanding on a Chicago morning.

"I'm glad I found you," Kat said.

"Sorry to get you killed."

"Was going to happen anyway."

The tracker winced as the drones closed with the tower, their jets flaring. In a second they'd crash through the windows, in a second they'd raise their cannons and fire. In a second, they'd—

"What?" Calvin said as the drones broke, veering like a bird swarm around the tower.

They weren't coming for Kat and Calvin after all. Kat let go the breath she held, gulping in air as the machines left them alive, left them alone.

A guard slipped around Calvin's lattice, weapon raised. Kat didn't think, just jumped in front of Calvin, reaching towards the guard's gun. She'd been shot once, felt it twice. How much worse would a third time be?

The world lurched, the guard fell back, his bullet going up towards the ceiling. The squawking alarms died as Kat's protective dive turned into a forward somersault. Calvin's shield fell apart as the anomaly joined Kat in a rumbling tumble towards the windows. Those big panes cracked and shattered as the tower, the whole damn tower, teetered back.

There are moments to slow down, to contemplate the next action and make the best choice. Kat hadn't lived too many of those. Instead, she'd run on snap judgments, on life-or-death instinct, and now that instinct told her to twist and fire her grapple up.

"Hold me!" Kat yelled as vials, office supplies, desks, and the hapless guards rolled towards her and Calvin.

The tracker's grapple went straight, striking the room's back, windowless wall and biting in. Calvin snared Kat's legs in a bear hug, swinging up his own to clear room for the passing debris. Their suspension didn't last long: the tower's top followed its bottom, sliding towards the ground.

Kat snapped her wrist, telling the grapple to reel them in. The device churned, pulled Kat up as they fell down. Calvin cursed again. The guards, still alive, yelled. Below and behind them, a monstrous roar rumbled, gnashing and tearing as if some giant creature feasted on Ziran's construct. Some force tugged at Kat's outfit, a light pressure bringing it back towards the building's center.

What the hell was going on?

"Get ready!" Kat said.

There wasn't time to explain what. As the grapple bit, Kat swung herself, using her momentum to give Calvin a lift. The anomaly caught up to the ceiling, the desert's rocky ground approaching fast below them. Wires dangled, broken floor drifted down around them, and Kat wrapped her arms around Calvin's chest, her grapple still keeping its hold.

The tracker felt Calvin's arm drop, his hand spread as Kat tucked up her legs.

Instinct gave her a chance.

Calvin gave her hope.

TWENTY-THREE

Downtown

RHIMES SAW five faces looking down at him. One he recognized; the intense yet somehow disaffected Regina, always seeming as though events weren't cool enough for her. Another belonged to a shirtless man with a fresh bird tattoo crawling up and around his chest.

The other three were the same. Exactly the same damn middle-aged man squinting at him three times over.

"Either I'm in the weirdest hell, or you're anomalies," Rhimes said.

As he spoke, Rhimes took stock of himself, the situation. Above him, the house's basement ceiling sat right where Rhimes had left it. Beneath him, the cement floor felt as stiff as ever. What didn't feel the same, frankly, was Rhimes himself.

His body *sang*. Aches and pains gone. The muffling stunning dart effects gone. A nagging sore throat from the flight to Chicago?

Gone.

"Hell? You wish." Regina pointed at the shirtless dude. "This man saved your life so you can save his. Get up."

"Yes, miss," Rhimes laughed, accepting a hand from one of the three clones to get to his feet.

"This," the shirtless anomaly said as Rhimes rose, drawing his hand around the beautiful, flying hawk tattoo, "is you. Only reason I had space for it, your company killed all the ones I saved before." The man deadlocked eyes with Rhimes. "She says you can pay us back for all that pain. You don't, I give it back to you."

Someone might've been intimidated, looking into that man's eyes and seeing the anger, the loss there. Rhimes had seen similar looks from his mercenaries, from his soldiers before them. Looking closer, Rhimes could see the odd, clean patches on the man's skin, spots that would've made perfect ink patterns. Everyone who lost someone carried the marks in a different way.

"Can't help what's happened," Rhimes said. Pity, excuses would be insulting to this one. "I can, though, make sure it stops."

With a nod, Rhimes turned to thank the triplet that'd helped him up only to see the man wither, skin-tight uniform and all, to shriveled brown dust. Rhimes stepped back only for Regina to balance him with her arm.

"Sorry," the only remaining copy said with a shrug. "Part of the game. They grow, they die. Name's Weed, and I gather you're going to get us inside?"

"Inside?"

"Ziran's headquarters," Weed said, nodding at Regina. "She said she has a passcode to disable the drones, but she needs a specific computer?"

"Not a computer, a place," Rhimes repeated to the group gathered around in the kitchen minutes later. "Ziran's only got two spots with access to the whole network. One's at the Factory in LA, put in after we,"

Rhimes coughed, "I mean Ziran, took it. The other's right here in Chicago, in Zhan-Yo's old office."

"Why?" asked Beth, the local Elemental head, a woman Rhimes had hunted more times than he cared to remember.

"Because Zhan-Yo didn't want anyone standing in his way when it came time to broadcast the revolution. We get Regina into that office, she can put in a code that'll hit every drone on the planet and knock'em out, at least for a little while."

"You know this code?" Beth asked Regina, all the faces in the kitchen swiveling her way.

"I do," Regina said. "At least, I have a good idea what it could be."

"Then tell us. If everything hangs on this code, then we all should know."

Regina shook her head, "I don't want my brother dead, and I don't want the world going back to the way it was. Get me in the tower and I'll call Wexley. If I don't like what he says, I'll put in the code."

Beth reached out, put her hand on Regina. Weed, across the makeshift circle in the cramped kitchen, frowned. Two other Elementals shifted their stances, getting their hands free. The Paragons did likewise.

"Hey," said a new voice pushing his way into the circle, a man Rhimes took a minute to recognize. He'd stared at too many files during his Ziran career, too many targets, to place Gordon Holyoak at first glance. "They're already attacking the Factory. We don't have time for games. Quit it, Beth."

The Elemental leader shot Gordon the iciest stare Rhimes had ever seen—and knowing Wexley, that was quite a statement—then released Regina, who sighed, then offered up her own glare back Beth's way.

"Manipulate me again," Regina warned, "and you won't like what happens."

"All right," Rhimes said, stepping into the circle's center. "Regina's keeping the code. I get you're all looking to help, and I'm grateful for it, but we're late. I'm escorting Regina up to the tower's top, and I'm doing it now. You wanna play a part, get in a pod and meet us there."

"Rhimes, Regina," Gordon said. "I've already got one ready, if you are?"

This time, nobody tried to stop them. Rhimes left the house a dead man brought back to life, and Chicago's early spring air, its night time chill, had never felt quite so wonderful.

GORDON'S POD ROCKETED DOWNTOWN, the evening streets quieter than Rhimes would expect. Then again, with every news broadcast focused on the conflict erupting in LA, both at the Factory and at a Ziran facility a little north, perhaps people didn't feel like going out. Drones, too, seemed to be in short supply: Chicago's skies were clear, city lights and the moon dueling for dominance.

"It's crisis protocol," Rhimes said when Gordon asked about the missing machines. "Ziran's not going to put the drones out on random patrols, but save them for defending critical infrastructure. People."

"Like the place we're going?"

"Actually no," Rhimes chuckled. "We didn't like the optics. The drones will be watching bridges, power plants. City hall. Ziran headquarters ought to be light tonight."

"You seem confident," Regina said, lounging on the pod's right side.

"Been scared enough today," Rhimes replied, folding

his hands behind his head in the pod's middle. In front, the vehicle jumped off the highway, running downtown. "Now we're rolling, better to focus on what's in front of me."

"I can get that," Gordon said.

"You can?" Rhimes asked. "Don't understand what a tracker's doing here?"

"Let's just say I'm invested in this turning out well for my side."

"Parasites," Regina muttered.

"Say again?" Gordon asked, doing an impressive job keeping any acid from his tone.

"Trackers, you bleed anomalies for your money. All you want is to keep the golden goose laying its eggs."

Rhimes had his hand on Gordon before Regina finished. His slight head shake met Gordon's bemused face. The tracker shrugged off Rhimes's hand, laughed.

"I've been called so much worse," Gordon said. "You're going to have to do a lot better to get under my skin."

Regina, though, kept her mouth shut until the pod rolled up, like some important affair, to the Ziran tower's entrance. A doorway wall greeted them, up off the wide sidewalk and beyond a casual courtyard with benches surrounding blaze-orange Z's on pedestals. Bombastic, just like Zhan-Yo and Wexley.

Rhimes followed Regina from the pod, his eyes flicking up the floors as he found footing on the sidewalk. Gordon joined them. At a wave from Rhimes, the trio advanced, heading across the wet concrete. White bulbs at their feet cast the orange statues in a soft glow, while lamps ringing the overhang covering the entrance mingled with Chicago's diffuse illumination to guide their way.

It being after hours meant two Ziran-uniformed security guards stood outside, no weapons visible. Both had their heads in their Tamas but looked up as the three neared the entry. Of the whole wall, only the middle two doors would be open after hours.

"Confidence," Rhimes said. "They won't know you."

"Isn't that the problem?" Gordon asked, but he didn't stop walking as Rhimes reached for the door handle.

"Evening," Rhimes said to the nearest guard and caught a nod in return, a placid face otherwise shadowed by the man's cloth cap.

Gordon went in first, Regina followed. Rhimes, expecting and not getting a reaction from either guard, let the door shut behind him.

And winced.

A large statue dominated Ziran's lobby, one showcasing Zhan-Yo's family, or at least a sculptor's idea of it. The fountains at its based churned continually, the shifting glow from the lights in the water's base mingling with the coins tossed in to create a sparkling effect. Rhimes never noticed it during the day, when natural light, the constant employee commotion combined to drown out and disappear the fountain's magic. At night, though, with low lighting throughout, the whole thing seemed magical.

Which made Brielle, Rhimes's best soldier, and the mercenaries standing with her inside the lobby all the more disappointing. This could've been a beautiful march to victory.

Instead it'd be a bloody battle to the end.

Brielle, her long gun slung over her shoulders while a shorter, close range weapon occupied her hands, started a slow clap. Rhimes counted eight other fighters with her in the lobby, all wearing grizzled Ziran gear meant for anomaly conflict. They followed their leader, letting their guns, their knives, their grenades hang to deliver a mocking greeting.

"Stay back," Rhimes whispered, putting a hand on Regina's shoulder and pulling himself in front. "We planned for this."

"A bad plan," Regina replied.

"Rhimes!" Brielle interrupted, her clap dying away, fingers returning to the trigger. "When Wexley told me to follow you, I thought he was being paranoid." She gestured with her gun at Regina and Gordon. "But you fooled all of us. Every one who signed up with Ziran to work with you, who believed in the mission, you got us, Rhimes. Congratulations!"

There were choices to make. Rhimes wanted to sit down with Brielle, sketch out in some bar somewhere all the little things that'd led to this moment. She had the smarts, had the savvy, had the humanity to see where Rhimes was coming from. She'd get it, might even join him on the mission.

But not here, not with her leading the group standing in their way. Every one of those men and women had lives to support with Ziran salaries and Brielle wouldn't throw that away just because Rhimes asked her to.

Hell, he wouldn't in her position.

Which meant a different tactic.

"Did you see what's happening out there?" Rhimes asked, spreading his hands out wide, giving no indication he had a weapon ready. "You see what Wexley's doing, what Adriana's doing?"

"Keeping us safe, that's what I'm seeing," Brielle replied. "You fought the Paragons. You captured anomalies for Adriana's experiments—"

"Experiments?" Rhimes heard Gordon ask, but Brielle

kept on charging away, layering evidence and allegation together into a hypocrisy cake.

"You're acting like you found God or something." Brielle shook her head. "We're not clean, Rhimes. This business is dirty. It's violent. But it's also necessary. We're giving the people their choice back."

"Nah," Rhimes replied, though Brielle's words weren't easy to shrug off. Rhimes figured he'd have to reckon with his own choices and where, exactly, the lines had been crossed, but that would come later. With whiskey. "We just took it from one maniac and gave it to another."

Brielle snapped her weapon up, flipped on a laser sight. Its red dot found Rhimes's chest, hovered over his heart.

"Last chance," Brielle said. "Fold, and I'll tell Wexley you had a psychotic break. You can join her in the home."

A man standing on Brielle's left, tall and intense, raised his own weapon, aimed the submachine gun over Rhimes's head. Brielle didn't catch it, didn't notice till the man held down the trigger and sprayed bullets through the tall lobby windows. Glass broke, rained down on the tile. The man turned, as if on a swivel, and opened up on the elevator shaft, blasting away its glass shell too.

Regina popping the signal, kicking off that bad plan right on time.

While Brielle yelled at the soldier, slapping away the man's gun, a form flew through the blown windows. A man and a woman, both in Paragon tactical gear. The man, his form bunched up, took the landing, letting the woman go. Holding a vape pen, the woman blew smoke towards Brielle's team as they noticed, finally, there'd been some new players added to the game.

Brielle's team fuzzed, blurred into shapeless swashes. Behind Rhimes, the two security guards thumped against the doorways, knocked out. The offending assaulters came barging through the unlocked doors a second later, Weed's many copies cascading by, a miniature man flood. The clones didn't stop at Regina, Gordon, or Rhimes: they kept right on going, through that blur and out the other side.

"Might wanna move," Smoke said, and she went right, forward.

Towards the elevators.

"C'mon." Rhimes practiced what he preached, Regina and Gordon joining up quick.

The plan called for a war to rage down here, fighting to keep the drones, the Ziran personnel busy until Regina and Rhimes could enter the shutdown code. The plan called for that and nothing else, because time meant they had to keep moving.

"Here," Rhimes said as Smoke escorted them to the elevators. He stuck his Tama up to the scanner, hoping Wexley hadn't blocked his account yet.

The scanner blinked back an angry red. Nothing.

"Nice," Gordon said. "This is off to a great start."

"Not helping," Regina replied.

"Get close," Lob, picking up the end, said. "Can't take more than two at a jump."

Rhimes and Regina fit in first, getting in tight as Lob wrapped his arms around them. Gunfire continued to echo around the lobby, Weed's clones attacking. Rhimes thought he heard, too, some other Elementals joining in. At least one bright green flash indicated another anomaly had arrived.

Hopefully Brielle would live. She'd been a good soldier, didn't deserve to die for choosing the wrong job.

"This is all your fault," Regina said as Lob had them squat down.

"I know," Rhimes replied. "I really know."

Without preamble, Lob jumped, carrying the trio up

several floors to the mezzanine, right where Regina's stolen soldier had shattered an opening.

"Hold on tight," Lob said, "This is gonna take a few jumps."

"Just make it fast." Rhimes looked at his Tama as Lob wrapped them up again.

Another message from Zhan-Yo:

Hurry.

TWENTY-FOUR

Soft Truth

THE PRINCIPLE CALLED her from the classroom. Cassidy flicked on an educational video for the students, had the assistant drone take over while she left the room. For the after-lunch period, the hallways were quiet, not a soul's sneakers squeaking on the laminated tile. On a normal day, Cassidy would've walked the passage to the office without a worry, confident the coming discussion would be about a difficult student, a curriculum change, a request to chaperone an event.

Today, Cassidy felt the voids. They sprang up along with her nerves, and, just like that morning, they were ready. The broken SUV meant her son survived, and while the kid hadn't made the connection, Cassidy saw her husband's look, knew he'd put the moment together clear enough.

He hadn't picked up her calls all day.

The principal sat at the desk, an exhausted woman with an apologetic frown on her face. The frown's reason for being came from the two men in blue-black uniforms standing in the room. They nodded at Cassidy as she walked in, and one extended his gloved hand. She shook, felt the strong leather and the grip beneath it.

Tried to picture herself in the same getup, failed.

"You know why they're here?" The principle asked.

She could guess, but Cassidy hoped instead for a miracle.

"Your husband," began the one on the left, sounding as apologetic as the principal looked, "sent us a message this morning, including some photos of a damaged vehicle. He said you damaged the car and claimed you've been hiding your anomaly abilities." The Paragon leveled his look at Cassidy. "There will be no consequences if you tell us the truth, Mrs.—"

The principle's office door opened again, loud enough this time for Cassidy to jump. She turned, saw someone she didn't expect, someone that didn't belong.

No Champion came for her. Not this early, at least. The memory fuzzed, the dream turning lucid as Cassidy tried to reconcile with Apinya, the Champion she'd come to know in Thailand, standing there. The Champion wore the nondescript white gown Cassidy had seen on other Ziran captives, but otherwise seemed no different. Apinya, for his part, fed her his trademark infuriating, endlessly patient grin.

"So this is where it all began," Apinya said, nodding past Cassidy to the two Paragons. "A discussion in an office creates the Void, and she, in turn, saves the very things she hates."

"Saves?" Cassidy asked.

Apinya waved a hand and the office disappeared, replaced with an island shore. Crashing waves, palm trees, salty brine on the air. The sand felt warm on her bare feet, grains tickling her toes. Blue sky, no clouds, the sun somewhere behind her.

"Take a deep breath, Cassidy," Apinya said, standing next to her. "Then I'm going to need you to wake up. There's much left to be done."

"I thought I would die," Cassidy replied. "That void should've burned me up."

"Perhaps, but if there is one time to push yourself, it's when you're surrounded by anomalies." Apinya laughed, light. "They will always surprise you."

CASSIDY'S EYES snapped open in the dirt. Her body ached, sweat pooled in her drenched clothes, and Cassidy would've done anything for some water. Instead, she saw a face covered with a Ziran visor, felt an armored hand on her shoulder.

"She's awake," the guard said to someone Cassidy couldn't see. "What now, sir?"

"Help her up, if you would be so kind," Apinya's voice, not quite the clear and calm speaker he'd been in Cassidy's mind. Out here he came through hoarse, soft.

Apinya's words rose over the continued fighting, screams, the velvet roars as drone jets kicked their machine bodies into the air. Cassidy smelled blood, the rich iron, on her tongue. Felt the guard take her shoulder and slowly, gently, ease the anomaly up onto her feet. Cassidy's knees buckled, as if the bones weren't quite ready to hold her up, so she leaned on the guard. The man, thankfully, had enough stability to help her without complaint.

Raised up, the battleground made a poor first impression. Cassidy saw the building, the tower, and gaped. Its top third had collapsed, leaving rebar spearing into the sky. Smoke boiled up from inside, its black undulating snake climbing high as drones buzzed the wreckage like bees. Ziran's machines lay out to Cassidy's left as well, corralling anomalies towards the train station in a closing trap marked by gunfire, by dying flashes as the few anomalies with dangerous abilities played them out.

Her gambit, the attempt to kill the leader, had apparently failed.

"Not quite," Apinya said, coming to stand next her. Cassidy didn't see anyone else with the Champion, clad in that same Ziran white robe—this one dirtier, with a blood stain around Apinya's knees—as before. "Your bold stroke set me free and saved several others already working to change this outcome."

"Others?" Cassidy looked back towards the tower. There were bodies in the dirt, yes, but nobody marching their way with victory at hand. "What others?"

"The ones we're going to go assist," Apinya said. "Can you walk?"

"Loosely."

"Then let's go." Apinya turned away from the drones, the anomalies struggling against them. "Time is passing."

The Ziran guard turned Cassidy to follow Apinya, but she resisted. Tried to focus, find some voids. They were there, those little black holes, nudging her fingertips, but quietly. A tickle, not an urge. That last one must've about killed her and, for once, Cassidy's voids seemed to be showing a little restraint.

"You're abandoning them?" Cassidy said, pushing off the guard. This time, her knees held, though repeated twinges cautioned against testing them much further. "The anomalies over there?"

"We'll help them more this way if we hurry," Apinya said. "You can throw yourself back into those drones and see how long you survive, but it would be such a waste if you did."

Apinya's disappointment with the idea cast a chilling

pall over Cassidy. Marching towards those drones felt, now, like the dumbest thought in the world. She'd be shot dead in seconds, never giving her a chance to see her family, to witness whether this whole grand mess would up-end the world.

A waste, indeed.

Cassidy, Apinya, and the guard had nearly reached the tower before the Void realized what she was doing, where they were going. Her feet moved without her active consent, shuffling along with Apinya while Cassidy struggled to get her head right. That dream had been so real: that office, those Paragons.

She'd left that office a prisoner, devastated and about to lose a decade and more.

"We're here," Apinya announced.

As the Champion spoke, the horrors dipped away from Cassidy's mind, a veil being dropped. The intrusion made clear.

"You bastard," Cassidy hissed, shaking her head. "Don't enter my mind again."

"Then don't give me a reason to," Apinya nodded to the guard holding Cassidy. "This poor man decided I should be dead. I'm not sure he'll ever think for himself again."

The Ziran guard stared, lost and numb. Cassidy clenched her fists.

"See, this is exactly the problem with the Paragons," Cassidy started, only for Apinya to lift a single finger and point it past her.

Cassidy's voice trailed off as she finished the line, calling the Champions the worst of the worse.

Coming out from the damaged tower's lobby was a strange collection. Three Ziran guards holding up a woman Cassidy recognized, one of Ziran's higher-ups whose fashionable clothes hadn't reacted well to a building falling apart around her. Behind them, equally battered but standing on their own power, came two others Cassidy couldn't place. They held guns of their own pointed at the Ziran guards and their backs.

"Calvin, Kat," Apinya said as the group approached. "I'd like you to meet Cassidy, the woman who blew a building out from beneath you."

"No offense, Apinya," Kat, a young woman on the left who looked real comfortable holding that gun, and who seemed to be wearing some sort of weird armor herself, said, "but there's a big fight going on over there that I feel we could stop."

"Agreed," Calvin said. "We got Adriana here." Calvin waved his gun at the Ziran guards. "You three hold her nice and steady. No fast moves. We're almost done."

At least these two had the right idea. Adriana, though, didn't look all that up to the task. A gash cut across her forehead, one of her arms hung at an odd angle. The Ziran guards didn't look much better, their armor battered and broken. Visors cracked.

"As you say." Apinya stepped over to Adriana, put a hand on that hurt forehead.

Adriana's eyes snapped open, their focus falling to the Tama on her wrist. The devices were nigh indestructible, and this one powered on as soon as it caught Adriana staring. Cassidy couldn't see the screen as Adriana held it near her face, but the woman winced, groaned as she tried to move her broken right arm to tap the screen. Apinya kept his palm on her forehead, like some somber nurse.

The three Ziran guards did as Calvin ordered and kept still. Apinya's own bodyguard did likewise. Kat and Calvin, bruised and bloodied themselves, settled for keeping their weapons ready.

"Cassidy, would you assist her?" Apinya asked. "Adriana, please tell Cassidy the steps."

Feeling a little like a teacher coming to assist a faltering student, Cassidy wedged her way into Adriana's space. As she did, Cassidy heard Adriana's whispers. Barely beating the breeze in their sound, Cassidy caught the weak missives and obeyed them, selecting a Ziran application on the woman's Tama and tapping in her code.

The first command made sense, an order recalling all the drones in the area back to the Factory. Stamped with Adriana's signature, the directive beamed out quick. The drones encircling the anomalies froze, then jetted up into the air. Tracker drones slithered away, angling south while gladiators and suppressors, those annoying orbs, flew off. Some anomalies took parting shots, scored hits the drones ignored.

The remaining Ziran guards, left without their mechanized protectors, made the right call: weapons fell, cheers rose.

"Wasn't so hard," Kat said. "Only had to bring down a building to win."

"You didn't live here for months," Calvin replied. "It was plenty damn hard."

Cassidy thought about chiming in with a quip about living in a Paragon prison for years, but Adriana started speaking again. This time Cassidy picked up the process as she swiped and typed: Adriana had Cassidy pulling in all the lab's data stored within Ziran's servers. All those tests, all those experiments, batching it all together in one big blob.

"Delete it all," Adriana said.

Cassidy paused, hand hovering over the Tama screen. Delete it all? Cassidy wasn't exactly a cop, but all these names, all these sacrifices over months of poking and prodding to see what a potential cure might be to the anomaly condition seemed like evidence.

"You heard her," Apinya spoke soft. "Delete the data."

"Why?" Cassidy asked. "This proves she's a criminal, this proves all the awful—"

"If she found something in there," Apinya interrupted, "something that could be used to create or sterilize anomalies, then releasing it into the world would do a far greater harm. Anomalies should be miracles, not products."

Kat coughed, exaggerated. Waggled her weapon Apinya's way, a motion Cassidy caught from her eye's periphery.

"See where you're coming from, Apinya, but I'm gonna have to disagree with you there," Kat said. "Don't know if you've been paying much attention lately, but seems to me that a whole lotta conflict could be resolved if we removed the mystery." Kat nodded towards Calvin. "Nobody's going to stick him in a lab like this again if we make the data public. And, speaking personally, the closer we get to turning off those anomaly bombs before they blow, the better."

"The old ways are over, man," Calvin added.

Apinya considered the pair, a scrutiny dwindling to quiet appreciation. The Champion drew in a long breath. Cassidy felt the nudge on her mind, a whisper telling her that deleting the data made the most sense, that the status quo would be the ideal, disappear. Like bursting from under the water, the world felt sharper, her sense, her thoughts all her own.

"Aegis said he planned to retire before all this fell apart," Apinya said. "Perhaps it is time to step away."

"Good idea," Kat said. "Now, what the hell are we doing here?"

Nobody had a great answer. Cassidy had been the last

of them to interact with Aegis and the other planning Paragons, but they'd kept her in the dark. Apinya had gone straight from the crashed jet to Adriana's lab prison, while Kat and Calvin never had a clue.

With the Champion keeping all the Ziran guards locked in mental stasis, the group rejoined the freed anomalies. The powered bunch took advantage of the fleeing drones to dump Ziran's remaining personnel into the old pens. Other anomalies went into the rubble to loot medical supplies, food and water for whomever wanted it.

To Cassidy, it felt a little like the towns on Mynx's island. Ad hoc camps with limited resources, everyone piecing together a life in circumstances they couldn't have imagined. Dusty, dirty, but hope lingered as conversations sprang up. Attention turned to the train station, to the closest town.

Avoiding Ziran once they returned to society.

Cassidy had a scavenged water bottle and an energy bar—Kat claimed the things sucked, but Cassidy's grumbling stomach wasn't going to be picky—when a new anomaly appeared from nowhere. Cassidy recognized the Paragon on sight, had seen the woman back in Thailand.

Back then, she'd been secretive, trying to get Apinya's band onto a jet to Pacifica. Now she ran towards the Champion and the anomaly crowd. Shouting something about an assault, about needing every anomaly that could fight to come with her to the Factory.

Thane's plan, the one that Celice wouldn't pass along. Send Cassidy up here to break out some anomalies?

Ridiculous.

"Isn't that where you just sent all those drones?" Kat asked Apinya, interrupting Cassidy's thoughts, as they stood to greet the Paragon.

"I thought I would buy us time to get away," Apinya

mused, one long, weathered finger on his chin. "It appears I was wrong."

"A Champion admitting a mistake?" Cassidy said. "I never thought I'd live to see the day."

"You might not live to see another if we don't go right away," the wind-running Paragon said, holding out her hands. "The wind's blowing hard today. If we get going, we won't be far behind."

"Then what're we waiting for?" Kat asked, looking at the assembled, battle-hardened anomalies. "Let's go break some drones."

TWENTY-FIVE

Claws and Maws

THE FACTORY BECAME A HATED NECESSITY. Mynx proposed it after the Champions had cemented their world conquest only to find ruling billions with a few million anomalies difficult. The choices were stark: either recruit normals—something the Paragons wound up doing anyway, albeit in more standard police roles—or supplement their anomalies with mechanical armies.

Aegis watched the first drones accompany his Paragons on patrols and missions. At first Mynx kept them passive, delivering observations to Paragons on the ground or reporting crimes in the offing so Paragons could catch those responsible. From there it became a math problem: two Paragons supported by drones could be as effective as five.

Then ten.

Then twenty.

Soon, they didn't need the Paragons doing the patrols, the minor work at all. The drones gained power and with that power came new concerns. Villains, anomalies and normals with big dreams and bad ambitions took over the early factories, ones run by manufacturing staples from pre-Paragon days. After too many crises brought about by would-be kings declaring some robotic revolution, Mynx moved the drones in-house.

Built this damn place and kept it all to herself.

"Could've used a few more windows, Mynx," Aegis muttered as the lift descended towards the Factory's main floor.

The lift cruised at a slow speed meant for lumbering metal, giving Aegis time to catch the drones, the defenses coming to life around the Paragons up above. While the drones already inside the Factory came in haphazard waves as Ziran techs activated them in a supposed panic, the turrets offered more efficient firepower.

The knife-like cannons popped from slits and spat lightning. Mynx hadn't designed the Factory for a human incursion so much as a machine uprising, so bright circuit-frying flashes spat out instead of bullets. Aegis hadn't been struck by the shots before, but given the pain coming through his earpiece, it wasn't pleasant.

Paragons hit back at the turrets as fast as they could, shrapnel raining down around Aegis. The metal pieces hit the shiny black floor, bounced off drone armor, and provided cover for the tracker drones seeking to ambush the Paragon's premier Champion.

Four centipede-like machines scrambled over the edges around Aegis. The lift offered a four-by-four meter-wide slab, bordered by a black-and-yellow line. Aegis planted himself in the middle, pacing around on loose heels, waiting to see which drone would make the first move.

"C'mon, cowards," Aegis said. "Once this lift hits bottom, I'm gone."

The drones rose like cobras, standing on their hind claws and clicking their mandibles at Aegis. An odd technique, and not one Aegis recognized. Defenders had the advantage when they could predict the attack, and this bunch wasn't making it hard.

A fifth drone hit Aegis's shoulders from above, driving him to the lift's deck. The tracker's claws bit into Aegis's vest, and he heard the other four start their skittering pounces. Soon they'd be clawing into him from all sides.

Not good.

Aegis threw his left elbow back, bouncing it off the tracker drone's metal face. With the added space, Aegis punched that same elbow forward, planting his palm on the lift and pushing. Aegis rolled, taking the drone slicing up his back and crushing it beneath him. The machine's four friends didn't seem to mind Aegis's belly getting exposed, their dicing claws gunning for Aegis's abdomen.

They might've hit too if Aegis hadn't been practicing his crunches. Bringing up his knees—collecting some nasty scratches on the way—Aegis curled into a reverse somersault, putting his palms down behind his head to roll off the crushed drone and buy himself some room.

His opponents, tireless and hungry, swiveled with the move and pursued. The foursome swarmed as Aegis backed up to the lift's edge. The Champion didn't have any weapons, much less time to draw them if he did. His fists wouldn't do much good against these steel creations either.

So Aegis cheated and jumped.

The lift had a good ten meters to go until the main floor, but compared to the plunge from the gladiator drone minutes ago, that felt like a bunny hop. Aegis rolled as he hit the spacious level, kept open for drone weapon demonstrations. Around him, the main floor's sides gave way to testing grounds, big arenas carved into the hills around the Factory so Mynx could test her creations without causing civilian fuss.

Aegis's real target lay behind him, a nondescript patch on the side left for a smaller lift going to the Factory's true basement. As Aegis turned towards it, the four remaining tracker drones dropped down, clacking his way across the floor. He couldn't outrun them, but here, with all this space, the calculus changed.

"Dad?" Celice's voice popped over the earpiece.

"I'm busy."

Aegis feinted left, kicked off right. He played an angles game, hoping he'd get to one drone just a bit faster than the others would catch him. The feint bought him enough hesitation, the drone algorithms doing some dance to figure where the human might be going. Turned out, he went for the one on the farthest right, the bug-like things twitching to track his new trajectory.

"We're getting trapped," Celice spoke as gunshots sounded around her, mixed in with curses. "There's more drones coming in from the outside. Too many. We need help."

Aegis reached the drone, had a second till the others caught up. The metal monster snapped at him, mandibles cutting for his throat. Aegis blocked the strike with his left arm while batting with his right. The force sent the drone rolling towards its friends. The other three trackers scurried over their pal, the delay giving Aegis time to break into a run.

As he did, Aegis told his Tama to change his communications channel.

"Thane?" Aegis asked.

A wordless roar filtered through in response.

Three seconds till the tracker drones caught up with him. Five seconds till Aegis reached the elevator.

"Get your ass back here and help my daughter," Aegis said. "You owe her that much."

Thane made random growls in reply, like a radio flip-ping frequencies.

Before Aegis could choose which insult to send Thane's way, something pulled his left leg. Aegis rolled forward with the fall, a somersault ending when two more talons speared his ankles. The Champion's momentum freed him from the drone's grasp but landed him on his back, staring down a clattering trio with their fourth not far behind.

Over a fighting life, Aegis had experienced more and different pain than most people could imagine. He'd been shot, punched, stabbed, and shocked. Burned and beaten. Dropped from heights and bitten by dogs, hyenas, and one particularly ornery donkey. On that long list, two knife-like strikes from the tracker drones didn't scale all that high.

"Switch back to squad general," Aegis said, keeping his voice even. Two drones rushed his legs while the third split to the right, angling for Aegis's head. His Tama chimed, the switch made. Aegis kicked hard at the drones as he scooted back with his hands. "Cover fire Factory floor!"

The command came off as desperate, the words almost unbelievable. Since the Champions split all too long ago, Aegis far preferred to run his missions solo. That way he didn't have to rescue anyone, didn't have to depend on anyone to get their job done.

And look at where that took him?

A world where his greatest allies ignored each other. All those former Champions, the ones who'd fought with him to build the Paragon future, stuck in their own regions fighting for their lives. Not together, not unified.

So many mistakes.

Aegis scooted his legs beneath him as the tracker drones lunged again. The shift saved him bites from the trailing two, but the third, the one going for Aegis's neck, came in a flying leap from his right. Aegis turned, brought up his arms to cover his face as the claws, already wet with his blood, came slashing in.

No bullets came. Aegis's call for help blended into a channel already crammed with similar pleas. Garbled yells for assistance, Zhan-Yo's sharp commands ordering this or that group to advance, Particle's target call-outs.

Aegis caught the tracker drone's claws on his wrists, felt them bite in deep. Stared into those gnashing silver blades in the tracker's mouth, made to break through the thickest anomaly skin and deposit, if possible, a tracer.

Instead, the reflection on all that metal gave Aegis an idea.

Whipping his arms out wide, Aegis crossed the claws over one another, the edge not biting into his skin serving to sever the claws from the tracker's body. Its leverage lost, the drone fell to Aegis's feet, already scrabbling towards the Champion's calves. A second drone took its own leap, a flash picked out in Aegis's periphery.

Feeling those claws stabbing in, Aegis punched down with his left arm, angling the swing so the claw's broken end, sticking out from his wrist, served as a jagged spear. At the same time, like some horrifying yoga pose, Aegis swung up his right arm, bringing that sharp edge up where his head ought to be.

The drone at his feet found itself with a new hole through its steel skull. Aegis's piercing shot drove the machine into the ground, sparks flying. The drone's remaining claws still tried to push the machine forward and Aegis would've repeated his shot except his right arm jerked, then pulled the Champion's whole body in a muscle-wrenching twist.

He'd caught a drone, hooked it on his arm. The torque launched him around, pulling Aegis down to his right side. Yanked free from its strike, Aegis felt his left arm pull along the ground, flashing a silver line as it scarred the black metal tile. The third drone followed its friends—did drones have friends? Did Mynx put that in?—and snatched at Aegis's feet.

Hitting the tile had an unexpected benefit: the bounce kicked Aegis's right arm free. The drone's claw still had its hold in Aegis's right wrist, though it came off bearing snagged wires, soaked in coolant. Electric shocks burned the Champion as the hook tore through the drone's middle. Aegis twisted as he fell, bringing his clawed arms across his body as his back hit the ground.

The third drone copied its earlier partner, diving in at Aegis's face. His wrists caught the drone on either side, capturing the writhing machine and locking it in the air. The machine extended, mandibles slicing down towards Aegis.

The EMP round struck, blue lightning arcing around the drone and settling it into a dead heap. Leftover jolts ran down the claws, zapping Aegis's arms and setting his hair up into a spike. His Tama chirped in protest, a static roar came over Aegis's earpiece.

"Want me to leave the last one for you?" Particle said as the roar died.

"No," Aegis said.

"Done."

Another EMP round flashed. Aegis couldn't see where it hit, but the drone must've been moving fast, because its dead body collided with Aegis's feet.

"What took you so long?" Aegis said, throwing the downed drone to the side.

His vision snapped up of its own accord, Particle forcing the Champion to see the Factory's upper levels. The clean look that'd been present every other time had vanished. Smoking ceiling panes told of turrets destroyed.

Suppressor drones hovered, firing stunning darts and worse at Paragons Aegis couldn't see. Two gladiators stood tall, their clawed feet firing jets to let them hover in place.

The only sound carrying over the screams, the called orders? A particular roar, one Aegis knew well. Closer now than after Thane's initial charge away.

Maybe the monster heard Aegis's call.

Maybe.

Aegis turned away from Particle's control, looked past the littered drones around him. For the moment, at least, the fighting up above left him alone. Nothing stood between him and the lift, and what lay at the bottom.

Zhan-Yo had his key, some code that would disable the drones until Ziran figured out a way around the block. Mynx would be the only end, the last chance to knock her own mechanized creations out for good.

Not that Aegis knew how Mynx would do that, but he had to hope, had to believe. If Mynx couldn't prove the key to the drones she'd created, then Aegis would have to destroy every last one. If Wexley gave up and left the machines disabled, great.

But wishing for that, depending on that, was a leap too far.

The lift had no Tama scanner, Mynx apparently believed the Factory's external security was good enough and Wexley concurred. Sometimes folly worked out in Aegis's favor, and he slapped the call button.

"Status?" Aegis said, speaking into the earpiece. "I'm at the lift, will be reaching Mynx soon."

"We hold the entrance," Zhan-Yo came in next, a dead tone. "For how long is uncertain. Hurry."

"We are hurrying," Celice said, gunfire and Thane's howling roar coming through strong. "Thane's bashing through everything, but I don't think Mynx is gonna like what he's done to her home."

"If we make it through this, I'll pay for the fixes myself," Aegis said.

The lift door dinged, slid open. The Champion backed into it, resisting the urge to look up one more time into the fighting above. It felt bad enough to hit the button for the Factory's basement, bad enough to leave friends and family holding the ground against an endless enemy.

It would feel worse to lose them all for nothing.

On The Hunt

KAT HIT CALVIN, who struck the ground first. The anomaly *bounced* off the rough, debris strewn grass, only for Kat to drive him back into the dirt. She rolled in the moment, instinct taking over as her bones, muscles crunched. Getting off of Calvin, momentum still throwing her down, Kat hit a pillow. An invisible pillow that sent her gently onto the saffron grass.

Looking up, glass and breaking beams rained down. They bent, flowed along around Kat, around Calvin as if hitting a roof. If not for the whole risk of death thing, Kat might've found the disintegration beautiful, the rubble spreading like industrial snowflakes as it crashed against the anomaly barrier.

"Calvin, tell me that's you," Kat said.

"Me," Calvin gasped.

"Sorry I crushed you."

"It's," another gasp, "fine."

Kat rolled to her right, looked at Calvin buried in the grass amid the wreckage. Beneath her, the earth rumbled as the tower, cut in half, settled. Calls for help rose up as the cracking, snarling collapse died, the dust falling. The night sky came through, stars littering the black in a way Kat hadn't seen since, well, since she'd done that late night trek through the snow after that rogue anomaly, the illusionist.

"You still alive over there?" Kat asked.

She could hear Calvin breathing or she might've been a little more alarmed. Most anomaly abilities took their energy away like running a sprint, so the guy might need a minute. Then again, she could use a minute herself.

Things had gone real weird over the last couple days.

Kat preferred introspection over a drink, preferably several. With a bartender serving as a well-tipped ear, she could spill out her concerns to someone she knew wouldn't give a crap after the night ended, someone who would, if nothing else, offer unfiltered advice.

Calvin groaned a reply.

"You know," Kat said. "I haven't had much luck with relationships, but since I've met you, I've nearly died several times. Had a bullet shot through my stomach. Had a milkshake while tied to a chair . . ."

"What?" Calvin coughed. "A milkshake?"

A hundred drones or more lingered beyond the tower's remnants. Surviving Ziran guards might be picking their way through the wreckage looking for survivors. Anomalies hellbent on destroying both and anything caught in the middle might be unleashing devastation.

All that was true, but for a minute, maybe ten, Kat just wanted to talk. Look at the stars. Breathe. Revel in being alive because, holy hell, it seemed like her lucky breaks would have to run out soon.

She told Calvin about trying to find him. About how she spent months tearing Chicago apart looking for any sign. She'd kidnapped, interrogated her way up the Ziran tree. Waited at bars where employees hung out and took the loners. All said they never heard of the anomaly, didn't know where Ziran might be taking them. Until . . .

"Gordon found me?" Calvin stretched out a hand, caught Kat's. "That dude. Coming through in the clutch."

"Almost killed him," Kat replied. "You owe him a beer when we get back."

"Done."

Kat smiled, felt the grass in her hair. "How'd you do it? Keep us alive?"

"Pushed air from one side to the other. Big pocket, like running into a wind tunnel." Calvin sighed. "Used to do that more when I was a kid. Jump off buildings for fun."

"Your childhood was weird."

"Says the girl that—" Calvin cut himself off. "Never-mind. Don't wanna go there."

The anomaly didn't have to. Rustling in the grass drew their attention, particularly when that rustle resolved itself into a battered Ziran guard. The man held a gun, aimed it down at the pair.

"Surrender," the guard said.

Kat glanced right, caught Calvin's little smile, how the anomaly had his right hand pointing at the guard's ankle.

"Sure," Kat said, and Calvin blew the man's leg out from under him.

Curling back, Kat disarmed the guard, taking up the gun and feeling her way around the trigger. Looking away from the stars gave a grim scene, with scattered bodies, broken drones, and debris burning holes in the landscape. One group caught her eye, a duo helping a woman to her feet. They weren't paying attention to Kat, to Calvin.

"Think that might be our ticket," Kat said as the anomaly stood up next to her. "Ready?"

"Never," Calvin replied. "Let's go."

. . .

NOW KAT HAD Calvin's hand again. They'd traded the stars for a collective, a few dozen anomalies with useful powers and enough stamina to keep on rolling. They'd all formed a circle, the new Paragon at one end closing her eyes and launching into a countdown. The wind the Paragon seemed to want picked up, rippling through the crowd. Behind the whole bunch, those anomalies too hurt or useless in a fight grouped up near the train station. A few brave ones continued in-and-out expeditions into the tower for supplies.

Whether Ziran would keep to a normal train schedule in this disaster seemed doubtful, but Kat wasn't going to waste too time much worrying about the refugees. She'd just met her first Champion, Apinya, and he'd walked out of legend to draft the tracker.

Kat might be cynical, but she couldn't say no to that.

Flying in a plane had nothing to literally *being* the wind. One blink, Kat had her feet on the ground. The next she'd disappeared, her body, her mind soaring up into the sky above the Ziran camp. She saw the tents, the tarps all torn down. The tower, its ruin smoldering, shrank against cliff-side hills.

The breeze carried Kat out over the ocean. Waves sparkled silver beneath the rising moon on a cloudless night. The direction and its Pacific ocean destination prompted a wonder whether the anomaly had full control over the wind she'd sucked them all into, but it was hard to get all that worried.

Maybe Kat and Calvin could ride the gust all the way out to Hawaii. They could enjoy some beachside cocktails, check back in when the Champions had finished saving the world. Or, if the battle went sideways, hide out in a lovely jungle shack. The grapple on her wrist might work real well for spear-fishing . . .

A gentle sway pushed Kat—and the others? Kat couldn't see anyone else, so she had to assume—south. LA's vast metropolis already conquered the horizon that way, its brighter, lifeless glow washing out the moonlight. The hills had their beauty though. Trees and canyons with the coastal highway weaving, pod lights forming moving specks.

Hawaii's daydream prompted another, bigger question. If Kat and Calvin survived, what would happen next? Not so much for the world at large—Kat figured the people making those decisions wouldn't include a tracker and a random low-level Paragon—but for her, for him. And Seeker, of course, stuck back in Chicago and no doubt wondering where everyone had gone.

First, she wouldn't change a thing. Keep her apartment until Kat saw where things would fall out. See if tracking stayed a job that existed. What her rep outlook might be. Calvin might take her out to dinner once or twice. To a baseball game. They'd see fights at *Carver's*. See if there was anything to the two of them beyond crisis intervention.

And if there was, well, Kat wouldn't be making that decision and the ones that came after alone. For the first time in a long time.

The thought wasn't as scary as Kat expected: compared to killer drones and monstrous companies, having to work with someone else didn't seem so bad.

The breeze picked up speed as it descended all too fast, swooping into another groove. This one led to a dominating concrete and solar-paneled structure. Vast sharp angles rose from the earth and Kat weaved around them without any effort.

Now she saw the drones. All the machines that'd fled

the camp landing, deploying into what Kat figured was the Factory. A mechanized horde crashing through massive open doors. The wind swirled in the entry, giving view to a desperate fight inside. Paragons, normals, firing and getting fried as they stood behind makeshift drone-body bulwarks inside that entrance.

From a wind-blown, body-less perspective, the combat looked like a movie. From Kat's more rational side, the battle looked like a place she really, really didn't belong.

The Paragon dropped them in anyway.

Thirty-some anomalies and one harried tracker filled in physical space amid chaos. Kat flung herself into a dive as soon as her feet hit the Factory's once-smooth, now dirt and dust and blood-coated tile. Anomalies hit the ground around her, struck by drones and their precision targeting as soon as they emerged. Others leaned into their abilities, Kat's ears and eyes shocked into ringing, half-blinded disaster as genetic mutations bent physical laws.

She crawled on her elbows. Ahead, smeared in her vision, Kat saw the Paragon line holding past the entry. The wind runner, whatever her name, had gone for shock and awe by dropping the new arrivals amidst the drones. Great for some anomalies, maybe, but not for her.

She had to get out.

Now.

Something grabbed her foot, pulled. Kat kicked, shook the reaching grasp. When the hand returned with a two-timed slap, Kat gave up her crawl to look back. Her left wrist and its ever-ready grapple were ready, while her right hand slipped to her waist holster, the Ziran gun she'd stolen occupying a slot in her makeshift armada.

Calvin looked up at her, the man and his shredded lab robe somehow more battered in the seconds since they'd been dropped. The anomaly's mouth moved but Kat couldn't hear a damn thing.

She could grab his hand.

Together they crawled to the anomaly line, denoted by a fluctuating, flimsy barrier that seemed to slow incoming projectiles as they passed through the Factory's loading dock doors. As Kat went through it, she felt her own pace go sluggish for a long second, as if she swam in honey.

"Get back and get out of the way," a sharp voice demanded.

Kat caught its owner, did a double take. That was freaking Zhan-Yo, wanted terrorist and the guy who started all this. What the hell was he doing here, helping the Paragons? The world's most wanted man didn't take offense at Kat's gaping face, instead using two commandos and their covering fire to slip through and yank Kat, and by extension, Calvin behind drone body cover.

Zhan-Yo took zero time to brief them, turning away from his rescued pair to head back to the front. Kat watched, noticed the man didn't have a weapon. Instead, Zhan-Yo focused on calling shots, directing the forces. A CEO turned battlefield general.

"You all right?" Calvin shouted in her ear, words that barely made it over her shell-shocked hearing.

"No!"

Kat wanted to curl up, wanted to dive off the upper floor they were on and hide somewhere in the Factory's deepest rooms. She wanted Seeker too, his barking, happy energy to bring her back to Earth.

Instead Kat was in the middle of a struggle with stakes larger than she'd ever cared to be a part of. Winning and losing meant more than reps, than tracing another rogue anomaly. Hell, it meant giving those anomalies Kat had traced a chance at a better life. Those horrifying machines, marching through delivering death on a whim . . .

Calvin stood, put a set look on his face, "I'm going in!"

Kat grabbed his arm, used it to pull herself up. A commando three meters away from them vanished as a drone-fired rocket struck home, heat singing Kat's eyebrows. Behind the flash, more gladiators stomped towards the barrier, more suppression drones hovered in the eaves. Far too many.

"We have to stop the source!" Kat shouted. "Not the drones, the hand behind them!"

Calvin looked confused as Kat pushed him down the Paragon line, off to the side of the hallway. Zhan-Yo, behind them, called for others to come forward and fill the gap. Someone moved in, another near-certain death.

One Kat might be able to prevent if they could get to Wexley in time.

All day Kat had been dealing with situations she decidedly *wasn't* trained for. All out brawls with drones? Falling buildings? Flying through the air in a blend with the wind itself?

Not exactly in the tracker handbook.

But finding someone in unfamiliar environments? That, Kat could do. The analysis ran quick as Calvin asked the tracker where Wexley could be, how they could find him in the Factory. The place had floors to spare, vast caverns lined with drones waiting to spring out like some horror creature and dice them up. Wexley might be deep inside the place, sitting in a secure room and waiting for the drones to finish their bloody jobs.

"Except he didn't know," Kat said as she kept moving away from the loading dock doors. Not towards the Factory's big lift, already on the bottom floor and well away, but rather the main hallway leading from the Factory's core.

"The Paragon's wouldn't have made it in here if Wexley had time to prepare."

"So he's surprised?" Calvin nudged Kat right, against the railing looking over the Factory's spacious center, as several more commandos headed back the opposite direction to reinforce the front line. "Wouldn't he still be, like, in the offices? Somewhere in here?"

They hit a branch, the Factory walkway splitting off. From the route on their right came nasty sounds, gunfire cloaked by nigh-constant roars. As if some giant tiger had been unleashed. That way looked like it headed deeper into the Factory, but Kat hesitated.

"Hear that?" Kat said. "We've got people down there already fighting. If Wexley was that way, we'd know. We'd probably abandon this door and go all in on the guy."

Straight ahead, though, came relative calm. The walls bore bangs and scratches, as if something big had rampaged that direction and then, if Kat could read the markings right in the fluorescent blue-white lighting, had come back. Odd, but the quiet pulled at her.

"So you wanna go where nothing's happening?" Calvin said, throwing Kat a skeptical look. "I get wanting to stay alive, Kat, but even I'm not this much of a coward."

"Then you can stay here, or you can follow me," Kat replied, pushing past the anomaly and breaking into a run. "If I caught you, I can catch this guy."

Mynx used to brief all the trackers a few times a year. Big video sessions Kat would click into from her Chicago apartment. Every time, Mynx joined from an idyllic ocean overlook. She said it was her home, and everyone knew Mynx lived at the Factory. Coming in on the breeze gave a clear lay of the Factory's land, including where the ocean sat relative to the loading dock doors.

In other words, the quiet hallway should lead right to

Mynx's residence. And, if Wexley took Mynx's home as his own, where else would he be during a dinner time attack?

Calvin caught up to Kat as the hallway turned into an upward stair, one ending in a closed, more normal door. Slate gray, with a golden Paragon P etched into its center. One big dent in that P showcased someone's only attempted entry.

The two stared at the door as Kat relayed her thinking to Calvin. The anomaly didn't argue this time, didn't do anything more than shrug.

"We're here, and it beats getting shot at," Calvin said. "Let's get in."

"That's the thing," Kat replied. "I don't see a Tama scanner."

"Mynx probably doing something fancy. I got it, though. Cover me."

The anomaly stepped forward, put his left hand on the door. He stuck his right hand out behind him, and Kat moved away when gray and gold globs began spraying from Calvin's fingertips like a cement firehose. The liquid sprayed down the steps, hitting and hardening in an instant. More interesting, though, was the door: where Calvin had his left hand, a widening concave scoop expanded, pushing through to the other side after a few seconds.

"You work fast," Kat said, drawing her gun and aiming it through the widening hole.

"Goes quick when I'm not trying to do anything with the material," Calvin replied, sliding his left hand along the hole's edge to keep it growing. "Looks downright nice in there."

The Factory's efficient decor died through the door. While Kat wouldn't call the residence homey, softer lighting poked through Calvin's hole first. As it widened,

Kat picked out marble tile leading into an entry with coat hooks, a shoe bench. Lighter spaces on the cream scalloped walls clued in the pair to art pieces gone missing.

Wexley's redecorating still in its early stages.

And no drones to speak of.

"Ready?" Calvin said as the hole hit a big enough size for the two to squeeze through.

"Never," Kat quipped as Calvin backed off from the opening. "Let's go."

The tracker slipped through, the anomaly followed.

Inside, Mynx's home opened up. Past the entry came the kitchen, with the big porch off on the right side and Mynx's bedroom—now Wexley's—off to the left. Inside stairs led to a lower level, one Kat ignored for now, ignored because she saw something on that porch, on the glass table dominating it.

An open wine bottle, white from the looks of it. Holding up a finger to her lips, Kat rolled her feet through the kitchen, aiming the gun towards the deck. Not a soul on it. The sliding door, though, had been left open wide. With Calvin on her heels, Kat stepped through outside, swiveled right and left, saw nobody on the deck.

But down on the beach stood a shadow caught in the house's outside lights. The waves washed up to the man's feet. He had an arm out wide, right where you'd hold a wine glass.

"Well damn," Calvin whispered. "Guess we found him. How do we play this?"

Kat leveled the gun at the shadow. Wanted to pull the trigger, but killing Wexley probably wouldn't stop all those drones from slaughtering the Paragons. They needed the man alive, afraid, and willing to surrender.

"Hit him hard, fast," Kat replied. "Don't let him call anyone unless it's to stop those drones. Try not to kill him."

"Easy."

Kat nodded, though as they started down the steps to the beach, instincts said otherwise. Wexley had the world in his iron grip.

They would have to rip it from him.

TWENTY-SEVEN

Transmission

LOB BOUNCED from floor to floor, pausing at each stop only to set his feet, squat, and leap to the next one. For a man who didn't look like he lived in the weight room, Lob nevertheless didn't seem to give a damn that he carried Rhimes, no small person himself, and Regina, more compact but still not a twig. Only when Lob hit the second highest floor—Ziran reserved its uppermost level for an observation deck—did he let Regina and Rhimes go with a heavy sigh. With his arms unloaded, Lob staggered over to a nearby chair and collapsed into it.

"You're up," Lob said.

"On it," Rhimes replied, already moving through the lobby towards Zhan-Yo's, no, Wexley's office.

The floor had a simple plan: the central elevator opened into a secured waiting room, a glass wall blazing with an orange Z separating visitors from the office trio on the other side. Ziran's CEO had the biggest one, while flanking spaces on the left and right were reserved for whichever employees the CEO felt had earned them.

Zhan-Yo, according to legend, had once given one

office to the building's housekeeping director as an honor for their hard work. That director had kept the view for a month before giving it up, declaring the elevator rides up and down too much of a hassle. Nonetheless, the point had been made: your title alone didn't give you access to the top.

And Rhimes had no title at all.

Normally, a secretary might sit on the glass's other side, ready to buzz in qualified visitors. Now that desk sat empty, the floor's lights flickering on as Rhimes and Regina moved into the lobby.

"We don't have another machine gun to break this glass," Regina said.

"Don't need it," Rhimes said, grabbing a chair. Lob watched as Rhimes hefted the big, wooden seat and launched it.

The furniture slammed into the glass, driving huge cracks up and down the central pane.

"Really primitive," Regina said, watching as Rhimes drove the chair into the glass again. "True caveman style."

"I'm a simple man."

Rhimes heaved the chair a third time.

The pane shattered, littering the nice tile with shards. Rhimes, waving Regina along, crunched those same shards as they went through. There, ahead, sat Wexley's office. A bold white door with a glass Z etched into the center. No Tama scanner, no security locks.

If you made it this far, the thinking seemed to be, you belonged here.

Rhimes reached for the handle, clicked the door open and swung it wide. Beyond it sat a sparse, huge office. A projector hung from the ceiling's center, ready to blast images up on the floor-to-ceiling windows blanketing the space. Chicago's nightlights showed through now, their glare splashing in against the office's own soft yellow lighting.

The dedicated workstation would be in there, ready to go.

The elevator dinged.

"Go," Rhimes said, letting Regina slide past him into the office. "Find the computer, enter the code."

"Like I know how to do that," Regina said, but she went in.

The elevator swung open, revealing one battered, angry Ziran soldier. She'd lost her big gun in the fighting below, but Brielle still had a close range pistol, and she raised it as she left the elevator. Lob lurched up from his seat, jumping at her, only for Brielle to pivot, fire, and down the anomaly with a quick shot to the man's chest. Groaning, Lob collapsed back into a chair.

"Brielle," Rhimes said, holding his hands up, stepping from the office. "Stop."

"Stop?" Brielle asked, coming forward slow, that pistol unflinching in her hands. "Stop? Is that really what you're saying to me right now?"

"What do you want me to say?"

"I lost a squad down there, Rhimes. Don't know how many are dead, but more than one," Brielle's voice stayed level, no panic, no hysteria. A soldier. "We all came here for you, a traitor, and they won't be going back. So I'd start with an apology."

The lobby and office entrance didn't give Rhimes much to work with. Throwing another chair, diving behind the secretary's desk wouldn't fly with Brielle's crack shooting. Rhimes couldn't turn and run, and Brielle halted her own advance well out of physical range. Any lunging punch, kick, or shoulder charge would be met with a fatal cap.

If he was going to die, then Rhimes might as well buy Regina all the time he could.

"Then I'm sorry," Rhimes said, keeping those hands wide. He didn't look at the gun, but right at Brielle. He was being honest and she had to see that. "I came here alone to keep anyone else from getting hurt."

"Tell that to my team."

"You can. And you can tell them why I'm doing this."

"Because you don't agree with Wexley. Fine. You could've quit."

"That's not who I am," Rhimes replied. "I don't run from what I believe in."

"Oh yeah? What's that, exactly? 'Cause it sure looks to me like you've been chasing reps and nothing else for a long time."

Okay, not a good direction. Rhimes had Brielle talking, which meant she really was curious, really wanted to know why things had gone so wrong. Now he needed to put her on a track that would get her finger off of that trigger.

"I was, I did," Rhimes said. "But first, I was a soldier. I served my country and its causes. When the Paragons took that away from me, I was lost. Ziran hired me in, private security." Rhimes took a breath, saw Brielle hadn't wavered. She hadn't interrupted either. "Wexley's efficient, strong. Zhan-Yo's hopeful, a prophet more than an executive. They both wanted the same thing, but went about it in different ways. When Wexley took control, I followed him because hey, it's fun being on the winning side. Profitable too."

"Until?"

"Until you realize all those reps won't mean anything if we're sitting under a drone's iron eyes all day." Rhimes shook his head. "How long you think you'll have a job,

Brielle? How long until we're all just doing to whatever the machines want us to do?"

"Yeah, well, we had that with the Paragons," Brielle said. "At least this has a chance at being different. Goodbye Rhimes."

Brielle aimed, Rhimes ducked forward. He reached out, knowing he wouldn't get there in time. Brielle pulled the trigger. The gun flashed, the bullet went over Rhimes's shoulder. A miss, and one that let Rhimes tackle Brielle full on. Rhimes drove her to the ground, slamming Brielle's wrist against the carpet and knocking the gun away.

Brielle kneed Rhimes in the stomach, used his flinch away to push out from underneath the man. Rhimes rolled, reached, and found Brielle's pistol with his left hand. His right side exploded in pain as Brielle kicked, forcing Rhimes to protect his head with his right hand while trying to bring the pistol to bear.

His student took Rhimes's defense as an opportunity to swing her right leg around in a slapping kick at Rhimes's left arm, one that numbed his shooting hand and, again, sent the gun skittering across the tile back towards the elevator.

Guess they'd be handling this one with hands and feet.

With his right hand, Rhimes pulled Brielle's left leg, wobbling her off balance as he rose into a head-butting charge, pushing Brielle back into a chair. She fell across, then over the furniture, backing into a roll. Catching against the leftover glass pane, Brielle rose up to her feet just in time to catch a Rhimes shoulder barge.

The two crashed through the weakened glass, landing on the tile beyond with shards raining around them. Rhimes pulled back a fist, saw Brielle's face as the target with cuts running along from the glass and hesitated.

He'd worked with her early on, on a dwindling police

force replacing its least effective officers with drones. She'd found the niche with the long range weapons, picked up the sniper's slack with up close training as a way to keep from being cut. She and Rhimes had sparred plenty in Chicago over the last few years, and while they'd punched and blocked and kicked and flipped on mats around the city, this . . .

Brielle growled, bunched her legs up beneath Rhimes and kicked him off. Rhimes crunched on the glass as he landed, saw Brielle run past him towards the elevator, the gun.

Another shot. Rhimes sat up, saw Brielle stagger back a step. Lob, sitting against the elevator, held the pistol in his hand. The man's aim was low, unsteady, but Brielle's motion made it obvious she'd been hit. Lob lifted the gun again.

"Stop!" Rhimes yelled, standing. "It's over. Don't shoot."

Lob coughed, glassy eyes looking Rhimes's way, shaking his head. Focused on the gun. Rhimes moved, put himself between Brielle, who had her hands cupped around her abdomen, and Lob.

"The body count's high enough as it is," Rhimes said. "Don't, man. Please."

"She's not gonna stop," Lob gasped. "She's gonna keep trying."

Rhimes glanced back at Brielle. Pain etched on a face already going pale. Her eyes went to his and Rhimes didn't see hate there anymore, didn't see a soldier's drive. He saw what he saw in everyone at the end: fear, and loneliness.

"It's over," Rhimes repeated, loud. "She's not going to try anything. Use your Tama, Lob, and get some medical help up here."

Facing Brielle, seeing back behind her, Rhimes

answered a lingering question. No way Brielle would've missed that first point blank shot. No way Rhimes shouldn't be lying in his own blood right now.

Regina filled in the blank.

Wexley's sister sat on the floor in the office entry, one hand on the open white door and the other pressing on a very red, very wet left shoulder. Her head hung low. Rhimes cursed, helped Brielle sit in a chair, then ran on to Regina.

Without her, without that code, none of this mattered.

"Hey," Rhimes said as he kneeled next to Wexley's sister. On a normal mission, loaded out with gear, he'd have aid kits, something that might stop the bleeding or delay shock. Here, with all the haste, he had jack. "You with me?"

"It hurts so much."

"Yeah, getting shot isn't fun." Rhimes winced at the injury. A shot that high shouldn't be fatal, but it all depended on what the bullet did, how Regina reacted. "We gotta focus, Regina. Did you get the code in?"

"Couldn't do it."

"Why?"

"No access."

A variable. Rhimes hadn't forgot about it, exactly, but he'd hoped Regina would have her own way in. Or that Wexley's personal workstation wouldn't have the security. Or that his own access wouldn't be curtailed that fast.

Instead he'd have to improvise.

Rhimes glanced back at Brielle, "Tell me the code, Regina. I'll get it open."

Wexley's sister looked up at Rhimes, pallid, breathing soft, "I tried to take her, to stop her from shooting you, but she's strong. She fought me, wanted to pull that trigger so much.

But she didn't want to kill you, Rhimes. That's why I moved the aim." Regina shivered, Rhimes hand on her uninjured shoulder. "I don't want anyone else getting hurt like this."

Regina said the code, a date and name mixture that meant nothing to Rhimes. He repeated it, Regina nodded to confirm, and Rhimes wheeled, dashed to Brielle. At the room's end, the elevator sped away down. Either for medical, reinforcements, or enemies. Rhimes couldn't wait for any.

Lob looked like he'd passed out. Or died.

"C'mon," Rhimes said, lifting Brielle. She shouted, then bit off the cry, burying her head into Rhimes's shoulder. "I know it hurts, but I need your Tama."

Brielle didn't struggle, let Rhimes carry her over Regina and into Wexley's office. As he moved, Rhimes felt warm sticky blood run over his own shirt. She'd been hit bad, with maybe minutes before things progressed too far to save. He'd try nonetheless.

In the office, Rhimes beelined to the left where Regina had the terminal up and running on Wexley's desk. The screen flashed a login requirement, waiting for a Tama to scan.

"Just need to borrow your left arm for a second," Rhimes said, settling Brielle into the white leather chair.

"You're destroying everything you fought so hard for," Brielle whispered, tight and clipped.

"I'm burning it down so something better can grow," Rhimes replied, getting the scanner to chirp.

The terminal unlocked, giving icons aplenty for Rhimes to pick. There was only one that mattered: the emergency beacon, a message that'd go out to all the drones in the area with a response code. Rhimes clicked on it, amplified the area to cover the globe. Most people didn't have access to that kind of broadcast, but Brielle, thanks to Rhimes promoting her up the line, did.

"Wexley," Regina's voice came from the office door as Rhimes set up the broadcast. "I'm sorry, but one of your people shot me."

Rhimes tapped in the code, double-checked the words, the numbers.

"Not her fault," Regina replied. "She was only doing the job you gave her."

He couldn't hear Wexley's reply, didn't want to. The code was set, Rhimes started the send. Looked back at Brielle. She'd folded just like Lob. Rhimes stuck a finger up to her throat, felt a pulse. Weak, but there.

Outside in the lobby the elevator dinged.

"I don't know if I'll be okay," Regina said. "That's why I called you. To say I love you, and I'm sorry."

Ziran's program confirmed the send. Transmission towers would be beaming out the signal across the globe, striking everywhere and sending every drone it found into stasis. Rhimes figured Ziran would, could reactivate them, but in those precious minutes the Paragons would have a chance.

Zhan-Yo would have his chance.

"He hung up," Regina said as Rhimes reached her side. "But not before he said he loved me anyway."

Outside, Rhimes saw Weed carrying a first aid kit, saw that tattooed Elemental along with an emergency medical drone hovering over Lob. The man would add a few more high powered names to his collection now, more strings to pull.

"Your brother got lost, Regina," Rhimes said, tearing off part of his own shirt to press against her wound. "I hope they find him."

"Me too." Regina coughed. "The code? You know what it is?"

Rhimes shook his head.

"My birthday, scrambled. Of all things, Wexley always cared about his family."

Regina leaned back into Rhimes's grip, and the man called out to the medical trio, told them two more needed attention in here. Then he looked right, out past Wexley's desk into the Chicago skyline.

Bright lights once again shining on a changing world.

TWENTY-EIGHT

Damage Control

THE WIND DROPPED Cassidy in the loading dock's middle, her body emerging from the air beneath a gladiator's towering form. Gliding in gave Cassidy a chance to scope out the battle, see the chaos before getting dumped into it, so the moment her fingers returned to feeling, those voids came up ready.

Cassidy threw a dinner plate void straight up, its swirling nexus carving and vaporizing the gladiator's central core. Minor explosions rippled as battery packs lost cohesion, as wires and tubes found themselves missing middles. Lubricants, shards, and heat fell on Cassidy, mashing her hair and getting her very bedraggled outfit coated in grime.

Then again, it'd been coated with dirt and dust a moment before, so c'est la vie.

The drone's meatier components teetered after Cassidy's shot, so she flipped a mental coin and broke towards the Factory's inside. That seemed to be where the anomaly attacks came from, where shouts in a human cadence called. The drones repeated their own orders to surrender amid all the beams, the gunfire, the static shocks, a steady undercurrent of insanity to couple with the moment.

A hand grabbed Cassidy's shoulder as she left the falling gladiator's shadow. A push and Cassidy found herself nestled against the loading dock's side, Apinya crouching next to her. Several stunning darts bounced off the floor where Cassidy had been, would've been without the Champion's intervention. Cassidy followed the trajectory to a floating suppressor drone and flicked another void, feeling sweat bead on her forehead.

The saucer-sized void blazed through the suppressor drone's side, the machine swerving and stabilizing, a perfect target holding still in the air. Three hard rounds crashed into the orb from the Paragon line, bullets shredding the drone's thin skin and sending the ball bombing to the debris-littered floor.

"Thanks for the save," Cassidy said as they both resumed walking towards the Paragon line.

"Likewise," Apinya replied, his head darting fast from their goal to the enemies around them. "These scenes are not my forte."

"No minds to control?"

"No chance to focus even if there were. My place is at the negotiating table, not the battlefield."

On their right, a Paragon looking like a boiling sun charged in at a gladiator. The short man darted around the larger drone's swiping claws, every dance leaving a fiery gout in its wake. The blasts scorched the drone, but didn't seem to do more than irritate the thing. With Apinya pulling her along, Cassidy didn't have a chance to get her voids back up, didn't have a chance to help as the Paragon darted the wrong way.

The flame shot up, the gladiator ignored it, and its

swinging kick caught the Paragon mid-stride. The strike sent the Paragon flying into the air where the gladiator, its gun-toting arms tracking the anomaly, lit it up with too many rounds to survive. By the time the Paragon hit the ground, his fire had already gone out.

"Then why did you come?" Cassidy said, gulping. Flashbacks to the island escape danced behind her eyes, all those drones swarming around their makeshift boat, anomalies dying one by one. "If you can't help—"

"I'm here for Wexley, not for his machines," Apinya said. "We need cover now."

Cassidy knew an order when she heard one. They'd reached the loading dock's end, where the Factory opened into a broad walkway. The Paragon line sat halfway back, drone bodies forming bulwarks for the fighters on the other side. Crossing that walkway meant a meters-long sprint under fire, a trek some managed—Cassidy caught that tracker and her anomaly friend scurrying over on their stomachs—while others died, pinned down by all-too-accurate drone fire.

Feeling the heat grow, Cassidy touched her fingertips together, creating a void several meters across. Other anomalies still fought behind them, teleporting and bashing and slashing amid the oncoming drone force. She couldn't just send a void spinning along the loading dock's width without killing ten or fifteen Paragons in the process.

Though if things swung enough, Cassidy might do it anyway. For the chance to see her family, very little crossed the line.

Instead, she popped the void up, holding it between her, Apinya, and the drones. The few machines bothering with the pair sent rounds, a laser blast, a stunning dart their way. All vanished into the void.

"Let's go before I pass out," Cassidy said. Maintaining

one void only felt like a bad fever, not the dire, hazy crash she'd experienced on the island boat or in Apinya's Bangkok hall. Nonetheless, this fight didn't exactly look like it'd be ending soon. Losing her energy right here, right now, seemed like a quick sprint to the next life. "Now!"

Apinya didn't question Cassidy's command. In a move that lacked the Champion's usual regality, Apinya crouch-ran across the walkway. His Ziran lab robe snagged and ripped on debris, making him look even more like a ragged disaster victim. Cassidy followed, dragging the void behind her.

The Paragon line offered makeshift protection. Walking towards it felt a little like sprinting into a movie scene. Gun-wielding people—who were they?—poked out between piled metal to squeeze off rounds, the bullets zipping over Cassidy's head. Anomalies swapped in whenever the gunners had to reload, putting hands together to send beams, toss blue-glowing grenades, or send gnashing, neon swarms swirling into the mix.

For all the panic, all the death, the rush came too. If the island escape had been a desperate flight, this was a true battle. The world's future rested on this little corridor here, anomalies doing everything they could to preserve themselves against a company, a power that wanted them dead.

And Cassidy was *here*, in the moment, at the nexus. Not on some beach, not trapped in a prison, or even just filing taxes over a clean cabernet at home. She cursed, more in wonder than anything else.

An arm reached out, grabbed Cassidy's wrist and pulled her over the drone wall. The Void let her void dissipate. She nearly stood until that same arm, belonging to one of the gun-wielding normals, pressed her back down.

"Stand and you're dead," the man shouted, then swiveled back to his post, fingers already on the trigger.

Right. No sense getting so swept up in the cause that she died before doing anything.

"Cassidy," Apinya was saying, "over here!"

The Champion had himself crouching with a face Cassidy recognized from the Internet. Zhan-Yo, the terrorist that'd bombed LA, that'd started this whole revolution. Somehow, Apinya didn't look angry, somehow Apinya wasn't trying to wring the man's neck. As Cassidy approached, she picked up words like position, strike force, and goals.

Was Zhan-Yo on their side now? And was he carrying *swords*?

"Listen," Apinya said as Cassidy crouched in with them. "Zhan-Yo says a group went to the Factory's control room. They're trying to take the place so when our ace comes through, Ziran won't be able to reset the drones so fast."

"Our ace?"

Zhan-Yo waved off the question, "No time. We need you to head down the walkway, take the first right. Follow the fighting. Go."

"Sorry, where do you get off giving me orders?" Cassidy snapped back.

"Cassidy," Apinya said, and the Void felt that calm pressure on her mind, the soft easing rubbing away her sharp edges. "We need you to do this. Thane's down there."

The real reason, then. Thane stuffed in a firefight's middle was a dangerous play. The anomaly was a wrecking ball, the more hits he took the angrier he'd get until anything turned into a target.

"You want me to sweet talk him or something?" Cassidy said.

"No," Zhan-Yo replied, and Apinya matched the man's grim stare. "Thane knew the risk when he came along. If he can't be stopped, if he starts killing his own, we need you to take him out."

Amazing how fast a heroic confidence could die. Being a part of saving the world suddenly felt less like a grand adventure and more like a sickening hit job.

"Please," Apinya said, and that pressure intensified. A headache's opposite, Cassidy's anger pulsed away into serenity, at peace with the ask. Despite all the violence around her, Cassidy felt like she could breathe, could nod, could understand the request made perfect sense. "We need you now."

She couldn't say no, even though she wanted to.

Cassidy picked her way along the walkway to the intersection. She'd followed the tracker and that anomaly this way, but they'd carried on straight ahead. Instead, she looked right, where the walkway turned into a standard hallway, its open air railing giving way to a two-walled corridor with a downward slant. Bodies, drone and otherwise, marred the path. Smoking ceiling panels showcased turrets that'd met their end.

Apinya's pacifying effects wore thin and Cassidy's frustration came back muted. The reasoning made sense: destroying the drones wouldn't matter if an invincible, mindless Thane murdered the Paragons right along with them.

Not that she'd kill Thane. Hell no. Better if she took out everyone making him mad first.

She took off, running.

The corridor dipped then cut sharp left. Another

several smashed wall panels displayed ruined turrets. A broken door had its middle bashed apart. Then another door after, and a third, each one bolstered by sparking, ruined turrets.

Mynx took her security seriously, or maybe Ziran put in the changes.

At the corridor's end, the hallway blossomed into a wider, black-tiled space. Cassidy caught the fighting as she approached, heard the gunfire, drone orders to cease and desist. And, most clearly, the echoing roars as a particular anomaly continued on his rampage. Unlike the loading dock, this big room had its space crowded with racks upon racks of servers.

Black cubes stationed on metal shelves, the whirring computers and the cold chill slicing through the room gave a different background to the combat. Tracker drones, commandos, and a couple anomalies seemed to be dancing through the racks, firing and slashing at one another. Across the room's middle, before the only other entry Cassidy could see, stood Thane. The big anomaly faced off against three gladiators, the drones combining their firepower to drive Thane back under a bullet and stunning dart hailstorm.

Cassidy could fix that. She strode forward, feeling the voids come to her fingertips. She swept back her arm, getting ready to cast a void wide enough to sever all three gladiator heads. And Cassidy would've launched it too, except a gun barrel pressed against her temple.

"Don't," said a woman, "we can't destroy anything in here."

The barrel pulled away and Cassidy glanced to her left, already shifting her voids to cut the offending person to ribbons. A young woman, icy and confident, stood there.

She had small guns in either hand, one tracking a snake-like tracker drone slithering their way.

"Sorry, had to get your attention," the woman said, swiveling both guns to target the drone. In a rapid-fire precision release, the woman sent six shots pinging into the drone's face, shattering its cameras and sending the machine veering into the room's back wall. "I'm Celice, and we need Thane to keep those gladiators occupied."

"Cassidy, and I can destroy them," Cassidy said, stepping past Celice and whipping a small void at the injured tracker.

The void split the drone in half, gouged a lovely line in the wall behind the machine.

"Nice, but not the point," Celice replied. "Past those drones there's a bunch of Ziran techs running computers we need access to. Thane gets past those gladiators, those techs are next."

Cassidy caught on, "And the computers get to be collateral damage."

In the same moment Celice's argument pieced together, the shots firing around the room died down. Drone clattering halted, with different bangs echoing as tracker drones plunged from walls, the ceiling, and server shelves to the ground. One landed at Celice's feet, claws extended and seemingly ready to make a fatal strike.

Instead the machine laid there, dormant.

"No," Celice muttered. "He actually did it."

"Did what?"

A roar cut off Celice's reply and the pair looked towards the gladiators facing off against Thane. The big machines stood stock still, and Thane's victorious howl bled into his rending and tearing. With each hand ripping apart a different drone and his head bashing in the third, the anomaly continued his berserker rage. The gladiators had no response, did nothing as Thane tore limbs off and threw them around the room, prompting commandos emerging from cover to dive back down.

"We need to calm him down," Celice said, moving past Cassidy.

"Easier said than done," Cassidy replied, following.

She'd seen Thane pull from these rages before, though not one so intense. The last time the anomaly had been so desperate, so deep in his own monstrosity, Cassidy had been unconscious. Thane swam with her for kilometers, dragging Cassidy all the way to a faraway beach. The way Thane told it, he'd finally died out due to exhaustion.

The anomaly didn't look tired now.

Beyond Thane, in the room those gladiators had been protecting, new voices called out. Confused, crying for help as their metal protection disintegrated and Ziran's staff had their first up-close look at a spit-flinging, roaring Thane. Seeing the drones dismembered, steel limbs snapped to pieces probably gave them good ideas of what was about to happen.

Cassidy, having seen Ziran's lab, the experiments up there, had trouble finding much sympathy.

Celice, though, shouted at Thane. Told him to stop, to calm down.

"This was the plan!" Celice called, the anomaly ignoring her, continuing to rip apart the last gladiator. "Get inside and stop Ziran from bringing the drones back, remember?"

"He's not going to hear you," Cassidy said, folding her arms and watching as the woman continued her approach. "He has to burn himself out."

"What if the people in that room know something we need? This is bigger than your anger, Thane! Bigger than these drones!"

With a final, laughing cry, Thane flung the last gladiator's split chest ahead into the control room. Some Ziran tech made a high-pitched howl. Another begged, loud, for Thane to show some mercy, that it wasn't their fault.

Just following orders.

Cassidy pressed her lips together, shook her head. These techs chose the wrong side, and they would've continued sitting here, spelling death and capture for anomalies day after day, year after year without this. Thane took a thundering step into the central room, then another. Bringing torture to the torturers.

The gunshot came over the cries. Came over the assembling, remaining commandos as they picked up each other, stayed on the sidelines. Came over Thane's growling, gruff approach.

Celice fired again, then a third time. Cassidy saw the rounds strike home, bouncing off Thane's thick skin and leaving little red welts where they struck. The last one hit Thane's head, a pinprick gash marring the man's wispy hair.

And earning Thane's attention.

Celice dropped one gun, settled her other weapon in both hands, aiming down the pistol as Thane turned fully 'round, the man's old and hardened face an insane picture. Wide bloodshot eyes, skin wrinkled and stretched, muscles bulging not just from the usual places but along his cheeks, his neck. What clothing Thane still had was ripped and burned, slashed by drone claws and spotted with bullet holes alike. Celice's fire only added to a complete scarring, so much that Cassidy couldn't hold back a gasp.

Alive or not, Thane's body looked black across his chest. Legs and arms bled where gladiator drone strikes had been strong enough to pierce skin. A tracker drone's leg spike stuck from Thane's left thigh, embedded deep in the anomaly.

So much damage, so much anger. This, this wouldn't end with a warning.

"Celice," Cassidy said, letting her arms fall free. "We need to run. Now. He's not going to stop."

"Then we need to stop him." Celice squeezed the trigger again. The shot hit straight into Thane's forehead, expert placement. The bullet bounced away. Thane's eyes narrowed. "Thane! You killed my mother! I don't give a damn if you die!"

Killed her mother?

Cassidy gaped. Thane roared. Celice fired again.

The anomaly charged. A single long leap. Celice shot a third time as Thane came crashing towards her. She would've been flattened, should've been, except a commando dove from the side and tackled Celice out of the way. The man flattened Celice with his own body as Thane landed on the floor, the tiles themselves cracking with his weight. The anomaly shifted, looked down at the normal pair. They had nowhere to go, nowhere to run.

"Thane!" Cassidy called, getting zero acknowledgement. "Don't make me kill you."

That word, that one word worked. Thane's eyes flicked Cassidy's way, saw her arms and hands spread. Voids waited, ready to carve into anomaly. He'd saved her once, twice, three times. Could she save him from himself?

"Please," Cassidy said. "Remember me, remember who you are."

Thane growled, his huge hands folding into fists, uncurling. Big breaths sent his chest up and down. Every blood vessel popped.

Cassidy knew where she'd throw those voids, had her own muscles tense.

"This isn't you," Cassidy said, quieter this time. She took a step, small and slow, towards Thane.

The movement broke the spell. Thane kicked, hit Celice and her protective commando and sent them flying. Then he turned his mad eyes at Cassidy, howled, and charged.

TWENTY-NINE

Rescue

As the elevator descended, Aegis pulled the tracker drone claws from his forearms. Dropping the metal pieces and shaking his wrists, the Champion felt the tickling sensation as his cells put themselves to work. Back before his internment in Mynx's tank and Mila restoring Aegis to basically brand new, healing up from cuts like this would take almost a whole day.

Now? When the lift doors opened, Aegis strode forth a whole human, ready to go.

The same could not be said for his tactical uniform, which looked like it belonged in the trash. Its ripped and holed fragments flitted along Aegis's skin. More a gothic shawl than a Paragon-ready outfit, but who cared. He'd reached the Factory's basement, the same long corridor leading to Mynx, to Mila.

To de-coupling Ziran from its drones.

Six Ziran guards—people in those white-and-orange armored suits—waited in the corridor. Their weapons, guns and what looked like electrified batons, sat ready in their hands. Two stood just beyond the lift's doors, aiming down their sights as the lift opened. Aegis saw the other four positioned deeper, nestled behind makeshift barriers, doors torn off hinges, a desk on its side.

"Evening, gentlemen," Aegis announced when the lift door swung aside.

He snapped forward and left as the guards hesitated. The usual reaction to a real-life Champion appearing in your face.

Aegis grabbed the left guard's gun and tore it from his grasp, whipping it into the right guard's face and sending that one falling back. The left guard went for his baton only to find himself lifted off the floor and propelled backward. Aegis used the man as a shield, charging forward.

Ziran's employees weren't totally homicidal. They held their fire as Aegis ran, a clock ticking in the Champion's head till the guard he'd knocked down back at the lift picked himself up and shot at Aegis's back. As he neared the second Ziran pair, both guards heading to the corridor's right side to dodge the rush, Aegis pushed off his hostage, throwing the guard into his two pals.

The three bodies collapsed behind an overturned table, one used a second ago for cover, and Aegis followed, diving on the pile as the guard back by the lift squeezed off a couple rounds. The bullets flew overhead as Aegis hit the pile. The back two guards held their own fire, again respecting the lives of their comrades.

A nice change from some villains Aegis had battered back in the good old days, ones that regarded their henchmen as fodder. Maybe Ziran wasn't totally evil.

Maybe.

With his right hand Aegis delivered quick knockout punches to the scrabbling guards, bashing skulls in helmets till the bodies went limp. With his left, Aegis pulled a gun free and held the trigger in an aimless spray towards the last two guards, forcing them behind their own cover. Rolling free from the pile, Aegis snapped up, rotated, and triggered rounds back towards the lift. The guard there panicked, dove into the elevator and slapped at the buttons, closing the lift's door.

Aegis could live with that.

A bullet hit his shoulder, spinning Aegis right. The metal round dug in, a sharp pain staying with it. A second shot went wide, and by then Aegis had his finger holding down the trigger, sending rounds towards the battered doors the two guards had for cover. They ducked back, giving Aegis free room to advance.

"C'mon guys," Aegis called, keeping the stolen rifle ready. "Two against a Champion? Bad odds. Throw those guns away and I'll let you walk on out of here. Keep 'em, and you'll get the fast and deadly kind of Paragon justice."

Quiet greeted Aegis's words, the Champion continuing his advance. Ahead and to the right he could see the capsule room, the tanks that would be holding Mynx and Mila. Almost there.

"Promise you'll let us go?" asked the guard on the left. "I have a family back home. Two kids. One's getting married in a month."

"Promise." Aegis felt a little surprised to find he meant it, but after the day's violence, the further fighting sure to come? He could let these clock punchers leave. "But you're quitting after today."

"Deal," came the same guard, and his gun flew back as he said the words, clattering to the hallway floor. "They don't pay us enough anyway."

"They never do," Aegis replied, shifting his aim. "Now your buddy."

A curse, a sigh, and rifle number two joined its brother

on the hallway floor. Hands up, both guards rose from behind their barriers. Aegis nodded back towards the lift.

"Take your pals with you. Tell the folks upstairs I said you could go," Aegis ordered. "If you're nice and they're not too mad, you might get home tonight."

THREE CAPSULES GLOWED in the room. Two, filled up with eerie liquid, held Mynx and Mila. A drone charged with monitoring the capsules with its all-too-many arms sat on the left. The machine didn't activate when Aegis entered the room, a sign Aegis chose to interpret as positive. Now he just had to figure out how to get these capsules drained, the two Champions released.

Each capsule had a Tama screen on it showcasing vital signs. Both had bright greens across the board as they floated, eyes closed and oxygen masks on. Also on those screens sat a simple button, one reading Release.

"Easy enough," Aegis muttered, and tapped it on Mynx's capsule.

The oxygen mask, the lithe mechanical arms keeping Mynx stable and afloat unsnapped. The Champion sank, her eyes popping open as she woke, totally submerged in a glass jar. Aegis cursed, looked at the Tama and saw only flashing red. No answers.

He'd have to provide his own.

Aegis stepped into a hard slug, bringing all his force to bear in a straight up punch into the capsule's glass. The hit struck, cracked, and, upon a second blow, shattered. Glass and water poured out everywhere, followed by Mynx. Aegis caught the Champion, coughing, and held her up out of the glass.

"What the hell are you doing?" Mynx gasped, blinking.

"Saving you," Aegis replied.

"Like an idiot," Mynx said, her hair soaked and matting to the sides of her head.

"It's not like there's instructions on these things."

Mynx shot him a glare, then shook it off, "If you're here and I'm out, I assume something stupid is going on?"

Aegis explained, going over the Ziran takeover, the current assault. The need to get the drones cut off from Ziran before they could be reactivated. Mynx, meanwhile, swiped and tapped away on the Tama affixed to Mila's capsule. This time, the water drained away, the arms settling Mila on the capsule's floor.

Then, and only then, did Mynx release her from the oxygen mask, the arms.

"See?" Mynx said, interrupting Aegis's digression into the many Factory assaults. "It's not that hard."

As the capsule hissed, opened, Aegis switched to his radio, holding up his Tama and confirming on the broad channel that he'd made the rescue. Two Champions in the bag, ready to head up and help.

"Drones just died," Zhan-Yo came back quick. "Get her to the control center. Celice, do we have it yet?"

Static.

Mynx helped Mila to her feet, rubbing the Champion's arms to help her wake up. Mila blinked, shook her head.

"We're back," Mynx whispered. "But there's no time to rest up. This isn't a snatch and grab but a full on takeover."

"Takeover?" Mila asked. "Of what?"

Aegis nodded towards the exit, "I'll talk on the way. Can you walk?"

"Slowly."

Any progress beat none at all, so Aegis went towards the room's exit. Zhan-Yo filled in the silence, saying how they were dismantling as many drones as they could while the machines stood frozen. The Paragons, the commandos had casualties aplenty and emergency pods were arriving to take who they could away to the hospitals.

More interesting, Ziran hadn't sent any humans, any police to assist. They'd established a perimeter instead, letting their robots do the work without risking other lives. A fortunate stance for the Paragons, a safe one for Ziran.

Loyal bodies never looked good on the news.

The hallway to the lift stayed empty, the guards taking Aegis's advice and fleeing far. That left a long stretch, time aplenty to get Mynx and Mila caught up while the two newly awakened Champions brought their muscles back to life.

When the shaking started, Aegis didn't even get alarmed. There'd been so much violence, maybe some system in the Factory, its air conditioning or water pressure had burst. The vibrations came from above as Aegis reached the lift, tapped the call button.

The rumbling grew. Mynx and Mila looked up, the former frowning.

"Nothing's falling," Mynx said.

"What?" Aegis glanced up, saw cracks forming in the ceiling, but looking more like folds, as though something above pinched the earth.

The shaking grew into a crackling, ripping roar. The lift beeped out an instability alarm, shutting itself down before its arrival. The cracks spread, and Aegis moved. He told Mynx and Mila to crouch and pulled himself over them, wrapping the smaller pair in a big hug. Not perfect protection from what seemed about to happen, but better than letting the two experience a cave in without the slightest guard.

"I can't believe I woke up just to die," Mynx said. "Your timing sucks, Aegis."

"At least he tried," Mila replied. "That's something, right?"

"All I know is, I was having some great dreams."

"This hall falls on us," Aegis said, yelling over the noise, "you'll get all the dreams you want."

A brief silence. The roaring vanished, the tearing stopped, and Aegis had that hopeful glimmer that things might turn out okay.

Until he felt the first rock hit his back. Saw a second strike the floor on his right.

Heard a different sort of roar, the kind made by an angry creature instead of industrial processes gone wrong. A gnashing, enraging sound Aegis recognized.

And with it, the ceiling fell.

Tile, rock, piping and metal didn't sprinkle, didn't rain, just collapsed. At once Aegis felt the debris bear him to the ground. He planted his wrists, did what he could to keep the mass off Mynx and Mila. Even with all that weight training, all that exercise, Aegis knew they'd be buried.

But after the first wave, little followed. As if someone had scooped out the Factory's flooring and left only a bit behind. Aegis straightened, shifting the rubble off him, and caught fluorescent light shining down through a slanted, neat shaft. As though some perfect drill had bored out a hole.

Through that hole thrashed a familiar figure. All ugly bone and gristle, muscle and mass, Thane howled towards the shaft. Debris collected up to Thane's waist, but Aegis could make out the anomaly's damage, the scars and burns and bleeding bits. The man's charge into the enemy hadn't gone perfect, though what Ziran had capable of creating that shaft, Aegis didn't want to know.

"Stay down there!" Came a shout, a voice Aegis

thought he'd heard before but couldn't place. "Don't come back, Thane, or . . . just don't, please."

Thane roared in response. Aegis felt Mynx, Mila squeeze out from beneath him, dig their own way to standing. Rock and tile crumbles, clattering around them, and Thane's rage cut off, his bloodshot eyes turning their way.

"Hey there," Aegis said, cracking his knuckles. After all this, fighting Thane hadn't been at the top of his list, but how often did the Champion get to choose his battles? "You going to calm down?"

"Aegis," Mynx said. "Now's not the time."

"Then I'd get some distance." Aegis stepped square into the hallway's center. "Don't think he's in a place to listen." The Champion turned his attention back to the monster. "C'mon, buddy. This was all your plan, remember? It's working like you said it would. Don't ruin it by being an asshole."

Thane pounded his fists into the rubble, clearing it out and forcing Aegis to cover his own face to deflect the rocks. The big anomaly pulled himself free, Thane's height forcing him into a half crouch as he snarled at Aegis. Those eyes flicked, caught Mynx and Mila backing away.

"No no," Aegis said, taking another step forward. "Those two are off limits. You going to fight someone, it's going to be me." He spread his arms. "After all, I'm the one that put you in that cage for all these years. You took my wife from me, and I took your years from you. You should hate me, Thane, because I sure as hell hate you."

Something in that monster still worked. Thane flipped his focus back to Aegis, opened his mouth to show off jagged teeth. And jumped forward.

The low, ruptured ceiling meant Thane's leap carried him into the rock, the tile. More debris rained. Aegis ducked forward, dodging into Thane's left and right haymaker to deliver one of his own. Not a blind punch but one that went right for a black burn scar. Aegis felt Thane's hide crackle with the hit, the anomaly howling.

Aegis threw a second jab, striking low and driving Thane back a step. The third swing in the combo went to Thane's right knee, bending it wide. Aegis felt Thane's mitts wrapping close for a hug he very much didn't want and dove beneath that bent knee, rolling on the broken beams, cracked cement and coming up in a crouch of his own.

Thane spun towards Aegis, those hands grabbing rubble and launching it at the Champion. Rebar hit Aegis like a star player's home run swing, knocking the Champion onto his back. Grit landed on Aegis's face, in his eyes and his mouth. Rock stuck between his teeth.

Not that he had time for a floss.

"Get outta here!" Aegis shouted towards Mynx and Mila, or where they had been, as he rolled to the side, dodging one Thane punch as the anomaly closed and taking another on his shoulder.

The dislocation hurt. The follow-up sending Aegis flying into the hallway's side hurt too. Thane's spit-filled battle-cry didn't hurt all that much, but the gut punch, a gnarled fist driving Aegis into the same wall he'd just slammed before spreading into an open-palmed pin, definitely added aches to Aegis's growing pain symphony.

The Champion blinked his eyes open, blurred vision looking into Thane's ugly mug. The anomaly had his left fist curling back, aiming right for Aegis's head. Aegis had to delay the thing somehow, give Mynx and Mila time to run.

"Know what," Aegis said, "she didn't want you dead. At the end, once we got her out of your claws, she made me promise."

Thane stuck his face in close, breathed foul air right at Aegis. Growled. Aegis coughed, continued.

"In that chair you were safe, we were safe," Aegis said. "You should've died there. At peace."

Thane roared, reared back, that fist ready to go. Aegis couldn't see the other two Champions. Hopefully they'd escaped.

Metal arms swung from the blue-washed shadows. Tentacles reaching out, grabbing Thane's pulled back arm and holding it in place. Thane whipped an angry look that way, Aegis doing the same, only to see the capsule maintenance drone in full drive. Mynx stood behind it, her hand on the machine's bulk.

And running around them, towards Aegis, towards Thane in a suicide move, came Mila. The Champion had her hands outstretched, one towards Aegis, one towards Thane. Aegis started to yell something, call them morons for staying, but stopped as blue-white filaments, little lines split the air between him and the monster pinning Aegis to the wall.

Those filaments stung, a pressure pain like giving blood. More and more spun out from Aegis and lanced into Thane. The anomaly howled, not with rage, but confusion.

"Hold on," said Mila, though Aegis couldn't tell who she was speaking to.

He felt his body war with itself, Mila's threads sucking Aegis's life away even as his healing put it back together. Thane, holding Aegis to the wall, shivered. His blackened skin peeled away. Bruises shrank, vanished. Red scars where bullets or debris had done their work pinked over with fresh, healthy skin. Wrinkles and blemishes disappeared, and new, fresh white hair poked from Thane's scalp.

The fall came without preamble. Thane's grip faltered and Aegis struck the floor, collapsed onto his chest. The Champion felt he could barely breathe, his muscles seemed to lack the will, the ability to squeeze, to move. But he wasn't dead, Aegis knew that much.

And Thane wasn't roaring anymore.

Gradually, the stings went away. One by one the pressures eased and Aegis's body began to win its battle to bring itself back. Aegis felt his fingers, felt his heart beat, felt that aching shoulder knit into position. He looked up and saw a man, a normal, older man staring at his own hands.

"Thane?" Mila asked, and the man looked at her.

Slowly, as if not believing how he'd come to be standing there, Thane nodded.

THIRTY

Waterfront

CROUCHING, the two hit the sand. Wexley still stood where the waves came in, a Tama's glow illuminating his face. This close, Kat and Calvin could hear Wexley's voice but the crashing waves washed out the words. Below and beyond the natural noise popped the drone-anomaly battle, its reverbs shaking the ground.

"Pretty calm for a man who's about to lose everything," Calvin whispered.

"He hasn't lost it yet," Kat replied. "Can you hit him from here?"

"A target like that? Easy," Calvin said.

The anomaly put his right hand on the cliff wall. Kat inched forward, dropped to her chest and leveled the stolen rifle. If Wexley had some trick, the tracker would make the fatal call. Wexley alive would be better for the world, but Wexley dead would be just fine.

Over her right shoulder, Kat caught Calvin forming a slender needle from the cliffside stone. The anomaly had his left hand wrapped around it, ready to fling the thing like a dart. A long toss, but Kat had seen Calvin spear enemies time and again from distance. This time shouldn't be any different.

"Ready?" Calvin said.

"For a shower. Let's get this over with."

Calvin lanced the limestone needle. Kat watched the dart fly, saw a dark blur slide down to catch it. Sparks flew and the intercepting drone smashed into the sand. Apparently Wexley wasn't alone.

Plan B.

Kat pressured the trigger, aimed down the sights. She didn't consider herself a sharpshooter but a standstill target, even in the dark, should be viable.

Then Wexley had the guts to turn, hands up, and face them.

"He's surrendering?" Calvin asked and Kat noticed the anomaly had another rock needle ready to throw. "That's different."

"Come on out," Wexley said. "My hands are up. No weapons."

Kat couldn't deny the visceral appeal in standing up to confront her one-time shooter. She had more than the upper hand now, had Wexley dead to rights with an assault rifle. Ziran CEO, rooftop murderer, a hundred other names Kat could probably dig up if she wanted, and here he was, blinking back at her as Kat walked down the beach towards him.

"Kat?" Calvin said to her back. "What're you doing?"

"You?" Wexley said, and his face, ghost-gray in the wash from the house lights, matched the shock in his voice. "How is it you?"

"Long story," Kat said, "and I'm really hoping for a quick ending. Turn off that Tama."

Wexley glanced at his left wrist as Kat nudged her rifle's nose in that direction. The man shrugged, reached over and tapped the thing's power button. The screen went dark.

"There. No more drones." Wexley looked around Kat, hunting for shapes that weren't there." I expected Aegis. Maybe one of the other Champions. Are they still alive?"

"Doesn't matter. We'll find out in a minute and you'd better hope they're not dead. Can't imagine whomever's left is gonna treat you kindly otherwise."

"If you think I'm going anywhere other than to the next life, you're naive," Wexley said. "I knew the risks when I took Mynx months ago."

The pops, the bangs, rattles, and roars died as Wexley spoke, a winding down demise in the distance. Kat froze, wondering if the change meant the anomaly line had fallen, if those Paragons had all succumbed to drone bullets and metal claws.

Wexley grinned, "Looks like the game's not over yet."

Calvin looked left, his hand gracing Kat's shoulder as if getting ready to spin her to face drones pouring forth from the Factory. As the anomaly turned, Kat kept her rifle leveled on Wexley. She had to hope the drones had lost and not the other way around, not the disaster.

She'd already fought one drone army today. Her luck wouldn't hold through another.

Sand flew up, crashing grit against Kat's eyes. She pulled the trigger by reflex, but Wexley ducked ahead off the kick, letting the rounds fly free over his shoulder into the ocean. Kat took the man's charge on the chin, Wexley barging into her neck and sending her flying back. She felt a tug on the gun too as she fell, her hands holding strong and keeping the weapon with her as she landed in the dunes.

Her inner lip burned where Wexley's attack knocked it into her teeth. Kat's eyes watered as she blinked, brushed sand free. She pulled the gun up, saw two dark shadows dancing a meter before her. Without Wexley's Tama, the moonlight served a grayscale bag. The rising cliffs around them cut the shine to slivers, Calvin and Wexley punching, kicking between them.

Calvin's ability might've been amazing, but Wexley refused to let the anomaly find a way to use it. Ziran's CEO adopted a brawler's stance, angling in with tight jabs designed to keep the man close. Calvin, as the fight in *Carver's* basement taught Kat oh so long ago, hung with the hits. The anomaly used his elbows, his longer reach to knock Wexley's blows aside and deliver some counters of his own.

Enough that Kat, tracing the fight with her fingers back on the trigger, held her fire.

"Isn't this what you wanted?" Wexley said, sparking up a conversation as he attempted a three-punch combo towards Calvin's ribs. "A chance to be a star all your own?"

"You don't know me," Calvin replied, grunting when one of Wexley's shots struck home.

The anomaly responded with a wicked left elbow, catching Wexley across the jaw, his jabbing arm too far from home to recover. Wexley stumbled, managed to keep enough wits to move Calvin between himself and Kat.

"I do, though," Wexley said, falling back into his stance. Calvin shook himself out, playing a wary game. "I took Mynx's data. I know all about you and your runaway life."

"Like I give a damn."

The anomaly threw a punch with his right hand, one far away from Wexley's face. Nonetheless, Wexley flew back, landing in the surf. Kat grinned. Calvin would've puffed some air behind that swing, given it a tiny hurricane's boost.

Calvin followed his air-filled swing with a slow walk up as Kat stood, shook off the sand.

"Stay wide," Kat said, "I've got the shot again."

Wexley sat up in the water as Calvin approached, "Going to let her do the work for you, anomaly? A normal ending our fight?"

"Man, where do you get off talking like that?" Calvin said, the waves splattering his shoes too. "You're over, done."

"Never," Wexley growled, curling forward in a dive at Calvin's legs.

Kat pulled the trigger. Heard a click, the gun jerk. Nothing fired.

Jammed. Too much sand.

A splash. Kat looked up, saw Calvin and Wexley wrestling in the waves. Throwing the rifle aside, Kat broke into a sprint towards the fighting pair. Flicking her left wrist, Kat armed the trusty grapple. Aimed it when Wexley scooped himself over Calvin, hands on the anomaly's throat. The Ziran CEO snapped a glare her way, caught Kat's raised wrist.

She fired.

Wexley flattened himself on Calvin's chest, the grapple sailing overhead and into the ocean.

"Seen that one before," Wexley barked, sliding his left arm into a tight bar on Calvin's throat.

"Have you?" Kat said, twitching her left wrist and dropping her arm.

The grapple retracted, shooting from the ocean a half meter lower than where it'd gone in. Wexley didn't catch the sound, didn't get down, and the grapple slapped his chest, caught in and tugged Wexley off Calvin's sputtering, gasping form.

Kat closed the distance, delivered a kick to Wexley's gut

that had the Ziran leader in the wet sand, on his back. The tracker didn't stop as the grapple clicked back into her wrist. With a twitch she sent the steel barb out again, this time sticking it into Wexley's leg.

Right where she'd hit him so long ago on those Chicago rooftops.

He yelped this time like he had then, but the man wasn't done. Wexley kicked the grapple leg back, a move that had to hurt like hell. The motion tugged Kat forward a step, far enough for Wexley to reach out and snag her ankle.

Like he'd done to Calvin a minute earlier, Wexley tugged, expecting Kat to fall in the dirt. Instead, Kat lunged forward with the ankle grab, landing on Wexley with a decided thump. With their faces close together, Wexley's wild eyes glared into her own. Kat saw all that desperation, all that panic, all that sickness she'd seen in so many anomalies as their own dreams dashed with her arrival.

Except those anomalies went on to newer, stable lives. Wexley, nah.

"It's over," Wexley said, bringing up his hands around her neck.

"For you," Kat replied, nodding ever-so-slightly.

Her suit caught the pressure, sent her faceplate, one still bearing the bullet scar from Rhimes's shot months ago, sliding over Kat's face. As Wexley's hands pressed in on her neck, Kat snapped her head forward, slamming it into Wexley's own.

Once had his grip loosen, had his eyes go cross. Twice had them rolling back, Wexley falling unconscious into the sand.

"This guy," Kat said, scooping in air, looking Calvin's

way. The anomaly sat up in the surf, hands massaging his own throat. "You all right?"

"Oh hell yeah. Never been better."

A wave hit, burying the anomaly beneath its frothy white.

THE PAIR DRAGGED Wexley back up the beach. Kat didn't have any stun cuffs, but Calvin took the plentiful sand and encased the Ziran CEO in a Sphinx-like coating. Then, for what felt like too little and too long, Kat and Calvin watched the waves, the stars, and waited. Either the Paragons had won and the heroes would come barnstorming, or Ziran's drones had claimed the day, in which case Kat and Calvin would either be dead or . . .

"An island," Calvin said. "Heard about it. Mynx owned it, I think. We can trade Wexley's life for a spot on the island if things go south."

"You mean leave everything to go live on a beach with a bunch of anomaly criminals?" Kat occupied her hands cleaning out the gun, digging out the grains. "What a paradise."

"You're talking like you wouldn't love it. We'd have no rent to pay, no taxes. Just a shack where we could watch the sun rise, the stars shine."

"No comic conventions on an island."

Calvin shrugged, "With all those anomalies, bet there'd be enough entertainment."

Kat considered, set the gun in her lap. Wexley's eyes were still shut, the man not adding any input to the conversation.

"If I could bring Seeker, I suppose."

"'Course the dog would come." Calvin nodded as if the whole idea was settled.

Footsteps on wood boards ended the conversation, with Kat rolling over onto her chest, the rifle up and steady in her hands. Several forms moved slow in the moonlight. As the leader came into view, saw Kat, he put up his hands.

A few thoughts crashed through in that moment. The first came with relief: Kat had never seen a drone, no matter how human-like, surrender. The second flashed recognition from video calls in Chicago, the Paragon's back-to-life leader dishing out orders from his patchy, gray-haired mug. And the third?

They'd won.

"Hello," Aegis said as Kat dropped the rifle, the Champion catching sight of Wexley in his sand prison. "Who are you?"

TO THE VICTOR go the complications. For all their work snaring Wexley, Kat and Calvin found themselves sidelined fast as Champions and other big-wigs clustered on the beach. At Aegis's direction, Calvin freed Wexley only for the man to get stun cuffs slapped on by an all-too-solemn Zhan-Yo.

"I'm sorry, my friend," the revolutionary said as he closed the cuffs on Wexley's wrists. "It shouldn't have come to this."

"I made the world you wanted," Wexley said, "and then you tore it apart."

"You made the world *you* wanted," Zhan-Yo replied as the others either watched or stepped aside, speaking into Tamas to handle ongoing details.

A drone, small and flying with a tray attached buzzed down near Calvin and Kat. Warm coffee-filled mugs graced its metal holders.

"Would you like some?" came an awfully pleasant

voice, one Kat recognized from tracker missives and meetings.

"Reeves?" Kat asked. "I thought Ziran deleted you."

"A bug in the system, I'm afraid. They tried, they failed."

"And that cost them," Mynx said, stepping over and picking out the one mug on the drone filled with tea instead. The Champion wore what looked like exercise clothes plucked from her closet. "Guess who fed Aegis data on the those shipments he kept raiding?"

Kats eyes flicked between the Champion and the drone. "Uh, Reeves?"

"Exactly." Mynx smiled. "For all the machines I've made, I think he's my best creation."

Calvin raised an eyebrow, Kat just nodded. As post-fight adrenaline wound down, Kat found herself without the stamina to keep up. These were power players attempting to put together a new world for the second time in months. Thane, Aegis, and Apinya, joined now by Mynx and Zhan-Yo, debated global structure, their Tamas aglow with joined callers from across the planet. Summits would be organized, governments built.

Kat watched the conversation with long blinks, the waves behind the talks looking inviting.

"Hey," Calvin said, tapping Kat's shoulder. "Don't know about you, but I'm thinking we're not necessary here."

Kat smiled, "You don't think we're important?"

"Oh, we're way important. Too important for crap like this," Calvin replied. "How about we let these chumps deal with the details while you and me get some good breakfast?"

"Good breakfast? You know a place around here?"

"Kat, trust me."

Turned out, Calvin did know a place. Turned out too, he knew the place because it'd been a frequent hideout during a long stint Calvin had pulled in the city during his teen years. He'd scrabbled together shifts at the buzzy, hallucinogenic Hollywood-themed breakfast haunt between independent drifts through LA's tougher enclaves.

In the early AM, after a pod ride from a Factory swarmed with emergency personnel, Paragons, and news crews, Kat found herself looking at a pancake stack dribbling over with butter. Eggs and lab-grown bacon on one side. Calvin had the same, knife and fork already going to work.

A TV played to mostly-full booths, night shifters on break and drifters grabbing cheap meals. Bleary-eyed newscasters, make-up and ties askew, delivered flabbergasted takes one after another. Footage from around the globe kept pulling Kat's eyes to the screen to see anomalies and normals dancing around defunct drones. Champions on other continents gave solemn speeches about better tomorrows.

And, best and worst of all, families streaming back together as loved ones emerged from Ziran's prison lab to the north. Buses brought reunions with every trip. Adriana came in on the first one, joining Wexley at a particular high security prison that, Mynx promised to a camera, would, despite Zhan-Yo's recent breakout, hold the pair without a problem.

"Hey." Calvin had his mouth filled with pancakes, the man looking like a goofy chipmunk, his words coming out mushy. "You better eat that before it gets cold."

Oh, yeah. Breakfast. Kat blinked, nodded, picked up her fork and knife.

The first bite tasted damn good.

THIRTY-ONE

Criminals

RHIMES WATCHED the Paragons across the lobby. The two looked battered, tired, pressed into official duty as the Paragons snapped into reflexive world control. Details, so the news said, were being worked out between factions and the future would look a little different. For now, though, the anomalies replaced the drones, back to the usual run.

The soldier gathered his coat around him, kept his baseball cap bill pulled low. Glanced towards the hallway, the elevator bank beyond. People poured in and out, central Chicago's main hospital not a quiet place.

Picking up his coffee from the magenta-sealed wood side table, Rhimes made the slow stand so often seen in places where people's time wasn't all their own. His move made him aware of his empty pockets, his wrists nudged the loose loops up his sleeves. No knives or guns here today. In Rhimes's left hand he held a small bouquet, yellow and white flowers bringing a bright spring shine.

At the elevators he joined a doctor, head buried in her Tama, and another worried-looking family. He punched numbers for each, wound up being the first off into a surgical recovery ward. Medical drones dominated here, backing up living nurses, doctors. They trundled around like warped families, following each other from one patient room to the next.

"Can I help you?" asked a greeter behind a walnut wraparound desk, computer monitors doing their best to hide her head. She managed to poke her eyes over, hunting for Rhimes's plastic Visitor badge until she found it.

"Regina Porter," Rhimes said.

"Family?"

"Friend." Rhimes raised the flowers. "Just dropping these by."

The greeter smiled, told Rhimes room seven. The soldier nodded, went on past. Hand sanitizer mixed with cafeteria breakfast foods to create a miserable anesthetic scent while a dozen different shows, movies, and songs burbled into an eclectic sonic clash. All that coupled with passing small talk, the robotic suggestions coming from drones rambling through their algorithms.

Almost as busy as Ziran had been in the days following Wexley's takeover. Everyone running around picking up extra duties, flush with a world fallen into their hands. It'd been exciting, it'd been hopeful, but even then nobody seemed to know what would happen next. Like the dog catching the proverbial car, Ziran achieved its goal and had no clue what to do with it.

Now the company would have nothing. Rhimes didn't know the ins and outs, but Zhan-Yo popped an occasional line or two his way. Ziran wouldn't survive the renegotiated landscape, a move designed both to discourage further bloody uprisings and to bring Tamas out of the private sphere and into the public one.

Communication was too valuable to hand to one company, apparently.

Room seven had a good window view onto a park. The rainy day gave everything inside a light blue hue, extending to the hospital bed and the gowned woman lying inside it. Regina Porter had her eyes closed. A connected monitor showed all greens across the board. Successful surgery to remove the bullet, a little anomaly juiced healing, and Rhimes figured she'd get discharged within a day or two.

He set the little vase with its flowers on the windowsill. Pulled a tiny card from his pocket and slipped it between the cut green stalks. Handwriting the thing had been amusing. Picking up a pen happened so rarely, but it'd been good to draw those curves, link him personally to the words.

He'd left no signature, but Regina would be smart enough to figure it out.

After all, how many lives had she saved? Couldn't be that many, right?

Rhimes left the room and made a left, going farther from the elevators and the exit. Towards the ward's far end, another Paragon sat in a chair outside room twelve. As Rhimes paced that way, a nurse, medical drone, and two doctors went by the Paragon into the room. The anomaly stood, followed.

Right on schedule.

On Rhimes's right, a fire alarm lingered as a possibility, but one he ignored. He hadn't flipped the table on Wexley to go back to hurting random people, and too many on this ward might need serious attention to warrant panic. And Regina looked so damn peaceful there on that cot.

Instead he kept up the walk until he passed room twelve, caught the conversation. Rhimes posted himself outside, pretending to read his Tama. Drink his coffee.

Brielle, unlike Regina, was plenty awake. The doctors were going over her treatment, how she'd need rehab, would need some significant follow-up given how the bullet had scraped some organs. The Paragon spoke over the providers then, saying Brielle would get enough treatment to survive, but she wouldn't remain here any longer.

That, too, Zhan-Yo had tossed Rhimes's way. Aegis and the other Champions were resolute in pushing against Ziran's more zealous fighters. Those that killed, hunted anomalies would be put up for their actions, tried and convicted. Rhimes himself would get a reprieve thanks to his efforts, but that didn't cover anyone else.

Didn't cover Zhan-Yo either, but when Rhimes asked the man what move he'd be making, Z ignored the ask. Had dropped off the grid entirely.

One who hadn't?

Gordon Holyoak had proved a good man, a better tracker. He'd helped get Rhimes set back up in that featureless white house, pushed for Rhimes to get his exemption, and when Rhimes asked two days ago, Gordon had found Brielle's information, clued in Rhimes to the discharge date and time.

Gordon had asked Rhimes, as had so many others, why he'd turned on Wexley. What'd been the final straw, and Rhimes had no real answer. It wasn't so much a single moment as a gradual flood, the washing away of ideals by hatred, desperation, power. Some, like Brielle, had been caught up in that storm. Not that she bore no responsibility, but she had talent, she had promise.

And Rhimes brought her into Ziran, dammit. He owed her a way out.

The doctors, drone, and nurse left the room. The Paragon followed, continuing to chat with the medical staff. Going over transfer details, anything necessary to keep Brielle from falling apart on the way. They moved down the hallway, not too far, but the Paragon had his back turned to the room.

Rhimes took advantage, slipping inside. He started a clock in his head.

Brielle, exhausted and pallid, stared out the window. Unlike Regina's room, Brielle's view looked out onto a highway coated with pods. In the distance, planes came and went from the airport in a staccato line.

"What'd you forget?" Brielle said, not looking over.

"You," Rhimes said, keeping his voice low.

Brielle turned her face his way, eyebrows going high. Rhimes ignored her for a moment, did a quick review. An IV bag, a monitor had their hooks in Brielle's left arm. Her right had a cuff around it, tying Brielle to her bed. Not an easy extraction.

"Why're you here?" Brielle asked, "and if you say 'you' again, I'm calling the nurse."

"You don't deserve what's happening here."

"Are you sure?" Brielle curled up a lip. "We all knew what we were doing. For the cause, for the cash, but we weren't stupid. You can't save me from the choices I made. The choices you made."

"I feel like I failed you."

"Oh, you did. You're a traitor, Rhimes. That's not gonna change no matter what you do now."

Rhimes nodded. He'd told himself there'd be two possibilities. Either Brielle would leap at the chance to run, they'd work together and make some desperate escape. Or she'd do this. Accept her fate, give Rhimes a bitter pill, and that'd be that.

Except.

"Have they said what they're going to do to you?" Rhimes asked.

Brielle shook her head, "Get me out of here. That's it. From there, I don't know."

"I do," Rhimes came up to the bed, sat in the chair next to it. His running clock already passed by the mark. The Paragon would be back any second, an escape wasn't happening. "The world doesn't need any more executions. It's not a good way to start, so they're going to ship out everyone they can. Get'em off the field and forgotten."

"Ship us where?" Brielle asked. "Antarctica?"

"Close." Rhimes lifted his Tama, swiped to pull up an image, a place. "Mynx, the Champion—"

"I know who Mynx is."

"She's got this island. Guess it used to house anomalies the Paragons didn't know what to do with, and now we're getting put there."

"We?"

Until he said the words, Rhimes hadn't planned to put himself in the group, but it made sense. He was a soldier, he'd fought his wars. No family to return to save the one he'd been working with for years upon years now.

Besides, dipping his toes in the warm surf didn't sound bad after so many Chicago winters.

"Wexley, Zhan-Yo," Rhimes said. "All the Ziran players, all the conspirators, and more than a few Elementals too. Wiping us off the slate."

"And sticking us together? On an island?" Brielle shook her head. "We'll kill each other."

"Maybe. Or maybe we'll do better than we ever did here."

The Paragon came in curious, too new to suspect someone of foul motivations here in this house of healing. Rhimes waved, said he'd be going along with Brielle. When the Paragon mentioned she was a criminal, Rhimes shrugged, said he was too.

. . .

THE BOAT TAKING them to the island looked like a fortress. Paragons and Mathieu's commandos covered every spare meter while the prisoners kept themselves to a sealed section in the center. Rhimes, wide-brimmed hat shading his eyes, watched the waves as the boat motored along. There'd be more following as the new governments rounded up criminals and decided whether to skate by slaughter to send them on to the island or not.

As a justice system went, Rhimes figured it was a little barbaric to dump a whole slew of folks, many who might've had families, on an island without a chance of return. On the other hand, they wouldn't be rotting in cells or facing a firing squad. He turned, looked out at the folks sharing the fate with him. Most had that hardened look that came with years spent at war. A few stared at the empty spots on their wrists where Tamas once lay.

Wexley sat with Adriana off in his own corner. Their hands sat on top of one another, the world's foremost leaders now the same as everyone else. Wexley still had those dark sunglasses, and when he caught Rhimes in those shades, Ziran's former CEO gave the soldier a slight nod. One Rhimes returned.

He understood, same as everyone else on the boat, that a life on the island meant a reset. Former grudges would only serve to get people killed. An idea easy to say, difficult to hold onto. Who knew how long the peace would last?

The other man, alone and opposite Rhimes, would no doubt fight to keep it going as long as possible. Zhan-Yo shared Rhimes's look out over the waves. Rather than Wexley's pensive, straight stare, though, Zhan-Yo's wrinkles held a small smile between them.

That morning, for the first time in so many decades,

the globe had started holding its first elections. Leaders, anomalies and normals alike, would find themselves in power not because of might, but because of freedom.

"Is this what you wanted?" Brielle, walking with a cane as her recovery continued, stepped up next to Rhimes.

"I didn't know it till now," Rhimes replied. "But it just might be."

THIRTY-TWO

New Plans, Old Homes

THE POD CURLED onto a street at once familiar and not. Houses bore a resemblance, but the paints had changed. New trees grew on lawns speckled with new toys. Kids far removed from her own enjoyed the morning sunshine. Cassidy leaned back in the seat and tried not to think about how fast her heart was beating.

"Nervous?" Thane said, fit and looking good beside her.

The anomaly's whisker-thin hair had turned a thick white, the wrinkles and blotches along his skin receding or disappearing beneath a healthy glow. Mila's effect, so he said.

That Thane sat there at all came as a surprise. After Cassidy directed her void down into the Factory floor, letting it tear a hole beneath the raging anomaly, she expected to never see the man again. He'd either be trapped in the rock or something else down in the Factory's depths would kill him. So long as she didn't have to make the final call.

They'd had their disagreements, she and Thane, but

without his endless ambition, she'd still be stuck on that island.

After ditching Thane down in the dirt, Cassidy had stayed with Celice and the other commandos while they took over the Factory's control center. Mathieu, the one who'd pulled Celice away from Thane's murderous advance, worked with Aegis's daughter on some computer wizardry to disable the Factory's remaining defenses. From there they'd put out a hold order to Ziran's human forces while blocking any attempts to re-activate the disabled drones.

Cassidy stood there in the room's back keeping an eye on the half-dozen Ziran techs shoved off into a corner. After all the day's chaos, playing guard to a terrified group felt like a nice break, a chance to catch her breath.

Then Thane came crawling back from that hole, followed by Aegis, Mynx, and Mila. The new Thane, back to his sensible size. He'd slipped Cassidy a thank-you look before the bunch went onward and outward: someone reported on the Tamas that Wexley had been found, apprehended on the beach.

Showers, hot meals, a chance to change clothes. Civilization came back almost too fast. Cassidy found herself put up in the Paragon's LA tower, a large spire with more than enough rooms due to, well, the obvious. Cassidy spent the next day putting herself together and, finally, getting in touch with the ones she most needed to see.

Thane found her that morning as Cassidy, simple Paragon backpack loaded with her few possessions, headed out to catch quick flight courtesy of a new Paragon-issued expense account.

Saving the world had its perks.

"You're not leaving," Thane said just inside the doorway.

"I'm going home," Cassidy replied, waving at all the bustle in the tower. "I played my part. This is all your game now."

"No. It isn't."

The pod pulled up and Cassidy went outside, Thane following. When she opened the door, Thane went to the opposite side and opened his.

"I'm waiting," Cassidy said as she sat down, Thane matching her.

The doors shut, the pod whirred away.

"On the island I had so many ideas for the world," Thane said. "So many ways I could make it better if only I was in charge. I could make the drones better, I could make the people love me." Cassidy rolled her eyes. Thane chuckled, a strange sound, as though the man wasn't quite used to making it. "See? That, right there, used to make me so angry."

"Because I think you're ridiculous?"

"I was. I am. And I didn't see it until Bangkok. Until Ziran took my idea and ran with it."

"You're saying you wanted to be a genocidal ruler?"

"In my head, no. In reality, perhaps that's what I would have become." Thane pointed outside to passing buildings, people walking to coffee shops, stepping into offices. "See how little's changed? In one night, the whole world order has shifted, but for most people it's something they'll barely notice. So long as they're able to pursue their dreams, their desires—"

"Hold on," Cassidy said. "It's a long trip to where I'm going, but it's not that long. Thane, you came into this pod with me. Why?"

Thane considered and Cassidy waited for the man's body to wither, to shrink down as his brain went into its galaxy mode. The pod didn't have a cane, didn't have a walker for the man to use, so hopefully he wouldn't go so far down a rabbit hole that she'd have to carry him out.

"I've spent so much time on the bigger picture, both in a cell, on that island, and in Apinya's camp," Thane said, "and seeing Wexley makes me think I've missed something more important."

"Like?"

"Mila gave me more time than I expected," Thane replied. "I'd prefer to spend it with you, rather than arguing with those old Paragons over who gets to run Siberia."

"I *would* be more fun than that." Cassidy folded her arms. "But who says I want you along? You sent me to that lab. I would've been tested, experimented on."

Thane scratched at his hair, "A gambit. I told the others that you'd save Apinya. Truthfully, I thought it would take too long for anything to happen. I wanted you removed, off the board. Safe."

"Safe? You think that place was safe?"

"Safer than a Factory assault? Yes," Thane replied. The pod swung onto the highway, a short jaunt now to the airport. "Ziran wasn't trying to kill the anomalies there. I figured we would succeed within a day, long before anything bad would happen to you."

"Or you could've told me to stay away."

Now Thane smiled, "But you wouldn't have."

No, she wouldn't have.

THEY ARRIVED at a bright yellow house. The same color it'd been on that morning when Cassidy left it for the last time. A trimmed yard, pear tree sitting center. Sunlight blasted off the cream driveway leading to a carless garage, open and filled with boxes. Cassidy read the labels as she walked up, Thane behind her.

"My things," Cassidy said, running her fingers along the cardboard. "He packed them all."

"A lot of boxes."

"Not just mine. Our children's toys, their old clothes. Everything from our life together is sitting out here."

"Not thrown away."

"Maybe he couldn't go that far." Cassidy considered. "Or maybe he thought I might come back and didn't want me to be so angry."

"Are you?"

"After all this time?" Cassidy sighed. "Yes, and also no. If that makes sense."

"I can understand," Thane replied, and Cassidy supposed he probably could.

The front door opened. Someone, a young man who could only be her son, said her name. Her real name.

Mom.

"Ready?" Thane asked, putting a hand on her shoulder.

"You know, I think I'm more ready for this than I've been for anything in my life."

THIRTY-THREE

The Time

For once, Aegis didn't play a part in the revolution. He started it, along with all the others on the beach that night, but beyond a few hopeful remarks to a confused media, Aegis kept himself from the spotlight. He made important deals in the dark, including ones to send Zhan-Yo, Wexley, and their cohorts off to Mynx's island, and when it came to put names forward for new leadership, Aegis only had one to suggest.

Celice.

"Your own daughter turned you down," Mynx said, joining Aegis out on her expansive deck. Tea and coffee, rolls and eggs floated out behind her courtesy of some small drones. "How does that make you feel?"

"Just fine." Aegis adjusted his cap to shade the sun. "She wants to run her own shadow show, that's her choice."

"That Mathieu is a bad influence," Mynx said, but the sparkle in her words cut the damage.

"You know, he's the first one that hasn't run away after meeting me. That has to count for something."

Mynx settled into a chair next to Aegis with a satisfied sigh. Together they took their own long moments, enjoying the waves, the breeze.

"Reeves thinks it'll take a couple months, but we'll have the Factory all reconfigured by summer's end. Just in time to have some real fun."

"Getting our hands dirty?"

"With real dirt, yes. Isn't that what you wanted?"

"Not just me." Aegis flexed his fingers. "I think you said you were tired of taking punches?"

From building gladiators to creating craftsmen, drones designed to work alongside carpenters, farmers, manufacturers to build, sustain, support. Mynx didn't want to scrap her Factory, so that'd been the next best thing. She and Aegis would be going out with the first wave, heading to hard-hit areas to help them rebuild.

Zhan-Yo had that idea, offered it up as something he'd seen so often leading Ziran, driving its own charities. Something the ex-CEO never had time for, something the old Champions might be able to enjoy.

Mynx nodded, "When you spend so long in a tube, you start thinking maybe it'd be nice to get out a little more. See the world without feeling like you're responsible for it."

"Not sure I'll ever get that far."

Being a hero, being on the front line had been Aegis's whole identity for so long. He could feel it now, the pressure urging him to get up from the chair, use his Tama to log into the Paragon's database, see what disasters existed around the planet and how best to deal with them. What new anomaly and normal villains needed bashing, what storm and earthquake victims needed assistance.

He'd tried, actually, before Mynx came out a minute ago. Pressed his finger to the Tama's little scanner and been rejected. Had its camera look at his face only to get the same red denial.

Celice doing what she promised.

Aegis was out. Mynx was out. All the old Champions evicted to make way for a new crowd, anomalies and normals both, coupled with regional elected officials. A massive overhaul unfurling over weeks, months, years.

"I think it will work," Mynx said, guessing what Aegis thought. "Better than what we did, anyway."

"Were we that bad?"

"We set out to do what we thought was best, and we did it," Mynx slanted a smile, "That gave us more confidence than we deserved."

"We bought peace for more than twenty years."

Mynx nodded, "Every one of those years was a desperate scramble to maintain what we'd created. It's time to let them try something new." A wave crashed, spray flying up and catching the sunlight in a micro rainbow. Mynx set down her fork, looked over at Aegis. "Have you ever tried surfing?"

"Never had the time."

"Guess what, old man? You do now."

THIRTY-FOUR

Retirement

FORGIVENESS CAME EASIER IN VICTORY. On that beach, Zhan-Yo asked for what he didn't deserve: a chance at a different, better life. He'd paved the path for Wexley, for Ziran. He'd detonated bombs inside a crowded stadium to make a point. By any reasonable measure, the revolutionary deserved to rot somewhere dark, damp, and decrepit.

Instead, he asked for redemption.

"There won't be another chance to remake the world like we have right now," Zhan-Yo said on that beach, deep in the night. "We've whipsawed civilization from one side to the other over the last few months, and it's time to let it settle on the better path."

Aegis, Thane, Mynx, Mila, Apinya, Celice, and Mathieu watched him, Tama glows joining starlight. The tracker and her friend sat on the beach next to Wexley, either uncaring or too exhausted to participate. The void-casting anomaly, the one Thane had sent to Ziran's prison, stood off on her own looking at the waves.

Not that every voice needed to speak up. Better to keep it small right now, when everything felt so fragile.

"And what is that path?" Apinya asked, though it sounded more like a prompt than a question.

Aegis folded his arms, Mynx glowered Zhan-Yo's way. The others ranged between curious and cautious. Suspecting if not outright knowing what Zhan-Yo would say.

He said it all anyway. Laid out the very idea he'd been living with since so long ago in Chicago, the one he would've spilled to Aegis and the Paragons without all the bloodshed if only they had listened. Equality, irrespective of anomaly and normal status. Carve the world up as it wished to be, with regions as varied as desired. Stabilized by a worldwide force made up of, yes, anomaly and normals.

"The Paragons," Aegis said then. "We keep the same name, strip out the anomaly-only parts. The transition will be easier."

"And no drones," Thane added. "Not anymore, not for any force."

Mynx shrugged, "Less work for me."

More bits and bobs danced between the players, a loose framework solidified as the hours creeped towards dawn. They snacked as they talked, Paragons and commandos occasionally running down refreshments in between reports on injuries sustained, Ziran resistance dwindling across the globe.

"One last thing," Zhan-Yo said as pink appeared behind the mountains. "We can't be a part of this. Me for obvious reasons, but you." Zhan-Yo pointed at Aegis, then Mynx, "And you. Thane. The other Champions. Our reputations precede us, will overwhelm what we're doing here tonight."

That the Champions agreed came as a shock, that it took several long minutes to extract that agreement did not. Nonetheless, the moment stuck with Zhan-Yo as the days passed, hanging with him on the boat as it arrived, finally, on Mynx's sun-swept island.

Around him on the horizon: clear water and clouds. Drones no longer hovered at the edges waiting to slaughter any escapees. Instead, as the passengers shuffled off onto the shore, their sentence would be monitored by a different sort of guard: human, with regular visits to bring food, fresh water. Medicine.

A prison, yes. A hell, no.

Zhan-Yo stretched, glanced around at the factions already forming. People striking off up the beach, some towards the rising volcano at the island's center, others to the east, where anomalies still lived.

"West?" Rhimes said, Brielle at his side as the two came up next to him.

"West," Zhan-Yo replied.

A certain anomaly told him she'd had a village over there once, with a nice thatched shelter and a perfect sunset view.

The Path

Manhattan spread beneath Bastion's giant windows. Celice stood near where her father often sat, scanning monitors as election results began to flow in from around the world. It'd been a hasty scramble to set anything up, but with Tamas being ubiquitous, they'd managed to get the online voting going without too much trouble. The first candidates were a mix, but sometimes you had to get the cart moving and worry about the path later.

"That sounds dangerous," Mathieu said, standing on her right and flicking through his own screens. "Shouldn't it be the other way around? The path paved before the cart?"

"Guess we'll find out," Celice replied. "Anything important for us?"

"There are a few anomaly breakouts here and there, but local Paragons have them under control. A couple bright minds stole some defunct drones and restarted them," Mathieu said, "but our recruitment's going well."

"The trackers?"

"A lot are jumping in," Mathieu replied. "I think we won't have a problem finding our agents."

Celice nodded. Someone else could run the main Paragon show. She'd be happy to stay behind the scenes, do what her father always wanted: stop the major threats without being buried in bureaucracy. And now, with the tracker program disbanded, there were a whole lot of skilled hunters looking for work.

"Now," Mathieu said, "Here's something interesting. Bangkok. Seeing reports about robberies, broad daylight. People going deaf, blind, then losing their wallets. Get all their senses back a minute later. Locals don't have any leads."

Celice looked over at Mathieu's screen, read over the summary.

"Something to delegate?" Celice asked.

Mathieu grinned, "Could. But I've always wanted to go to Thailand."

"We do have that nice jet Mynx gave us." She shared his smile. "How fast can you pack?"

An Excerpt from DROP ZONE

Aurora heard Rovo's warning call and responded with habit, "Set them up and let them loose."

Three Severs sat at the back, in their crash harnesses, and each of them pressed a small button under their right hand. The shuttle's ceiling held drop-down screens hanging from metal bars. The displays swung right in front of the Sever's faces, each one perfectly aligned thanks to micro-cameras measuring appropriate eye level. Each screen flipped to show a cannon's feed. Two on the bottom —split to the bow and aft of the shuttle—and one on top, all charged and ready to fire.

Aurora's snapped on first, giving her the front-facing lower cannon. Showed the world of stormy, musty yellow-gray fog they were descending into as the shuttle went lower and lower. Nothing appeared on her scopes. Who knew whether Dynas had any kind of defense, but survival dictated acting as if the planet bristled with death.

"I'm picking up a heat signature, looks like energy use," Eponi said through their transponders. "Gonna land on top of it. Feel it's as good a spot as any."

"Just don't get us killed," Sai said.

"Do I ever?"

"Any sign of threats?" Aurora snapped. She had no problem with squad banter, so long as it didn't distract in a dangerous moment.

"No," Eponi replied, but her voice trailed even as she spoke. "Wait—coming behind. A pair of Darter-class skiffs."

Skiffs? If they flew open top craft like those here, then Dynas had a thick atmosphere. Breathable. Skiffs also meant Dynas didn't understand who they were dealing with. Sure, not having a plated hull or windshield might make for pretty views, but it also made for an easy target. Couldn't shield open space. Aurora would have loved to trigger a few shots and let go the tight knots that always formed in her muscles as missions began, but Gregor had the rear cannon, and the first chance to speckle Dynas's fog with the enemy's bits and pieces.

The drop ship didn't shudder when Gregor fired his cannon, a total lack of feedback Aurora should have been used to by now. No projectiles, like in the old models, so no recoil. Just a hum. A draining battery's whine.

As battle went, lasers made the whole thing feel artificial, like they were playing a game. Aurora knew that feeling would vanish with the first casualty showing what a laser's direct strike could do to a person, but Gregor's fire didn't deliver that absolution.

"They're splitting their approach. Lightly armed," Gregor said after his initial volley. "I see two cannons on each one, mounted bow and aft. I've already neutralized the front cannon on mine."

"Only because your pilot doesn't know how to dodge," Sai added. "Mine at least understands the concept of a maneuver."

The soupy fog broke as Eponi soared the shuttle down. Lush deep green poked through, caught by the drop shuttle's lights, which Eponi switched on as the clouds, now above, consumed most light daring to try and get this far. If Aurora had to guess, the reason Dynas had life at all came down to its heat trap of an atmosphere boiling up biologic sludge from whatever unlucky rock collection collided to form Dynas in the first place.

"Keep your eyes open for ground defenses," Eponi said.

The shuttle rattled as Eponi finished. Something popped and smoke flooded into the cabin. No, not smoke. Fog from outside.

"What was that?" Aurora snapped.

"The skiffs." Sai replied. "Not the main cannons. Something weird. From handheld rifles. My guess, homing drones with explosives attached. Can we move any faster?"

"This is a drop shuttle, Sai. We're basically falling." The cocky sass vanished from Eponi's voice, signaling a pilot focusing on her flying.

Which meant a serious situation. Aurora cut off her own urge to ask Eponi for details—one of the hardest parts about leading Sever lay in trusting the crew, holding off the urge to question their every action, ask for and approve of every detail.

"The second skiff is cutting overhead!" Gregor yelled.

Aurora didn't need to hear anymore. Her view screen flashed bright yellow in the upper left corner; the shuttle's scanners indicating a target. Aurora used her eyes, dragging them to the target's position. The move aimed the cannon, and she stared back up into that fog. Waited. The active contact between Aurora's eyes and the screen kept the feed active, the cannon primed.

A long dark shadow cut across the screen. Aurora

blinked both eyes and the cannon fired a bright green bolt into the ether. Aurora blinked again and again and again, sending a series of shots towards the shape, which flared into a beautiful orange and red rose. Skiff down.

"Took care of it," Aurora said.

But the fog kept flowing into the drop shuttle. Aurora couldn't see the hole, and unstrapping during a potential crash landing scenario would put Aurora on the wrong side of every DefenseCorp guide. And common sense—the drop shuttle still continued doing what it had been made for: dropping. The ship wouldn't have to hold up for much longer.

"Sorry, Sever, seems like that shot killed my coolant. Engines are overheating. Going down here because, uh, otherwise we're all getting cooked." Eponi said. "Brace for a wet landing."

Aurora aimed her cannon down in time to see massive branches, trees, and vines snag the shuttle and swallow it up. The cannon feed held, then shook and went dark. The shuttle filled with roaring, wrecking, tearing as Sever shook in their seats. Seats that didn't break, because DefenseCorp bolted every drop shuttle chair to the floor with heavy metals. Meant to handle an impact, and to stop a sharp object from piercing through the floor and hurting its occupant.

Aurora had been in plenty of crashes, a standard hazard in this line of work, but most had been on land. One on a beach, as part of a rescue in a resort overtaken by discontent alien tourists. But none into a swamp. So when the shuttle smacked into the water, bounced forward, and settled into a noxious mix of slimy water and terrible gasses, Aurora had a new candidate for worst place ever. She unclipped, clocked the power readings on her armor — all greens—and made for the shuttle's opening sides.

Swamp water had the same idea, flooding into the ship to greet Aurora with frothy filth.

"Pop out!" Aurora said the words that nobody needed to hear. Gregor and Sai, following her, scrambled through the open door in the left hull, made larger courtesy of a now-downed tree that'd taken its final stab through the drop shuttle's side.

Eponi and Rovo had already evacuated, having climbed out through the shattered cockpit window. Rovo looked towards the sky, hunting for any further skiffs, while Eponi leaned back into the cockpit, swatting at buttons. Protocol said it'd be best to shut down the drop shuttle's systems, drain the batteries in the event of a harsh landing to prevent bad things like enemy scavenging and random explosions.

"What happened?" Aurora yelled to Eponi when the pilot settled back on the drop ship's nose. "You didn't make the hit sound serious?"

"Whatever they fired at us?" Eponi shot back. "It kept going. I lost systems one by one. Had to take us down fast or we would have run right through these trees."

Aurora looked out over the desolate swamp stretching as far as she could see, which, given the dark, misty conditions, wasn't all that far. Their attackers, whomever lived on Dynas, weren't looking for visitors. They were ready to kill keep their world quiet, but they'd missed their chance.

Sever wouldn't give them a second one.

Start a brand new adventure with DROP ZONE, *book one in the Sever Squad series, available at your favorite retailer:*

336

Liberator's Light concludes a series that branched off some ideas I had years ago but never had the opportunity to grow into full novels, much less an arc like this one. The idea of 'crappy' superheroes always sounded like fun: what would happen to these purveyors of the slightly extraordinary?

If the powers were the fun part, the human element grew to become the most interesting. What would happen if parts of society, so long entrenched in their security, found themselves robbed of it by genetic lottery winners? How would the world react to a very clear divide between those who have abilities and those who do not?

The Hero's Code played in that sandbox, and as I wrote it, I found its villains, its heroes, its bystanders to be (as I often do) less black and white, going far more to the gray. At the end, we all want what we want, and whether we can erase a building with a snap of our fingers or if we fumble our morning coffee, we will strive to get it within whatever reason fits our ideals. In these stories, Kat, Wexley, Calvin and Aegis were trying to do what they felt was the right thing.

I hope you found their journey as interesting to read as I did to write.

About the Author

A.R. Knight spins stories in a frosty house in Madison, WI, primarily owned by a pair of cats. After getting sucked into the working grind in the economic crash of the 2008, he found himself spending boring meetings soaring through space and going on grand adventures.

Eventually, spending time with podcasting, screenplays, short stories and other novels, he found a story he could fall into and a cast of characters both entertaining and full of heart.

A.R. Knight plans on jumping through to other worlds and finding new stories to tell in the limitless borders of our imagination.

Thanks, as always, for reading!

For more information:
www.adamrknight.com

To DJ